Charles Frederick Bradley, Francis Dana Hemenway, Charles
Macaulay Stuart

Life and Selected Writings of Francis Dana Hemenway

Charles Frederick Bradley, Francis Dana Hemenway, Charles Macaulay Stuart

Life and Selected Writings of Francis Dana Hemenway

ISBN/EAN: 9783337416010

Printed in Europe, USA, Canada, Australia, Japan

Cover: Foto ©Andreas Hilbeck / pixelio.de

More available books at **www.hansebooks.com**

LIFE AND SELECTED WRITINGS

OF

FRANCIS DANA HEMENWAY,

LATE PROFESSOR OF HEBREW AND BIBLICAL LITERA-
TURE IN THE GARRETT BIBLICAL INSTITUTE,
EVANSTON, ILLINOIS.

BY

CHARLES F. BRADLEY,   AMOS W. PATTEN,

CHARLES M. STUART.

———— ••• ————

CINCINNATI AND CHICAGO :
CRANSTON & STOWE.
1890.

PREFACE.

• ──

THIS work was undertaken as the result of a suggestion made at the annual meeting of the Alumni Association of Garrett Biblical Institute in May, 1887. The committee appointed were left without special instruction as to matter and form, and free also to make their own division of labor. From his special intimacy with Professor Hemenway, the biography was assigned to Professor C. F. Bradley, D. D., of the class of 1878, who, to perfect his labor of love, spent part of the summer of 1888 in the scenes of Professor Hemenway's boyhood and early manhood, and secured reminiscences from friends who remembered him as student, teacher, and pastor. Former students, friends, and parishioners were also laid under contribution through correspondence, and a careful and thorough examination made of diary, letters, and tributes of contemporaries, to portray, as characteristically as might be, the features of one whom all alike loved and honored. The committee acknowledge gratefully the kindness of all friends who responded to the request for reminiscences; and especially the unfailing

3

and sympathetic assistance of Mrs. Hemenway, who placed at their disposal her husband's diary and letters, and in many other helpful ways made easier and more intelligent the work committed to them. To the Rev. Dr. Amos W. Patten, of the class of 1870, was assigned the preparation of the general lectures, sermons, and addresses; and to this writer, the lectures on hymnology. The work is now sent forth to perpetuate, in some degree, the labors of an able, devoted, and accomplished minister and teacher. May it reach many, to help and to bless!

CHARLES M. STUART,

CHAIRMAN OF THE COMMITTEE.

EVANSTON, ILL., April, 1890.

CONTENTS.

————•——

PART III—LECTURES AND SERMONS.

EDITED BY REV. A. W. PATTEN, D. D.

Biographical Sketch.

BY

PROFESSOR C. F. BRADLEY, D. D.

BIOGRAPHICAL SKETCH.

CHAPTER I.

THE HOME AMONG THE HILLS.

THE country east of the center of Vermont is marked by huge ridges of hills running north and south. In a pleasant valley between two of these, through which flows the First Branch of White River, nestles the village of Chelsea. Up to the present day no railroad train has disturbed its rural quiet. A yellow coach drawn by four horses brings mail and passengers once a day from South Royalton, thirteen miles down the valley. West of the village green rises the noble West Hill, whose highest point is not less than seventeen hundred feet above the sea-level. A mountain road, starting from the north end of the village street, climbs up this ridge. There are dense woods on the left, and glimpses of vale and hill on the right as one ascends, until higher ranges of hills, with intervening valleys, are attained. After about two miles, an abrupt turn to the right and another half mile bring the visitor to the Hemenway homestead. It is a small but comfortable house, surrounded by the ordinary buildings of a New England farm. Behind is a wooded hill, and in front a meadow with its brook. Undulating hills and a blue peak in the distance complete the pleasing picture.

2

In this farm-house, on the tenth day of November, 1830, Francis Dana Hemenway was born.

The father, Jonathan Wilder Hemenway, was born in Barre, Massachusetts, in 1784, and came to Chelsea in 1810. His first wife bore him three sons and four daughters. The mother of Alpheus and Francis was the second wife, Sarah Hebard. As is so often the case when a distinguished son comes from an otherwise unknown family, the boy inherited from the mother his marked mental and moral traits. She is described by those who remember her as above the medium height, with large, dark and expressive eyes. Her manner was quiet and sedate. Though not a church member, she was a religious woman, and, having a sweet voice, sang in the church choir. The whole family felt the inspiration of her intelligence and character. Her mother, Sarah Davison, was also a woman of superior mind and manners. She is said to have been a Congregationalist. Such glimpses, slight but gratifying, we get of "the grandmother Lois and the mother Eunice."

Given a New England stock, a simple New England country home, and the influences of New England village life, and what will be the result? As well might we ask what carbon will become in Nature's laboratory. The Vermont and New Hampshire farmers' boys in those days had possibilities. Webster, Marsh, Chase, and many others, prove that. The humbler Puritan stock had the strength of granite, and contained here and there veins of gold-bearing quartz. The district schools and the rural academies discovered the gold, and the country colleges gave it a stamp which made it current in the markets of the world. It is interesting to note the contrast between the conditions of the country-boy of unusual talent, born in an undistinguished home, and the son of a family of the New England "Brahmin caste." The latter had great odds in his favor; inherited talents, culture from the cradle, a literary atmosphere for daily breathing, family influences—which were often in themselves a liberal education—the best schools and colleges, the stimulus of family pride, and often foreign travel and study to widen the horizon and finish the training. Yet the country lad would often win in the long race. He had his peculiar advantages. The simpler state offered fewer temptations. The out-of-door life favored freer development of mind and body, and furnished solitude for thought and intimacy with Nature. There was less conventionality, and more chance for maturing individuality. The New England farm and village life was the mold of some of our greatest and best Americans. .

Fortunately we have some descriptions of life on the West Hill of Chelsea during the boyhood of Francis Hemenway in his own words. Its circle embraced the farm-house, the school, the neighborhood and village society, and the church. Its main features may be quickly sketched. There was a simplicity about it which might seem to us to involve hardship. This embraced cold bedrooms in winter, early rising, plain fare, hard work, meager expression of affection, few holidays, and few papers and books. Yet there were lofty ideals connected with this plain living. There were strict integrity, high devotion to duty, deep though undemonstrative family affection, Puritan morality, high intelligence and practical good sense, and noble types of manhood and womanhood, such as have ever lifted the poorest of our New England native homes immeasurably above the cottage of the ordinary European peasant. The Hemenway home lacked only family religion to make it typical of the best New England family life. Even this lack was to a large extent supplied by the mother, who taught her children to pray and read the Bible. Her death, when Francis was nine years old, left him deeply bereaved, but permanently benefited by her teachings and example.

Francis developed rapidly in body and mind until his fourteenth year. He was then a robust and merry boy, large for his age, and with a growing reputation as a precocious scholar, fond both of fun and of his books. One old neighbor, now eighty-three years of age, remembers him as "a first-rate boy — an extra boy; bound to make his mark." A proof of this recognized precocity is the tradition, cherished in the family, though not fully vouched for, that when seven years old he read the whole New Testament in a week. Certain it is, that before he was eight, he had read the entire Bible through.

A severe illness in his fourteenth year marks a crisis in his life. The nature of the disease is not certainly known. He himself, in his later life, regarded the improper treatment of an ignorant physician as more serious than the disease. Some years of ill-health followed. He could do little work or hard study. Yet this serious check, which seems to have put a ball and chain henceforth upon his physical strength, and which doubtless shortened his life, brought blessings too. Relieved from the necessity of working on the farm, he had leisure for study. His life became more solitary and introspective, and habits of religious meditation and prayer were formed, which gave wings to his spirit. The depth and originality of his spiritual life owed much, no doubt, to the quiet hours he spent in the woods and in the little chamber with its one south window, which is still cherished as " Francis' room. "

CHAPTER II.

THE SCHOOL-HOUSE AND CHURCH AT THE CORNERS.

"THE Corners," which formed the center of social and religious life for the neighborhood, were about a mile and a half south-west of the Hemenway farm. They could boast neither post-office nor store, and but few dwellings. The plain, typical Vermont district school-house, which stood at the cross-roads, had no comeliness of form or feature; but that its surroundings and influence were held in grateful remembrance by this man whose boyhood was blessed by them, we know from the following sketch, written in the early days of his last illness:

"There it stood, turning its homely but honest face toward me, as I made my weary journey of a mile and a half from my childhood home to this scene and center of my early toils and triumphs. There was no paint on the walls, either outside or inside; no inclosing fence; no friendly shade of trees; and no shrubbery of any kind, except that on one side the original underbrush had never been fully cleared away. Fortunately, however, the woods were not far away, and here were found inexhaustible resources in climbing the trees, getting spruce-gum, and hunting the squirrels and rabbits. Indeed, they were to us boys a veritable Arcadia. I have heard a good deal about 'classic groves' and 'scholarly retreats,' and have seen some of the most famous of these on both sides of the sea, but have found nothing that has brought to me more exhilaration, or a more delicious sense of freedom and wealth, than came to me in that oft-frequented forest. Our play-ground was, to appearance, rather restricted; for, in the good old utilitarian times, no heresy could have been more radical than that of actually providing a play-ground for the children. But human nature is wiser than puritanical rules, and stronger than the barriers which the unthoughtfulness and poverty of our parents had thrown about us; for we took, as our rightful domain, 'all out-doors,' finding our only limits in the length of the nooning or recess. . . . Of course each day of the winter's school began by the building of the fire by the boy whose turn it was, for we were our own janitors. The young hero had to make an early start; had to do all his own chores at home—feed the horses, milk the cows, feed the cattle, clear the stables, eat his breakfast, put up the doughnuts and apples for his dinner—take his walk of half a mile, or mile, or mile and a half, and get a rousing fire started by half-past eight o'clock. At nine the work began. The staple of the work for the first hour of each session was reading. The first class, made up of all the full-grown boys and girls, read in the 'American First Class Book,' compiled by John Pierpont. This exercise consisted in calling upon each individual in turn to stand up at his seat and read a paragraph, which, with the aid of the teacher's prompting, he would generally be able to do. The second class would be distinguished by being called out to sit together on a front seat to repeat substantially the same programme as the first, except that a different reading-book was used, which, for many years, was 'Emerson's Second Class Reader.' The days of the 'Scott's Lessons,' the 'English Reader,' and the 'Art of Reading,' had gone by, and the above *avant-couriers* of the coming multitude had taken their places. The other classes were called up into the floor, and had to stand with their toes exactly to the crack in the floor, while they went through the same original and exciting exercise. Then came the time for the master to go round to each one who 'ciphered,' and ask him if he had any difficulty in doing the 'sums,' and when any one was pointed out, he was expected to take slate and pencil, and work out the example for the benefit of the lazy dunce. And now there is a lull. The master seems to be getting through, and the boys are all awake and under a common spell. Suddenly the word is spoken, 'Boys may go out,' and upon the instant the door flies open, and with an explosion like a bottle of pop, the school-house discharges one-half of its contents into the street. Had a pound of dynamite been exploded under the seat of each individual boy, the movement would hardly have been more prompt. But when, after five minutes, the rapping of the master's ruler upon the rattling window-sash called us again to duty, the effervescence had all departed, and we came back with exemplary sedateness.

"We had little apparatus in the old school-house. I well remember when our first blackboard put in an appearance—a rather diminutive specimen, about two feet by three—and we had to wait a year or two before anybody could find a use to put it to. As for a globe, or outline maps, we had never seen them, and had no idea of any purpose they could serve. Even a call-bell was an unnecessary refinement; there was more character, and more ominous suggestiveness, in the birch ruler. The only absolutely indispensable article of apparatus was this same ruler. Whatever else the teacher had, or did not have, it would not do for him to be without this. You might as well have a mason without a trowel, a barber without a razor, or a policeman without his club. At all events, I have a pretty distinct memory that, in my days, this particular article of school apparatus was put to constant and faithful service.

"What did we do in that old school-house? Just about every thing. If there was any thing we did not do, it was because it had not been invented. We strained every nerve, exercised every muscle, practiced every sense; took all the studies from the alphabet to algebra, geometry, rhetoric, chemistry, and 'Watts on the Mind;' carved in the soft basswood desks all possible grotesqueness in form; upset the benches; experienced about every form of penalty which pedagogic ingenuity could invent, from 'ferrilling' to standing on the floor. or sitting among the girls. In the evenings we had debates, spelling-schools, and exhibitions.

"But how can I recount the histories which were made there? As my mind dwells upon it, I feel the flow of infinite numbers, and take warning from the inexhaustibleness of my theme to constrain myself into limits. That old house

BIRTHPLACE OF F. A. HEMENWAY

becomes, in my memory, a world peopled with innumerable forms of beauty and life. Never may I, this side of heaven, realize intenser experiences than in the days when my life revolved about this center. This old house represents one of the mightiest forces which have come into my own life. I have seen many good schools, and have taught some of them myself, I may say in all modesty, and yet I have never known any school that was more loyal to its own work, or one in which the lines of progress were more directly drawn. If I interrogate my own experience, I am constrained to the conclusion that some of my most important school-work was done in this old Vermont school-house before I was twelve years of age. The decisions which have determined the hue and coloring of my life, so far as I can now judge, were, in large measure, made in that early time."

Not far from the school-house stood the church, or, as it was then called, the "West Hill Meetin'-house." This was a unique institution, which served a variety of purposes, and was not the home of any one Christian organization. The Methodists of the neighborhood formed a class, which met in some private house, but held their membership in the Church at Chelsea village. Their pastor preached a certain number of Sundays in the West Hill Meeting-house, according to an arrangement described below. The following sketch, written by Dr. Hemenway for the *Vermont Messenger*, gives us a charming picture of this peculiar sanctuary:

"It was a union church; such an one as a good old Episcopalian minister used to call a Pantheon—that is, a place where all the gods are worshiped. But this was by no means true of this dear old church. Many indeed, and various, were the 'performances' of which it was the scene and witness, striking every chord of human experience, from pathos to bathos.

Funerals, weddings, sermons, lectures on temperance, lectures on phrenology, lectures on mesmerism, magic-lantern exhibitions, school exhibitions, revivals, prayer-meetings, Sunday-schools, singing-schools, and lyceum debates, have all presented themselves in turn in this community kaleidoscope. Methodists, Congregationalists, Universalists, Adventists, Baptists—Freewill and Calvinistic—and Christians (with the first *'i'* long), held places in the ecclesiastical procession. And yet the difference was mainly in the minister and the name; the congregation, the choir, the hymn-books, and the order of service were, for the most part, the same. This can also be said of the subject-matter of the preaching, if one or two of the denominations be excepted. And it is my belief that, notwithstanding the various names and creeds represented in the services, the worship in that humble country church, as constantly and truly as in any church I have ever attended, was paid to the living and true God.

" It had just fifty-two pews, divided among fifty-one owners (except that one man, with a very large family, went to the extravagance of owning two), one for each Sunday in the year. A most fortunate circumstance was this, for it furnished a ready and perfect solution of the problem of occupancy. At the beginning of the year, subscription papers were circulated among the pew-owners, and they, according to their denominational preferences, signed their Sundays to Baptists, Methodists, etc.; the number of names on each paper indicating the number of Sundays that denomination might control the house that year. Generally, as already intimated, the same congregation would be present, whoever preached; though, as must be confessed, when the Universalists 'occupied,' the congregations were 'pretty slim.'

" Few spots on this green earth are to me as this old church. I have sat on its hard benches (for never were seats constructed with a more sublime unconsciousness of the anatomy of the human frame) for many dismal hours, and ofttimes with a burning indignation against the minister for his bad faith, in that he had finally come to say 'once more,' and then, after thus raising my hopes, had rudely dashed them again by keeping on, as I thought, a good many times more.

My most sacred and most cherished memories center here. Here I first became accustomed to the services of religion, for the voice of prayer and praise was not wont to be heard in my childhood home. Here I recited my first Sunday-school lesson; here I first knelt as a 'seeker' at the 'anxious seat;' here I stammered out my first words of Christian testimony; here I was baptized and licensed to exhort; here I spoke my first words as a Christian minister; and here, too, I was married. Here, with an ineffable sense of desolation, a pitiable boy of nine, I last looked on the dear face of my mother; and fifteen years later, in the very same place, the words of religion were spoken at the funeral of my father. In the old burying-ground, in the rear, sleep my parents, my wife's parents, a sister of each of us, together with many a friend and playmate of our childhood years.

"Various, indeed, have been the 'gifts' which have been exercised in that pulpit. Sermons of the 'vealy' type, sermons of the traditional 'hard-shell' variety, and sermons as keen and resistless as one ever hears, would follow each other in close order. The holy tones of the 'Freewillers,' the 'roarations' of the 'Campaigners,' and the affectations of the college-bred ministers, were all familiar to the people who worshiped there. The singing ranged from such minor fugues as 'Complaint,' 'Russia,' and 'New Durham'—any one of which was doleful enough to start tears from anybody who had tears to shed—to 'The Old Granite State,' which was made to carry such choice and devotional lines as—

> 'You will see your Lord a coming,
> You will see the dead arising,
> We'll march up into the city,
> While a band of music,
> While a band of music,
> While a band of music,
> Will be sounding through the air.'

By way of an awful warning to all choristers and choirs, I must relate what once happened because of a fugue tune there.

"It was on a bright afternoon in midsummer that the minister, from his tub-shaped pulpit, which was just a little

lower than the singers' gallery, gave out that most searching
hymn of Joseph Hart:

> ' O, for a glance of heavenly day.'

The faithful chorister had already before him his list of tunes,
and the moment the minister said 'long meter,' set to work
looking up the tune. His choice was telegraphed to the various sections of the choir, and the singing began. The hymn
was solemn, and the tune in keeping with it, while a fugue arrangement of the last line added to its expressiveness. But
alas! little did we expect what was before us; for when we
reached the third verse, it came upon us in this fearful fashion :

> ' Thy judgments, too, which devils fear,
> Amazing thought! unmoved I hear;
> Goodness and wrath in vain combine
> BASS—To stir this stu—
> TENOR—To stir this stu—
> ALTO—To stir this stu—
> ALL—To stir this stu-pid heart of mine.'

" But, after all, my main interest, as I look back to that old
church, centers in the people who used to worship there. As
I think of one after another who used to tread those aisles·
and sit in those pews, what an interesting, and ofttimes grotesque, panorama passes before me! Here is Deacon H——,
who invariably came to meeting late, and marched up the aisle,
hat in one hand and whip in the other, with his thoroughly
dried calf-skin boots squeaking like a band of music. And
Deacon L——, who, as the reward of long, faithful practice, had
come to that rare state of harmony between body and soul that
he could sit bolt upright, and close his eyes at the beginning of
the sermon, as if for divine communion, sleep soundly and
sweetly as an infant in its mother's arms, and wake up promptly
at the 'amen' without any starts or false motions. Not so ex-
pert, however, was a son of another of the deacons—Deacon
S——. His name was John, and on one occasion, during sermon time, he leaned forward, resting his head on the back of
the pew before him, in which unhealthy and uncomfortable
position he fell asleep. Soon, however, the preacher having
occasion to refer to the beloved disciple, called out in a clear

and somewhat dramatic tone, 'John.' Our friend, being suddenly brought back to consciousness, and thinking his father was making his last and most peremptory call for him in the morning to get up and 'do the chores,' startled all about him by calling out: 'I'm coming, father!' It was not, however, in this church, but another, that the preacher, having become fairly discouraged and desperate at the universal stupor of the congregation, with a boldness (in expedients) to which we were not accustomed in our New England churches, suddenly stopped, and called upon the people to stand up and sing:

> 'My drowsy powers, why sleep ye so?
> Awake, my sluggish soul.'

But he must have experienced some laceration in his own breast, as he heard them calling out in the very words which he had put them to:

> 'Nothing hath half thy work to do,
> Yet nothing's half so dull.'

"Blessings on the memory of the ministers who used to look down upon me from the pulpit of that old church! The first Methodist preacher I ever heard—and that was too early for me to distinctly remember—was the Rev. James M. Fuller, who is still * doing good service as presiding elder of the most important district in the State of Michigan. What a throng of sacred memories cluster about the name of Elisha J. Scott! One of my most distinct and vivid recollections is of a baptismal scene in which he officiated. Twenty-eight young men and women marched from this church to the pond, which had been extemporized as a baptismal font, singing,

> 'On Jordan's stormy banks I stand,'

and were all immersed.

"But I may not call the roll of all the precious names which are inscribed on my memory and graven on my grateful heart. Again I say, blessings on the memory of the dead

---

*In —— —— ——. Dr. Fuller is now (1889) a superannuate of the Detroit Conference, and lives in Detroit.

and on the hearts and lives of the living! What would have
been the history of that community without that humble
church? What would I have been? My soul shudders with
fear as I look down into the abyss of dark possibilities."

Among others who preached in this old church
was the Rev. Amasa G. Button, of whom Dr. Hemenway wrote: "I heard him preach often, and under
a great variety of circumstances—in the village church,
in the little country meeting-house on the hill, in
school-houses, and in private residences—and always
with much satisfaction. I do not think it is often
given to a minister to make a more distinct and permanent impression on a boy of twelve, than I have
retained from those important years. He led the
first Methodist class-meeting I ever attended."

CHAPTER III.

EARLY RELIGIOUS LIFE.

TO form a complete picture of the outward conditions of Francis Hemenway's early life, we need only add the additional features of the neighborhood and village society. The neighboring homes were substantially like his own, though in some of them there was a more positive religious and intellectual life. This was exemplified in the household of Mr. Ichabod Bixby, a man of excellent mind and marked religious character, and the class-leader for this neighborhood. His home was about three miles from the Hemenway farm. Besides the Sunday and week-day religious meetings and social gatherings, there were lyceum meetings and lectures, to bring the neighbors together. The village life, which formed the connecting link between the West Hill and the outside world, differed mainly in degree from that already described. Chelsea Green supported two churches, a court-house, a small academy, and a more compact community.

Amid the environments already described, began that inner life which gives to this biography its chief interest. Soon after his fifteenth birthday, Francis Hemenway commenced a journal, devoted almost exclusively to his religious states and feelings. This was continued, with slight interruptions, for about five years. Its set phrases for religious things contrast strangely with the terse and manly utterances of his later life, and are to be attributed to the books of devotion then in vogue, and to language then used in relating religious experience, which almost constituted a dialect. The journal tells us, in a sort of introduction, that the habit of reading the Bible and of daily prayer had been early fixed by the instructions of his mother. After her death, in his ninth year, he had many serious thoughts, and was convinced that he ought to become a Christian, but the fear of ridicule kept him from open confession. After describing this condition of mind, his journal says:

"Such was the state of my mind when a protracted meeting was commenced at this place in February, 1843; and while I was present one evening, an invitation was given to all who felt their need of a Savior to come forward for prayers. I immediately rose and went forward, and continued so to do for several successive evenings; and, although I could not specify the precise time, place, or even day, yet I felt that in the course of the few days, dating from the time I first went forward for prayers until the termination of the meeting, a change had come over me. St. John says, ' We *know* we have passed from death unto life, because we love the brethren,' and I felt that such was my own case; but when I heard others relate the wondrous exercises of their mind, and the marvelous change instantaneously wrought in them, my mind would revert to my *own* case, to think how different had been *my* feelings, and a doubt as to my genuine conversion would sometimes arise; but I could not see why the apostle spoke of *knowing, because* we love the brethren, if the feelings of all Christians were always thus clear. But my feeling towards Christians was not the only particular in which I observed a change. I felt that I loved religion; I loved secret prayer; I loved devotional books—those which perhaps would have been the most irksome to me before, I now delighted in; and, although I did not feel so clear in my mind as I wished, yet I felt warranted in concluding my conversion real. Yet I had some misgivings, lest the change I had noticed might be something short of genuine conversion; and I would sometimes retire, and endeavor to examine myself, and see whether I were in the faith or not, and usually after a period of self-examination, I felt strengthened and confirmed, though not always fully satisfied."

Believing himself a Christian, he now considered the matters of baptism and of uniting with the church. At that time the Methodists of that community practiced immersion almost as exclusively as the Baptists. The ceremony of "going forward in baptism," as it was called, being performed in a pond near the church, was somewhat formidable. An opportunity of being thus immersed having passed by without his knowing it in season, he felt at liberty to postpone the act for a time. Thus two years passed, at the end of which came the loss of health referred to in the first chapter. As his journal says: "It was deeply afflicting at this important season of life to be compelled to remain inactive in body and mind." Yet he sought for the bright side of this providence, and found his affliction drawing him nearer to Christ.

"As by my sickness I was in a measure shut out of the world, and worldly sources of enjoyment were cut off, my only resource consisted in the smiles of that Friend that sticketh closer than a brother, and he did not forsake me. As my disease precluded much exercise, either of body or mind, yet did not wholly confine me, I was left with no employment which might interfere with any regulations I might adopt, and therefore I instituted four stated seasons of secret devotion daily; and I did find true comfort and consolation, in this season of deep affliction, in unbosoming my cares to Him who can 'be touched with the feeling of our infirmities.'"

At intervals, perplexing doubts concerning the reality of his conversion gave him great trouble. Like many young Christians, he feared that his religious experience was not genuine, simply because it did not correspond to a particular type deemed essential by some others, and set up as a standard in his own mind. Careful self-examination would reassure him that he had really experienced the saving mercy of God. The first year of the journal presents an affecting picture of this invalid boy, struggling against his doubts, and earnestly striving for a higher Christian life. On the 7th of January, 1847, he prepared and formally signed a written self-dedication. He was apparently led to this act by a devotional work called "The Convert's Guide," which he found among the few books in his father's home. This contains a form of self-dedication which is credited to Doddridge's "Rise and Progress of Religion in the Soul," but which is really a rearrangement of portions of two examples of such covenants given by Doddridge. This self-dedication, as Bishop Ninde has said, furnishes the key to his whole religious life. It is given here entire, both for its own sake, and because of the profound influence its adoption exerted upon his character:

SELF-DEDICATION.

"Eternal and unchangeable God, thou great Creator of heaven and earth, and Lord of angels and men! I desire, with deepest humiliation and abasement of soul, to fall down in thy awful presence, deeply penetrated with a sense of thy glorious perfections. Trembling may well take hold upon me, when I presume to lift up my soul to thee on such an occasion as this. Who am I, O Lord God, or what is my nature and descent, my character and desert, that I should speak of this, and be one party in the covenant, where thou, King of kings and Lord of lords, art the other? But, O Lord, great as is thy majesty, so is thy mercy. And I know that in and through Jesus Christ, the Son of thy love, thou condescendest to visit sinful mortals, and to allow their approaching to thee, and their engaging in covenant with thee; nay, I know that thou hast instituted the covenant relation between me and thee, and that thou hast graciously sent to propose it to me. I am unworthy of thy smallest favors, and having sinned against thee, I have forfeited all right of stipulation in my own name, and thankfully accept the conditions, which thy infinite wisdom and goodness have appointed, as just and right, and altogether gracious.

"And this day do I, with the utmost solemnity and sincerity, surrender myself to thee, desiring nothing so much as to be *wholly* thine. I renounce all former lords that have had dominion over me, and I consecrate to thee all that I am and have; the faculties of my mind, the members of my body, my worldly possessions, my time, and my influence with others, to be all used entirely for thy glory, and resolutely employed in obedience to thy commands, as long as thou shalt continue my life; ever holding myself in an attentive posture, to observe the first intimations of thy will, and ready with alacrity and zeal to execute it, whether it relates to thee, to myself, or to my fellow creatures. To thy direction, also, I resign myself, and all I am and have, to be disposed of by thee in such manner as thou shalt, in infinite wisdom, judge most for thy glory. To thee I leave the management of all events, and say without reserve, ' *Thy will be done.*'

"And I hereby resolve to take thee for my supreme good and all-sufficient portion; that I will acknowledge no God but thee—the Father, the Son, and the Holy Ghost; that I will depend alone on the mediation of thy dearly beloved Son for wisdom, righteousness, sanctification, and redemption. And may it please thee, from this day forward, to number me with thy peculiar people. Wash me in the blood of thy dear Son, and sanctify me throughout by the power of thy Spirit, that I may love thee with all my heart, and serve thee with a willing mind. Communicate to me, I beseech thee, all needful influences of thy purifying, thy cheering, and thy comforting Spirit; and lift up the light of thy countenance upon me, which shall put joy and gladness into my soul. And when I shall have done and borne thy will upon earth, call me from hence, at what time and in what manner thou pleasest; only grant that, in my dying moments and in the near prospect of eternity, I may remember these, my engagements to thee, and may employ my latest breath in thy service; and do thou, Lord, when thou seest the agonies of dissolving nature upon me, remember this covenant, too, even though I should be incapable of recollecting it. Look down, O my Heavenly Father, with a pitying eye, upon thy languishing, thy dying child; place thy everlasting arms under me for my support; put strength and confidence into my departing spirit, and receive it to the embraces of thy everlasting love. Welcome it to the abodes of them that sleep in Jesus, to await with them that glorious day, when the last of thy promises to thy covenant people shall be fulfilled in their resurrection, and to that abundant entrance, which shall be ministered to them, into that everlasting kingdom, of which thou hast assured them by thy covenant, and in the hope of which I now lay hold on it, designing to live and die as with my hand upon it. Amen.

"As a witness whereof, I hereunto set my hand and seal, this, the 7th day of January, A. D. 1847.

Francis D. Hemenway."

On March 16, 1847, he refers again to his distressing doubts, and says: "Two weeks ago last Saturday, while reading Watson's 'Life of Wesley,' I thought my present state exactly corresponded to Mr. Wesley's before his conversion; indeed, I never read any man's experience that seemed so exactly to correspond with mine as Mr. Wesley's. I concluded I was striving to become justified by the deeds of the law, or at least

by something short of that living faith which is requisite to our justification. I, indeed, was seeking after
holiness of heart, and even delighted in the law of
God after the inward man; but yet I was carnal, sold
under sin. Since I have concluded this to be my
state, I have been endeavoring to seek religion by
faith in the Great Sacrifice for sin, but as yet have
been unsuccessful. I see I am by nature evil, only
evil, and that continually, and my only hope of salvation rests in the merits of the sacrifice of Christ;
but yet some accursed thing keeps me back. O,
Lord, show me what it is, and help my unbelief!"

On April 25th his troubled heart found expression in the following verse of Charles Wesley's—an
early token of that love for devotional hymns which
characterized him in later life:

"O, Love divine, how sweet thou art!
When shall I find my willing heart
    All taken up by thee?
I thirst, I faint, I die, to prove
The greatness of redeeming love—
    The love of Christ to me."

On May 16th he says: "I have not as yet attained to the certain knowledge of my sins forgiven,
but I intend never to let go my hold until I do; for
if I stay here I die, and if I go back I die; there-,
fore, my only hope is in going forward." In this
painful condition of mind he continued for months.
The first light came from religious conversation with
a good sister in the church, which greatly restored
his confidence. "She seemed to be of the opinion,"
he writes, "that I had really experienced religion,

and she encouraged me to persevere, for Jesus would
surely reveal the light of his countenance. Such is
my intention."

The following extracts from his diary trace his
deliverance from this despondent state:

"*July 12.* I related some of the exercises of my mind to
Brother Copeland. He advised me to go forward in the duties
of a Christian, as I have some evidence that I am a Christian, and that it is my sincere and chief desire to be one. For
some time before, I had felt some misgivings lest, after all, I
were doubting away the grace of God, and had begun to
notice some discrepancy between my experience and that of
Mr. Wesley, the reading of which was the principal occasion
of the conclusion that I had been the victim of self-deception;
while the state of mind he spoke of seemed to be produced by
religious education, in a great measure at least, I had experienced a change which did not result wholly from religious
training. I feel that I do delight in the law of God, that I
love religion, that I love Christians as such, that sin is hateful
and holiness pleasing in my sight; but as yet I do not see
very clearly.

"*July 13.* This evening, for the first time in my life, I
lifted up my voice in social prayer, and felt that the Lord did
bless me, though the clouds of doubt and unbelief still hovered
around. How can I be so faithless, when Jesus has loved me
so well?

"*July 19.* Spent some portion of the day in reading Phil-
lips's 'Christian Experience,' which served to confirm and
strengthen me in the faith. The past has been a season of
bitter trial to me, and I pray that it may not be altogether
unprofitable. The conclusion that I had been the victim of
self-deception was indeed a bitter one, and after I arrived at
it I truly passed through a season of affliction. I had made
it my constant practice, for more than two years, to observe
four stated seasons of secret prayer daily; but after I gave
up the hope that I was a Christian, I more frequently observed seven or eight each day, than less. My usual prac-

tice was to read a portion of Scripture and a hymn before prayer, and in so doing, during the season of trial and doubt, at my seasons of prayer I read all the penitential hymns in our Hymn-book at least twice, and many of them eight or ten times, besides many others that I thought particularly adapted to my frame of mind. I thank the Lord that, although I was thus doubting, his loving-kindness was still over me, and he did at last permit me to feel that my feet were established on the rock, although as yet I do not see with all the clearness I desire. But my deliverance from this state was certainly far different from what I expected. I suppose my state of mind concerning this was something like Naaman's, for I really thought the Lord would do some *great thing;* and even after I began to think I was really converted and was now doubting away the grace of God, I thought the Lord would grant me such a clear evidence of my conversion as would leave no further room for doubt. But in this I was disappointed, and I, at last, was obliged to accept that which I had once rejected as spurious. I have found that very many Christians have been in similar circumstances.

"*August 8.* This day I followed my Savior in the divinely constituted—but by me long neglected—ordinance of baptism, which I received by sprinkling. As I had become fully satisfied that I had been genuinely converted, and, after careful examination of the subject, was thoroughly convinced that sprinkling was valid baptism, I saw no reason why I should not obey the command which says, 'Arise, and be baptized!' Immediately after being baptized I partook of the Lord's Supper.

"*August 19.* Though I feel the evidence of my justification quite clear, yet I want to be holy; to know, by experimental knowledge, that the blood of Christ cleanses me from all sin."

This longing for a richer Christian experience soon led him to adopt a set of formal rules for the regulation of his time and actions. The devotional books which he used doubtless suggested this course, and his ill-health gave him the requisite time for keeping the rules. Dated August 31st, they are as follows:

"1. I will observe at least five seasons of devotion daily: The first immediately after rising, the second at 9 A. M., the third at 1 P. M., the fourth at 4 P. M., and the fifth just before retiring. 2. I will endeavor to read three chapters, and commit at least five verses daily. 3. I am resolved to spend at least some portion of each day in self-examination. 4. Respecting my actions—(1) I am resolved to commit no known sin; (2) I will omit no known duty. 5. I am resolved to be watchful; to watch constantly against the enemies of my soul, and against all evil thoughts and idle words. And finally, I will endeavor, at all times and places and under all circumstances, to observe that rule given by the apostle when he says: 'Whether, therefore, ye eat or drink, or whatsoever ye do, do all to the glory of God;' and each night, before I retire, I will call myself to an account respecting the observance of these rules.

"*November 28.* I would be so perfectly united to Christ that his blood may circulate all through me, as the sap of a living vine through the branches. I would have such a communication open between Christ and my heart, as shall entirely cast out sin from my heart, and exclude it forever."

Shortly after passing his seventeenth birthday he began teaching a district school in the adjoining town of Brookfield. An old lady, who remembers him as he was at this time, recalls his habit of practicing on the bass-viol, and also that she found him one day deeply absorbed in reading the "Merry Wives of Windsor." He experienced the usual cares and perplexities of a young school-master, yet he recorded, at the close of the term, his thankfulness that improving health permitted him to engage in the useful activities of life.

On March 2, 1848, he was received into the church in full connection, and a few days afterward, commenced attending school at Chelsea village, which boasted a small academy. At his boarding-place, for the first time in his life, he enjoys the daily privilege of joining in family prayers. He is surprised that the class-meetings are so thinly attended, considering the large numbers of church members, and does not understand how a Methodist can absent himself from this invaluable means of grace. He says: "If I know my own heart, my desire is for religion, and the blessings it confers, in preference to any and all other blessings." At the close of this term, he speaks of it as the first term, for three years, which he has attended without injury to his health.

In an entry, dated May 23d, he speaks of reading the rules which he had adopted, and finds that they have been too much neglected. He still intends to carry out their spirit, though he may not be able to follow them to the letter. During this summer he had his first experience of an annual conference. On Sunday, July 9th, he listened to a sermon by Bishop Hedding, from 1 Timothy iv, 10. He says: "The bishop gave a brief but interesting history of his life, as far as his conversion and the commencement of his ministry were concerned, and then proceeded to his discourse, from what he said was the first text he ever used." The boy-critic adds: "His remarks were sound and weighty, and characterized by much mental acumen." No one could enjoy this bit of patronizing criticism more than the author of it in his later life.

The following entry marks a most important epoch, as it gives the first intimation of his desire for a thorough education, and of his thoughts concerning the ministry :

"*August 3.* I am highly favored this summer with respect to my health, so that I am able to study considerably, and engage in light manual labor to some extent. I regard it my privilege and duty to acquire a good education, should circumstances permit, and for this I am striving daily. I know not what employment my Lord will assign me in future life, but I frequently look forward with some anxiety, and perhaps with vain conjectures. My mind has been frequently directed toward the holy ministry; but I almost fear it is sacrilege to indulge a thought concerning it, believing, as I do, that it should not be entered by human caprice. but only by a special divine call. I have sometimes tried to forbid my mind to dwell on this subject, but I can not."

In the autumn of 1848 he taught in the old school-house on the West Hill, where he had received his own earlier education. He expresses profound gratitude that he has health to engage in purposes of usefulness. In the winter of the same year he taught again in Brookfield.

CHAPTER IV.

SCHOOL-DAYS AT NEWBURY AND CONCORD.

1848-1853.

WE have seen that at eighteen years of age Francis Hemenway had improved health, an increasing desire for a thorough education, and serious thoughts concerning a call to the ministry. His teaching, to procure the means for a higher education, was in accordance with the custom of the time. Tradition has preserved a significant incident of this early apprenticeship as teacher. The big boys in one of the schools, hearing a rumor that the new master was intending to open the morning session with prayer, leagued together to make a disturbance; but the young teacher's prayer was so manly, tender, and appropriate that the plot was at once abandoned.

The spring of 1849 introduced him into a larger world, whose influences were potent in developing his character and talents, and shaping his future. At that time he entered the conference seminary at Newbury. Both the place and the school became very dear to him. The village itself possesses rare charms. Built upon a high terrace of the Connecticut, its long street follows the direction of the river, while two shorter streets, at right angles, mark out the village green. On the west side of this common

stand the seminary building and the Methodist
church, back of which rises the steep side of Mount
Pulaski. The view eastward is one of the fairest in
all picturesque New England. Beyond the quiet
hamlet are spread broad and fertile meadows, through
which the Connecticut sweeps in a series of graceful
curves. Wooded hills across the river reveal here
and there a prosperous village, while along the eastern horizon extends a range of noble mountains, from
the ragged outlines of Lafayette, on the north, to
Moosilauke, lifting his gigantic shoulders in massive
and magnificent beauty on the south. Without questioning the wisdom of the subsequent removal of the
seminary to Montpelier, no Methodist can fail to regret the necessity of abandoning this charming place,
which, in summer at least, is little less than an earthly
paradise. The seminary, attracting students at that
time both from New Hampshire and Vermont, was
in a very prosperous condition. "If there is any
happy combination of circumstances on earth," wrote
the young student, "calculated to assist our conception of heaven, it is surely to be found at Newbury."
The Rev. Dr. Joseph E. King, now at the head of
Fort Edward Collegiate Institute, was principal, and
the late Professor Henry S. Noyes was one of the
teachers. The buildings and other appliances of the
seminary would seem meager now; but the men in
charge, from its beginning, had fixed a high standard
both of scholarship and piety. Enthusiasm for education and religion pervaded the place. Besides that
of men already mentioned, it had felt the inspiring
influence of Osmon C. Baker, Charles Adams, John

Dempster, and Clark T. Hinman, who had established
here in 1845 the first theological school of the Methodist Episcopal Church, which, two years later, was
removed to Concord, N. H. The ardent and heroic
spirit of pioneer days animated both teachers and
students. Almost every term witnessed a revival of
religion, in which many students were converted and
the Christian workers were trained for future service.
Two entries in his journal show the purposes with
which Francis began his life here, and the impression which this large company of Christian young
people made upon him:

"*February 26, 1849.* I have come to Newbury to spend
the spring term at the seminary. I expect to enjoy many
privileges—educational and religious—and I pray that this
may be a season of improvement in every way, that in all
things I may grow up into Christ my living Head."

"*March 1.* Attended the seminary class-meeting, where a
very large number was assembed. How delightful to see so
many young people who are willing to take upon themselves
the yoke of Christ!"

Amid these new scenes and influences his own religious life is greatly quickened. He records hearing
"an excellent and moving discourse on Zech. xii, 10,
by Professor Hinman," from which he expects abundant fruit. The next Sunday he goes from public
service to the band-meeting, and thence to prayer-
meeting. At the last, nine came forward for prayers.
This was on the first of April. On the third, nine
more rose for prayers; on the eighth, twelve; on the
fifteenth, seven or eight. On the sixteenth of May
he wrote: "The work of revival in the seminary still

continues." To one who loved both religion and
study ardently these surroundings were most congenial; and amid them he increased in wisdom "and
in favor with God and man."

In the summer vacation he expressed to his pastor
thoughts concerning his life-work which he had before committed to no other confidant than his journal.
The subject of the ministry, he said, had, at times,
pressed with great weight upon his mind. Mr. Hill
assured him that it had been his impression, and that
of others in the church, that he was divinely called
to that work.

The autumn of 1849 was spent at Newbury in
study, and the winter at Williamstown in teaching.
The following entry describes his final decision with
regard to his life-work. The meeting referred to was
held in the old parsonage at Williamstown:

"*January 13, 1850.* I have had deep anxiety for a long
time with regard to the ministry, to which I have before al-
luded, and I set apart last week for especial prayer on that
subject, if by any means I might obtain satisfactory light
with regard to my duty. I have long entertained the impression that it would be my calling, and that it was my present
duty to prepare for it, but as yet I was unsatisfied with regard
to it. In this state of mind I remained until to-night, though
seeming gradually to approach an affirmative decision. I
went to the meeting praying for some convincing manifesta-
tion of duty. I had not long been there before I began to
feel the especial workings of the Spirit, while, at the same
time, this subject came up before me. Soon it assumed the
aspect of present duty, and, regarding it as such, I commenced
mentally an act of personal dedication. I was interrupted by
the singing of the hymn, 'When for the eternal worlds,' etc.,
which seemed as a celestial voice. Again I dedicated myself,
which done, they sang the verse, 'Prone to wander,' etc.,

every word of which was in harmony with my feelings. Thus, by this act, am I the Lord's in an especial sense. May I draw still closer to him!"

In March he was again at Newbury, where the spring term was marked by another revival. In May he had his first experience in leading class, of which he quaintly says: "Contrary to reasonable human expectation, I had a tolerably good season."

On June 16th he attended the Sabbath exercises of the conference at Bradford. He describes the conference love-feast and the testimonies of the veteran ministers with delighted enthusiasm. He heard Bishop Morris preach in the grove "a very instructive and practical discourse from the text, 'Cease to do evil.'"

During the winter vacation of 1850–51 Mr. Hemenway traveled through Orange County, introducing a new series of text-books into the schools. His journal was neglected, and the regularity of his religious exercises interrupted, yet he found this new mode of life not unfavorable to religious experience.

On February 13th he records his recommendation by the class for an exhorter's license. The following entries describe his first experiences as a preacher:

"What a solemn thing it is to stand between God and man! I have consented to speak to the people Tuesday night before I leave for Newbury. May it be in simplicity, and assisted by the Holy Spirit's influence!

"*February 18.* Found an unexpectedly large number assembled, to whom I had a good degree of liberty in speaking, and am sure, by the united prayers of the praying ones, the presence of the Most High overshadowed us. Many appeared affected. Three rose for prayers. May this first seed, sown in tears and weakness, produce abundant fruit!"

A friend, who was present at this latter service, remembers that he gave out as the first hymn, "Soldiers of the Cross, arise," which he started himself to the tune of "Caledonia."

Once more he returns to Newbury for his last term as a student there. On March 23d he preached his first Sabbath sermon at North Haverhill, from the text, "The effectual fervent prayer of a righteous man availeth much." He says: "It was to me a memorable time, and also a good time." The Rev. Mr. Cushing was with him. The next Sunday he consented to "improve a part of the day" at Swiftborough, where he had more freedom and less embarrassment than before. The next Sabbath he preached at South Newbury, with special freedom, which he attributed to two causes: "1. I was enabled to resign myself more implicitly into the hands of God, and rely more fully on his power. 2. My subject was better matured and more familiar."

The term passed pleasantly. He enjoyed the work in school, and apparently even more his Sabbath labors in the little churches and school-houses of the vicinity. Throughout his school-days at Newbury he maintained high rank as a talented and industrious student. He was one of those selected by the authorities for occasional service as tutor. The reputation achieved at the home lyceum as a speaker and writer was increased at the seminary. When he finished his course at Newbury in May, 1851, he left with an enviable record and with sincere regret.

The following summer was spent at home. His

journal shows that he preached several times, and with increasing enjoyment. The part he took in a Fourth of July celebration of the Lyceum caused him some uneasiness, "because of the prejudice which is abroad in this immediate vicinity against literary societies and every thing connected with them." He adds: "I fully believe it to be a Christian's duty to deny himself sometimes, in view of the consciences of his brethren; but in this matter, after looking at it carefully and considering my obligations to all classes, it did not seem that any departure from my own ideas of right and propriety was required." August 29th he left home to teach in Waitsfield, and wrote: "I shall not probably return to it again until, in a certain sense, it shall cease to be my home. I love my home, *passionately* love it."

After preaching for the first time in Waitsfield, he says: "There are a thousand sources of uneasiness as I appear before a public congregation; but the greatest is lest, for some reason, my ministry should not be *efficient*—lest, by some apparent inconsistency which may have been seen in me, the word should be neutralized, and fail of producing its legitimate effect. I pray that I may be holy, discreet, entirely freed from everything which would operate, in any manner, as a hindrance to the word of God."

In October he received news of the death of his intimate friend and former room-mate, A. K. Carter. Obliged to go immediately to the school-room, he gave out the hymn:

"O, what is life? 'T is like a flower that blossoms and is gone,"

4

"to be sung to that favorite tune of mine, Stepney."
He says of this friend : "From our first meeting our
sympathies, secrets, and hearts seemed to flow spon-
taneously together. We were bound together by the
strongest and most sacred ties of sanctified friendship. Had he lived he would most certainly, it seems
to me, have become a minister of great usefulness."

On his twenty-first birthday he reviews his blessings and anticipates the future :

"I am oftentimes tempted to despond, yet as often encouraged to hope. From the responsibilities which may probably devolve upon me in future, should I live, I ofttimes
shrink, yet the promise is always available: 'My grace is
sufficient for thee.' May I be sanctified and fully prepared
for all the will of God! If I know my own heart, my ambition is not to be great nor honored nor famous, but to be
just what the Lord would have me be. O that I may be
able to acknowledge the Lord in all my ways, that he may
direct my paths!"

He was recalled to teach the winter district school
at Waitsfield, and received no little discipline himself in this work, which tests about all one's powers
of ingenuity and endurance. He had forty scholars,
and over *thirty* exercises a day. One morning he
was called from the school-room to see a young man
who was lying upon his death-bed. The conversion
of this man stirred him profoundly, and he preached
his funeral sermon with deep emotion and "unusual
liberty."

In a letter of December 16, 1851, he asks of a dear
friend : "Do you think it best, all things considered,
for me to go to Concord in the spring?" In Janu-
nary, 1852, he wrote to the Rev. Justin Spaulding,

asking advice on this matter. The letter describing the correspondence says:

"He knows something about me and almost everything about the Methodist itinerancy. He himself is a self-made man, yet a close student. He gives his decided opinion in favor of entering the Institute, and assigns *seven* reasons, the substance of which is: In order for one to be prepared to fulfill the mission of the Methodist minister, one must possess a cultivated intellect, a mind prepared to meet and grapple with the various engines which Satan may use to advance his work, a mind furnished with knowledge which shall answer to the present improved state of society. The opportunities for that close, consecutive study which alone can make us what we should be are very small on a circuit or station. He also noticed the objection that an educated ministry will be a proud and lazy ministry, urging, in answer, that the most humble and active ministers in the Church have been the best educated. I have not, as yet, reconsidered that question, but do not know but I shall to-morrow. Pray for me, that the Lord, by his counsel, may guide me. I have just commenced reading Upham's 'Interior Life,' of which, perhaps, you may have heard me speak. Already my soul burns more ardently for *holiness*. I am daily convinced that I know too little of the deep things of God to be prepared to explain them properly to others."

His presiding elder strenuously opposed his going to the Biblical Institute, yet, influenced by Mr. Spaulding's sensible advice, and his own high ideal of a minister's requirements, he decided to take a theological course. The first of March, 1852, found him in Concord. A letter describes his first meeting with Dr. Dempster:

"*Concord, March 2, 1852.* Arriving at this place a perfect stranger, as I was, I had myself driven immediately to the Institute boarding-house, where I found a Brother Moore in charge. He directed me to Dr. Dempster. I went and rang

the bell at his door, and was conducted by a young lady into
the sitting-room, where she left me, telling me she would call
Dr. Dempster, who would soon be in. I was alone, awaiting with
palpitating heart the appearance of the great Dr. Dempster,
whom I had imagined to be not only great in mind and name,
but in body too. I was expecting to see a large, bland, portly-
looking Doctor of Divinity. Imagine, then, my surprise when
a small, quite ordinary-looking man, dressed in the plainest
and oldest style, appeared, calling himself Dr. Dempster. He
received me very cordially, and gave me all the information
necessary for me."

He describes the Institute as located " in a retired
part of the village, entirely removed from the noise
and bustle, yet situated at the head of the two principal streets, and especially convenient of access to
all parts of the village." The lofty elm-trees lining
the streets are a great attraction. We may get a
glimpse of him at work. He says: " Improvement
is now with me the paramount aim." On April 15,
1852, he writes :

"Since I last wrote I have been at work with all my
might taking in pieces the Hebrew and Greek languages, and
dissecting Butler's and Watson's Theology, so that I am now
almost covered with rubbish. In Greek we are reading the
Gospels harmonized; in Hebrew we are now in the third
chapter of Genesis. We have been translating Hebrew but a
short time, yet I think it is quite an easy language, although
its characters appear so unintelligible. In theology we have
a lecture one day and recite the next. Dr. Dempster is now
delivering a course of lectures on the connection of geology
with revelation. His last was respecting the universality of
the Flood. He takes the negative position.

"I preached last Sabbath to an Orthodox* congregation

---

*Some readers may not know that in New England "Orthodox"
is commonly used to distinguish the Trinitarian from the Unitarian
Congregationalists.

in an Orthodox meeting-house in Loudon, about seven miles from this place. The Lord was with me. I had a blessed season. I am to go there next Sabbath. My turn will come to preach before the school two weeks from to-morrow, at nine o'clock. Let me then have an especial interest in your prayers."

He leads a class in the village, and preaches frequently in Concord, Barnstead, Hookset, and other neighboring towns. This work he enjoys more and more.

"It is blessed to feel that we are accomplishing the important work of the evangelist. I mean not merely to go through the formality of preaching, and contemplate a delighted congregation hanging upon your words, if by chance it should be so, but to know that God is sending out his word through you, with the certain promise that 'it shall accomplish that whereunto it is sent.'

"*June 19, 1852.* I am enjoying myself very greatly here this summer. I have plenty of work, agreeable companions, convenient accommodations, and the blessing of God. I have but a single object in view in all my labors,—*immediately*, my preparation for the work of the ministry; *ultimately*, the glory of God; and while I have the evidence that this end is being answered, I can not but feel satisfied. I am thankful that I ever came to Concord; that, green as I was, I did not conclude to take upon myself immediately the responsibility of performing the work of the Christian minister.

In writing of his theological instructors he speaks of Professor Baker as "a modest, quiet, easy, good-natured, corpulent man, but a most *rigid* Greek teacher." Professor Vail "is considered a Hebrew scholar of the highest order." Dr. Dempster "is a man full of thought, and is very suggestive in all his teaching. In the department of mental and moral science he is the greatest man I ever knew." As to the students, though "there must of necessity, among a company of forty human beings, be some things to which the fastidious might take exceptions," yet he is convinced that the fears concerning a decline in religion among theological students are baseless, and that the "sacred fire does burn here in its purity." He boards in a club, and gives the assessment for one week as one dollar and sixty-one cents. In August he listens to lectures on the Discipline by Professor Baker, already elected bishop, and performing his last service in the Institute.

By November he has received a temporary appointment at Pittsfield, and begun his first pastoral experience. He feels an "especial sense of weakness" in making pastoral calls, and yet believes that "at least half of the preacher's work lies in this direction." The winter passed pleasantly and successfully, and in the spring he returned to Concord.

In May, of 1853, at the Conference which met at Newport, N. H., he heard an excellent sermon from Bishop Janes; and from Abel Stevens a speech, which he had "rarely, if ever, heard equaled." His topic was "The Tract Cause," and, in response, over $1,200 were pledged by the preachers for themselves and their charges.

He now has applications for preaching which would fill all his Sabbaths two or three times over, and finally arranges to preach regularly at Hill and Barnstead. In June he is present at a musical convention, conducted by Lowell Mason. A letter written this summer indicates two prominent traits, which all his students will remember. It speaks of his "love for perspicuity and systematic arrangement," and discusses the proper pronunciation of "Goethe."

In July he attended the Commencement exercises at Dartmouth College.

"Wednesday morning last took the cars for Hanover— Dartmouth College. . . . The 'natives' had already begun to assemble, so that when we arrived the peddlers' carts, victualing tents, and 'congregated thousands' told, in language unmistakable, that Hanover was realizing a signal day. The announcement that the Hon. Rufus Choate would speak on that day had called together an unusually large number to attend the exercises. As the exercises were not to commence till 9.30, after seeking out my special friends, I went with them to visit the curiosities of the college cabinet, libraries, etc. Quite interesting. At 9.30 the procession was formed at the college chapel to march to the church, where the first address was to be delivered. Falling into the procession, as all 'professional gentlemen' and 'distinguished guests' were requested to do, after more jamming than I ever before suffered in the same length of time, I succeeded in entering the church. A very good address was then delivered by Hon. Ogden Hoffman, of New York. At 3.20 P. M. a procession was again formed, to be conducted to the church. Never before have I seen such a press to gain admission. A very strong police force had to exert itself to the utmost to prevent the people from rushing in *en masse* even before the 'dignitaries' were admitted. Mr. Choate spoke between two and three hours. Subject, 'Eulogy on Daniel Webster.' The elocution and oratory were good; but Webster, mere *man* as he was, was almost *deified*.

"Thursday was the regular day for the graduation exercises. Between twenty and thirty young men spoke. About fifty graduated. The exercises were quite interesting—more so to me, as a whole, than those of the day before.

"Some distinguished guests were present at the exercises— Hon. John Wentworth, of Illinois, commonly called 'Long John' (seven feet in his stockings), Dr. Mussey, Rev. Dr. Barstow, and others too numerous to mention. I saw quite a large number of the old Newbury students."

In October he visited an Adventist camp-meeting, which appears to him "a sickening exhibition of the fruit of ignorance." The same month he writes: "What do you think of my going West next year? The Doctor [Dempster] is going out to the college of which he is president, and wishes me to go with him. The West is a great field, you know. Would it not be just the place for me?"

With ten others, he graduated from the Concord Institute in 1853. As the Institute afterwards became the School of Theology of the Boston University, he is, in this sense, an alumnus of that school. His graduating address was on "The Imperishable Record." In this he said:

"The true testimonial of the faithful minister is not to be sought in the favorable notices of public journals, nor the popular voice concerning him, nor even in the reported conversions, so ardently coveted. His true record is found in the hearts and characters which he is instrumental in molding into the image of the heavenly. Happy shall he be who shall so unite in his character human excellence with divine grace, that he shall be able to produce upon plastic yet immortal natures impressions so true and beautiful that he can confidently appeal to them before the judgment-seat of the Omniscient One."

CHAPTER V.

PASTORATE AT MONTPELIER.

1854-1857.

PROBABLY the majority of young men who have thus far been educated for the Methodist ministry, have had no clearly defined boundary between school-life and the pastorate. Apprenticeship in preaching and pastoral work has been interwoven with academical and theological training. This course has both advantages and perils, but the former probably preponderate. The experience gained by the young preacher in school-houses and little churches, the practical knowledge of work and people acquired in actual service, is of inestimable value. However exact scholarship may be impeded, there is, ordinarily, an increase of zeal for useful discipline and available acquisition. The temptations lie in the direction of a low ideal of preaching, a failure to complete one's course of study, or of superficial work in the theological school. Mr. Hemenway yielded to none of these. Although he graduated in the autumn of 1853, he returned to Concord in the spring of 1854, to complete some studies which had been interrupted by enforced absences.

During the winter of 1853–4 he served as pastoral supply at Shelburne Falls, in northwestern

Massachusetts. The Methodist church in this picturesque and prosperous manufacturing village was regarded an important one. It had formerly enjoyed the ministrations of the Rev. William Butler, who became afterwards the founder of Methodist missions in India and Mexico. The outgoing pastor, an able and eloquent man, had been convicted of untruthfulness, and suddenly left the Methodist ministry. His defection had naturally thrown a shadow over the congregation. The young pastor found "the church and people quite a burden for a boy to carry." His letters, though very modest, contain abundant proof that he won the admiration and love of the people. They gave him substantial gifts, and urged him to remain as their regular pastor. He writes: "I used to think of the pastoral visiting as an unpleasant work, but I find it quite the reverse. In the sick-room, especially, our religion shines with a superadded luster."

In February, 1854, he received an invitation to become teacher of Greek and Latin in a seminary in Fulton, N. Y. About the first of March, though urged by presiding elder and people to remain at Shelburne Falls, he steadfastly adhered to his resolution to complete his studies at Concord. He found awaiting him there an invitation to join the New England conference, from the Rev. Amos Binney, presiding elder of the Charlestown district. "So you see," he writes, "that if the calls of the church are the calls of God, his kingdom is divided against itself. There are openings enough, and there is work enough. The greatest point is grace and ability to do it." A letter written to an invalid friend at this time contains this characteristic passage : " I think it my province to proclaim Scripture to you. *' Be careful for nothing.'* Live as though to live *now* was *all your business.* Have no providence for the future, except what you have in that very thing; *i. e.,* living carelessly. I know living so may not seem to consist with one's interests religiously or intellectually, but it may do both. When that course of life becomes a *duty,* and is allowed as such, it will not harm us in any regard."

April 15, 1854, he writes : " I have, this very morning, had a long talk with Bishop Baker with reference to my further course for one or two years. He decidedly advises me to join conference, as the first course; of the others, I 'll tell you when I see you. Doctor Dempster, on the other hand, wishes me to go West, and take a place, or as he calls it, a ' chair,' in an institution there. Of course it will be my privilege to ' decide, when doctors disagree.' My present opinion is that the chances are in favor of my teaching for a year or two, and that the place will be west of Vermont, though the question still hangs ' in even scale.' "

The summer of '54 was spent in preaching and study, and in visiting friends in Chelsea, Pittsfield, Barre, and other places. The first of September found him at Newbury seminary in the position of a teacher. The work was intended to be temporary only, and rendered advisable on account of his health, which work and study had somewhat impaired. There were two hundred and seventy-five students, and he taught arithmetic, grammar, algebra, geometry, mental philosophy, reading, Latin, and Greek. In writing about the teachers, he said: "Miss —— has n't quite enough *sparkle* about her to render herself available to the fullest extent. What a desirable quality of character is *assurance*—not that which produces forwardness, but that which enables us to rest *easily* in the right place! Energy, vivacity, and decision, as it seems to me, depend very much upon confidence as a basis. Prof. Taverner,* a distinguished teacher of elocution, has been with us for the last two days. His terms are very high—twenty dollars for a course of private lessons, and two dollars and a half for admission to his class."

The letters indicate that Mr. Hemenway preached almost every Sunday in neighboring towns. But more interesting than teaching or preaching were the plans and arrangements for his approaching marriage to Miss Sarah L. Bixby, of Chelsea. They had now been formally engaged for four years; but when their attachment began ·it would have been difficult for either of them to have told. The families had long been neighbors and friends. As children they had gone together to the old school-house, and to the meeting-house on the hill. Miss Bixby's father had been Francis Hemenway's class-leader and spiritual adviser for years. The two young people had also been at Newbury as students together. Companion-

* This unique, peripatetic teacher, a philosopher in the science of reading, was at Evanston as late as 1884, but has since died. Probably no man ever gave instruction in elocution to so many and so distinguished ministers.

ship, sympathy in the best things, and friendship, gradually ripened into a devoted love, which proved the greatest of earthly blessing to both, and endured all tests. The one shadow which darkened these bright days is described in a letter dated October 27, 1854. After speaking of the beauties of the October scenery, he says: "Our community was very much saddened, one week ago, by a telegraphic dispatch announcing the death of the Rev. Dr. Hinman, president-elect of the North-western University, of which Brother Noyes is chosen one of the professors. His funeral was attended here Tuesday. Bishop Baker preached the sermon. The four teachers were bearers. It was a very solemn time." October 31st he left Newbury for Concord, to attend the first alumni reunion of the Concord Institute.

On the 19th of November, 1854, the long-anticipated marriage ceremony was performed, in the West Hill meeting-house, by the Rev. Elisha J. Scott, then presiding elder of the district. The young couple established their home in pleasant rooms in the seminary boarding-house at Newbury. During a pilgrimage, last summer, to the scenes of Dr. Hemenway's early life, the writer spent some days in Newbury, and stopped in this building, which has now been transformed into Sawyer's Hotel, a cool and attractive summer hotel, and, by a strange coincidence, was assigned to these very rooms, the most pleasant in the whole house. Here began a home-life which ever seemed to him, and the nearest friends who knew its beauty, as near the highest ideal as can be hoped for this side heaven. But happy lives and the steady monotony of faithful school duties, however significant and influential, afford little material for historian or biographer.

The next spring brought an important change. May 28, 1855, he writes from Plainfield, where the Vermont conference is in session, as follows:

"The appointments are to be read at five o'clock. . . . I suppose the die is now cast! My appointment you will find, among others, upon the inclosed slip.* It can not be more surprising to you than it is to me; and it is in spite of my personal remonstrance, which I had never expected to express, that I am stationed there. Still, now it is done, and can not be remedied, I see much that is desirable about it. You remember the pretty parsonage, and know what a pleasant home it may be for our first. Quite a number of the people have expressed themselves in favor of the arrangement, or, in other words, petitioned for me."

The appointment of Mr. Hemenway to the State capital was unwelcome to the seminary. Professor Noyes did "not know how to have it so." A letter to Bishop Ames is contemplated to break up the arrangement; but it is a fixed fact, and irrevocable. Though feeling deeply the separation and the added responsibilities, he writes to his wife: "Let us look to the bright future. I shall have more time to devote to Biblical and theological study than heretofore."

The story of the two years' pastorate at Montpelier must be briefly told. Nature, discipline, and divine grace had now made him a preacher and pastor of rare attractiveness. His sermons were clearcut, interesting, helpful, and inspiring. Congrega-

---

* Montpelier, Vt.

tions increased, the church was quickened, and souls were saved. By his manliness, sympathy, and holy character he won the respect of all classes in the community, and the warm affection of those to whom he ministered. He devoted himself with ardent enthusiasm to his work in study, pulpit, and parish. A letter, written from Montpelier in February, 1889, bears testimony to the results of these labors :

"His was surely a marked pastorate in the history of this church. There are not a few living still who can bear witness to the wealth and beauty of the intellectual treasures he lavished upon this people, and the great spiritual power which emanated from his life. Some remember, with a gratitude too deep for words, his influence while here, and the proofs of his continued interest given long afterward. One of our recent pastors said, in alluding to Dr. Hemenway, whom he never personally knew, that the fruits of his ministry could still be seen here after the lapse of so many years."

A notable event in the home-life at Montpelier was the birth of the first child, a son, born December 20, 1856, and named Henry Bixby. New springs of thought and feeling were thus opened in the father's nature, enriching his own life and greatly increasing his usefulness.

In one respect only was the young pastor unsuited for the work before him. He had not that robust health which is almost essential to great success in a city pastorate. And the work was very taxing. The ordinary Sunday services began with preaching at half-past ten in the morning. This was followed immediately by the Sunday-school, at which the pastor's presence was desired and most desirable. There was preaching again at half-past one. In the evening, at early candle-light, there was held a mammoth prayer-meeting, for which special preparation was necessary, and which brought no small strain to the tired pastor's nerves. In the winter many members of the legislature were constant attendants upon his ministry, and the house was generally packed with hearers. It was a successful pastorate, but the success was dearly bought. A few such victories would have utterly ruined his health. He completed the full term, but felt obliged to ask a location at its close, that he might look about for less taxing work.

Two testimonials to his great service to his people will be appropriate here. The first is a selection from some verses contributed to a local paper. They are presented, not as poetry, but as a hearty and worthy expression of the impression made by his early ministry. They were written by the daughter of a leading member of the Church, a former student at Newbury :

" Youth's fair light was on his forehead,
    Genius flashing from his eye,
And the hopes of early manhood
    In his heart were beating high.
Not a worn and weary soldier,
    With the battle almost done;
But a young, fresh-hearted warrior,
    All his trophies yet unwon.

God had lent him brilliant talents,
    Which could charm the listening throng;
Worldly paths had often wooed him
    With their wildering, siren song;

But he laid each fond ambition
  Lowly at the sacred cross,
Heeding not Fame's proffered laurels,
  Boldly 'counting all things loss.'

Words of life seem doubly precious,
  Falling from his hallowed tongue,
And rich treasures of affection
  From his people hath he won.
He is with us when our loved ones,
  Earth-tired, sink to dreamless sleep,
And in those dark, trying moments
  He can 'weep with those that weep.'

Walking close with God, he leadeth
  Tenderly his little flock,
Pointing, when the storm-clouds gather,
  To the 'Shadow of the Rock.'
Faithfully he does his mission,
  Faltering never by the way,
Knowing a reward awaits him
  In the land of cloudless day.

Let us then, when, morn and evening,
  Bending low to breathe our prayer,
Ask for him, our youthful pastor,
  Our Good Father's kindly care;
That life's harvest-field may yield him
  Golden sheaves, a rich reward,
And at last a crown of glory—
  A 'forever with the Lord.'"

But no biography of a Methodist minister would be complete without a view of his gifts and graces from the stand-point of one of his presiding elders. Under the date of July 24, 1857, the Rev. Elisha J. Scott, presiding elder of the Montpelier district, wrote to a leading member of the East Genesee conference:

"Understanding that the Rev. F. D. Hemenway, late a member of the Vermont conference, proposes to offer himself for readmission into the traveling connection in the East Genesee conference, I feel it a privilege, no less than a duty, to furnish you such a representation of him as shall enable you to introduce him fairly and truly to your conference. Brother Hemenway is believed to be deeply and uniformly pious, and possessed of intellectual powers which entitle him to rank among the first young men in the country. Indeed, he exhibits a rare *ripeness*, intellectually, for one of his age. His mind has been thoroughly and extensively trained. He is a scholar in the best sense of the word. It may properly be said that he has a liberal education, though not a collegiate. He has passed through the prescribed course of studies in our General Biblical Institute, and graduated with its highest honors. He does not regard his education as finished, however, but is an ardent student—perhaps too much so for his delicate constitution. His talents as a preacher are of a superior order. Sound in doctrine, clear and eloquent in its enunciation, and pleasing in style and manner, he can hardly fail to be popular. The two years last past he has spent in this place, as you are aware, and to say he has been highly esteemed and universally beloved but feebly expresses the real position he holds among us. Many deeply regret, and none more than myself, that our law does not allow him to remain longer. The conference consented to his location, with a view to his removal from us, with extreme reluctance. Nothing but a belief that a milder climate, and especially that your system of ministerial work would contribute to his health, and thus promise a longer period of active service to the church, reconciles us at all to his removal. We need many just such men in Vermont. He is a man to be trusted anywhere. Whatever he does is well done.

"Trusting that you will pardon this *volunteer* representation, I am," etc.

From a letter, written several years later to an intimate friend in Montpelier, we get a satisfactory glimpse of the spirit and results of this pastorate. He had just learned of the death of a young lady of this Church, and says:

"There has been no moment of time in my ministerial life, filled with so true and deep a joy as that in which she said to me, as I took her hand to bid her good-bye: 'Brother Hemenway, won't you pray for me? I wish to be a Christian.' I had long felt that she stood on the very verge of life, but in my extreme fearfulness I dared not venture to address her with reference to personal religion, lest I should break the spell that seemed to be drawing her to the Savior. And the bliss of that glad moment, in which I was first assured of her purpose to be a Christian, was the truest and deepest of my ministerial life. Her thoughtful and earnest look, which had confronted me so many times as I stood in the sacred desk, had burned itself into my very soul. I knew that she was an earnest seeker for the true center of rest and the unfailing source of consolation. And in the silence of this night, as I think of her, I feel a gratitude I can not express, but which fills my eyes with tears and my heart with joy that she found them."

CHAPTER VI.

NEVER was a man's spirit more willing to continue for life the work of a Methodist preacher
and pastor. Mr. Hemenway loved to preach, and he
delighted in the pastoral relation. But the flesh stag-
gered under its heavy burden, and rest and change
became imperative. He decided to ask for a location
at the approaching conference of 1857, and to seek
recuperation among the Chelsea hills, while he should
await the directing voice of Providence. The first
intimation of the call came in the form of a letter
from Professor Henry S. Noyes, of the Northwestern
University, at Evanston, Ill., dated April 13, 1857.
It stated that the writer had recommended Mr. Hemenway for the position of principal of the preparatory
department of the Garrett Biblical Institute. It says:
"Dr. Kidder has told me what kind of a man they
want, and I have informed him that you exactly fulfill all the required conditions. He is favorably impressed, and desires me to write you to ascertain
whether you would favorably entertain such a prop-
osition." The annual income of the institute was
stated to be nineteen thousand dollars. The question
of his joining the East Genesee Conference was under

consideration at the same time. A later letter of Professor Noyes's says: "The lake breeze keeps us from miasma. The range of study in the preparatory department of the Institute comprises common English branches, rhetoric, elementary Greek, elocution, and possibly Hebrew. I am greatly desirous to see you in this position. Dr. Dempster speaks of you in the highest terms. We are not entirely 'out of the woods' yet, but this is no drawback, and all our visitors are charmed with our delightful scenery." Bishop Baker, and many others, uniting in commending this appointment, it was formally made by the trustees * and accepted by Mr. Hemenway, and in September, 1857, he left the hills and valleys of Vermont for his new home on the shores of Lake Michigan. His admiration and love for New England never decreased. Twelve years after this removal, he wrote to a friend in Montpelier, Vt.:

"We think of you with peculiar interest in these unrivaled summer days. What a lovely home you have! Do you know how grand is the panorama before you every time you ride to town? Your hills and mountains standing about you, clothed in their summer beauty, are worth a pilgrimage to see. I express no disloyalty to the magnificent country in which our lives are cast, when I confess my profound sense of its inferiority, in variety and beauty, to yours. May God continue you, for many long years, to drink in his goodness through channels so appropriate!"

Yet Evanston, too, had its peculiar natural charms, to which even the early Indian inhabitants were not

---

* The trustees at this time were the Hon. Grant Goodrich, Orrington Lunt, John Evans, and Revs. Philo Judson and Stephen P. Keyes.

indifferent. To the gently rounded cape, covered with noble oaks and jutting out into the blue waters of Lake Michigan, which now forms the main campus, they gave, if the tradition is trustworthy, the name of "Beauty's Eyebrow." Just north of this, and beyond the "Rubicon," the first building* of the theological school was erected in 1854, on the location now occupied by the Swedish Theological Seminary. The remarkable series of events which led to the establishment of the Garrett Biblical Institute might well be considered romantic, if it should not rather be regarded as providential. The history can not be related here. † The first term of instruction, under a temporary organization, began in January, 1855, with four students, under the tuition of Dr. Dempster and Professors William Goodfellow and William P. Wright. When Professor Hemenway entered upon his duties, in the autumn of 1857, he came to an Evanston very different from that of to-day. Up to that year the mail was received but once a week. The present main campus did not contain a single building. The Northwestern University found ample accommodations in a portion of the present preparatory building, which then stood at the north-west corner of Davis Street and Hinman Avenue.

Actual work in the Northwestern University had

* After the erection of Heck Hall, this building became a university boarding-house, and was known as Dempster Hall. It was burned to the ground in 1879. Special mention is here made of it because of its historic interest, and of the memories associated with it in the minds of the older alumni of the Institute.

† See the historical sketch, by the late Hon. Grant Goodrich, in the catalogue of the Institute for 1889, and "The History of Evanston," by Miss Frances E. Willard.

begun November 5, 1855, with ten young men, who
constituted a Freshman class. The Rev. Dr. Randolph S. Foster was the President; Henry S. Noyes,
A. M., Professor of Mathematics; Rev. W. D. God-
man, A. M., Professor of Greek; and Daniel Bonbright, A. M., Professor of Latin. The name of the
Rev. Abel Stevens, A. M., appears as Professor of
Rhetoric and English Literature, but he never came
to Evanston for active service. A sister institution
had also been established by Professor W. P. Jones,
bearing the somewhat cumbrous name of "The Northwestern Female College and Male Preparatory."

The circular of the University for 1857-8 has the
additional name of J. V. Z. Blaney, M. D., as Professor of Natural Sciences, and states that Professor
Bonbright is absent in Europe. By this time there
were three small collegiate classes, and two thousand
volumes in the library. It adds naïvely that " Mr.
Kennicott is collecting a museum of natural history," and that "the community comprises, with few
exceptions, professors of religion." The circular of
1858-9 claims a population for the village of twelve
hundred.

Rooms for Professor Hemenway were provided in
the building of the institute named above. Fifty-
three theological students were registered for the year
1857-8, of whom thirteen were engaged in preparar-
tory studies. The Rev. Dr. John Dempster, the noble
founder of Methodist theological institutions; the
Rev. Daniel P. Kidder, an acknowledged leader in
theological training; and the Rev. Henry Bannister,
in the full vigor of his powers, and with a well-

earned reputation as a Biblical scholar, constituted
the regular faculty. The capacity of the original
building had been nearly doubled by a large addition. A glimpse of the interior is given us in the
reminiscences of the Rev. Thomas R. Strobridge, A. M.,
who says: "When I first took my seat in the chapel, and
swept my gaze about me, I was amused at the coats
of many colors which the students wore. But I grew
sober as I observed the central figure upon the plat-
form, an aged man, not large of stature, with a genial,
thoughtful face, wearing the same kind of a garment,
made of dark, red-figured calico. This was Dr.
Dempster, whom I frequently saw afterwards working at his wood-pile. There also sat Dr. Bannister,
whose sturdy form, strong face, and noble character
were in perfect harmony; Dr. Kidder, whose erect
carriage denoted the courteous gentleman and methodical student; and Professor Hemenway, accurate,
clear, industrious, and upright in form as in soul."*

The conditions of life and work in these pioneer
days, in what Miss Willard calls the "rural and
idyllic Evanston," were simpler than now, but, if the
testimony of the old settlers is trustworthy, were not
only satisfactory but delightful. A brief extract
from a letter, written by Professor Hemenway June
11, 1859, gives us a picture of the social enjoyments:
"Last Wednesday I took dinner at Dr. Foster's, only
two or three being present beside the family. That evening I attended a tea-party at Professor Noyes's, with
the Willards, Bannisters, Professor Bonbright, Mrs.

---

* From the Evanston *Press*, 1889.

White, and Mrs. Evans. The same day I had the supreme honor and felicity of being introduced to 'The Little Giant' [Senator Douglas]. On the same remarkable day I visited the Art Union at Chicago." The same letter states that "the community is excited over the prospect of Bishop Simpson's coming to Evanston to reside."

Professor Hemenway entered upon his work with an enthusiasm and equipment which assured success. He manifested those peculiar excellencies as a teacher for which he afterward became conspicuous. After an interval of housekeeping on Michigan Avenue, the family found a congenial home at Dr. Bannister's, until, in the summer of 1859, he built his own house, on Clark Street, between Judson and Hinman Avenues. By this time the paralyzing effects of the panic of 1857 had checked the promising growth of Evanston, and greatly reduced the resources of both University and Institute. Times grew worse rather than better, and in 1861 Professor Hemenway decided to relieve the general embarrassment by temporarily re-entering the active ministry. He was granted a leave of absence, and was appointed pastor of the Methodist church at Kalamazoo, Michigan. The following year his valued services were desired and secured by the First Methodist Church of Chicago, the old mother church, then in the full vigor of her prime. His ministrations there were most acceptable; but the heavy duties and cares overtaxed his strength, and, at his own desire, he was returned to Kalamazoo to fill out his three years' pastoral term. The impressions and influences of these years are

cherished both by the local church and the Michigan
Conference in sacred and grateful remembrance.

These four years spent in the pastorate were those
of the Civil War. That his utterances in regard to
it were not uncertain is evident from the following
extract from a sermon, preached in the autumn of
1864, at the close of his second year at Kalamazoo :

"The year now closing has been one of the most exciting
and perilous in the history of this nation. It has been a year
of doubt and darkness, of tears and blood and suspense, of
fearful peril and sublime patriotism. The terrible strife that
has been raging in our land has continued with unabated fury.
The cause of public order, involving every thing dear to the
patriot and Christian, has been in imminent peril; and I could
not be silent; I could not if I would, I would not if I could.
Treason is a capital crime, and I have judged that mere indifference at such a time as this partakes of the nature of treason.
If I could stand by with a cold, calculating selfishness when my
country is in a death grapple with her foes, I should be unfit to
live, how much more unfit to stand in this sacred place! And
I have spoken, not as a politician, but as a patriot; not as a partisan, but as a Christian. I have spoken with the single purpose of making the government strong. As a minister, I have
felt that I have nothing to do with men or measures, with ad-
ministrations or policies, except as connected with a divinely-
established government. For the interests of truth, of humanity, of religion ; for the love of the past and the hope of the
future ; in view of my allegiance to my country and my God,
I have spoken. Never as the friend of any party; never as
the advocate of any policy; never in view of any merely
earthly interest. It is possible, though I have received no
such intimation from any quarter, that the words I have
spoken on this subject have sometimes been felt to be narrow
and bitter and partisan, or, at least, too earnest and emphatic.
If I have ever spoken harshly or bitterly; if I have ever os-
tracized from the pale of my sympathies any truly loyal man ;
if plainly or obscurely, directly or by implication, I have been

understood to teach anything more than unconditional, unswerving, unyielding devotion to our God-given government,
I deeply regret it and humbly beg your pardon. But if, on
the other hand, my words have been, as they were intended
to be, true to the Union, to humanity, to God, to the past and
to the future; if they have been such words as the Christian
soldier would speak with the inspiration of his heroic death
upon him; if they have been such words as those sublime
patriots of our Revolution would speak, could they come down
amid the ruin and darkness of this great civil strife, whose
stake is the very government founded by their wisdom, consecrated by their prayers, watered by their tears, and baptized
with their blood, I do not wish them changed. I am grateful
to have been permitted to speak, though feebly, in their behalf. I could only wish that my utterances had been more
emphatic and influential. If I could speak coldly or doubtfully in behalf of a cause for which, in the same hour, hundreds and thousands of my brethren may be dying, I should
be unworthy of the American name. Brethren, it is only the
sacrifice and union, the faith and firmness of the loyal people
of the North that can avert an issue, the result of which must
be the scorn of men, the curse of God, and calamities in comparison with which war itself would be light. Better that a
generation perish than that the tyranny, corruption, and bar-
barism of a slaveholding government be permitted to sweep
over our land! And if this result may be averted by prayer,
by suffering, by concession of everything but principle, let us
not falter."

The character of his preaching may be fairly
judged from the sermons included in this volume.
These selected examples may surpass his average sermon in finish or special interest, but they lose im-
mensely more in lacking the living voice and impressive personality of the preacher. He ordinarily wrote
rather full notes in preparing to preach, and then
spoke extemporaneously from a brief outline. Occasionally, however, he would read from a full man-

uscript with marked effect. His illustrations were frequent, fresh and pointed. His main divisions were clearly marked, forcibly stated, and hence easily remembered. More than one minister has avoided using a text from which he has heard Professor Hemenway preach, from fear of plagiarism, which could not honestly be attributed to "unconscious assimilation."

The general influence and results of his pastorate in Kalamazoo are described in a letter from a prominent member of the church :

"One beautiful October day, in 1861, there came to our then village a young man of medium height, clear-cut, intellectual face, cultivated manners, and pleasant voice. He sought out the trustees of the Methodist Episcopal church, and introduced himself as Mr. Hemenway, and was at once recognized as the newly appointed pastor. That October day marked an era in the history of the Methodist church of Kalamazoo. The church he came to serve was a small society, worshiping in an old wooden building. It was singularly wanting in all those external things which tend to make a church a refining and uplifting power in a community. After a three years' pastorate he left us well on the way to the high position of influence and usefulness to which the church has since attained. The missionary and other collections were increased phenomenally, and the membership largely added to, though there was no wide-spread revival. He made possible the large church-building enterprise on which we entered the next year. Indeed, the church experienced a true renaissance—religious, intellectual, and social. He found us weak and small; he left us strong, united, and growing. Never before were the relations of all the pastors of the Kalamazoo churches so fraternal; and never before was a Methodist pastor in Kalamazoo so respected, beloved, and sought after by other denominations. But my poor pen can never tell all he was to us, and all he did for us as individuals and as a church. The story may be partially read in our material growth and prosperity, but a fuller and more enduring record exists in the hearts and lives of those to whom he was an inspiration and a guide. And now, though more than a quarter of a century has passed, and many of those who were blessed by his ministrations here are, we trust, enjoying the 'liberty of the sons of God,' there are still many among us to whom his name stands for all that most perfectly characterizes 'a minister in the church of God,' and his memory is, in the Kalamazoo church, 'as ointment poured forth.'"

An important event of this period was the death of Dr. Dempster, which occurred in November, 1863. The Rev. Dr. Thomas M. Eddy preached his funeral sermon at Evanston; and memorial services were held in the Clark Street church in Chicago, December 13th, which were participated in by Professor Hemenway, Dr. Kidder, Dr. Bannister, Rev. C. H. Fowler, and Dr. Tiffany. Professor Hemenway was asked to speak of Dr. Dempster as a minister. A few sentences from his address will show his admiration and affection for this honored man:

"I feel that I do no injustice to the living when I say that there are regards in which Dr. Dempster stood alone in my affection, as he now stands, and must ever stand, alone in my memory. It is not for me to speak of his genius, his varied and extraordinary attainments, his unsurpassed industry, his rigid parsimony of time; his steady inclination toward whatever might improve the condition, elevate the character, and promote the efficiency of that church in which he was a happy member and honored minister for fifty years; the simplicity and modesty with which he bore the distinguished honors so worthily conferred on him; that uniform courtesy of demeanor and kindliness of heart which made him more than welcome in every circle. . . . . He was sometimes overwhelmingly eloquent. . . . . In the devotional part of the minister's work he was pre-eminent. I have heard many men pray, but no man like Dr. Dempster. In the fitness of his terms, the delicate gleams of imagery, the vigor and comprehensiveness of the thought expressed, and, above all, in the fervor, the unction, the rapt inspiration of his style, he was most remarkable. . . . . For two years I was under him as a student, and for several years as a subordinate teacher, and during these years I can recall no instance of an unnecessary wound to my feelings, not a single exhibition of infirmity of temper, no harsh or careless or unfeeling word; but always the most tender regard for the rights, interests, convictions, and even prejudices of those with whom he had to do. The sweetness of his temper, his perfect self-control, the affability of his manners, his rare conversational powers, and keen and ready wit, made him a favorite in every circle."

The vacancy caused by the death of Dr. Dempster was most wisely filled by the election, in 1864, of the Rev. Dr. Miner Raymond to the chair of Systematic Theology, who, in addition to his work in the Institute, served as pastor of the Evanston church for three years, to the great enjoyment and profit of the congregation. The finances of the Institute having materially improved by 1865, Professor Hemenway then resumed his duties in the school, not, however, as instructor in English Literature and Greek, but as adjunct Professor of Biblical Literature.

A substantial and visible proof of the improved conditions was the laying of the corner-stone of a new building for the Institute in 1866. The Rev. James S. Smart, of Michigan, who was financial agent at this time, labored efficiently to make this a worthy centenary memorial, and was nobly aided by the Ladies' Centenary Association. Miss Frances E. Wil-

lard was introduced to public life as corresponding
secretary of this association. The new building was
appropriately named "Heck Hall," after Mrs. Bar-
bara Heck, of blessed memory.

During this period such history was being made in
his family circle as must remain unwritten, and yet is
recognized in every home as more important than all
which can be recorded. He had watched, with unut-
terable anxiety, for the returning health of the one
who was dearest to him, and whose life was threatened by disease. Once death had entered his home,
and taken away his second child, little Willie, who
seemed, in the father's eyes, the most beautiful thing
he had ever seen. In joy and sorrow, his home was
to him the center of his affection and life. Yet he
was ever faithful to his duties as a friend and neighbor, as a citizen, and as a member and minister of the
church. He made it a rule to be present at the
weekly prayer-meeting, and most of the time he
served either as a class-leader or Sunday-school
teacher. During the years spent at Evanston he was
frequently called for occasional service as preacher,
and served as a regular supply, for longer or shorter
periods, at Winnetka, Rogers Park, and some other
places. These years, though outwardly rather uneventful, were filled with beneficent activity, which
brought discipline and happiness to him, and incalculable blessings to others.

In 1859 Professor Hemenway had received the
degree of Master of Arts from the Ohio Wesleyan
University, an honor most fittingly bestowed, since,
by private study, he had mastered a range of collegi-

ate studies more extensive than the ordinary college curriculum of the day. In 1870 the Northwestern University honored him with the degree of Doctor of Divinity, and he was elected by the trustees to the chair of Hebrew and Biblical Literature. This latter year, therefore, is marked by the public recognition of the maturity of his powers both as a scholar and teacher.

CHAPTER VII.

AT EVANSTON.

1870-1874.

DR. HEMENWAY was now forty years old. The portrait accompanying this volume will recall to friends and reveal to others the attractiveness of his face, with its broad brow, clear-cut features, and bright and kindly expression. His eyes and complexion were dark; his hair and whiskers, originally black, were now well silvered with gray, and becoming fringed with white. A little under the medium height, his carriage was erect 'and his step quick and peculiar. His dress was " neither distinctively clerical nor noticeably otherwise, but simple, sober, and manly." He had a rich and pleasant voice, and a manner generally reserved, yet always courteous. His bright smile and occasional hearty laugh will be remembered by his intimate friends. He was now living in his own house, on the corner of Chicago avenue and Clark street. His family consisted of his wife and two sons, Henry and Frank. Of this home it is enough to say that it reached his own lofty ideal of "a place of rest and peace and freedom—a holy place, a place of brightness and warmth, the clearest and fullest revelation of the best possibilities of human experience." If he appeared reserved to others, he poured out upon his family a

6

veritable wealth of affection. He cherished also the
neighborhood ties which had been forming for many
years, and he was, in turn, greatly beloved.

Many remember well his accustomed seat at the
church prayer-meeting, which was seldom vacant.
Some will never forget how heartily he used to sing
the hymns he loved so well. His voice in prayer
and testimony was ever most welcome. Of the words
he spoke these sentences are characteristic: "No
man was ever happier in his church relations than I
am." "The religion of Jesus Christ meets every
want of my nature and condition." One friend* has
treasured in his memory the following remarks, and
has reproduced them substantially as they were
uttered by Dr. Hemenway in a Wednesday evening
prayer-meeting:

"It is in their human qualities that the life and character
of the Savior afford to me the greatest helpfulness and hope.
The fact that Jesus was a *man*, and that as a man he can enter
into, understand, and sympathize with all the experiences of
men, enables me to come into closer relationship with him
than would be possible under any other conditions. As a
Divine Being I adore and worship him. His power impresses
me with wonder and with awe; his condescension fills me with
amazement, and his goodness and mercy with gratitude. In
all these respects, however, he is infinitely removed from me.
He is my Lord and Master, the God whom I reverence, the
Sovereign whose loyal subject I strive to be, and believe that
I am.

"But it is the human Christ to whom my heart cleaves
when temptations beset me. When disappointments and afflictions and sorrows press heavily upon me, I remember that
Jesus, in his human character, became familiar with all of these

---

* Mr. Frank P. Crandon.

experiences; that under conditions and limitations similar to those which surround me, he worked and walked and talked and lived and died. He is literally *my brother*. He knows all about my trials and my necessities, not as the ministering angels know these things, not even as God the Father knows them, but as they become known to one who has shared them—one who has borne the burden they impose, and who, through these experiences, can understand my case, and afford me the exact assistance and strength which I need. In this Elder Brother's presence I am no longer conscious of the distance which intervenes between an infinite God and a sinful man. The Savior talks with me, and as we commune together he seems to enfold me in his arms. He bears me upwards out of the region of despondency or of doubt, dissipates every cloud and every fear, and so identifies me with himself that I am made a partaker of his strength; and as I go forth to the duties and labors which await me, I am constantly encouraged by the admonition, ' Be of good cheer, I have overcome the world.' "

Dr. Hemenway was a regular attendant of the Saturday evening teachers' meeting, which he frequently led. Referring to this, Mr. William Deering, a layman of great experience in this line, and of ripe judgment, has said: " Dr. Hemenway was the best Bible teacher I have ever known."

His great life-work, however, was done in the class-room. The teacher's chair was his throne of power. The old Dempster Chapel in Heck Hall will ever be sacred in the memory of many students, because of the intellectual stimulus and spiritual inspiration received in his classes there. A former student writes: " Nothing that he said is so vividly remembered by me as the prayers with which he opened each recitation hour. These were brief, fervent, pointed, and so suited to the circumstances of student life that I am sure others must have felt as I did, that they were the voicing of desires which I had deeply felt but found no words to express. There was always more light after he had prayed."

Another former student,* noticing the remarkable brevity, thoughtfulness, and finish of these prayers, formed the habit of taking them down. Among those thus preserved are the following :

"Inspire us with a regard for thy law as it applies to every thought of the mind, to every emotion of the soul, and to all the energies of the will."

"We bring unto thee an imperfect service; but we ask thee to accept it, not because of what we have obtained, but because of what we desire to obtain. Bless us, O Lord, evermore. Amen."

"O God, help us to recognize thee as the King of truth—truth which is not only external in its relation, but first of all internal. Assist us to be ever loyal to the truth, both in the decisions of our intellect and the affections of the heart, and in the decisions of the will, and in all the acts and forms of our life. Bless us at this time, and reveal to us thy truth according to our need. Help us to call upon thee with full purpose of heart, for Jesus' sake. Amen."

"We come unto thee, O Lord, asking thee for the blessing of which thou seest we stand in need, in order that we may properly do the work of this hour. O Lord, we thank thee for the bright shining of thy light upon us. We thank thee that we have our existence in the fullness of thy revelation. We pray

---

* Rev. Register W. Bland, class of 1884.

thou wouldst help us to see the eminence upon which thou hast placed us. Enable us to understand our high privileges. Help us to realize that to whom much is given, of him much shall be required; that as ability increases responsibility increases. And, O Lord, help us to be faithful to the responsibilities which are upon us."

Mr. Bland adds: "Sometimes his prayer was a single sentence, ending with an abrupt 'Amen.' His prayers had no hackneyed, worn-out, pious phrases. His phraseology was always fresh, clear, and condensed. He abhorred cant and Pharisaism. He said it seemed to him that the interior communings of the soul with God were too sacred to be invaded by the questions of our most intimate associates, and sometimes too sacred to be uttered aloud."

Another old student * has recalled these sentences from his prayers:

"O Lord, we are driven to thee by a sense of our need, and we are drawn to thee by a sense of thy love."

"As the leaf of the flower opens to receive the light of life from the sun, so, O God, we open our hearts to thee, the author of all life."

"Shine upon our darkness and dispel it. Subdue our sins and cast them out."

"Help us to recognize the solemn responsibilities that confront us every hour of our mortal being."

Another† writes: "In those prayers Dr. Hemenway talked with God as a man talks with his friend.

---

* Rev. Wm. H. W. Rees, D. D., class of 1883.
† Rev. O. L. Fisher, class of 1871.

One such prayer I can never forget, in which he thanked God that we could know his Son, Jesus Christ, better than Peter and James and John did, while they walked and talked with him in the flesh. As the prayer continued there came to me such a revelation of Christ that we seemed almost to be on the Mount of Transfiguration." Rev. L. M. Hartley, of the class of 1884, recalls this incident: One day, when the nature of God was under discussion in the class, a student questioned the propriety of attributing emotion to the Almighty. At this Dr. Hemenway kindled, and exclaimed in his peculiarly emphatic way: "Remove emotion and feeling from the idea of God, and *you have taken away my God.*"

Dr. Hemenway's principal work was in Hebrew and Biblical literature. He was not enthusiastic in the drill required in teaching the elements of a foreign language. The new methods of teaching Hebrew had not yet been introduced. Yet his instruction in the elements was thorough and satisfactory. His expositions were free, clear, and suggestive. Written notes were seldom taken, and written examinations were not required. In his lectures on Biblical Introduction he exhibited and aroused greater enthusiasm. He was accustomed to write an outline of his lecture on the blackboard, and then, standing before the class, he would enlarge upon this in forcible and well-chosen language; so that the hour proved not only instructive, but interesting and inspiring. During several of the years of this period he gave instruction, also, in homiletics and pastoral theology. His ideal of a Methodist preacher and pastor was clearly defined and high. From his own experience, and his observation, he had accurate and extensive knowledge of a Methodist minister's field of labor. He had carefully studied the conditions of success, and was peculiarly fitted, by his sound judgment, warm sympathy, and descriptive powers, to present these conditions vividly to the minds of his students. While he described this lofty ideal of a Methodist minister—as a man, a student, as a preacher and pastor—many who listened formed a new and higher conception of their calling, and accepted the directions and inspiration offered them as among the greatest and best of their lives. The notes taken on this subject were cherished and consulted in later years, in the midst of the active duties and perplexities of responsible pastoral life.

Some extracts from his utterances, concerning the Methodist preacher and pastor, will show the force and clearness of his views:

"The Methodist minister should have some special adaptations. For instance, to the masses. It is the special glory of Methodism that it is eminently the religion of the people. To be suited to her ministry one must be capable of adjusting himself, not merely to the cultured and aristocratic few, but to the hard-working, practical masses, who make up the bone and sinew of society. He must not be dainty and fastidious in his tastes. He must be able to wield an influence over men incapable of judging of the quality of his culture and indifferent to the beauty of his diction, but who, nevertheless, may judge very correctly as to the quality of his teaching and the spirit of his ministry. He should distinctly aim at power over the people. Monarchists cry, 'God save the king!' American politicians, 'God save the Union!' ecclesiastics, 'God save the church!' but let it be the cry of Methodists, everywhere and always, 'God save the people!' for if they are saved, every thing else worth saving will be saved also. There is a kind of clerical exclusiveness, which many indulge or affect, and which stands in the way of this practical adaptation. Some clergymen—of what George MacDonald calls the 'pure, honest, and narrow type'—seem, in every point and line of their countenances, marked as priests, and hence apart from their fellow-men. By their dress, the tones of their voice, and their general demeanor, they proclaim: 'Stand by yourself, come not near me, for I am holier than thou.' They are, they would seem to say, as the Sabbath to common days, or the church to common houses; but, more correctly, they are like funerals to common events, or corpses to living beings. In the unsullied whiteness and the unwrinkled blackness of their costumes, in the cold stateliness of their aspect, and their hollow and priestly tones, they remind us of the dead rather than of the living. They move among men with a mingled pomposity and solemnity, 'as if the care of the whole world lay on their shoulders ; as if an awful destruction was the most likely thing to happen to every one, while to them is committed the toilsome chance of saving some.' As they enter the places where men congregate—market, shop, railway depot, public hall—the language of their manner is: '*Procul o, procul este, profani!*' They flow into the sea of common humanity like streams of holy oil. When they speak to common men they bless, or patronize, or tolerate, or endure. Their ministrations have a mechanical efficacy. Men are to be regenerated by their magical, priestly touch, or by their grand and impressive ceremonial manipulations. Men of this type, though found in every denomination, are specially out of place in our ministry. The Methodist minister should be every inch a man. He should be more broadly, profoundly, and intensely human than common men. He must be able to give other men his hand and his heart—to 'rejoice with them that do rejoice, and weep with them that weep.' Not by pompous ceremonies, but by vital influences will he expect to save men. . . . . There must be adaptation to the Methodist pulpit. The Methodist pulpit, however numerous and marked may be the individual exceptions, is a place where the gospel is preached freely, earnestly, plainly, pointedly, effectively. It is not a place for essays—theological, moral, literary, or any other kind. It is not a place for lectures or orations, be they political or religious. It is not a place for abstrusities, profundities, or platitudes. It is not a place for dry and harsh polemics. It is not a theater for oratorical display, or word-painting—for intellectual gymnastics. The preaching of the Methodist pulpit must be nothing suited to the few merely, but to all. It must address, not the intellectual nature mainly, but the spiritual nature. Its profiting must not respect mainly the life that now is, but that which is to come. If it be said that all these characteristics pertain to the Christian pulpit as such, in every denomination, I reply that they characterize eminently the Methodist pulpit. There are those who would be acceptable in other pulpits who would not be acceptable in ours; just as there are many who do effective work among us, but would not be equally successful in any other denomination. The typical Methodist preacher is a man positive in his convictions, fervid in his feelings, plain and downright in speech, simple in manner, of broad sympathies, and capable of wielding a fair measure of popular influence. Extemporaneousness of address, also, is commonly associated with these qualities, and is their most natural mode of expression." . . .

"And so, too, should be corrected all tendencies towards priestly charlatanism—ghostly, priestly tones, denominational cant, stock phrases, and affectations of all sorts and kinds. The clergyman who is faithful to himself, and thoroughly genuine in his individual life, will, in the end, slough off all such excrescences, and stand forth a truthful expression of the religion which he assumes to teach." . . .

"Especially offensive to a cultivated and spiritual worshiper is *ministerial egotism*. The minister who, like Æsop's fly, seated on the end of the carriage axle, is continually exclaiming, 'See what a dust *I* raise!' thus constantly thrusting his important self upon the attention of those whose 'heart and flesh are crying out for the living God,' wearies and baffles the spirit of devotion sometimes to the point of positive disgust or absolute defeat." . . .

"If I have room to mention another clerical vice which mars the beauty and lessens the interest of public religious

service, it shall be *affectation.* In the case of the minister, it
hides more excellencies than charity does sins. There is nothing we so much demand in men, and especially those who
'minister and serve the altar,' as genuineness—a thorough
conformity of the outward life to the inward spirit. Strained
allusions, disgusting finery, pompousness of demeanor are especially out of harmony with the office of him who stands
before the people 'in Christ's stead.'" . . .

"Here, then, is a prime qualification for a Methodst pastor. He should know the peculiar genius of his denomination,
and be in full sympathy with it. He should enter into this
great evangelic movement. He should feel that his business
is not to instruct men as an end, but to save them. He should
seek to follow worthily in the footsteps of the fathers, and
tone up his soul by studying their heroic lives. He should
practice the same simplicity, earnestness, directness, evangelic intensity which God so honored in Wesley's time. He
should remember, as he stands up to speak to the people, that,
in the case of many of them, he has but a half hour out of
the week to raise the dead in, and this reflection should nerve
his arm to strike the most vigorous blows. Then shall every
sermon be a battle—short, sharp, decisive, victorious."

No pen-picture of this great teacher would be
complete without some reference to his sense of
humor, and the sarcasm which he wielded in the
class-room in an effective and sometimes startling
way; yet it is impossible to give any idea of the
quality and power of his wit. All his former students remember it well, some doubtless ruefully.
But few can recall definite examples, and those preserved, apart from the remembered situation, give
no adequate impression of their original pungency.
Some of the alumni of the Institute may, however,
enjoy the following, as reminders of the old seminary
days. In the Hebrew class, one day, a student trans-

lated Gen. ii, 3, as follows: "And God blessed the seventh day and sanctified it, because that in it he had done all his work." "That rendering," remarked Dr. Hemenway without a smile, "is for some preachers—on the seventh day they do all their work." To a student whose irregularity and unfaithfulness had greatly tried his patience, and who came to him one day with a lame excuse, he said: "Brother ——, I believe that you are *a much better man than you seem to be.*"

He used the Socratic method freely and effectively in his classes. He once defined teaching as "the vital and helpful contact of one stronger and better furnished with another who has a conscious need." His method of questioning was calculated to draw real knowledge into adequate expression; but it was equally well fitted to expose ignorance and make conceit ridiculous. He sometimes made the contact vital by first cutting to the quick, and aroused the "conscious need" by making a student smart for a time for wounded vanity. Some of these wounds were long in healing, but the great majority of students soon understood the underlying kindness of this spiritual surgery, and were grateful for it. His questions called forth some strange answers. A student, being asked whether the English or Hebrew language was the warmer, gave his opinion in favor of his mother tongue. "Why do you think so?" asked the Doctor. "Because the Hebrew is a dead language," was the ready reply. Doubtless Hebrew was made warmer for him after that. It may be that Dr. Hemenway learned the value of occasional severity from Dr. Dempster. It is related of the latter that he said to a student who had just attempted to recite: "Your thought has been buried in the tomb of your words;" and that after announcing that a certain man would not return to finish his course of study because he had been married, he pronounced his sentence in a deep voice thus: "Plunged into the bottomless gulf of oblivion!"

Dr. Hemenway sometimes followed an incorrect answer by a peculiarly emphatic "Never." An examiner once perplexed a student about the word translated "beginning," in the first verse of Genesis, which the examiner spoke of as a "participle." Coming to the student's rescue, the Professor asked him if the Hebrew word in question was a participle. "Not here, I think," was the response. "No," said Dr. Hemenway, "not here nor anywhere else." But as a rule it was a scimiter and not a sledge-hammer which he wielded. I have been more than once reminded of the Arabian story of a Damascus blade, which its owner would swing swiftly around the head of his enemy. The unconscious victim sat smiling until a pinch of snuff made him sneeze. At this his severed head rolled to the ground. The laugh of the class was sometimes the first intimation a student had of his sudden execution.

In social intercourse he had many a hearty and good-humored laugh over the incidents of his pastoral and school life. He told me once, with great enjoyment, of an old shoemaker in one of his parishes into whose good graces he found it exceedingly difficult to win his way. The old man kept station-

ery and other articles to sell in his shop, and Dr.
Hemenway went out of his way to purchase there.
At length the old man thawed. "I like you," he
said. "I'm glad to know it." "But I couldn't
bear that other preacher who was here. He was so
close. He asked me, one day, what the price of a pack-
age of envelopes was, and I says, 'I'll let *you* have
them for five cents.' 'What,' says he, 'has envelopes
riz?'"

The following, from a member of the last class he
taught,* represents the experience of a large number:

"My first impressions of him were not favorable. He
appeared stern and unsympathetic, seldom speaking to or recognizing us on the street or in the post-office when we chanced
to meet him; but I soon learned that underneath this exterior,
which was calculated to inspire awe, there was a warm, sympathetic nature and heart which could but win the affection of
his students when they came to know him well."

An earlier student † writes:

"I was but fourteen years old when I registered as a student for the ministry, and took a room in Heck Hall. Dr.
Kidder cordially encouraged me when I timidly told him my
boyish wish to become a preacher. I grew up on the old
campus, and during those years when a boy is most deeply
impressed was strongly influenced by Dr. Hemenway. I never
saw him walking the old paths to and from the hall, with his
peculiarly emphatic gait, without wishing to be what he
seemed to be so thoroughly—a Christian gentleman. I think,
by his manly deference in manner and address, he knocked off
many a rough corner from us boys without knowing it himself, and without our being aware of it. He was especially
considerate of those who were trying, as I did for two years,

---

* Rev. E. M. Glasgow, class of 1884.
† Rev. R. G. Hobbs, class of 1878.

to do that very hard thing, keep up with a class and carry on
the work of a pastoral charge at the same time. He seemed
to appreciate the fact that the fellows who were thus burning
the candle at both ends needed special encouragement, and he
never withheld it. His sympathies were quick and warm."

Another alumnus * bears this testimony:

"It took some time to get acquainted with him, but an
acquaintance with such a character was something to be highly
valued. How he prized faithfulness! 'A lazy student,' he
said one day, 'may have a call to the ministry, but not a divine call.' He emphasized the word 'divine' as only Dr.
Hemenway could. In more than one of his classes he said
things severe and deservedly severe. On one of these occasions he said: 'Brethren, you are fitting yourselves to be am-
bassadors for Christ. If you are unfaithful to your studies in
the Institute you will be unfaithful to your duties in the ministry.' Who can forget the tone of his voice and the flash of
his eye in administering reproof? No cannon-ball was ever
more direct than his words at such a time; yet how warm and
sympathetic was his nature! The night that Dempster Hall
was burned I barely escaped with my life. When I appeared
next morning in the Doctor's recitation-room the earthly house
of this tabernacle was not in a very presentable shape. His
sympathy, expressed in words and *deeds*, I can never forget."

Perhaps there was no part of his teaching enjoyed
more by Dr. Hemenway and his classes than his lectures on hymnology. His love for Christian hymns
began in early life, and his critical and enthusiastic
study of them extended through many years. And
in the minds of many, his memory is most vividly
associated with his expositions of this subject in the
delightful praise-meetings which he led. A part of
the results of his hymn-studies will be found in this
volume; but the richest fruitage, garnered in the

---

* Rev. John Lee, class of 1882.

Hymnal, has long benefited the entire Methodist
Episcopal Church.

For some years he led the Tuesday evening class-
meeting, held in Dempster Chapel. Many students
have borne testimony to the rare helpfulness of the
spiritual counsels given there. From the wealth of
his knowledge of the Bible, of Christian hymns, of
religious literature, and of human life, but most of
all from his own inner life, he was able to counsel,
warn, and inspire his younger brethren. In these
meetings he seemed to come closer to the students,
and exhibited a pastor's solicitude for their welfare.
Some, who thought him cold, distant, and severe as
an instructor, discovered in the class-room the warmth
and tenderness of his heart.

Those students who went to him for advice in
times of perplexity and trouble, could never again
doubt the sincerity and warmth of his interest in
them. And by some, such interviews are cherished
in memory as turning points in their lives. To such
applicants he opened the secret treasuries of his mind
and heart. His interest in individual students was
far greater than was generally understood, and it did
not cease with their graduation.

In the meetings of the faculty the expressions of
his judgment concerning students and alumni had
especial weight. When some alumnus was to be recommended for an important position or an honorary
degree, Dr. Hemenway generally had the fullest
knowledge of his course and success since graduation,
and his discriminating judgment seemed almost infallible.

In estimating his personal influence, account should also be taken of his visits to the Western conferences to represent the Institute; of his services at Sunday-school assemblies; of his articles contributed to the religious press, particularly the *Northwestern Christian Advocate* and the *Methodist Review.* These fugitive writings related mainly to Biblical subjects and practical discussions of a pastor's work. It was largely through his efforts that the Pastors' Theological Union was organized and held annually for several years at Evanston, meetings which were most profitable both to its members and to the Institute. In 1875 there were present six bishops and two hundred and twenty-seven pastors, representing thirty-three annual conferences.

The witnesses already summoned bear testimony to the unique influence which Dr. Hemenway exerted. Others will, in a later chapter, emphasize this fact. But no description can adequately represent this power. It was as subtle and undefinable as life. It was the result of unusual character, in which genuineness, unselfish devotion, and deep spiritual experience were the ruling elements.

CHAPTER VIII.

IN LABORS MORE ABUNDANT.

1874-1884.

AT the session of the Michigan conference, in the autumn of 1875, Dr. Hemenway was elected a delegate to the General Conference, which convened in Baltimore May 1st of the following year. Like many of the ablest men in great representative bodies, his voice was not heard in public debate. He rendered valuable service in the Committees on Education and Conference Boundaries, and his letters from the conference show his devotion to all the interests of the church, and his discriminating judgment of men and measures. The questions of the color-line, of woman's place in the church, and of the presiding eldership, were especially prominent. On each of these he had clear convictions, but made no public expression of them beyond his vote. If we regret this reserve, we can not fail to admire the modesty which caused it. He took a deep interest in visits to Alexandria, Washington, and Mt. Vernon, and especially in the new phases of life which these places presented. He enjoyed lectures by Beecher, Simpson, and Fowler, and the rich succession of great sermons and eloquent addresses which a Methodist General Conference always affords. He made a pilgrimage to the graves of Asbury and Lee. This month, spent in Baltimore, extended his influence through the friendships strengthened and formed with leading men in the church; but the matter which made it possible for him to render an important service to every member of the Methodist church, for decades to come, was the action of the conference ordering the revision of the church Hymn-book. When a committee to do this work was appointed by the bishops, it was a matter of course that Dr. Hemenway should be a member of it, and it caused no surprise that he was chosen chairman of the Western section.

By poetic temperament, practical judgment, and long-continued study of hymnology, Dr. Hemenway was peculiarly fitted for this service. It is no injustice to the other members of this excellent committee to say that few of its number did so much as he, and no one more, to make the Hymnal the admirable book it is. From the first he gave himself to this labor of love with untiring enthusiasm. He attended all the meetings of his section and of the general committee. From the early summer of 1876, until the publication of the Hymnal in the autumn of 1877, his heart and mind seemed full of this subject. Two summer vacations were devoted almost exclusively to it. He is obliged to confess it a "prodigious job." The entire committee met twice in New York, and once each in Cleveland, Ohio, and East Greenwich, R. I. The work was done with great thoroughness and system. Every hymn passed in review three times, once privately and twice in the committee, where "debates arose and sometimes continued for

hours on a single hymn or part of a hymn." The
sessions often continued until late at night. Dr.
Hemenway was detailed more than once for special
services. He was one of the sub-committee which
submitted the results to the Board of Bishops, and he
was one of the two selected to arrange the Hymnal
with tunes, in conjunction with Dr. Eben Tourjée
and Mr. J. P. Holbrook. Dr. Hemenway prepared
the greater part of the report on the revision
which was presented to the bishops, and which
forms a valuable contribution to the history of hymnology.* The chapters on hymnology contained in
this volume took shape soon after the completion of
the revision.

The period during which these labors on the
Hymnal were in progress was one of the darkest in
the financial history of the Institute. Yet, as he devoted the usual time for summer rest and recuperation to severe and gratuitous toil for the good of the
church, he wrote courageously of this gloomy outlook
for the school: "I have faith that God will do his
work if we do ours, and certainly it is not our work
to determine the conditions of our own labors."
Speaking of his spirit and counsels at this time, Dr.
Raymond says:

"In the darkest hour of our history, when the trustees informed us that the entire resources of the institution would be
absorbed in the payment of the interest on its indebtedness,
and there would not be a dollar left with which to continue
the school, and when the faculty were called together to con-

---

* The first twenty-two pages of the report, as printed, were written
by the Rev. Dr. J. M. Buckley.

sider the communication from the trustees, Dr. Hemenway said at once, most emphatically: 'Whatever it may cost us as teachers, the doors of the Institute must not be closed.' He proposed the measure which was adopted, and which, so far as the faculty was concerned, was the means of tiding the institution into the broad seas of its present prosperity."

In addition to his other work, Dr. Hemenway also supplied the church at South Evanston, which, in loving memory of faithful and fruitful service, upon the completion of its handsome new edifice, named it the "Hemenway Memorial." The Hon. M. D. Ewell, LL. D., contributes this concerning Dr. Hemenway's pastorate there:

"I think I was the first person who had an interview with him respecting his coming to serve this church, and I well remember the then depressed condition of the society. There were no striking events during his service, but our intercourse with him, from first to last, was characterized by the utmost fraternal feeling, and I may add, affection. His work was faithful and prospered from beginning to end. I have never known a man more universally beloved and respected than was Dr. Hemenway by this society. I have never known a man more entirely unselfish in his relations with his people than was Dr. Hemenway. Whenever any benevolent or church enterprise was being canvassed, he always quietly but firmly insisted upon doing more for it than we thought he ought to do. In making these statements I feel sure that I represent the feeling of all who knew him. Personally I had the utmost respect for his ability, the most unbounded confidence in his piety, and very great affection for him as a man and a brother."

There is reason for believing that the extra exertion required for this gratuitous work upon the Hymnal may have shortened his life. At all events, the slow decline of strength began about this time.

After the publication of the Hymnal the usual duties of his chair were supplemented by the completion of a commentary, which had been begun some two years earlier. This was Dr. Hemenway's most important individual publication. It treated of the books of Jeremiah and the Lamentations, and, together with the Commentary on Isaiah by Dr. Henry Bannister, forms the seventh volume of Whedon's Commentary. It is a noteworthy fact that no one of the three distinguished men, whose names appear on the title-page of this book, lived to see the completed volume. This commentary exhibits the same qualities which marked Dr. Hemenway's instruction. It is clear, scholarly, independent, and spiritual, and takes rank with the best in this valuable series.

In 1879 Dr. Hemenway was again chosen by his brethren of the Michigan conference to represent them in the General Conference which met in Cincinnati in 1880. Here he did quiet but efficient service, especially in the Committee on Education, of which he was secretary, and Dr. E. O. Haven chairman.

Dr. Hemenway's entire public life adds another exception to the rule that a powerful physique and robust health are essential to great usefulness in responsible positions. He never excused himself from duty on the ground of invalidism, nor did he seem to regard himself an invalid; yet it was only by the most careful regard for the laws of health, and the concentration of his forces upon a few lines of effort, that he was able to accomplish what he undertook without overtaxing his strength. He waged a forty

years' war with disease, and contested every point
with wisdom and courage; and if a slow retreat was
inevitable, it was masterly and honorable. With a
cheerful courage, recognizing the early and irreparable impairment of his constitution, he carefully con-
served his strength and devoted it to the highest
ends. In the spring of 1881, however, it became
manifest to his friends and to himself that his health
was seriously threatened. He planned to spend the
summer months at the sea-shore, but was finally induced to try the effects of an ocean voyage and a
short tour in the Old World. He sailed for Europe
the latter part of July, in company with his son,
Henry B. Hemenway, M. D. In a hurried trip, oc-
cupying less than three months, they visited parts of
Scotland, England, France, Germany, and Switzerland. His letters show that he was a good traveler,
tempering an intelligent enthusiasm with sensible
moderation. He did not wear himself out in the effort
to see everything in every place, but sought to select
and study typical specimens of the various objects of
interest. Facing the Atlantic voyage for the first
time, he writes home: "I know you are more or less
solicitous for me, but I hope you will not be at all
anxious. It seems evident that I am walking in the
way of Providence, and if so I must be safe. And
I want to say that even if it should be God's will
to overwhelm me and remove me by some unforeseen
dangers, which are always liable to come, I believe it
will be well with me. I have a vivid and ofttimes
oppressive sense of my sins and shortcomings, and
never, perhaps, was that sense more vivid than now,

as I write; but I do honestly seek to give myself to
Christ, and I believe he accepts and saves me. I
never felt more unqualifiedly determined, living and
dying, to be the Lord's."

Writing in 1882 to a friend who was starting for
a foreign trip he said: "How this year, under God's
blessing, may be made to enrich your whole life, and,
through the work you shall do, the lives of many
others also. There is a supreme instant in the pho-
tographer's art when what had been a mere cloud,
with dim and scarcely distinguishable outline, becomes a perfect picture, so truthful and so expressive
as to be beyond all price. So will this year, which
is before you, be made up largely of such moments.
The places and scenes which are old in your memory
will come again into your life as new creations."
After mentioning some of the principal places he had
visited abroad, he added: "We had the satisfaction,
also, of standing by the graves of many of God's
heroes, of whose names this sheet is not worthy; and
some glorious visions entered our souls, which, I am
sure, will be lost only, if at all, in the beatific state."

One of these visions is described in a letter which
he wrote home from Interlaken: "We have had
glory enough for one day. At ten o'clock we left
Basle and came through Berne into this Alpine
region. I can not tell you what I have seen since
then. It is an experience of a life-time. All the
way from Berne the Alps were coming more grandly
into view, until as we took the boat on Lake Thun
the culmination was realized. The beautiful water of
the lake was broken into fine ripples, which sparkled

in the sunbeams like a pavement of precious stones. In the near foreground were the bold, precipitous mountains. A little farther off the peaks rose above them, streaked with white; and just beyond, and yet so near us as to seem absolutely startling, were the great forms which wear an eternal livery of white. It was almost like confronting the Great White Throne. They looked down upon us and drew near to us like the Infinite Presence. I never had any just conception of mountain scenery before."

Dr. Hemenway returned from Europe with his health decidedly improved, and resumed with ardor his accustomed labors. If he had premonitions that there remained but three years more in which to finish his work, he gave no outward sign of them. In the home, the Institute, and the church he bore his part as before. If any change was noticed it was that the fruitage of his mind and heart seemed more abundant and rich. Perhaps he was more careful to take rest and exercise, yet he could accomplish more in the same time than in earlier years.

The letters written to his sons during the last decade contain, in a condensed form, the results of his experience, and one might almost say his philosophy of life. Two characteristic utterances from these letters are the following:

"I always want you to feel that you represent us, your parents, and are to represent us when we have ceased working; and so I want you to be strong and true and high-minded, cherishing at all times a vivid sense of the dignity and the sacredness of life."

"I wish you may feel deeply and always, and that you may live it out continually, that no life is worth living that does not spend itself mainly in helping other people."

A long letter is preserved, written to his elder
son when he was absent from home, pursuing his
medical studies. It would prove a safe chart to any
young physician and helpful to any student. The
product of wide observation and deep thought, it is
written with the simplicity and warmth which it received in the depths of an affectionate father's heart.
As expressing his mature judgment upon the conditions of a truly successful life, it may fitly close this
chapter :

"I write, then, at this time, not to administer to you a
lecture, nor to change you from what you really are, but to
suggest some things which may possibly be of some practical
value to you this coming term of school, which will be to you
of superlative importance.

"First of all, let me charge you to look wisely and watch-
fully after your *physical* well-being. The importance of this
is being constantly impressed upon you, both by what you
learn and what you see. Be sure and dress yourself warmly
this winter, and see that the best conditions of warmth and
pure air are supplied in your room. Allow of no strain too
severe on your nervous system. Do not permit your laudable
zeal in study to induce overwork. It is better for such as you
to make haste slowly than to kindle the fire too hotly. I
would then make this first point with myself, that I will look
after the body first, and let other things rest on this as a ground
condition; and whatever is necessary to this I want you to have,
suitable clothing, wholesome food, a pleasant room, and generally comfortable conditions of living. All this is, as you know,
consistent with rigorous physical discipline. It does not mean
that you are to live a life of luxury or indolence, or of uncertain
and nerveless exertion, but it is consistent with patient industry and vigorous effort. It only means that you are to carefully consider your bodily habits, and adapt your habits of life
to your capital of strength and vitality. With your lithe and
active temperament, you are capable of the best things physically under judicious care; without this, you can very easily

make shipwreck. I am the more careful to speak of this because I am entirely certain that I have lost fully ten years of
my life simply because I did not know how to use myself at
the very start. I would repeat it, then—make it a point to
take good care of yourself physically. If you have not now
and do not secure a room-mate, so as to make it better for you
than to be alone, by all means keep the room you have rented
for yourself alone. The better arrangement, however, when
your social and intellectual character is considered, is to have
a room-mate, provided he is of the right stamp.

"Let me say a word as to your *intellectual* life. Probably
more than ought to be the case, you are likely to be judged by
your fellow-men by purely intellectual and practical standards.
The question will not be, What are you? but, How much do
you know? and, What can you do? Your power to influence
and benefit your fellow-men will depend largely on the breadth
and fineness of your culture, as well as your acquaintance with
the principles and practice of your profession; and inasmuch
as the best results in this direction can come only from a correct ideal and an *established habit or course of life,* I am sure
that any well-considered suggestions on this subject may be,
to some extent, serviceable. Of course you must know your
profession. Common honesty requires this. There is no man
before the public more really dishonest than he who professes
a science and a practice like that of medicine without understanding it. Be more careful to know than to seem to know.
Discriminate with the utmost care between the great things
and the small. A thousand little things may wait for your
knowledge until you need them, and then you will know just
where to find them ; but the great and fundamental matters
in your calling should be as familiar as household words. The
office of the school is simply to *inaugurate* a course of life, not
to carry it forward to perfection; hence, in the school, it is
vastly more important that your work be thorough than that
it be brilliant or extensive.

" But it is of your intellectual life in general that I would
speak. He who knows only the matters of his profession and
is noticeably ignorant on other matters can not succeed
People want *a man* in a physician—one who has some breadth
of adjustment in the kingdom of the truth. He who is a

good practitioner, and, in addition, is a cultured and manly man, will be likely to realize in any community, in the long run, many times more patronage and more influence than the man who is equally skillful but lacking in the more general and outside qualifications to which I now refer. Hence I would urge upon you the importance of keeping up your literary culture. Do this as a settled and inflexible principle. Do not allow any supposed press of duties to stand in the way of it. Just as nothing should be allowed to crowd out your Bible and your religion, so let nothing stand in the way of those great duties which you owe yourself as a man. What is needed for this is not much time, but a little time faithfully and wisely employed. Keep up a knowledge of the authors you have read in the school. Take some Latin author, as Virgil, and read it so frequently and regularly that you shall keep fresh your acquaintance with the language. It would be well, also, to do the same with the French and the German. You will find, in the end, that all this will tell immeasurably on your well-being as a man among men. It is your most sacred duty, as well as your just privilege and honor, to fit yourself to sit down in the company of the learned. You can only do this by patient, faithful, and laborious culture.

"All this applies also to English literature. Form the habit of reading the best authors. Do not attempt too much at once, but have constantly in reading something that will bring you nearer other men. Your great hope in this life will consist in cultivating the society of cultured people, most of whom must be drawn to you by considerations outside of your profession. The well-known and standard works in English literature may become links of union between yourself and all who speak the English language. In this there is a hint as to your *evenings*. In so far as possible, I should prefer to turn away from medical matters during the evening hours. Take up something of an entirely different character, and it will give tone and zest to your whole mental experiences. You will do better work in your studies if you turn away from them habitually every day for something higher or more general in its bearing on life.

"I wish I could say some helpful word to you on another and a much higher subject. I mean that of *character*. In this

word is contained all of real worth in any individual. Without any reference to mere qualifications, whether of this kind
or that, the amount of real character in a man is the measure
of his worth. And this is certainly under our personal decision and control as nothing else is. Rich or poor, learned or
unlearned, influential or obscure, it is possible for him who
wills to form a positive, clean-cut, decided character. Here is
his real personality, and here is to be his real value to himself
and to his fellow-men. What we *do* is important, but what we
are is ineffably more important.

"One of the main factors in character is what we call
judgment. This, combined with the power to do and to con-
serve, practically makes up the man as an actual force in society. To say that any person has good judgment is to bestow
on him a high commendation ; to say that one has a weak judgment is to make of him a fatal impeachment. It is well, then,
for any man to direct his own special attention to the conditions of strength in this regard. Avoid hasty and superficial
judgments—mere impressions, which we take up simply because they suit our moods or our prejudices. Judgment is
mainly a matter of thought, not feeling. Cultivate, then, a
judicial habit of mind. Make it a point to give every one his
due. Be candid, but be thorough and positive. In a word,
see to it that you become a man of *convictions*, and that your
convictions are sound.

"This quality of mind comes out into what we call *practical sense*, a thing upon which our own success depends as
upon nothing else; for, after all, it is not what we wish or
purpose or say that determines our adjustment to our fellow-
men, but the decisions we do actually make and the things we
actually achieve. . . . In your own consciousness, then, lay
greatest emphasis upon your judgment, and the way in which
it can be carried into effect. Do not make it so much a matter
of word as of deed. Not what we *promise* ourselves or others,
but what we *effect*, will fix our standing with our fellows.

"In this matter of character, of course, the most vital
element is the *moral* one. Be satisfied with nothing short of
the most thorough *truthfulness*, not merely in business and in
language, but in thought and feeling. Cultivate and maintain
a downright honesty. I fully believe you are doing this, yet

too much emphasis can not be placed on this matter. I hope that you will begin your life with the resolution that nothing foul or impure shall pass your own lips, and, in so far as you can prevent it, your ears too. As you move among men and families, let there be no taint or foulness because of your presence.

"And I would say one word touching the matter of personal religion. Cling to it and maintain it as for your life. Do not in this thing be time-serving and compromising. Your best interests for time and eternity lie in the direction of positiveness and consistency in this regard. Calculate, then, on doing your duty fully and regularly in this regard. Make it a matter of principle to be in your place in the church, the prayer-meeting, and the Sabbath-school. Let it be understood as a matter of course that you will stand in your lot and place in all religious assemblages that have a just claim upon you. Even this winter I would make it a point to attend the prayer-meeting every Wednesday evening, unless there are imperative reasons against it.

"One other thing I would call your attention to; namely, your *social* character and adjustments. It is a great thing to be admitted into good society. In order to do this it is necessary to cultivate the qualities which render your presence desirable. It is also necessary to observe carefully the social opportunities and facilities which are afforded you. Make it a point to cultivate any relations which are likely to be helpful to you and to elevate you. Do not throw away a valuable acquaintance or friend. If any door is open to you for social intercourse, especially with families which would help and raise you, be sure and enter; and when you go out, leave it ajar for another occasion.

"But I had not thought to write at such length. My special wish was to put down some thoughts which have been running in my mind, more or less, with reference to you. In my early life I had to stumble and blunder along as best I could, with little help from any one. I clearly see how it might have been much better with me, and so I feel a desire that the very best may come to you."

CHAPTER IX.

IN MEMORIAM—1884.

THE close of the Institute year, in the spring of 1883, was darkly shadowed by the sudden death of the Rev. Dr. Henry Bannister, who had been Professor of Exegetical Theology since 1856. In describing this event, Dr. Hemenway wrote: "It is safe to say that no other death has so stirred our community to its very foundations. The influence he has exerted in shaping and developing the inner life of the Institute has been most potent, so that in its present form the institution is as much the expression of his mind as of any one who has had a share in its work." The resolutions adopted by the faculty were prepared by Dr. Hemenway, and contained this testimonial : "For twenty-seven years he has been associated with the instruction and conduct of the school, and in all these years his career has been distinguished for the thoroughness and zeal with which he devoted himself to the work of his department and the general welfare of the institution. He brought to the chair which he so long and usefully filled rare qualifications, uniting the experience of the teacher with the aptitudes, habits, and attainments of the scholar. By unremitting study, he kept abreast of the most recent results of Biblical criticism. He was a wide reader and an accurate and profound thinker. Hundreds now preaching are indebted to his teachings for the evangelical scripturalness and the simple directness which characterize their preaching."

At the beginning of the summer vacation of 1883 Dr. Hemenway found himself not only unusually worn by the year's work, but warned by serious symptoms of disease to take active measures for recuperation. The summer months were, therefore, mainly spent at Saratoga and Clifton Springs, with favorable but not wholly satisfactory results.

In September he entered with zeal upon the new school year. An additional class was organized by him in the Biblical Theology of the Old Testament, and his lectures on this subject were listened to with marked enthusiasm. Although his work wearied him to an unusual degree, he sought relief from no duties. He would often return from the class-room or pulpit so exhausted as to be unable to do his usual study and writing. He expressed to Mrs. Hemenway the growing conviction that his public work must soon be given up. Yet, outside the home walls, his courage and activity gave no sign of flagging, and precluded apprehension. In the spring of 1884 he yielded to an urgent request to take a Bible-class in the Sunday-school. The book of the Revelation was taken up, and the numbers in attendance rapidly increased. Among the words spoken here, which proved to be among his last public utterances, these may be quoted:

"It is possible for me, on this first day of February, 1884, unimportant as I am, to live the life of God, to live just as he would have me, as truly as for the martyrs and the great men of the Church.

"The great fact of God's personal love to us is the one supreme truth which heaven has for us, and one great use of earthly loves is to reveal to us, in some measure, this love of God. If my mother had had the resources of Christ, how much she would have done for me! Christ loves me more than my mother. The best earthly love may fail me, not that of Christ."

On the evening of March 13th, a meeting of the faculty was prolonged to a late hour. Returning home, Dr. Hemenway was unable to sleep. The morning brought further symptoms of illness, and yet only a few days' absence from his classes was anticipated by any one. As he did not improve, the expedient of a visit to his son in Kalamazoo was recommended by his physician. This was followed by greater weakness. The best diagnosis indicated a slight but constant intestinal hemorrhage as the probable cause of this slow but steady decline. As he was able he directed the affairs of the home and his classes. He assigned private work to the latter, saying that they should not meet again until called. I saw him often, and part of the time daily, during the five weeks of his illness. He usually lay upon a lounge, noticeably weak, yet calm, cheerful, and possessing all the vivacity and clearness of his mind undiminished. It was in these days that he wrote the description of the old school-house, contained in an earlier chapter. He reviewed lists of books to be purchased for the library, of which he had been custodian for many years. According to a request of the faculty in a recent meeting, he marked in a cat-

alogue the names of those alumni whom he regarded
as suitable candidates for special honors. But the
exhausting disease was slowly doing its fatal work,
and on Wednesday, the 16th of April, it was fully
recognized that the end was near. During this last
week his old and valued friend, the Rev. Dr. R. M.
Hatfield, called and prayed at his bedside, to his
heartily expressed satisfaction. The last night came
at length—that of the 18th of April. It may be best
described in the words spoken by Bishop Ninde at
the funeral services:

"It was a night of great prostration and suffering. His
extreme weakness made respiration very difficult, and his efforts to speak were very seldom intelligible. Toward morning
he touchingly said: 'I did not know I was so sick.' After
prayer had been offered at his bedside, he reached out his
arms and embraced each of his sons, and then the wife—whose
devotion had been so untiring—kissing them his last farewell.*
Thus he died, in that home which had been to him the most
delightful of all earthly retreats, surrounded by the loved and
loving, whose society had more than satisfied his heart's
earthly cravings, and in the midst of a community where he
was widely known and universally revered and honored."

The funeral services were held at the First
Methodist Episcopal Church of Evanston, April 22d,
and were attended by the faculties and students of
the Institute and Northwestern University, and by a
large number of alumni, ministers from neighboring
conferences, and friends from Chicago and Evanston.
The Church and family pew were appropriately

---

*The other surviving member of his immediate family was Ruth
Lillian, infant daughter of Henry B. and Lillie Bradley Hemenway.
The latter died about a year before Dr. Hemenway's decease, and,
anticipating death, had requested that her little daughter should be
baptized by him at her funeral. This touching ceremony was the
last baptism at which he ever officiated.

draped. Many floral offerings had been sent as tokens of affectionate remembrance, prominent among which were a chair from the faculty and students of the Institute, a cross and crown from the Sunday-school, a harp from his Bible-class, a sheaf and sickle from the South Evanston Church (his last pastoral charge), an open Bible and a broken column from personal friends. The casket was borne by students of the Institute, and followed by the pall-bearers, Judge Goodrich, Mr. Orrington Lunt, Mr. Frank P. Crandon, and Drs. Hitchcock, Bonbright, Marcy, Axtell, and Sheppard.

The services began with the singing of the hymn, "My Jesus, as thou wilt," which was read by Rev. Washington Gardner, of Kalamazoo, Mich. President Cummings, of the Northwestern University, then read the selections from the Scriptures which had been prepared and read by Dr. Hemenway at the funeral of Dr. Bannister a year before.

President Ninde, of the Institute, read an admirable biographical sketch, which need not be reproduced here. In closing, he said:

"The characteristics of such a man can not be summed up in a brief paragraph. His intellect was penetrating, incisive, and luminous. He seized truth with the promptness of intuition, and developed it in the orderly methods of the most rigorous logic. He rarely revealed the materials of his thinking in the rough. He disclosed only the finished product. This was true of small matters as well as great. Thus his views were uniformly expressed with a certain sententiousness that made them impressive upon other minds. He was very positive in his conclusions when reached, and held them with great tenacity, yet with no disposition to obtrude them upon others who might differ from him. His learning was copious, choice, and serviceable. In the line of his special studies his scholarship was critical, profound, and accurate. Every intellectual task was performed with the most conscientious fidelity. As an instance of this, when he accepted his appointment as one of the revisers of the Church Hymnal, he gave to the work his absorbed attention through an entire vacation—possibly by these strenuous labors hastening that fatal event which makes sad so many hearts to-day.

"But, back of the rich and cultured intellect, was a spirit so pure, so elevated, so genial, so unselfish, that words seem empty and powerless to express its nobleness. A more unselfish soul I never knew; never asking aught for himself, ever considerate of the interests of his associates and friends. Words and acts of this sainted man, too sacred for publicity, wonderfully drew my own heart toward him. And so there is upon me to-day—and doubtless others share the feeling—an oppressive sense of loneliness. Bannister gone, Hemenway gone! The old familiar places seem vacant and unutterably sad without them. The Holy Oracles themselves seem almost mute, now that their voices are hushed in the stillness of the tomb.

"I can not close without referring in a word to the religious character of our departed friend. He has been well-nigh a life-long Christian. The religious life in him was thoroughly pervasive. It seemed to penetrate every fiber of his moral being. Without being demonstrative or strongly emotional, his nature seemed thoroughly possessed of an intelligent, genial, soul-satisfying piety."

Rev. Dr. Miner Raymond was the next speaker. He said that, having been associated for nearly a score of years with Dr. Hemenway in the work of teaching, it seemed not inappropriate that he should say a few words of him as a teacher:

"A successful teacher is familiar with what he teaches; not merely with those outlines of fundamental ideas which thinkers, not specialists, are wont to have, but he must be familiar with the minutiæ and the details of his profession. More than this, all sciences interpenetrate, yet they may be classified in clusters, since some of them are more intimately related to each other than they are to others. The teacher must, therefore, be qualified to point out both these intimate and these remote relations. In a word, he must be a man of broad culture.

"Again, the successful teacher must be 'apt to teach ;' he must have what is in common parlance called 'tact,' which is more of the nature of an endowment than of an acquirement. It is a sort of genius, by which its possessor can come down from above to the plane of the pupil, and, through sympathy with the pupil's requirements, get power to direct his thinking and lead him upward.

"The successful teacher must be an enthusiast in the specialty that engages his attention. It is true, a man otherwise qualified for his work may, from a conscientious sense of duty, be so faithful and efficient as to be successful, but evidently it will be far better if his heart is interested in what he does. This is true in any avocation in life. One whose work is drudgery to him will accomplish but little that is valuable. Even if a worker's enthusiasm is inspired by an overestimate of the relative value of his work as compared with that of other employments, still it will be no detriment to his efficiency and success, but contrariwise will be every way advantageous. But, be this as it may, surely the teacher of religion has, in the intrinsic value of his work, a rational basis for the most intense interest.

"Dr. Hemenway possessed all the endowments and attainments of which we have spoken, in an eminent degree, so that it may be said that he had few equals.

"I wish to say a word of his interest in the personal welfare of the students. Somehow he succeeded in making an early acquaintance with them, sympathized with them in their wants and wishes, aided them as opportunity and ability allowed, was their friend while here, and followed them in their after history; always evincing an undying, all-absorbing, unselfish interest in their welfare.

"As an associate, I may say of him: His counsels were wise and were usually adopted; but if conclusions were different, his co-operation was invariably cordial. In all these years of my association with him, never an action performed, nor a word said, nor an intimation, look, or expression, has come from him that has made upon me the least unpleasant impression. Our intercourse from the beginning unto the end has been characterized by unsullied, undisturbed reciprocity.

"As I stand here to-day, I ask myself—can any one inquire, Is life worth living? If the inquiry be made, surely the only answer possible, looking upon that coffin, and mindful of the history of him whose remains it contains, is that life may be made not only worth the living, but of incalculable value to him who lives it. But we can not avoid the reflection that that which makes our earthly existence of value to us, is the fact that it is inseparably connected with immortality. The present can not be adequately conceived apart from the future. Hence we think of the body here and of the spirit yonder. I seem by faith to see the three who have gone—Dempster, Bannister, and Hemenway. If the lives these have lived, the histories they have made, be the first-fruits of man's being, what must the full harvest be? If this be visible in the early dawn, what shall these be in the perfect day? Dr. Hemenway has gone, and we would not call him back—our hearts say, Go, my brother; to thee to die is eternal gain; go, and farewell till I come to thee."

Professor Bradley spoke in behalf of the alumni as follows:

"It is my privilege to bring here a brief tribute to the teacher we revered and the friend we loved. I know I cannot represent all who have been blessed by his instructions or inspired by his friendship. Yet imperfect and hasty as this offering to his memory must be, it is at least fragrant with precious recollections and inspired by the sincerest admiration and love.

"First among the powerful impressions which Dr. Hemenway made upon us, his pupils, I place the emphasis which he ever laid, by precept and example, upon the sacred and precious character of truth. 'Buy the truth and sell it not;' 'buy it at all cost and sell it not at any price,' were his injunctions. Because God's word is truth, because Christ is 'the truth,' they deserve absolute allegiance from us. Sham, pretention, and deception he abhorred. As in doctrine so in character, he demanded, as chief and fundamental, genuineness, sincerity, and truth. To many of us, I am sure, he made the truth more sacred and supreme. From this characteristic and unswerving devotion to truth sprang, I believe, other important traits of character, such as his fidelity to duty, loyalty to his convictions, his skill and justice as a critic, his clear and accurate judgment, and his marvelous power of analysis.

"For some years delicate health has combined with other causes to bar him from any regular attention to general society. His home, the Institute, and the church are the three points through which the perfect circle of his life has been drawn. But how minutely faithful he was to all his duties in these! No man could love his home and his family more devotedly. In the public and social services of the church he was ever active and ever welcome; but for more than twenty-five years the class-room in the Institute has been the center of his life. The professor's chair has been his throne of power. In my experience East and West, as student and teacher, I have known of no one who seemed to me more accurate, more inspiring, or more impressive as a teacher. He did not emphasize forms and methods, he did not relish the routine of a drill-master, but the spirit and power of the subjects with which he dealt were ever present in his lecture-room. He imparted to us his life, his spirit, his experience. It was living truth which he wished us to appropriate—truth to be experienced by the heart, to become vital and capable of imparting life, so that the preaching might be, in substance, the preacher's own testimony, a personal experience of Him who is the truth and the life.

"It is not easy to be intensely loyal to one's own church and still broad and just in one's appreciation of other branches of the church of Christ. Dr. Hemenway's example helps us solve this problem. He could enjoy the silence of a Quaker service; he warmly admired the character of the Congregational ministry; he preferred the simple rites with which the Presbyterians celebrate the Lord's supper; he commended for imitation the spirit of reverence and worship so prominent with the Episcopalians; he warmly cherished his own cordial relations with sister churches here and elsewhere; and yet how intensely loyal he was to his own beloved church! 'No one,' I have heard him say, 'no one could be happier or more perfectly contented in his church relations than I am.' He loved the apostolic spirit and fervent hymns and testimonies of Methodism, and was in perfect accord with the doctrines of his church. He was catholic in his sympathies and loyal in his personal allegiance.

"He taught his pupils to value and use logical analysis. Every subject he took up was divided with such clearness and discrimination that we felt he was not applying an artificial system, but, with wonderful insight, discovering the actual joints and cleavage of the truth.

"In all Dr. Hemenway's instructions he held before us clearly defined and lofty ideals. And then how sound was his practical judgment! He had extensive and accurate learning; but he had more than knowledge—he had wisdom. The power 'to see things as they are, and to do things as they ought to be done,' was his in a marked degree. His strong common sense, sanctified and consecrated to the holiest ends, was a tower of strength to all who sought its help.

"I think that no one part of Dr. Hemenway's great nature was less widely understood than the depth of his sympathy and the warmth of his heart. He was not demonstrative, and he did not ask demonstration in return. He had a warmer appreciation of his students than they generally knew. He seldom praised them to their faces, but in this he was consistent. No doubt he valued appreciation; but it would have been impossible to deceive him with flattery, and it was most difficult to praise him. He would turn aside the sincerest words of admiration. He was naturally reserved; but let the slightest appeal of real need touch what seemed a wall of reserve, and there came forth refreshing streams of wise counsel and heartfelt sympathy. Where shall we turn for one to fill his place when we desire again such sympathy and advice as he has given us? Perhaps the freest sign of the inner warmth of his nature came out in his use and exposition of our hymns. He cultivated in the hearts of some of us a new love for these expressions of Christian feeling; and among his favorites were those which breathed the most ardent love for Christ.

"There is a deep regret to-day, mingled with our sorrow, that more of the results of Dr. Hemenway's rare powers and great attainments have ·not been written and published, so as to be more wide-reaching in their blessed influence. How well we recall the hours when he stood before us pouring forth a wealth of thought enshrined in the choicest forms of expression, 'apples of gold in pictures of silver,' or like showers of pearls, a few of which we saved, while the greater part was lost. We can hardly endure the thought of such a seeming waste. We treasure our small savings as more precious than jewels. But our very regret should be to us an inspiration. I think that Dr. Hemenway underestimated the unique force of his own utterances, but he held the truths which he presented as immeasurably precious. Nothing would have more fully met his wishes, or proved a more fitting memorial to him we love and mourn, than our grasping those truths and living them in his spirit. So shall his influence live as he would most desire. We may overestimate the influence of books, but not of living epistles. In and through our lives the teachings of our translated instructor may live and multiply till the end of time. To-day many a one of us makes the prayer of Elisha his own: 'I pray thee let a double portion of thy spirit be upon me.'"

Rev. Lewis Curts, pastor of the Evanston Church, spoke of the relations of Dr. Hemenway to the church and to the pastor in Evanston:

"We could think of him as a man of broad culture; but we may thank God that he was not too broad for the prayer-meeting. The Sunday-school teachers, the superintendent, and the church thank God that Dr. Hemenway never grew to be above the Sunday-school. He was one of the most cultured in the art of sacred song, and yet he did not become so refined in his ideas of music that he was not willing to sing with the great congregation or the little class-meeting or the little prayer-meeting. We think of him as a great teacher; and yet every one who has been his pastor will thank God that Dr. Hemenway was willing to sit in his pew and be taught, imperfect as his teachers might be. How the pastor will miss his encouraging look, miss his voice in song! How he will be missed in the Sunday-school, missed everywhere! How appropriate is this harp of flowers! He has in his hands a golden harp to-day, and sings the song of Moses and the Lamb. This beautiful chair is a symbol of his throne of power while here; but I hear the word of the Master saying: 'To him that overcometh will I grant to sit down with me in my throne.' He has gone from us, but he is with the church of the first-born and the spirits of just men made perfect. It will be but a little while before we shall meet him."

The services in the church were concluded by singing the hymn, "Rock of ages, cleft for me." The burial took place in Rose Hill Cemetery, where the services were conducted by the Rev. Dr. Ridgaway.

The following minute was drawn up by Dr. Ridgaway at the request of the faculty of the Institute:

"Within the short space of another year we, as a faculty, mourn the loss of another one of our colleagues. A year ago it was the veteran and revered Dr. Bannister, who was suddenly removed from our side, at the end of a career longer than that which is usually allotted to diligent workers; now it is our beloved Dr. Hemenway, who falls in the fullness of his powers, and at an age when, in the course of nature, there was reason to hope for him many more years of active usefulness. Words are insufficient to express the deep sense of sorrow which we feel in view of the loss we have sustained in this added bereavement. The fewness of our numbers as a faculty, the closeness of our relations, the identity of our work, the sympathy of our aims, and the oneness of our faith, bring about an intimacy and kindliness of intercourse which make us like one family, so that we grieve for his death as for a near kinsman, as though, indeed, the dark shadow had fallen upon the hearth-stone of each of us.

"We grieve the more, however, because of the immeas-urable loss which the Institute has sustained. While gratefully recognizing the immense and truly admirable work which he accomplished, a work in which he lives to-day in hundreds of his former students, and which is his most fitting monument, yet we had fondly anticipated that the work hitherto done was but the broad foundation for a still nobler superstructure He had acquired a ripeness of scholarship, a richness of experi-ence, a facility of expression, an ascendency over mind—that comes alone from thorough mastery—which must have made his instructions, in the very difficult and important department of Biblical exegesis, of inestimable benefit with every succeed-ing year. To speak of the loss sustained in his own particular department, is but meagerly to state the whole calamity which has befallen our cherished school. His entire being was wrought into its structure and history. Identified with it from youth, he was with it in its small beginnings, had stood by it in all its vicissitudes, and through all his vigorous manhood he served it with a zeal that knew no abatement, a wisdom which was never at fault, and a conscientiousness that allowed neither slackness nor diversion. He could not for a moment separate himself from Garrett; and, consequently, all that he was —in the spiritual and moral excellence of his character as a man and Christian, the force and beauty of his eloquence as a preacher of the gospel, the exactness, depth, and variety of his attainments, in his marvelous power of Biblical exposition, both as writer and teacher, in his scrupulous fidelity to all the public and private duties of life—he belonged to the Institute, and helped mightily to augment its fair fame and usefulness. His life is another striking illustration of the law that con-centration is the grand element of strength, and that he lives the most who most truly loves God and serves his fellow-creatures.

"In parting with the bodily presence of this our honored co-laborer in the sacred employment to which the church had called him and us, we cheerfully bear this tribute to his memory to be recorded on our minutes. We would also assure Mrs. Hemenway, the sons, and all surviving kindred, of our heart-felt sympathy in their affliction, and of our sincere prayers that the God whom he adored, Father, Son, and Holy Spirit, may be their unfailing strength."

The news of Dr. Hemenway's death caused widespread surprise and sorrow. Letters and resolutions of sympathy sent to the family showed the extent of this public bereavement. The Vermont conference, his old home conference, received the intelligence while in session, and hastened to express its sorrow and sympathy and high appreciation of his character.* An eye-witness wrote: "Such a thrill as went through the Vermont conference, when the telegram announcing Dr. Hemenway's death was read, I never witnessed before." (Rev. Ezra Walker.) The trustees of the Institute resolved "that the school, where he has so long and faithfully labored, and to whose interests he was so thoroughly devoted, has sustained an irreparable loss, and that the cause of sacred learning has been deprived of one of its brightest ornaments. By his thorough scholarship, marvelous analytical and critical methods, hundreds of young men, preparing for the ministry, have gained a clearer insight into the divine word. By the singular nobleness of his character, he has illustrated the power and blessedness of divine grace."† The Chicago Preachers' Meeting‡ and the Alumni Association of

---

*The committee consisted of Rev. Drs. J. C. W. Coxe and A. L. Cooper.

†Signed by Mr. Orrington Lunt, Secretary.

‡Their committee was: Revs. A. W. Patton, D. D., N. H. Axtell, D. D., and W. H. Holmes.

the Institute* passed similar resolutions. The Congregational church at Glencoe, and the South Evanston Methodist Episcopal church, expressed in strong terms their love and admiration for their former pastor.

The press of Evanston and Chicago, and the Methodist papers throughout the church, gave suitable recognition to the public and connectional interest in Dr. Hemenway's life and death. Yet even the notices in the Methodist *Advocates* showed that his modest and retiring nature had prevented an adequate appreciation of his unique character. The following is condensed from an article in the *Michigan Christian Advocate*, by the Rev. Charles M. Stuart:

"It is almost impossible for one with the freshness of the loss upon him to speak calmly or judicially of his qualities as a man and teacher. So striking were they that, even under circumstances less trying to the judgment, it would be difficult to set them forth adequately without seeming, to those not acquainted with him, extravagantly eulogistic. No man, however, could better afford to dispense with obituary honors. His undying eulogy will be found in the hearts of a generation of students into whom he breathed the love of virtue and the enthusiasm of a true science.

"As a teacher, perhaps nothing was more characteristic than his *precision.* In every detail of the class-room he was exact, methodical. Upon the stroke of the hour he was at his desk, and his mild look of rebuke to late comers was in itself a picturesque lecture on punctuality. Prodigal enough of his own time, for the sake of his students he never traded a moment upon theirs. This habit was carried, with excellent effect, into his use of language. His lectures on Biblical Introduction, could they be reproduced as he delivered them, would be models of precision and lucidity of statement. He recog-

---

* Revs. T. B. Hilton and A. W. Patten, D. D., committee.

nized that no two words were *exactly* synonymous, and his selection seemed to us little less than the choice of a conscience profoundly impressed with the moral quality of speech. So, too, in thought. In him there was no confusion of ideas. He knew what he knew, and the grounds of his knowledge; and he was quick to discern the student's uncertainty about the things he thought he knew. His precision in quoting authorities was also notable. He fully shared Sumner's high scorn of the trick of quoting a man's words to the distortion of his idea.

"As a teacher, Professor Hemenway was not only precise, but positive and conservative. One element of his strength was the tenacity with which he held to old and tested truths. Novelty was not with him a reason for change of opinion. So-called 'new' truths were canvassed and weighed. If their claims were valid he gave adherence, not because they were new, but because they were true. Eager for all light which modern research might throw upon Biblical questions, he was conservative of the old standards, and duly impressed his pupils with the value, in times of agitation and controversy, of making haste slowly in forming conclusions different from the old and well-established. To an information which to us students seemed encyclopedic, he added the teacher's crowning quality: the ability to inspire enthusiasm for study. A poor recitation in his class was the exception, and anything like indifference to the subject under consideration was impossible.

"Highly valued as Professor Hemenway was as a teacher, he was not less esteemed as a man. Only by his intimates could the real beauty of his character be appreciated. He was prevented, by ill-health and family duties, from being distinguished in the social circle, which he would have adorned by his disposition and attainments. His interest in the personal concern of the students was unremitting and almost womanly in its tenderness. Many a young man carries to his work to-day the inspiring remembrance of this good man's cheerful and helpful counsel and advice. His virtues were of the rugged order. The wells of affection were deep in him. His emotional nature was rich and profound. His lack, if lack it be considered, was in the display of his feelings. He was self-contained to a fault.

"Once only did I hear him preach. It was during a revival in First church, Evanston. The exhortation was most touching. He spoke extemporaneously. His sentences were short, direct, simple; his elocution at first nervous and somewhat over-accentuated; his gestures few but emphatic. When fairly launched on his subject the periods lengthened, the voice became charged with emotion, and the climax reached in thrilling impressiveness.

"And now he is gone! But he is not dead to us who knew him as man and teacher. He gave us his own best nature, and by so much made us better. The grave receives his mortal body, but the immortal self lives'

> 'Embalmed in memory, with things that are holy,
> By the Spirit that is undying.'"

The number of letters received from the alumni and other friends by the family and the Committee of Publication is very large, and there is a remarkable unanimity in the expression made. A few might well stand as types for all. They have deepened and confirmed the impression made by the man himself. Since all can not be quoted without filling the volume, we must content ourselves with typical extracts from a limited number. I know he sometimes felt that the students misunderstood him, and that the relation of a teacher seemed to him less cordial than that of a pastor. We may hope that he knows now the gratitude and affection which the following extracts express. A missionary in China writes: " I owe to him a lasting debt of gratitude for the exactness and thoroughness of his instructions. The example of his devoted and sensible Christian life is a constant help to one who is called upon to deal with all sorts and conditions of men, especially in a heathen land."[1] From India comes this testimony: "The class-meetings in Heck Hall were always rich seasons to my soul because *he* led them."[2] From other letters we cull the following brief tributes: "His exposition of hymns, the sweetness of his singing, and the *cheerfulness* of his religious experience made the class-meetings of the Institute most enjoyable."[3] "His sermons were models of pith and purity, and would invariably draw an exceptional audience."[4] "His words, his singing, and every movement have been a precious inspiration to me many times since I left Evanston."[5] "I learned to love him ardently, and his instruction and personality produced a greater impression upon me than those of any other man, except my father."[6] "I learned to prize his teachings so highly that I tried to preserve in writing almost everything which I heard from his lips."[7] "I have ever remembered the service he rendered me by wise counsel at a critical time with sincere gratitude."[8] "The fragrance of his holy life has gone out into all the church."[9] "I shall ever feel thankful to God for having known him as an instructor and friend."[10] "His clear discernment of truth and precise statement of it, his warm and genuine sympathy, and his personal interest in me, made him the one man of all living to whom I have looked for instruction, counsel, and help in my life-work."[11] "He was one of the great standard-bearers of the church. No

---

[1] Rev. M. C. Wilcox.   [2] Rev. J. C. Lawson.   [3] Rev. E. G. W. Hall.
[4] Prof. John Poucher, D. D.   [5] Rev. Wm. Dawe.   [6] Rev. E M. Glasgow.   [7] Prof. E. M. Holmes.   [8] Rev. A. L. Cooper, D. D.   [9] Rev. O. L. Fisher.   [10] Rev. J. S. Chadwick, D. D.   [11] Rev. A. E. Griffith.

death outside of my family could have come nearer to me."[12] "My beloved teacher, my true and gracious friend, my trusted counselor, my inspiring exemplar."[13] "His firm, calm simplicity of manner and conversation, and his exalted Christian character, made a deep impression on my mind."[14] "The influence of a few words he spoke to me one day, years ago, in the library of the Institute, has been the source of almost measureless support and encouragement during trials since. Some day I hope to tell him how much he did for me."[15]

The expressions of other friends were not less emphatic. Names can not well be given here, and only a few sentences may be quoted. A gentleman in whose home he was entertained during a General Conference wrote: "His presence with us was a benediction." A parishioner at Montpelier, Vt.: "How much my life has been enriched by his ministry here, only the eternal years can measure." A minister who was never his pupil wrote: "I, among thousands, am also a debtor to Dr. Hemenway, whose influence I felt long before I met him."

From other letters are culled the following: "Whenever he spoke, his words came to me like a benediction." "To Dr. Hemenway I owe more for spiritual progress and insight than to any other one person." But the veil can not be drawn from the personal sorrow and love which such a death discloses to those most deeply bereaved. A neighbor and friend for thirty years said: "O, if you could only tell how

---

[12] Prof. E. L. Parks, D. D.   [13] Rev. C. H. Morgan, Ph. D.   [14] Rev. M. M. McCreight.   [15] Rev. J. W. Richards.

much we loved him!" But when we attempt to express the deep things of life, the value of pure and unselfish character, the power of noble and consistent Christian living, the delight one feels in the fit embodiment in words of true and beautiful thought, the affection which a great and good friend inspires, then we realize that we are attempting the impossible.

To the alumni of the Institute, whose admiration for Dr. Hemenway has occasioned this volume, no words spoken here will seem extravagant. They are much more likely to be regarded inadequate. They might appear to other readers the unstinted praises of admiring pupils, unless accompanied by the testimony of those not under such obligations, and with a broader knowledge of men and things. Such witness we have from the Rev. Dr. Arthur Edwards, editor of the *Northwestern Christian Advocate;* the Rev. Dr. J. M. Buckley, editor of the *Christian Advocate;* Miss Jane M. Bancroft, Ph. D., formerly Dean of the Woman's College, in Evanston; Miss Frances E. Willard; the Rev. Dr. Isaac Crook, of Louisville, Ky.; and Mr. Frank P. Crandon, of Evanston. Each contribution tells its own interesting and valuable story.

DR. EDWARDS.

One's regard for a man like Dr. Hemenway is very sure to be of the most genuine quality. Certain men attract irresistibly; and he who is attracted, sometimes finds at last that he has been a victim of his own self-interest. Other men seem to attract because they are unselfish, and you may be sure that your regard for them is solely a tribute to their genuine worth. Dr. Hemenway won his friends slowly, but they were quite sure to remain friendly to the end. I knew him at arms'-

length for some years, but our common service on the committee to prepare the Hymnal, now in use by the church, brought us closely together. Of course I found him true in all our formal relations, but I felt drawn to him by reason of the deeper man which lay concealed at first beneath the surface of the outer personality. To most people he seemed reticent; but he was, in fact, one of the most sociable and ready talkers I have ever known. Once you broke the outer crust, you were sure to discover a thorough companion, if indeed you were entitled to the discovery and the confidence it implied. Our long journeys to the committee's meetings, and protracted service together, revealed to me, and to all the committee, one of the rarest men in our own or any other church. The Doctor was grave in demeanor; but in the restful moments we gave ourselves in the intervals of close work, he joined in the fun with a zest which is one of the best proofs of the genuine dignity in a confident, self-poised, and candid man. True humor often consists in the intentional violation of logical relations; and the genuine humorist, by the very excellence of his fun, manifests the firm texture of his mind. In the moments of which I speak, the heart and brain of Dr. Hemenway were often revealed at their best, and I am sure that those of the committee who survive enjoy the memories of our recreation somewhat as they do those of our soberer work. Some men "go to pieces" in your estimation because of what is revealed when humorous intercourse has put them off their guard. Look into Dr. Hemenway's heart or head, however, through whatever window, you were sure to discover nothing but the strong, the good, and the pure. He was instinctively a devout man. Sometimes, to try a hymn, or to get at the "understanding" with which it should be sung, we often gave it voice in two or three or more verses. I can now see him, with head thrown back, perhaps with closed eyes, as he entered into the spiritual interpretation of the lines we were preparing for the use of the church. His heart would take fire, and his strong voice was our leading soprano as we rolled forth the noble words of the poets of Methodism. Dr. Hemenway worked with a conscience. No labor was too great or protracted when needed to place the text of a disputed line in proper form. He had a genius for painstaking investigation, and, like all the rest of the world's busy men, he was called upon to do the world's extra work. He did not appear at his best when on parade, but in the uneventful corners of vital efficiency he made the success of the church's armies possible. When God promoted him to his reward, the world lost a really great man. I held him in highest estimate and loving regard. I would have freely trusted him in the highest place within the gift of the church. He was a pastor, and has aided to shape hundreds of pastors, and he was equal to the office and work of our pastors of pastors. Dr. Hemenway was pure in heart, simple-minded, devout, ambitious only in the highest and best sense, and he had that highest type of genuine catholicity which prefers his own church for the sake of all the churches. I hallow his memory, for, in all best respects, it is as ointment poured forth.

DR. BUCKLEY.

The request to write a few words concerning the late Professor F. D. Hemenway, preferred to me by the compilers of this memorial, has respect doubtless to that intimate relation subsisting between us in the work of revising the Methodist Hymn-book; for, prior to that time, it had not been my fortune to have more than a passing acquaintance with him. I consider it an abundant reward for the time and labor expended upon that work, that it brought me into contact with so many earnest and devoted representatives of different sections and spheres of activity in the church.

It soon became apparent that the design of the bishops to make the committee of fifteen truly representative, had been accomplished. The place filled by Professor Hemenway could not have been taken by any other. His death, or inability to serve, would have left the revisers without the counsel of a critic than whom none was more discriminating, painstaking, conscientious, or kindly.

During the first few weeks after the organization, to a stranger he might have seemed somewhat finical; but this resulted from a transient reserve, which exhibited only his intense devotion to truth, even in details, without the *bonhomie* which on further acquaintance lit up his communications, as rays of sunlight bring out the colors in a somber landscape, and change its whole aspect.

Many students exhaust their energy in sedentary habits and laborious application to monotonous work. Chronically languid, they are not able to display their knowledge attractively, or to hold attention while they present carefully formed opinions. It was not so with Professor Hemenway. He spoke upon recondite points with the vivacity of earnest conversation; received contradiction meekly, defending his positions strongly; and acknowledging an error, if found in one—which was rarely the case—with thanks.

Understanding music, he considered every hymn, not only with respect to its sentiment, but its adaptation to Christian song in the family, the Sabbath-school, the prayer-meeting, and the worship of the great congregation. Yet he often remarked that the Hymnal served an important purpose as a volume of devotional reading; and that it should not be forgotten that many an invalid would read these compositions, and they would be the delight of the aged and infirm, and the instruction and entertainment of many who are not able to sing.

His taste was exquisite. We learned to look for the exhibition of the hidden beauties of a composition, if there were any, and for a prompt and convincing exposure of essential defects. Nor did he lose sight of the substance of truth. He was not one of those who would sacrifice for a beautiful figure a strong statement. If possible, he would unite them; but I recall several occasions when he said: "The hymn is metrically and musically almost perfect; but it is too weak—it contains nothing nourishing." Professor Hemenway distinguished between sentimentality and spirituality, and desired that, without the loss of true sentiment, ever helpful to spirituality, every hymn sung by the church might be a proper vehicle for devout aspiration, thankfulness, petition, or penitential confession.

To speak of his reverent spirit will seem to those who knew him well superfluous; but as the purpose of these words is not merely to remind his friends of him, but to enable others to know why they loved him, I will definitely state that in two years and a half close intercourse with him, by correspondence and in conversation, in hours of work and hours of ease, I never heard from him a word which would have been incompatible with an immediate transition to the most solemn act of devotion. Yet there was nothing somber; the "light of smiles" often played upon his features. His tenderness was not weakness, his strength not coarseness, his wit not lightness, nor his mirth levity.

Upon questions of expediency he was not pertinacious; upon those of principle he was immovable, yet more solicitous to be convinced of truth than to prevail in controversy. In the report submitted to the bishops and published to the church, the discussion of new hymns was committed to Dr. Hemenway, and in its preparation his qualities as a thinker and writer appear at their best.

On an important sub-committee he was associated with Professor Harrington and the writer, who alone survives, and writes these words with feelings in which a sense of the uncertainty of life blends with an encouraging conviction of the permanence of work done for Christ, and the value of a hope that personality is not destroyed when this "mortal shall have put on immortality."

MISS BANCROFT.

In the various relations of daily living, Dr. Hemenway was honored and loved by all. A sincere and faithful friend, a professor of careful and exact scholarship, a Christian of unobtrusive yet fervent piety, the record that he left is plain and open—it can be read by all.

Yet there is no personality that completely reveals itsel to another; "as Thebes of old, so has the soul her hundred gates;" and when one swings ajar, and we have glimpses within, yet they are but glimpses, and we can only wonder and conjecture as to what we do not see. Yet by combining the glances of insight of many friends of varying nature, we shall obtain a more complete conception of a rarely lovable personality—a personality that veiled itself in a degree by reticent dignity and quiet composure.

I had the privilege of counting Dr. Hemenway among my friends for a number of years; and yet I ever remember him by preference on the few occasions when I reached below the surface, and obtained a slight knowledge of the thoughts he was thinking, or the motives which impelled him.

One day we were returning from church together, and were talking of the sermon, with its lesson of trust in Divine Providence—a trust that should stand firm, even if the outward conditions of life failed to bring home the conviction of a loving Father's care.

"It is the eternal question," I said, "coming anew to every generation, fresh to every human soul, as though long centuries of tired, troubled men had not struggled to attain the certain assurance—'God is my Father; he has personal, loving care for me.'"

"Yes," he answered; "and what a blessed truth it is that so many seeking souls have found the answer! It was meant to come home to every one; each man must face it for himself. God presents us difficulties in life so as to educate us in trust. It is a ceaselessly recurring question, because it is the vital one of life."

"Yes, there is witness of this in all countries and at all times," I responded, and then quoted Whittier's poem on the German mystic, Tauler, of mediæval times:

> "Tauler, the preacher, walked one autumn day,
> Without the walls of Strasburg, by the Rhine,
> Pondering the solemn miracle of life;
> And as he walked, he prayed even the same
> Old prayer, with which for half a score of years—
> Morning, noon, and evening—lip and heart
> Had groaned: 'Have pity upon me, Lord;
> Thou seest, while teaching others, I am blind.'"

"O, that is one of my poems," he said. And taking up the lines where I left them, he quoted stanza after stanza, showing a wonderful exactness of verbal memory. "This is the heart of the poem," and he repeated in a slow and measured way:

> "What hell may be, I know not; this I know—
> I can not lose the presence of the Lord.

One arm, Humility, takes hold upon
His dear Humanity; the other, Love,
Clasps his Divinity. So where I go,
He goes; and better fire-walled hell with him
Than golden-gated paradise without."

" And this, a most beautiful conclusion of the whole matter:

'So darkness in the pathway of man's life
Is but the shadow of God's providence,
By the great Sun of Wisdom cast thereon;
And what is dark below is light in heaven.'"

As he spoke I felt with subtle sympathy, "That poem has had its message to you as it has to me—a comforting one—giving the assurance that to his own, God will reveal himself."

Then there is another glimpse I cherish well in memory. I had asked Dr. Hemenway to come to our Wednesday evening service at the Woman's College, to give us, some of the treasures of his rare knowledge of the hymns of the church. He accepted the invitation, and when he came, the entire evening was devoted to a song-service, made up of the hymns that had been written by women authors. Each hymn had its own explanation as to how, when, and where written; then followed gentle words of encouragement to the young college girls, inciting them to service for Christ's church, and, if possible, also to write words of praise and thanksgiving to be treasured in sacred song. They were only a few words, but listened to with closest attention.

Afterward, as I considered the thoughtful tact in the choice of the hymns, and the wise, stimulating words of encouragement that had been said, I obtained another glimpse into a nature quick to see and ready to respond to every opportunity for working good.

These facts may seem but slight testimonials when compared with the far wider tributes that many will give—tributes of words and deeds that were known and recognized as sources of power in a wide range of influence—but such as I have I give; fragrant, blessed memories, that will be treasured by me, and shared by others, while life lasts.

MISS WILLARD.

The life of Dr. Hemenway was set to music. His dome-like head, trim figure, quick, measured step, and voice remarkable for rhythm, were the insignia of a spirit full of cadences and melody. I used to think that in him a tone-master was spoiled to make a scholar. Had his physical vigor equaled his psychic sensibility, he would have wrought out in a long life something in music beyond the realm of Methodism. As it is, he takes rank, for our time, as the first hymnologist of the church, concerning which he often said it was "beloved by him beyond his chief joy." When he raised the tune for us in love-feast, prayer- or class-meeting—and I heard him do so hundreds of times—we all felt that the act was one of worship.

Dr. Hemenway was of a rarely reticent nature, and persons of frank and enthusiastic make-up did not always feel sure that he approved of them; but it was only the surface recoil of unlike temperaments. Take my own case: Our homes were but a block or two apart for twenty years, yet, beyond the kindly greeting of passers-by, we almost never met except in class-meeting, where for some time he was my leader, and beloved as almost no other has been since I became a daughter of the church. In my journals of those days, as in my sister Mary's, allusions to him are frequent, and always in appreciative terms. Take the following from mine by way of illustration:

Autumn of 1869: Evening. Have just returned from class-meeting, where I went with Oliver as in the pleasant days of last spring. Professor Hemenway was as kind and candid as ever. The room was cozy, the lamp and table and pictures were just as usual. But the one with whom I used to go to class-meeting was far away. My brother prayed very sweetly and earnestly. Professor Hemenway uttered one sentence that particularly attracted my attention. He said: "We have strength only because we are joined to him who is strong."

In appearance and conduct, in character and achievement, this unique and noble man gave to all who knew him a sense of symmetry hardly paralleled in my acquaintance. He was one whose presence warmed the spirit. The ray was not of sunshine, but of purest starlight, and I always felt it was a beam so true and kindly that it was good to follow, even as that at Bethlehem, which led always straight to Christ.

He was a man to be confided in. When three of my best beloved—father, sister, and brother—passed away, Dr. Hemenway's presence, his voice, his participation in the last services, brought solace to the hearts that sorrowed, though we saw him only in the pulpit and at the grave. Tuneful and sweet, that remarkable voice has memorably fallen on my ear in tender cadences as Dr. Hemenway walked up the church aisle, leading the funeral procession, and uttering the words, "I am the resurrection and the life; he that believeth in me, though he were dead, yet shall he live." There was the steadiness of absolute conviction in those tender tones.

He was a man to trust—a man to seek in time of trouble. He was a royal counselor and a choice critic. When I started out to speak without manuscript or notes, I asked him to let me rehearse before him, and, at his suggestion, we went up to University Hall, where, in Professor Cumnock's recitation-room (in which that generous friend and brother had trained me many a time), Dr. Hemenway seated himself, paper and pencil in hand, carefully noting his points of commendation and of criticism for an hour or more. Meanwhile I pictured him to myself as a large audience, and tried to speak precisely as I would have done had he needed to be saved from the errors of his ways, or aroused to the exigencies of the situation and enlisted as a soldier in "every body's war." Nothing could exceed his gentle faithfulness in telling me the impressions made upon his trained and well-poised mind, from which statements I have tried to profit. When I had heard all that he had to say, we went our several ways, and I had few other opportunities for conversation with him.

But there are hymns that I shall never sing without perceiving him before me with his lofty brow and spiritual countenance, and chief among them is his favorite:

> "Lead, kindly Light, amid the encircling gloom,
> Lead thou me on."

DR. CROOK.

I write not as a pupil, but as a learner and admirer. I met Dr. Hemenway at Minneapolis, at a theological conference. He was its very able conductor. There, as often elsewhere, there seemed to me an exactness and precision, bearing the appearance of coldness and severity; but there was withal an affability and manliness very admirable. In the progress of the discussions he occasionally gave clear-cut statements, which I have carried and found entering into my ministry. Among others he said in substance: " I accept the Bible because I find Christ in it and indorsing it. I do not accept any thing primarily because I find it in the Bible." I may not represent him precisely, but he made it clear and precise. He gave one evening to the then new hymnal, to the compiling of which he had devoted possibly more rea hard work than any one of the committee. It was a great feast to hear his rich comments and look at many of the hymns through the light of his intelligent enthusiasm. He afterward said to me, at our place of entertainment, that Lytle's hymn, " Abide with me," was the finest composition in English hymnology. I never behold the hymn without seeing his clear-cut, pensive features, and hearing the tones of " a voice that is still."

MR. CRANDON.

For several years Dr. Hemenway was actively associated with me in Sunday-school work. As a Bible-class instructor, and as the leader of our teachers' meetings, I never knew his peer. His exposition of Scripture was clear, forcible, and exhaustive. His diction was elegant, and his method of discussion secured the undivided attention of his audience. He never seemed to utter a superfluous word, yet at the close of any of his exercises, every person who had listened to him felt that nothing which was worth the saying had been left unsaid.

His resources seemed to be almost illimitable. Our teachers' meetings occurred on Saturday evenings. As a matter of course it often happened that the Doctor taught a Bible-class on Sunday the lesson which he had expounded at the teachers' meeting the evening before. The two audiences would be composed in part of the same persons. I never knew him to pursue the same method of exposition, or to use the same illustrations, or to repeat to any considerable extent, in his Sunday teaching, what he had said to the Saturday evening class. None the less, however, would he seem in each exercise to cover the entire scope of the text. Aside from his marvelous powers of instruction, he was in many other ways most helpful in all our Sunday-school work. He was particular, even in minute details, to observe all the general regulations of school, and this conformity on his part resulted in a similar conformity on the part of those who would otherwise have been somewhat refractory.

To Dr. Hemenway I am personally greatly indebted. I came to regard him as the ideal Christian. Generous, sympathetic, scholarly, devout—it would be difficult to suggest any desirable characteristic which he did not possess.

To have known him was a benediction. To be like him would be to be worthy of the profound esteem of good men. I cherish his memory as a most precious inheritance, and I recognize in his life and character an ideal exemplification of the attainments which, under Divine guidance, are possible to humanity.

The truest and best memorial of such a man as Dr. Hemenway is to be found in the characters and minds of those whom he has influenced for good. Two material monuments, however, should be mentioned. When the South Evanston church replaced its building, destroyed by fire, with a more beautiful structure, it was decided to call the new house the Hemenway Methodist Episcopal Church. The graceful edifice stands as a fair and fitting memorial to this pastor of pastors. It was built under the leadership of the Rev. Dr. T. P. Marsh, now president of Mount Union College.

As the Institute grew in numbers, a new hall became a necessity, and President Ridgaway, in planning for it, proposed that it should be a memorial hall, to commemorate the noble men and women who had been connected with the seminary, and especially the three deceased professors—Drs. Dempster, Bannister, and Hemenway. In the exquisite chapel, the triple south-window has been especially dedicated to their memory. The alumni of the school gave the portion inscribed to Dr. Dempster, and the First Church of Evanston gave two thousand dollars on condition that the side windows should bear the names of Drs. Bannister and Hemenway. The plan of the design for this "teaching window" was made by Professor Charles W. Bennett. The dove—symbol of the Holy Spirit, who inspires all true Christian teaching—is at the top. The next panels contain three emblems of Christ, the Revealer of Christian truth. Suitable symbols of the different departments of theological instruction in which each professor was engaged, form the three parts of the next section. A figure of St. Paul, bearing the Sword of the Spirit, is the central figure in the window. The artistic drawing and coloring, and the richness of the glass, render these windows an object of interest to many visitors, and daily emphasize to the students the beauty of that holiness exemplified by the noble men whose memory is thus fitly honored.

The study of such a life as Dr. Hemenway's strengthens the belief that the highest character is really indescribable. Its quiet force is subtle and indefinable, yet so powerful and so unspeakably valuable that even an imperfect biography will doubtless deepen and extend its holy influence. The history of the great religious teachers of the world shows that personal influence, exerted first upon a comparatively small company, and then extended through them to others, has been the saving leaven of the world. Such lives prove life worth living. They give a silent but severe rebuke to sordidness and selfish ambition. They do much to convince men that there is a blessed immortality. To the Christian they make heaven seem real and near. He whom we loved and who helped us so in the best things, is now with Christ, "whose he was and whom he served." He who so prized and taught us to value the songs of Zion, now joins in the eternal harmonies of the song of Moses and the Lamb.

> "O sweet and blessed country,
>   The home of God's elect!
> O sweet and blessed country,
>   That eager hearts expect!
> Jesus, in mercy bring us
>   To that dear land of rest—
> Who art, with God the Father,
>   And Spirit, ever blest."

Studies in Hymnology.

EDITED BY

REV. CHARLES M. STUART.

INTRODUCTORY NOTE.

D R. HEMENWAY believed the Hymnal to be the third in the trinity of books which ought to constitute the basis of every Methodist pastor's library. The other two were, of course, the Bible and the Discipline. To stimulate an interest in, and further a discriminating appreciation of, the best in hymnody, he gave occasional lectures on the subject; which lectures he was preparing to issue in book-form at the time of his death. It is interesting to note, as illustrating the method and orderliness characteristic of all his work, that he left a memorandum naming the book, enumerating the chapters, and outlining the contents of the preface.

The book was to be called "Our Hymns, and Their Authors," and to consist of the following twelve chapters:

    I. Hymns and Lyric Poetry in General.
    II. Hymns of the Ancient Church.
    III. Earlier Mediæval Hymns.
    IV. Later Mediæval Hymns.
    V. Hymns from German and French Authors.
    VI. Earlier English Hymns.
    VII. Watts and the Wesleys.
    VIII. Other Hymn-writers of the Eighteenth Century.
    IX. Later English Hymns.
    X. American Hymns.
    XI. Modern Catholic and Unitarian Hymns.
    XII. Woman in Hymnody.

The manuscript was complete to the end of the seventh chapter, and was in perfect order. The only change which the editor has taken the liberty of making is to divide the seventh chapter according to the very obvious lines laid down in the title.

The design of the work included only hymns in common use "in the congregations and homes of America," and "to say only so much as was necessary to identify and individualize the author and to introduce the hymns." Where anything special was known concerning the origin or history of a hymn, it would be mentioned. The book should be popular in style, but special pains would be taken to insure accuracy of statement. In this latter respect the author thought the work would "contrast favorably with anything of its general character in our language."

The work speaks for itself. It is only to be regretted that a work so useful, so well planned, and so thoroughly, intelligently, and conscientiously begun, could not have been completed. One does not think of the lamented author without associating with him a favorite hymn. That he had many favorites, the varying testimony of friends implies; and that testimony is at once an evidence of his discriminating taste, catholicity, and ample knowledge—it shows that he always loved the best.

His students and parishioners remember the singular felicity and aptness with which he used hymns in public discourse, and the rarely beautiful and impressive elocution with which they were delivered.

The General Conference of 1876 ordered a revision of the Hymnal, and authorized the appointment of a committee of fifteen to undertake the work. Among the number selected was Dr. Hemenway, and his name appears first in the list of five who constituted the Western section. Of the quality and extent of his work on the revision, the Revs. Dr. Edwards and Dr. Buckley, also members of the committee, write elsewhere. The elaborate report of the committee to the bishops, a pamphlet of seventy-five pages, was the joint work of the Rev. Dr. Buckley and Dr. Hemenway, the latter writing that part of it embraced in pp. 23–75. In this, under the discussion of "New Hymns," he adds historical notes of great interest and value. In nothing, perhaps, was this delightful accomplishment of Dr. Hemenway's used to so large and fruitful advantage as in impressing upon prospective pastors the dignity of hymn-singing as an element of worship. To him music was divine, not diversion; and as divine, to be treated as all divine things are treated, with intelligent reverence and devout consideration.

One wish was dear to him. It was that a knowledge of hymns and hymn-writers might be popularized. Not for the sake of its pleasing and curious information, but that the psalmody of the church might be "in the spirit and with the understanding," and that the song service might accomplish something more of its mission among the people as a kind of spiritual dynamics. It would delight him, even where he is now, to know that his work in this direction was being used to that end. We venture to suggest the use of these lectures for an occasional Sunday or weekday service. It would not fail to interest, instruct, and inspire. With Augustine, many have testified, and many will yet testify: "The hymns and songs of thy church, moved my soul intensely. Thy truth was distilled by them into my heart. The flame of piety was kindled, and my tears flowed for joy."

STUDIES IN HYMNOLOGY.

CHAPTER I.

HYMNS AND LYRIC POETRY IN GENERAL.

A S we turn our attention to lyric poetry in general, the first thing which impresses us is its *antiquity*. The oldest human literature has come to us in this form. The most ancient books of the Hindoos, and, as many think, the most ancient of all human books, are the famous Vedic hymns, which, by the most moderate calculation, are nearly three thousand years old. The entire number of these is 1,028; and as early as 600 B. C. their verses, words, and syllables had been carefully enumerated. The oldest of the Chinese sacred books is the third of the ante-Confucian classics—called by them the " Book of Odes "—fragments of which are seen scattered over tea-chests and other articles of Chinese manufacture. As to the relative antiquity of the Vedas in Hindoo literature, and the Book of Odes in Chinese literature, there is no difference of opinion; but it is impossible to determine with certainty, or even a high degree of probability, the absolute age of either. The general estimate of those most competent to form an opinion on the subject is, that both may date from 1000 to 1200 years B. C.; thus, in the matter of age, ranking with the Davidic Psalms.

The oldest fragment in our Bible, and probably the oldest bit of poetry—and, indeed, of literature of any sort—in the world, is the song of Lamech, which is recorded in the fourth chapter of Genesis:

> " Adah and Zillah, hear my voice;
> Wives of Lamech, hearken to my speech;
> For a man have I slain for smiting me,
> And a young man for wounding me.
> Surely seven-fold shall Cain be avenged,
> But Lamech seventy and seven."—Gen. iv, 23, 24.

Herder, with whom Delitzsch substantially agrees, calls this "a song of the sword." It articulates that spirit of pride and atheistic self-confidence which culminated in the rebellion and catastrophe of Babel. Lamech virtually says, and with so much of passion that his utterance is crystallized into poetry: " I will protect and avenge myself with the weapons which my son, Tubal-Cain, can forge. I will avenge myself more terribly than God threatened to avenge Cain."

> "Surely seven-fold shall Cain be avenged,
> But Lamech seventy and seven."

It is interesting to find, in this one specimen of antediluvian literature which has come down to us, all the peculiar characteristics of Oriental, and particularly of Hebrew poetry—rhythm, assonance, parallelism, and poetic diction.

Coming to Christian lyric poetry, we are at once struck with its vast extent and incomparable wealth. It is estimated that in the German language alone there are 80,000 Christian hymns, [1] and in the English 40,000. Even as early as 1751, says Kurtz in his

Church History, J. Jacob V. Moser collected a list of 50,000 printed hymns in the German language.

Not only is the gross amount so considerable, its diffusion is still more to be noted. Next to the Christian sacred books, nothing in literature has been so multiplied as copies of Christian hymns. The multiplication of certain choice and popular books—such, for instance, as the " Imitation," the " Pilgrim's Progress," and the "Thousand and One Nights," in many languages, and in every variety of form, cheap and costly, plain and elaborate—is something wonderful; for the highest proof which life can give of its own existence and fullness is its continuous creative energy; and yet all this falls immeasurably short of the truth touching the choicest hymns. Copies of some of these may be counted literally by the million. They rival the Lord's Prayer and the Ten Commandments in their hold on human memories. There are not a few into whose memories verses of hymns came earlier than verses of Scripture, and they will be more likely to speak them with their dying breath.

A hymn is the most subtle and spiritual thing which a man can create. It must be in *fact*, if not in *form*, a transcript of his highest and holiest experiences; for the distinguishing characteristic of lyric poetry is the stamp it bears of the personal consciousness. The most perfect expressions of the Christian creed and life are found in the hymns of the church. As influences for good they are at once subtle and powerful, swaying our natures as nothing else can. " What care I," says Falstaff, " for the bulk and big assemblage of a man? Give me the spirit, Master

Shallow, give me the spirit." Now, the spirit of humanity, and of the Christian church, in a sense infinitely higher than Shakspeare's hero could understand, are found in lyric poetry as nowhere else. The subtle essence, the delicate hues, the delicious fragrance, and ethereal beauty of spiritual character, are here most variously and beautifully exhibited.

Bishop Wordsworth, in the somewhat elaborate essay on Christian hymns prefixed to his "Holy Year," complains that while the ancient hymns are distinguished by self-forgetfulness, the modern are characterized by self-consciousness. "In ancient hymns man is always elevated to God; in modern, God is too often depressed to man. In these last, the individual often detaches and isolates himself from the body of the faithful, and in a spirit of sentimental selfishness obtrudes his own feelings concerning himself; and claiming, as it were, a monopoly of spiritual privileges for himself, makes it to be the theme of praise to God the Father of all that he has had mercy on *him*, and to Christ the Savior of the world that he has died for *him;* and he comes forward to speak to God concerning his own spiritual state, contrasted with that of others, in a tone of self-congratulation which sometimes seems to be not far removed from that of the Pharisee in the Gospel; and he does this in public worship, in the house of God, and makes his own individuality to be, as it were, the axis around which all the congregation, and even the heavenly sphere itself, is caused to revolve." As illustrative examples he cites the following: "When I can read my title clear," "When I survey the wondrous cross,"

"I hold the sacred book of God," "My God, the spring of all my joys;" and he also quotes, as illustrating not only this egotistical character, but also a certain reprehensible self-assurance, and a familiar and even amatory style of address—

> "Jesus, lover of my soul,
>   Let me to thy bosom fly,"

which he says he has heard "given out to be sung by every member of a large, mixed congregation, in a dissolute part of a populous and irreligious city."

Seldom were words ever written which betray a more absolute want of comprehension of the whole subject of lyric poetry. Its one grand, distinguishing characteristic is the fact that we see here, as nowhere else, the glory of individual life and experience. It must be confessed that there are hymns which illustrate some of the objectionable tendencies pointed out by the distinguished prelate; but certainly the hymns he specifies show very clearly how a hymn can be a genuine lyric, reflecting most clearly and vividly the individual consciousness, and yet be thoroughly free from obtrusive egotism. The most perfect and most universally intelligible model of religious poetry holds such language as the following: "The Lord is *my* shepherd; *I* shall not want. He maketh *me* to lie down in green pastures; he leadeth *me* beside the still waters." Wiser was Luther, who used to thank God for these same little words—these words of personal confession and appropriation. It is comparatively unimportant whether the hymn stand in the singular or plural number; the one thing essential is that it be a crystallization of personal thought and experience. The great hymns of the church—the hymns of the ages—hymns which stand pre-eminent as expressions of the life of God in the soul of man—are almost uniformly such as come most directly out of the experience of the writer. Charles Wesley's hymns are eminently autobiographic. That grand hymn which has so long held the place of honor in both English and American Methodist hymn-books—"O for a thousand tongues to sing"—was written on the first anniversary of Mr. Wesley's spiritual birth. Equally evident is it that his holiest aspirations and his most blissful experiences are given voice in such hymns as: "O love divine, how sweet thou art;" "Love divine, all loves excelling;" "Vain, delusive world, adieu." Two of his hymns, very familiar to Methodists, were addressed to his wife on her birthday:

"Come away to the skies, my beloved, arise,
    And rejoice in the day thou wast born."

"Come, let us ascend, my companion and friend,
    To a taste of the banquet above." [2]

The connection of the hymn "God moves in a mysterious way" with Cowper's personal history is well known.[3] John Newton's most characteristic, though by no means most famous or most beautiful, hymn is a mere transcript of his spiritual autobiography: "I saw one hanging on the tree."[4] The hymn of Anne Steele, which is most universally known and most frequently used, "Father, whate'er of earthly bliss," is beyond question the simple outbreathing of her personal trust and submission beneath the heavy burdens of sorrow which she, more than others, was called to bear.[5] Charlotte Elliott's "Just as I am" is the expression of the experience into which she herself had come, after long and painful preparation. John Keble's most frequently used hymn, "Sun of my soul," exhibits the very characteristic which is so offensive to Bishop Wordsworth.[6] And, as we look through the whole range of hymnology, and consider the hymns which all agree to understand, to love, and to use, we shall find the great majority of them to be couched in the language of personal confession and appropriation, such as shows them to be the outpouring of the most sacred and most spiritual experiences.

As a *means* of *Christian influence* hymns are most serviceable, and sometimes well-nigh irresistible. The pure waters of holy song will sometimes make their way into places dark and deathful, which no other influence from heaven can reach. A few years since a little party of American travelers, happening to be in Montreal, took occasion to visit the celebrated Grey Nunnery, one of the wealthiest religious houses on this continent. As we were being conducted through the establishment, we came to the school-room containing the orphan children, kept there as one branch of their charities. For our entertainment, the children were set to singing. What was our surprise and delight to hear them sing our common Protestant Sunday-school hymns, such as "I have a Father in the Promised Land," "I want to be an angel," "There is a happy land!" What other form of evangelical influence could have made its way so successfully through the bolts and bars of that convent?

There is a familiar incident connected with one of Phebe Cary's hymns which may well be taken as representative of a very large class of similar instances showing the power of sacred song. A few years since two men, Americans—one middle-aged, the other a young man—met in a gambling-house in Canton, China. They had been engaged in play together during the evening, and the young man had lost heavily. While the older one was shuffling the cards for a new deal, his companion leaned back in his chair, and began mechanically to sing a fragment of Miss Cary's exquisite hymn, "One sweetly solemn thought." As these words, so tender and so beautiful, fell on the ear of the man hardened in sin, dead memories in his heart came to life again. He sprang up excitedly, exclaiming: "Where did you learn that hymn? I can't stay here!" And, in spite of the taunts of his companion, he hurried him away, and confessed to him the story of his long wanderings from a happy Christian home. At the same time he expressed his determination to lead a better life, and urged his companion in sin to join him. The resolution was kept, the man was reclaimed, and the story of his recovery came back to bless Miss Cary before she died. This hymn, God's invisible angel, had gone with the man, through all those weary years of sin, and finally led him back to purity and salvation.

An oft-repeated incident connected with one of the best hymns of Charles Wesley well illustrates the

power of this means of influence. The only daughter
of a wealthy and worldly nobleman was awakened
and converted at a Methodist meeting in London.
This was to her father an occasion of bitter grief and
disappointment, and he at once set about winning her
back to her former associations. Having vainly tried
other means to draw her away from her newly found
faith, he at last formed a plan the object of which
was to bring to bear upon her the combined influence
of her former most intimate associates and friends,
and that, too, under such conditions that she would
be unable to resist it. He arranged to invite to his
own home a number of her gay and worldly associates, hoping, by their influence, to entangle her
again in the meshes of fashionable dissipation. The
company assembled, and all, in high spirits, entered
upon the pleasures of the evening. According to the
plan preconcerted, several of the party took their
turn in singing a song, of course selecting such as
comported with the gayety and worldliness of the
occasion. Then the young lady herself, being an accomplished musician, was called upon. She distinctly
saw that the critical hour had come. Pale, but composed, she took her seat at the piano, and, after running her fingers over the keys, sang these verses of
Charles Wesley's incomparable hymn :

> "No room for mirth or trifling here,
> For worldly hope or worldly fear,
>   If life so soon is gone ;
> If now the Judge is at the door,
> And all mankind must stand before
>   The inexorable throne.

No matter which my thoughts employ,
A moment's misery or joy;
But O, when both shall end,
Where shall I find my destined place?
Shall I my everlasting days
With fiends or angels spend?

Nothing is worth a thought beneath
But how I may escape the death
That never, never dies!
How make mine own election sure,
And, when I fail on earth, secure
A mansion in the skies.

Jesus, vouchsafe a pitying ray;
Be thou my guide, be thou my way
To glorious happiness.
Ah! write the pardon on my heart;
And whensoe'er I hence depart,
Let me depart in peace."[7]

She had conquered. Truths so solemn and
weighty, borne on soul-moving music, and illustrated
by the humility and heroism of her who now sat in
her own father's house, in the midst of this joyous
company, alone with God, could not be resisted.
The father wept aloud, and afterward himself became
a trophy of his daughter's courage and fidelity.

As an *instrument of expression* song is equally
serviceable. It gathers up into itself our sweetest,
saddest, most heroic, and most spiritual experiences.
When the soul comes to its divinest heights, song is
sure to be there. If it is not already in waiting, the
inspired soul at once creates it, as did Mary the *Magnificat* and Simeon the *Nunc Dimittis*. Rarely was
there ever witnessed a scene of more thrilling interest than that of the reunion of the Old and New

School divisions of the Presbyterian Church, which took place in Pittsburg in May, 1869. On the day appointed, the two bodies met in their respective places, and then, having formed in the street in parallel columns, joined ranks, one of each assembly arm in arm with one of the other, and so marched to the place where the services were to be held. As the head of the column entered the church, already crowded, save the seats reserved for the delegates, the audience struck up the hymn, " Blow ye the trumpet, blow;" and, when all were in their places, " All hail the power of Jesus' name!" After the reading of the Scriptures came the hymn of Watts, " Blest are the sons of peace." The interest of the occasion culminated when Dr. Fowler, the moderator of the New School Assembly, at the close of his remarks, turned to Dr. Jacobus, the moderator of the Old School Assembly, and said : " My dear brother Moderator, may we not, before I take my seat, perform a single act symbolical of the union which has taken place between the two branches of the church ? Let us clasp hands!" This challenge was immediately responded to, when all joined in singing the grand old doxology of Bishop Ken, " Praise God, from whom all blessings flow!" And at the conclusion of Dr. Jacobus's remarks, amid flowing tears and with swelling hearts, the thousands present joined in singing the precious hymn, written just about a century before, by that grand and tuneful Baptist minister, John Fawcett, himself a convert of George Whitefield, " Blest be the tie that binds." Little did those happy Presbyterians think or care that two of the hymns for this hour of their supreme gladness were furnished by Methodists, one by a Congregationalist, one by an Episcopalian bishop, and one by a Baptist.

And so do hymns bear interesting and conclusive testimony to the catholicity of Christianity and the essential unity of the church. In them we see what is essential and permanent as contrasted with that which is merely formal and ephemeral. They do, indeed, reflect the surface of the Christian consciousness, whose phenomena are continually changing; but the hymns which have a life so permanent as to be accounted the "hymns of the ages" come out of the very depths of that consciousness. For the most part, such hymns do not so much illustrate the variety and separations of the church as its oneness. Christianity is simply the one life of Jesus Christ, and, however multitudinous may be the channels through which it flows, it is everywhere and always one. And so our hymnody is a visible evangelical alliance, where Catholic and Protestant, Oriental and Occidental, the ancient and the modern, Calvinist and Arminian, Unitarian and Evangelical, blend indistinguishably in the one grand and universal song. What Protestant hymnal would be felt to be complete without the hymns of such eminent Catholics as Gregory, Bernard, King Robert of France, Faber, Newman, and Bridges? What Arminian would think of dispensing with the hymns of such distinguished, and some of them high and extreme, Calvinists as Watts, Doddridge, Toplady, Newton, Baxter, Bonar, and multitudes of others? What Calvinist would think of dispensing with the hymns of the Wesleys, Perronet, Olivers, Heber, Keble, and Lyte? Who would think the hymn-books intended for the use of orthodox and evangelical churches to be quite perfect if all the hymns of Barbauld, Bowring, Adams, Holmes, Longfellow, and Sears were left out? What Churchman, during the present century, has been satisfied to leave out of his hymnal all hymns from such Dissenters as Doddridge, Watts, and Wesley? On these heights of sacred song the atmosphere is so rare and so pure that, for the most part, the voices of earthly strife and discord sink away into silence, and only the harmonies which are borne down to us from the upper sanctuary are distinctly heard.

One of the best illustrations of this is furnished in the history of a hymn which all Protestant Christians agree to place in the very front rank of hymns: "Rock of Ages, cleft for me." Its author, Mr. Toplady, was one of the best and bitterest of Mr. Wesley's opponents, the points of difference between them being mainly such as were involved in the Calvinistic controversy. Especially was he disgusted at the Wesleyan doctrine of Christian perfection as being, in his view, inconsistent with the doctrines of grace; and so he wrote this hymn, which expresses the utter nothingness of human merit, and represents the soul as finding its only refuge in the merit of Christ, giving to it this controversial title: "A living and dying prayer for the holiest believer in the world." The hymn was at once caught up by Christian people, and by none more eagerly than by the Methodists, against whom it was written, and who to-day sing it

11

as heartily as they do the hymns of Charles Wesley
himself. Thus did Mr. Toplady, the hymn-writer,
demonstrate his oneness with the very people against .
whom Mr. Toplady, the polemic, had leveled his
keenest shafts.

CHAPTER II.

HYMNS OF THE ANCIENT CHURCH.

IN our attempts to illustrate this subject of hymnology we must labor under one embarrassment. Many of the most notable hymns were written in other languages than ours, and a lyric poem never bears translation well.[1] That adjustment of sound to sense, of rhyme and meter to thought, which makes a poem perfect in one language, if once it be disturbed for purposes of translation, can never be perfectly restored. When these beautiful crystals of thought and feeling are broken, their high and peculiar value is gone. At the best we can only use the fragments, in each of which may be seen some gleam of the original glory, to help us to conceive what that glory really was. Some of the best and most eminent hymns, whose names are as household words, have never been known, and can never be known by us in their true and proper character. We do not see them face to face; and that image of them which is reflected in the best translation is more or less distorted and imperfect. They have lost in great measure their distinctive poetic character—the music of numbers, the nice adjustment of epithets, the delicate hues of spiritual beauty, and many of those gleams of personal life and experience which constitute the peculiar charm of lyric poetry.

The oldest hymn of the Christian Church outside of the Bible is that known as the "Trisagion," or, more commonly, by its Latin name, "Tersanctus," "Thrice holy." It is the earliest of the many echoes which the song of the seraphim, as heard by Isaiah, has awakened in Christian literature. Neither its precise date nor author, nor the circumstances of its origin, can now be ascertained.[2] All we are quite certain of is, that it goes back to the second century of Christian history—to that age which touched upon the work of the apostles themselves—and that it has from the first held its place in the holy of holies of Christian worship; for it is found in all the anti-Nicene liturgies as well as in the principal ones of later times. With the exception of one or two brief doxologies, it contains the oldest uninspired words of Christian praise in any language. It runs through the Christian centuries like a thread of gold, joining in one the praises of devout hearts in every age and clime. Even in the words of translation in which we know it, its simplicity and beauty, its strength and majesty, are most evident:

"It is very meet, right, and our bounden duty that we should at all times and in all places give thanks unto thee, O Lord, holy Father, almighty, everlasting God. Therefore, with angels and archangels, and all the company of heaven, we laud and magnify thy glorious name, evermore praising thee and saying: Holy, holy, holy Lord God of hosts, heaven and earth are full of thy glory! Glory be to thee, O Lord, most high!"

What a perfect religion is here! How catholic, how universal! It contains a glorious vision of the "all-temple" state. It shows the whole family, in earth and heaven, united in one song. Though it had its birth in a time of fiercest persecution—when any public act of Christian worship might end in martyrdom, when the song of praise begun on earth might be finished, "after a brief agony," before the throne of God—yet it rises sublimely above these dark and dreadful conditions. The gloom, the strife, the scorn, and the bitter injustice of their earthly lot, their spiritual anguish and their mortal agony do not even cast a shadow upon it. As this song of the seraphim goes back to heaven from men, poor, despised, and hunted even to martyrdom, it gathers into itself a wonderful sweetness and power, such as must make even the angels lean silent on their harps to hear !

With this hymn should be mentioned another not unlike it in spirit and history. It also originated probably in the second century, though, if we give much place to internal evidence, we must assign to it an origin somewhat later than the Tersanctus. From the earliest times these have been associated together, both having held a place in the communion service. We refer to the "Gloria in Excelsis," [3] a longer hymn than the Tersanctus and more emotional; of wider scope and more burning utterances, "with whose ringing accents of praise mingles the miserere of conscious sin." It begins among the angels, taking up the strains of angelic rapture which once it was permitted to mortal ears to hear, "Glory to God in the highest, and on earth peace, good-will to men ;" but speedily does it come down into this mortal and sinful life, taking up with solemn iteration

the one prayer of guilty humanity, "Have mercy
upon us." We are told that the early martyrs
were wont to sing this hymn on their way to their
death; and yet, like the blessed Christ, whose nature
and offices are in it so distinctly reflected, it is equally
suited to all who dwell in this mortal body:

"Glory be to God on high, and on earth peace, good-will
to men. We praise thee, we bless thee, we glorify thee, we
give thanks to thee for thy great glory, O Lord God, heavenly
King, God the Father Almighty! O Lord, the only begotten
Son, Jesus Christ; O Lord God, Lamb of God, Son of the
Father, that takest away the sins of the world, have mercy
upon us! Thou that takest away the sins of the world, have
mercy upon us! Thou that takest away the sins of the world,
receive our prayer. Thou that sittest at the right hand of God
the Father, have mercy upon us! For thou only art holy;
thou only art the Lord; thou only, O Christ, with the Holy
Ghost, art most high in the glory of God the Father."

There is still another hymn, which is, in many
regards, more notable than either of those already
mentioned. It is at once a hymn and a creed; or,
rather, as Mrs. Charles beautifully says, " It is a
creed taking wing and soaring heavenward; it is
Faith seized with a sudden joy as she counts her
treasures, and laying them at the feet of Jesus in a
song; it is the incense of prayer rising so near the
rainbow round about the throne as to catch its light
and become radiant as well as fragrant—a cloud of
incense illumined into a cloud of glory." We refer
to the "Te Deum Laudamus," [4] perhaps the grandest
anthem of Christian praise ever written. It is not
necessary to give it in full in this place, for scarcely
anything in Christian literature is more familiar; but

we will not forego the satisfaction of transcribing a
few of its grand sentences—sentences which have
been heard in every great cathedral in the world, and
wakened the echoes of every clime beneath the sun :

" We praise thee, O God; we acknowledge thee to be the
Lord. All the earth doth worship thee, the Father everlasting. To thee all angels cry aloud, the heavens and all the
powers therein. To thee cherubim and seraphim continually
do cry, Holy, holy, holy Lord God of Sabaoth! Heaven and
earth are full of the majesty of thy glory. The glorious company of the apostles praise thee. The goodly fellowship of
the prophets praise thee. The noble army of martyrs praise
thee. The holy church throughout all the world doth acknowledge thee. . . . Day by day we magnify thee; and
we worship thy name ever, world without end."

These three great anonymous hymns of the early
church never assumed a perfect metrical form, but
only that of measured prose, in this regard resem-
bling the songs and snatches or fragments of song
which are found in the New Testament itself. But
what is wanting in poetical structure is more than
made up in dignity, simplicity, and universal intelli-
gibleness. With little loss, they have been translated
into many of the languages into which the Bible itself has gone; and everywhere they stand to express
the catholicity of Christianity and the unity of believers. They belong peculiarly and exclusively to
no sect or section of the church, but equally to the
entire church. Neither Churchman nor Romanist
can claim exclusive proprietorship in them, but, like
the Bible itself, of which they are so evidently the
offspring, they belong to all who " profess and call
themselves Christians," of every tongue and clime.

We may not leave these earliest Christian hymns without reflecting upon the grand and sacred mission they have fulfilled. They have lifted heavenward the worship of countless millions. They have gone through the world like sweet-voiced angels, leading our discordant natures into harmony. In the cathedral, the humble village church, the cell of the monk, the palace of the king, the tent of the nomad; in the catacombs, by the martyr's stake; beneath arctic skies and torrid suns; in Asia, Africa, Europe, America, the islands of the sea; wherever the angel having the everlasting gospel to preach has gone, there have this blessed trio gone too. And in the supreme hour of mortal life they have been uttered by the bedside of the dying, lifting the soul into heavenly rapture even from the depths of mortal agony. So is it that men are

> " Learning here, by faith and love,
> Songs of praise to sing above."

The oldest uninspired Christian hymn which can with certainty be traced to its author was written by Clement of Alexandria, who died not later than 220, A. D. Of his personal history we know comparatively little; but as to his intellectual and spiritual life we have better information. He represents the famous city of Alexandria, which, more than any other, was the meeting-place between the life of the East and the West. Here was originated the Hellenistic dialect of the Greek language, which has for its precious contents the Septuagint version of the Old Testament, the writings of Philo and Josephus, and the books of the New Testament. One of his teachers came from Ionia, the birthplace of the grandest poem in all literature; another from Cœle-Syria, the vigor and glory of whose civilization is to-day most eloquently attested by the wonderful ruins at Baalbec; another still came from Assyria, a name suggestive of all that is venerable in antiquity and illustrious in achievement; while yet another came from Italy, but originally from Egypt. He became familiar with Jewish lore at the school of Tiberias, and he learned Christianity from Pantænus, who stood at the head of the Academy in Alexandria. When Pantænus left this position to enter upon a mission to the heathen of India and the East, Clement became his successor, and he, in turn, was succeeded by his own disciple, Origen, the most eminent and learned of all the Christian fathers of the third century. It is probable that the persecution under Septimius Severus, A. D. 202, compelled Clement to flee from Alexandria, and we hear of him about ten years later visiting Jerusalem, and from thence to Antioch, commended to the Antiochans by the Bishop of Jerusalem as "a virtuous and tried man, and one not altogether unknown to them."

Three works from his hand have been preserved to us: "An Exhortation to the Heathen," "The Instructor," and "Miscellanies." The object of the first seems to have been to convert the heathen, and it draws a vivid and powerful contrast between the impurity, the grossness, and sordidness of heathenism and the pure and exalted character of Christianity. The second was intended for those already converted, and consisted mainly of rules for the formation and development of Christian character and living a Christian life. The third was called "Stromata," or "Miscellanies," and was a collection of speculative notes bearing upon true philosophy. One or two extracts from these works will serve to illustrate the tone of Clement's thought and the spirit of the times in which he lived. Speaking of marriage, he says: "What a union is that between two believers, having in common one hope, one desire, one order of life, one service of the Lord! . . . They kneel, pray, and fast together; mutually teach, exhort, and bear with each other; the harmony of psalms and hymns goes up between them, and each vies with the other in singing the praise of their God." Again he says: "Prayer, if I may speak so boldly, is intercourse with God. Although we do but lisp; although we address God without opening the lips, in silence, we cry to him in the inward recesses of the heart; for when the whole direction of the inmost soul is to him, God always hears." He draws the following picture of a devout Christian: "He will pray in every place, but not openly to be seen of men. He prays in every situation—in his walks for recreation, in his intercourse with others, in silence, in reading, in all rational pursuits. And although he is only thinking on God in the little chamber of the soul, and calling upon his Father with silent aspirations, God is near him and with him while he is yet speaking."

There is a special interest connected with Clement's hymn as being the earliest *versified* Christian hymn, and so the distinguished leader of a shining host. It has been very justly described as "a collection of images interwoven like a stained window, of which the eye loses the design in the complication of colors, upon which may be traced, as in quaint old letters on a scroll, winding through all the mosaic of tints, Christ all in all." There are several metrical versions accessible to the English reader, but the strictly literal rendering of Mrs. Charles will give a more just idea of its substance, though none at all of its poetic structure and beauty:

> "Mouth of babes who can not speak,
> Wing of nestlings who can not fly,
> Sure guide of babes,
> Shepherd of royal sheep,
> Gather thine own artless children
> To praise in holiness,
> To sing in guilelessness,
> With blameless lips,
> Thee, O Christ! Guide of children.
> .   .   .   .
>
> Lead, O Shepherd
> Of reasoning sheep!
> Holy One, lead,
> King of speechless children!
> The footsteps of Christ
> Are the heavenly way!
> Ever-flowing word,
> Infinite age,
> Perpetual light,
> Fountain of mercy,
> Worker of virtue,
> Holy sustenance
> Of those who praise God, Christ Jesus,—
> The heavenly milk
> Of the sweet breasts
> Of the bride of graces
> Pressed out of thy wisdom!

These babes
With tender lips nourished—
By the dew of the Spirit replenished
Their artless praises,
Their true hymns,
O Christ, our King!
Sacred rewards
Of the doctrine of life,
We hymn together;
We hymn in simplicity,
The mighty child,
The chorus of peace,
The kindred of Christ,
The race of the temperate;
We will praise together the God of peace." (5)

The eminent Biblical scholar, Rev. E. H. Plumptre, has made an excellent metrical version, which may be helpful in bringing us face to face with the original. We transcribe two stanzas:

"Shepherd of sheep, that own
Their Master on the throne,
Stir up thy children meek
With guileless lips to speak,
In hymn and soul, thy praise.
O King of saints, O Lord!
Mighty, all-conquering Word;
Son of the highest God,
Wielding his wisdom's rod;
Our stay when cares annoy,
Giver of endless joy;
Of all; our mortal race,—
Savior of boundless grace,—
O Jesus, hear!
.   .   .   .

Lead us, O Shepherd true!
Thy mystic sheep, we sue.
Lead us, O holy Lord,
Who from thy sons dost ward,

> With all-prevailing charm,
> Peril and curse and harm;
> O path where Christ hath trod;
> O way, that leads to God;
> O word, abiding aye;
> O endless light on high,
> Mercy's fresh-springing flood,
> Worker of all things good;
> O glorious life of all
> That on their Master call,—
> Christ Jesus, hear."

But that version of the hymn which is most distinctly lyrical in its character, though it departs very widely from the archaic simplicity of the original, is the one commencing

> Shepherd of tender youth.

It was made by the Rev. H. M. Dexter, D. D., editor of *The Congregationalist* newspaper, published in Boston. This version is now very widely used, and is met with in most of the leading hymnalsboth of America and Great Britain. It is of special interest and significance that this oldest of our versified hymns is so full of Christ, and, at the same time, so clear in its recognition of his relation to children. May the singing of it by the churches in this latter day bring us into more perfect sympathy with that Savior who pronounced upon childhood the benediction which carries in its bosom all blessed possibilities: "Of such is the kingdom of God!"

But the most conspicuous figure in ancient hymnody is that of Ambrose, the famous bishop of Milan and pastor of Monica, the mother of Augustine. He was a man of unusual breadth and energy

of character, and it was given him to achieve a remarkable history. The son of a prominent civil officer, he was himself governor of the province of
Milan, and as such was present to keep the peace in
a large popular assembly convened to consider the
matter of electing a bishop, when, by the voice of a
child, he was himself designated for the office. After
what was doubtless a sincere but ineffectual attempt
to resist the will of the people in this regard, he was
baptized, distributed his property to the poor, and
eight days after was inducted into the episcopal office.
He performed the duties of this high office with zeal
truly apostolic, asserting, as no man had ever done
before him, the loving intolerance of Christianity as
against heathen religions. Over more than one emperor he exerted a strong, if not absolutely commanding, influence. Theodosius the Great venerated him
as father, and openly declared that he was the only
bishop worthy of the title. When, in a fit of passion, this same Theodosius inflicted terrible cruelties
upon the rebellious Thessalonians, Ambrose refused
to admit him to the altar until he had done public
penance.

A special interest attaches to Ambrose because of
his connection with the personal history of the distinguished Augustine, one of the greatest men of his
time or of any time. For thirteen years had Monica
carried on her heart the great burden of a wayward
son, waiting upon God in faith and prayer, and ministering to him with maternal patience and tenderness.
The stubbornness and rebellion of the young man
seemed to mock all her hopes, and she sought refuge

and strength in the sympathy of the good Ambrose. With bitter weeping, she poured her solicitude and sorrow into his ear. "Wait," said the man of God, "wait patiently; the child of these tears can not perish." The event justified the prophecy; for before Monica's star went down the sun of Augustine rose.

Of all the men of the ancient church, the impress of Ambrose upon her hymnody is deepest. Though the tradition which connects his name with the "*Te Deum Laudamus*" is not to be trusted, yet to him must be accorded the higher honor of having introduced the singing of psalms, and especially antiphonal and responsive singing, in the Western church. There are about a dozen hymns extant which the Benedictine editors ascribe to Ambrose, besides a very considerable number of the same general character which are designated Ambrosian. They are all remarkable for dignity and simplicity, both in style and structure, and the permanence of their life and wide extent of their influence would seem to indicate that a hymn "when unadorned is adorned the most." Born in the midst of theologic strife, these hymns have served not only as instruments of devotion, but as weapons against heresy, and for fifteen hundred years have been counted among the choice treasures of Christian literature. Among the best of these hymns of Ambrose, in their most approved English translations, are:

Now doth the sun ascend the sky,

translated from the Latin original, which Daniel calls Ambrosian, by the Rev. Edward Caswall; this hymn was chanted by the priesthood, in full choir, at

the déath-bed of William, the Conqueror, in A. D.
1087.

The morning kindles all the sky,

translated by Mrs. Elizabeth Charles, the gifted author
of the "Schonberg Cotta Family." Another version,
by Rev. Dr. A. R. Thompson, begins:

The morning purples all the sky. [6]

O Lord, most high, Eternal King.

The Lord on high ascends.

O mighty joy to all our race.

O Jesu, Lord of light and grace.

Ere the waning light decay.

O God of truth, O Lord of Might.

O God of all, the strength and power.

Now that the daylight fills the sky.

O Trinity, most blessed light.

Redeemer of the nations, come. [7]

Come, Holy Ghost, who ever one.

Creator of the stars of night.

Above the starry spheres.

It is difficult for us fully to appreciate the mission
and influence of these ancient hymns. They served
not only as channels of devotion, but as witnesses for
the truth and as safeguards against error. The testimony which Augustine himself gives as to the influence of the church-music on his heart, may well be
taken as truthfully illustrative of the value of this

feature of public religious service. "The hymns and songs of thy church moved my soul intensely. Thy truth was distilled by them into my heart. The flame of piety was kindled, and my tears flowed for joy." [6] This practice of singing had been of no long standing at Milan. It began about the year when Justina persecuted Ambrose (A. D. 386). The pious people watched in the church, prepared to die with their pastor. Augustine's mother sustained an eminent part in watching and praying. Then hymns and psalms, after the manner of the East, were sung with a view of preserving the people from weariness; and thence the custom spread through the Christian churches. [9]

12

CHAPTER III.

EARLIER MEDIEVAL HYMNS.

FROM the testimony of Augustine, quoted at the close of the preceding chapter, we are led to understand that hymns and music were all the time coming into greater prominence in the services of the church. As was therefore to be expected, the number of hymns representing the medieval period of Christian history, which, in round numbers, may be taken as extending from the close of the fifth century to the close of the fifteenth (500–1500), is many times greater than those representing the ancient church. At the beginning of the sixth century it is doubtful if there were in all one hundred Christian hymns in addition to the Jewish Psalms, which were then, doubtless, widely used. When Luther arose, it is estimated that there were at least one thousand. As compared with those of the ancient church, medieval hymns are less extensive but more intensive. They comprehend less but express more, and so are more likely to be used with loving interest. As was to be expected, the development of church-life continually tended to more elaborate and impressive ceremonial, and hence church-music seems to have undergone a process of rapid development. Hymns began to appear in greater numbers, and were appropriated to a greater variety of ecclesiastical uses. But they came very widely to be regarded as intended mainly for public service, the exclusive property of the church and choir. Hence, instead of simple lyrical effusions, as were many of the Jewish psalms, suited to the individual, the family, and childhood, we recognize a tendency to make the hymn a stately and formal matter, fitted to hold a place in grand and impressive church ceremonials. In the earlier part of this medieval period we find the hymns clustering about the person and offices of Jesus Christ and of the Holy Ghost; but in the latter part of this period some of the most famous—such, for instance, as the " Celestial Country " and the " Dies Iræ "—look forward to the second advent and the future life, though others were devoted to the praise of saints and the celebration of relics. But in all this period, as well as in the preceding, the hymns which have become universal and permanent are those which express, in directest and simplest manner, the deep aspirations of the devout heart for salvation and life through the offices of the Savior and the power of the Holy Ghost. Bernard's "O sacred head, now wounded," Gregory's "Veni, Creator Spiritus," King Robert's " Veni, Sancte Spiritus," and the " Veni, Redemptor Gentium," of Ambrose, are illustrations in point.

The earliest of these medieval hymns which have come to a wide celebrity were written by Venantius Fortunatus, an Italian gentleman, scholar, priest, and finally bishop, who was born about A. D. 530, and died A. D. 609. As in many other instances, these songs are more famous than the singer. Indeed it is

not probable that his name would have come down
to these later Christian centuries had it not been
made illustrious by his justly celebrated hymns.
That hymn of his, called from its opening words
" Vexilla Regis Prodeunt," has been pronounced by
Dr. John Mason Neale " one of the grandest in the
treasury of the Latin church." It was composed to
celebrate the reception of certain relics by his pa-
troness and friend, Queen Radegund, and Gregory,
Bishop of Tours, previous to the consecration of the
church at Poictiers. It came at once to be used as
a processional hymn, and, from the character of the
theme, in those services of the church devoted to the
memory of our Savior's passion and death.[1] Several English versions of this hymn have been made,
among the best of which is one by Rev. John
Chandler :

> The royal banner is unfurled ;

and one by Dr. John Mason Neale :

> The royal banners forward go.

Of these, the first is best suited for general use as a
hymn, though the second represents the original more
faithfully and vividly. We transcribe some verses of
the latter :

> " The royal banners forward go,
> The cross shines forth in mystic glow
> Where he in flesh, our flesh who made,
> Our sentence bore, our ransom paid,—
>
> Where deep for us the spear was dyed,
> Life's torrent gushing from his side,
> To wash us in that precious flood
> Where mingled water flowed, and blood.

Fulfilled is all that David told
In true prophetic song of old;
Amid the nations God, saith he,
Hath reigned and triumphed from the tree.

O tree of beauty! tree of light!
O tree with royal purple dight!
Elect, on whose triumphal breast
Those holy limbs should find their rest;

On whose dear arms, so widely flung,
The weight of this world's ransom hung,
The price of human kind to pay,
And spoil the spoiler of his prey."

The last line of the third verse, "Hath reigned and triumphed from the tree," is an allusion to the tenth verse of the ninety-sixth Psalm, which, in the old Italic version, reads, "Tell it out among the heathen that the Lord reigneth from the tree."

It seems extraordinary that from an occasion created by the errors and superstition of the church a product so pure and spiritual as this hymn should have arisen. It may be that through this, as through a loop-hole, we look into the real character of the great Romish church of this time, and see that, along with its idolatries and corruptions, moves the current of a divine life.

There is another hymn of Fortunatus—"Salve Festa Dies"—some of the associations of which are still more notable. It was the most widely used of all the processional hymns during the Middle Ages. It was sung by Jerome of Prague in the midst of his dying agonies. Cranmer translated it into English, and wrote a letter to King Henry the Eighth requesting its formal authorization for use in the churches, together with other similar hymns and litanies. This translation of Cranmer has been lost, but the letter is still preserved among the state papers of Great Britain. Several English versions of this hymn have been made, one of the best of which is that commencing

> Welcome happy morning! age to age shall say.[2]

Contemporary with Fortunatus was Gregory the Great, born of a noble family in Rome about 550, and dying 604—a man equaled by no other of his time and by very few of any time. Whether we consider his relations as a man, his devotedness and self-sacrifice as a Christian, his depth and clearness as a theologian, or his grand ability as a bishop, we find him worthily exercising a strong and commanding influence. Though not altogether free from the errors of his time, yet he must be accorded the credit of having done more than almost any other man in giving unity, vigor, and power to the Western church. A monument of his relation to church-music is the Gregorian chant, which places him not by the side of Ambrose in this regard, but clearly above him. This was intended for the choir and the people to sing in unison. It is one of the many interesting facts connecting the name of Gregory with Great Britain that the first attempt to introduce this chant into the churches resulted in a tumult in which many lives were lost.

On his accession to the episcopacy he directed his earnest attention to elevating the character of the clergy and improving the services of the church. He complains that the bishops of his time neglected too much the business of preaching for outward affairs, and confesses that in this he accuses himself; for, in spite of his own wishes, he had been compelled by the exigencies of the times to immerse himself in these external affairs. That his clergy might be suitably impressed with the dignity and sacredness of their office, he drew up for their use a "pastoral rule," in which he endeavored to show in what temper of mind the spiritual shepherd should come to his office, how he should live in it, how he should carefully adapt his methods to the end to be reached, and how guard against self-exaltation as he contemplates the happy results of his labors. On preaching he says: "Words that come from a cold heart can never light up the fervor of heavenly desires; for that which burns not itself can kindle nothing else."

As intimated above, there are many links of interest binding the name of Gregory to the English church and people. Having one day gone into the slave-market, his interest was excited at the sight of some Anglo-Saxon youths exposed for sale there. He inquired who they were, and being told that they were "Angli," he is related to have said, "Si Christiani sint, non Angli essent sed angeli forent." "If they were Christians, they would not be *Angles* but *angels*." He at once purchased some of them, and had them educated for missionary work among their countrymen. Some time later, when the way was more fully opened by the espousal of a Frankish princess to Ethelbert of Kent, he sent the Roman abbot

Augustine, with forty monks, on a mission to this land, and on the Pentecost of the following year the king and ten thousand of his subjects were baptized. Another of the most interesting associations of Gregory with English-speaking peoples is through the great hymn which is prevailingly ascribed to him, " Veni, Creator Spiritus." By many this hymn has been attributed to Charlemagne, but by most, and with better reason, to Gregory.[3] No other hymn has had more honorable recognition in the services of both the Catholic and Protestant divisions of the church. It has been used at the coronation of kings, the creation of popes, the consecration of bishops, the opening of synods and conferences, and the ordination of ministers. After the Reformation it was one of the first hymns translated into both German and English, and has doubtless in these versions come to its best and most spiritual uses. Bishop Cosin's English version was introduced into " The Book of Common Prayer " in 1662, and later into the Methodist Discipline, the ordinal of which was taken substantially from the English prayer-book. At no point in the services of either the Episcopal or Methodist church is the effect more impressive than when, after the solemn hush of silent prayer, the bishop and clergy take up responsively,

> " Come, Holy Ghost, our souls inspire,
> *And lighten with celestial fire,*" etc.

On account of a slight irregularity in the meter of the last two lines this version of Bishop Cosin is not found in many of the hymn-books, though it has very properly been given a place in the Methodist hymnal. Many other versions of this hymn into English have been made, most of them within the last half century. One of the best is that commencing

O come, Creator, Spirit blest!

Still another hymn of Gregory, translated by Ray Palmer, is found in recent collections:

O Christ, our King, Creator, Lord!

With Gregory's "Veni, Creator Spiritus," should be associated one of somewhat later date, but almost equally notable in character and history; namely, the "Veni, Sancte Spiritus," which has been pronounced by an eminent authority "the loveliest of all the hymns in the whole circle of Latin poetry." Its author was Robert II, king of France, who was born 972, came to the throne 997, and died in 1031. We know little of his life; but it has been well said that if we knew nothing, the hymn itself gives evidence of having been composed by one "acquainted with many sorrows and also with many consolations." Of the former, the history of the troublous times in which the king lived is sufficient proof; of the latter, the hymn is sweetly expressive. The king was a great lover of music, and used sometimes to go to the church of St. Denis and take direction of the choir at matins and vespers, and sing with the monks. It is said by Dean Trench that some of his musical as well as hymnic compositions still hold their place in the services of the Catholic church. The extraordinary perfection of the hymn "Veni, Sancte Spiritus," has made it exceedingly difficult to produce a

satisfactory version. For this reason we give it in
full as it came from the pen of its royal author:

> "Veni, sancte spiritus,
> Et emitte cœlitus
> Lucis tuæ radium.
>
> Veni, pater pauperum,
> Veni, dator munerum,
> Veni, lumen cordium.
>
> Consolator optime,
> Dulcis hospes animæ,
> Dulce refrigerium.
>
> In labore requies,
> In æstu temperies,
> In fletu solatium.
>
> O lux beatissima,
> Reple cordis intima
> Tuorum fidelium.
>
> Sine tuo numine
> Nihil est in homine,
> Nihil est innoxium.
>
> Lava quod est sordium,
> Riga quod est aridum,
> Sana quod est saucium.
>
> Flecte quod est rigidum,
> Fove quod est frigidum,
> Rege quod est devium.
>
> Da tuis fidelibus
> In te confidentibus
> Sacra septenarium.
>
> Da virtutis meritum,
> Da salutis exitum,
> Da perenne gaudium."

Of the many excellent versions of this precious hymn, that of Ray Palmer is one of the best and most musical, though it departs from the very simple measure of the original :

Come, Holy Ghost, in love.[4]

Two hymnists of lesser note stand about midway between Gregory the Great and King Robert; namely, Andrew of Crete, who was born about 660 and died in 732, and John of Damascus, who died about a half century later. Both were born in that oldest of cities Damascus, which, from the time of Abraham, has stood forth, always with distinctness and sometimes with commanding influence, in the history of the world. The former, in his later years, was Archbishop of Crete. He participated in the monothelite controversy, which even then agitated the church in some localities, at first giving his influence in favor of this heresy, but afterward strongly against it. One of the best known of the hymns from his pen, which are still retained by the churches, is that commencing

Christian, dost thou see them?[5]

The original was written for use in the second week of the great fast of Lent, and this fact is very clearly reflected in the hymn itself. The translation is by Dr. Neale. One other hymn of similar character, from this same author, has found a place in some modern hymn-books :

O the mystery passing wonder.

More interest attaches to the personal history of John of Damascus, as he is also more eminent as a

hymn-writer. Born at Damascus, he was for some
years a priest in Jerusalem, where he also held an
important civil office under the caliph. He was an
accomplished scholar, and entered into the theological controversies of his time with great zeal and eloquence. But, as many another has done, he held
"the unsheathed sword of controversy until its glit-
tering point drew down the lightning." He retired
from the lists, and spent the last years of his life in
literary and religious exercises in a convent between
Jerusalem and the Dead Sea. He has been called
the greatest poet among the Greek fathers, as he is
also the last. His best known hymn,

> The day of resurrection,[6]

was written as a hymn of victory, and was "sung at
the first hour of Easter morning, when, amid general exultation, the people were shouting, 'Christ is
risen.'" Its intrinsic excellence is only equaled by
its appropriateness to the soul-stirring occasion. "Of
the many hymns of the church which celebrate the
resurrection, perhaps no other one in common use
was written so near the very spot where this crowning miracle of our holy religion actually occurred."

St. Joseph of the Studium, born in the Island
of Sicily 808, and dying 883, is represented in our
modern collections by several hymns; such, for instance, as

> Stars of the morning, so gloriously bright.
>
> Let our choir new anthems raise.
>
> And wilt thou pardon, Lord?
>
> Safe home, safe home in port.

The most popular of his hymns, however, is the one commencing

O happy band of pilgrims.

The version is by Dr. Neale, and is a general favorite—a bright and joyous Christian hymn. Joseph was early driven from his native island to Thessalonica, where he was first a monk and ultimately an archbishop; but, in consequence of the fierce iconoclastic persecution, was obliged to betake himself to the covert of the Western church. Later he was taken by pirates, and enslaved in the island of Crete; but it is said of him that he "made use of his captivity to bring his captors in subjection to the faith." Afterward he betook himself to Rome, from which place he went into exile with his friend Photius. Recalled from this, he devoted himself to literary pursuits, and wrote many hymns, most of which, however, being in praise of saints, are little known.

In this general period of Christian history lived that man who may rightly be designated the illustrious leader of the most of hymn-writers in our own language—the Venerable Bede. Few men of this period stand so fully commended to our attention and our admiration. Noble in character, profound in scholarship, unwearied in labors, wise and zealous in his devotion to the church, he was a man to be both revered and loved. Not easily can England estimate her debt of obligation to such as he, who laid so carefully and wisely the broad foundations of Biblical culture upon which the church, in the later centuries, has so successfully built. Few pictures of that dis-

tant time are so significant and so suggestive of what
was vital in the work of the church of that period
as that of the closing scene in the life of this eminent
man. The history of this quiet and sublime death-
scene is by no means an unfamiliar one; and it is of
special interest because it furnishes a setting for the
oldest uninspired words of praise in any language
which have been crystallized into permanent form—
the Gloria Patri. The venerable scholar and monk
had been ill for several weeks, but not so as to interrupt his work of translation, on which he had become
so intent. About Easter, 735, he saw that his end
was approaching, and looked forward to it with cease-
less gratitude, rejoicing that he was accounted worthy
thus to suffer. He quoted much from Holy Scripture
and from Saxon hymns, but kept himself busy with
his translation of the Gospel of John. Ascension-
day drew near, and his illness had greatly increased,
but he only labored the more diligently. On Wednesday his scribe said: "One chapter remains, but I
fear it must be painful for you to dictate." "It is
easy," replied Bede. "Take your pen and write
quickly." The work was continued for some time,
but again interrupted. Bede directed his servant to
fetch his little treasures from his casket—his pepper,
kerchiefs, and incense—that he might distribute them
among his friends. He passed the remainder of the
day in holy and cheerful conversation. His boy
scribe, with pious importunity, again reminded him
of his unfinished task. "One sentence, dear master,
still remains unwritten." "Write quickly," he answered. The boy wrote and said: "It is completed

now." "Well," Bede replied, "thou hast said the truth. All is ended. Take my head in thy hands. I would sit in the holy place where I was wont to pray, that, so sitting, I may call upon my Father." Thereupon, resting upon the floor of his cell, he chanted the Gloria Patri—"Glory be to the Father, and to the Son, and to the Holy Ghost"—and while the name of the Holy Spirit was on his lips he passed away.

If not conspicuous in the realm of sacred song, yet certainly the Venerable Bede is deserving of honorable mention. Among his works were a "Book on the Art of Poetry" and "A Book of Hymns in Several sorts of Metre and Rhyme." It is said of him that he took great delight in the singing of hymns, and in his last sickness, when his asthma prevented his sleeping, he was wont to solace himself in this way. Among the hymns for which the modern church is indebted to Bede are:

> The great forerunner of the morn.
>
> A hymn of glory let us sing.
>
> A hymn for martyrs sweetly sing.

This last is perhaps the best known. It was inserted in the earlier editions of the "Hymns Ancient and Modern," the version being changed from that of Dr. Neale. The original has stanzas of eight lines, each of which begins and ends with the same line. To illustrate, we transcribe two stanzas:

> "Fear not, O little flock and blest,
> The lion that your life oppressed;
> To heavenly pastures ever new
> The heavenly Shepherd leadeth you;

Who, dwelling now on Zion's hill,
The Lamb's dear footsteps follow still;
By tyrant there no more distressed,
Fear not, O little flock and blest.

.   .   .   .

And every tear is wiped away
By your dear Father's hand for aye;
Death hath no power to hurt you more
Whose own is life's eternal shore.
Who sow their seed, and sowing weep,
In everlasting joy shall reap,
What time they shine in heavenly day,
And every tear is wiped away."

Another of these hymns shows still more power
of lyrical expression, and is not unsuited for use in
the congregations:

"A hymn of glory let us sing:
New hymns throughout the world shall ring;
By a new way none ever trod
Christ mounted to the throne of God.

The apostles on the mountain stand,
The mystic mount in holy land;
They, with the virgin mother, see
Jesus ascend in majesty.

The angels say to the eleven,
Why stand ye gazing into heaven?
This is the Savior, this is he;
Jesus hath triumphed gloriously.

They said the Lord should come again,
As these beheld him rising then,
Calm, soaring through the radiant sky,
Mounting its dazzling summits high.

May our affections thither tend,
And thither constantly ascend,
Where, seated on the Father's throne,
Thee, reigning in the heavens, we own!"

CHAPTER IV.

LATER MEDIEVAL HYMNS.

IN a desolate region near the River Seine, in the north-easterly part of France, is a wild valley inclosed by mountains, which in the eleventh century was a nest of robbers, and for that reason was called "The Valley of Wormwood;" but after the banditti were driven out, it was called *Clairvaux*—"Clear Valley." Here, in 1115, was established a monastery of the Cistercian Order, with a young man of twenty-four as abbot, famous in history as Bernard of Clairvaux. So magical was his influence that speedily this sterile valley became one of the great centers of power for all Europe, rivaling even Rome itself. From it were sent out missionaries to all parts of France, Italy, Spain, Switzerland, Germany, England, Ireland, Denmark, and Sweden, for the establishment of new monasteries, or the reformation of old ones; so that at the time of Bernard's death, thirty-seven years later, there were no less than one hundred and sixty monasteries which had been formed under his influence.

Bernard was born in a small town in Burgundy, in the year 1091, and was educated at the University of Paris. His father was a knight, his mother a saint. To this superior woman, as to the mothers of Augustine and the Wesleys, must be attributed much

13

of the strength of character exhibited by her remarkable son. She brought all her children—seven sons
and a daughter—as soon as they saw the light, to the
altar, that she might solemnly consecrate them to
God; which consecration she followed up by wise,
tender, patient, and loving instruction. As a result,
strong religious impressions were early made upon
the mind of Bernard, who was the third of her sons,
and after his mother's death they matured into his
taking the vows of monastic devotion.

Bernard was altogether the grandest man of this
dark time. Luther calls him "the best monk that
ever lived." In his personal influence he was mightier than kings or popes, and was often the chosen
and trusted counselor of both. He was repeatedly
sought as bishop for influential centers in the church,
but steadily refused all ecclesiastical preferment.
Trench says: "There have been other men—Augustine and Luther, for instance—who, by their words
and writings, have plowed deeper and more lasting
furrows in the great field of the church, but probably
no man, during his own life-time, ever exercised a
personal influence in Christendom equal to his." It
is hardly to be wondered at that, in this time of popular ignorance and superstition, he should be credited
by the common people with the power of miracle-
working, nor even that he himself should seem to
share that belief. Indeed his whole career seems to
have been one continuous and splendid miracle. His
brothers were at first violently opposed to his entering upon a monastic life, and for a long time a fierce
struggle was kept up in his own breast. But as he

was going one night to visit one of his brothers, who was a knight and at that time engaged in beleaguering a castle, the memory of his dead mother came to him with such resistless force that he was constrained to enter a church by the road-side, and, with a flood of tears, he poured out his heart before God, and solemnly consecrated himself to his service in a life of monasticism. Such was the fervor of his zeal and the force of his personal influence that all his brothers but one, who was then a mere child, together with others of his relatives and friends, were induced to join him in this course of life. That this humble monk, at the head of a new monastery, in an obscure and uninfluential region, should so suddenly have risen above all crowned and mitred heads, is truly marvelous, and evinces extraordinary qualities of personal nature and character.

What distinguished Bernard above all other men of his time, and most men of all time, was the union in his character of a piety singularly ardent and spiritual with transcendent administrative ability. Almost the only man fully worthy to be compared with him in this regard is John Wesley. He was both contemplative and practical. He felt the full power of the forces of the invisible world, and under their pressure he brought to bear upon the outward world a many-sided activity. He felt himself to be in the world on God's errand. "I must," he says, "whether willing or unwilling, live for Him who has acquired a property in my life by giving up His own for me." "To whom am I more bound to live than to Him whose death is the cause of my living? To whom

can I devote my life with greater advantage than to
Him who promises me the life eternal? To whom
with greater necessity than to Him who threatens the
everlasting fire? But I serve Him with freedom,
since love brings freedom? To this, dear brethren,
I invite you. Serve in that love which casteth·out
fear, feels no toils, thinks of no merit, asks no reward, and yet carries with it a mightier constraint
than all things else." In such words as these do we
see the secret of his wonderful and sublime life.

Seven poems from the pen of Bernard have been
preserved; but most of his hymns which are in use
are from one of these—different versions of different
parts. The best known of these hymns are:

O sacred head now wounded.

Of Him who did salvation bring.

We sinners, Lord, with earnest heart.

Jesus, thou joy of loving hearts.

Jesus, the very thought of thee.

O Jesus, King most wonderful.

O Jesus, thou the beauty art. [1]

The first of these is the most famous, and indeed
one of the most distinguished of all medieval hymns.
In its present form it is a translation of a translation,
and hence is, in a special sense, a monument of the
unity of the Christian church. Its first translator into
German, and in some sense co-author, was that prince
of German hymnists, Paul Gerhardt; while the translator into English was the distinguished American
Presbyterian, Dr. James W. Alexander. In this ver-

sion the hymn is adopted in most English hymnals of recent date; the only ones showing any disposition to pass it by being those of the so-called liberalistic faith, it being unacceptable in them because of the prominence it gives to the death of Christ. Dr. Philip Schaff says: "This classical hymn has shown an imperishable vitality in passing from the Latin into the German and from the German into the English, and proclaiming in three tongues, and in the name of three confessions—the Catholic, the Lutheran, and the Reformed—with equal effect, the dying love of our Savior and our boundless indebtedness to Him." It was this hymn which the missionary Schwartz sung, literally with his dying breath. Indeed he was thought to be already dead, and his friend and fellow-laborer, Gericke, with several of the native Tamil converts, began to chant over his lifeless remains this hymn of Bernard, which had been translated into Tamil and was a special favorite with Schwartz. The first verse was finished without any sign of recognition, or even of life, from the still form before them; but when the last clause was over, the voice which was supposed to be hushed in death, took up the second stanza of the hymn, completed it with distinct and articulate utterance, and then was heard no more. His spirit had risen on this hymn into the society of angels and the presence of God.

By an eminent authority, Adam of St. Victor is pronounced "the greatest of the Latin hymnologists of the Middle Ages." So little is known of his personal history that it is still a matter of uncertainty whether he was born in the island of Great Britain

or in Brittany in France, though probably the latter.
He pursued his studies at Paris, and his works show
him to have been a man of thorough literary and theological culture.   He was contemporary with Bernard
of Clairvaux, but seems to have outlived him by at
least a quarter of a century.   He was the most prolific as well as elegant hymn-writer of the medieval
period, leaving behind him about one hundred hymns,
of which at least one-half are of acknowledged excellence.   As often happens, however, his hymns have a
special charm and subtlety which seems almost indis-
solubly connected with the language in which they
were written, and so has baffled the translators.   Very
few of them have come into our own language in a
form which either does justice to the original, or is
well suited for use in public worship.   Miller, in his
"Singers and Songs of the Church," quotes two from
the " People's Hymnal :"

> The church on earth with answering love.

> The praises that the blessed know.

Both are translations by Dr. Neale.   We quote one
verse of the latter, which reminds us of a verse of
Watts, as do both remind us of a verse in one of
David's Psalms:

> "One day of those most glorious rays
> Is better than ten thousand days,
> Refulgent with celestial light,
> And with God's fullest knowledge bright."

We also transcribe a portion of the former, which
may serve to suggest something of the peculiar qualities of this eminent hymnist:

"The church on earth, with answering love,
Echoes her mother's joys above;
These yearly feast-days she may keep,
And yet for endless festals weep.

In this world's valley, dim and wild,
That mother must assist the child;
And heavenly guards must pitch their tents,
And range their ranks in our defense.

That distant city, O how blest!
Whose feast-days know nor pause nor rest;
How gladsome is that palace-gate,
Round which nor fear nor sorrow wait!

Nor languor here, nor weary age,
Nor fraud, nor dread of hostile rage;
But one the joy, and one the song,
And one the heart of all the throng."

But it is agreed on all hands that there is a subtlety and grace in the original that even this eminent translator fails to represent. Possibly a more just conception of the author may be gained from Mrs. Charles's version of his poem—it can hardly be called a hymn—on Affliction:

"As the harp-strings only render
    All their treasures of sweet sound,
All their music, glad or tender,
    Firmly struck, and tightly bound;

So the hearts of Christians owe,
    Each its deepest, sweetest strain,
To the pressure firm of woe,
    And the tension tight of pain.

Spices, crushed, their pungence yield;
    Trodden scents their sweets respire;
Would you have its strength revealed,
    Cast the incense in the fire.

> Thus the crushed and broken frame
> Oft doth sweetest graces yield;
> And through suffering, toil, and shame—
> From the martyr's keenest flame—
> Heavenly incense is distilled." [2]

The famous hymns of this period are: "The Celestial Country," "The Stabat Mater," and the "Dies Iræ;" which have been pronounced, and in the order given, the most beautiful, the most pathetic, and the most sublime of medieval poems.

The author of the first was Bernard of Cluny, of whom we know almost nothing save the name, and that he lived in the first half of the twelfth century. Even the place of his birth is a matter of uncertainty, most authorities placing it in Morlaix, in Bretagne; others, in Morlas, in the Pyrenees Mountains; while one author gives his birthplace to England, and classes him with her illustrious writers. He was a monk, and though this type of life was not likely to be eventful, so as to admit of very definite and individualizing record, yet we may with safety take the general picture of monasticism in this period, and write under it the name of any individual monk in whom we have come to feel an interest. There is a beautiful tradition of another monk of this time—the author of the "Imitation," as well as some hymns which for his sake are cherished—that may serve to suggest one characteristic feature of a monastic life, and one secret of the wonderful power which some of these men, separated from the world, have actually wielded. It is said of Thomas à Kempis (1379–1471) that he was wont to walk with his brother monks in the cloisters and retreats of his order, but would sometimes suddenly stop, and exclaim: "Dear brethren, I must go. There is some one waiting for me in my cell." That some one was the Lord Jesus, whose name, as Bernard himself said, is "honey in the mouth, melody in the ear, joy in the heart, and medicine in the soul."

Bernard's great poem—"De Contemptu Mundi"— contains three thousand lines, written in a meter so difficult as to give color to the claim of the author that he could never have written without the special help and inspiration of God. Each line in the original consists of the three parts, the first two of which rhyme with each other, while the lines themselves are in couplets of double rhyme. The music of the original is easily recognized, even by those who are not familiar with the Latin tongue:

"Hora novissima, tempora pessima, sunt vigilemus
Ecce minaciter, imminet arbiter, ille supremus,
Imminet, imminet, et mala terminet æqua coronet
Recta remuneret, anxia liberet, æthera donet." [3]

A portion of this poem was translated a few years since by Dr. Neale, and given to the public under this title—"The Rhythm of Bernard de Morlaix, Monk of Cluny, on the Celestial Country"—from which version have been taken the hymns in common use from Bernard. These are:

The world is very evil.

Brief life is here our portion.

For thee, O dear, dear country.

Jerusalem, the golden.

Dr. Neale in his notes on Bernard says: "Thankful am I that Cluniac's verses should have soothed

so many of God's servants. The most striking instance of which I know is that of a child, who, when
suffering agonies which the medical attendants declared to be almost unparalleled, would lie, without
a murmur or motion, while the whole four hundred
lines of the translation were read to him."

The editor of "The Seven Great Hymns of the
Medieval Church" calls this poem "a description of
the celestial land, more beautiful than ever before
was wrought out in verse." "The hymn of this
heavenly monk," says Christophers, "has found its
way into the hearts of all Christians, and into the
choirs and public services of all Christian churches."
Perhaps no other hymns on heaven are more widely
used, or more strictly ecumenical, than those which
have been made from this poem. It may not be
without interest to read the testimony of the author
of the version as to the music to which these words
should be sung: "I have been so often asked to
what tune the words of Bernard should be sung, that
I may here mention that of Mr. Ewing, the earliest
written, the best known, and, with children, the most
popular; that of my friend, the Rev. H. L. Jenner,
perhaps the most ecclesiastical; and that of another
friend, Mr. Edmund Sedding, which, to my mind,
best expresses the meaning of the words." Of these
the tune Ewing is in common use in the American
churches, and is certainly fully deserving of the honor
of being permanently associated with "Jerusalem,
the golden."

The "Stabat Mater" was written a hundred years
later by Jacobus de Benedictus, a man of a noble

Italian family, and a jurist of eminent distinction. Broken-hearted at the death of his wife—who lost her life by an accident at a theater—he renounced the world to join the order of St. Francis, seeking by self-inflicted physical tortures to chastise his soul into submission and peace. It is also related, though this has been questioned, that his sorrows drove him to insanity and death. He was certainly a man of rare zeal and courage. He so vigorously attacked the religious abuses of his time as to bring him into collision with Pope Boniface VIII, who caused him to be thrown into prison, from which he was only liberated at the death of his papal enemy. A single anecdote of this imprisonment shows the spirit of the man. When the pope sent to him a taunting message—"When will you get out?"—he answered by sending back the reply: "When will you get in?"

The hymn is characterized in a pre-eminent degree by tenderness and pathos; in these regards surpassing all other hymns of the Latin church. One of the best translations of it is that made by our own distinguished scholar and statesman, General Dix, late governor of the State of New York. Simply to illustrate the hymn—which, though it holds a conspicuous place in sacred music and in the literature of the church, is yet, on account of a certain tinge of Mariolatry, not ordinarily found in Protestant hymnbooks—we quote a few lines of the above-mentioned version, which is faithful and felicitous in diction and measure: [4]

> "Near the cross the Savior bearing
> Stood the mother lone, despairing,

Bitter tears down-falling fast;
Wearied was her heart with grieving,
Worn her breast with sorrow heaving,
Through her soul the sword had passed.

Ah! how sad and broken-hearted
Was that blessed mother, parted
    From the God-begotten One;
How her loving heart did languish,
When she saw the mortal anguish
    Which o'erwhelmed her peerless Son!

Who could witness, without weeping,
Such a flood of sorrow sweeping
    O'er the stricken mother's breast?
Who contemplate, without being
Moved to kindred grief by seeing,
    Son and mother thus oppressed?

For our sins she saw him bending,
And the cruel lash descending
    On his body stripped and bare;
Saw her own dear Jesus dying,
Heard his spirit's last outcrying,
    Sharp with anguish and despair.

Gentle mother, love's pure fountain!
Cast, O cast on me the mountain
    Of thy grief, that I may weep;
Let my heart, with ardor burning,
Christ's unbounded love returning,
    His rich favor win and keep."

There is a companion hymn to this, written by
the same author, which has but recently been brought
to the attention of the Christian public.[5]   It is
called the "Mater Speciosa," as might the other be
called the "Mater Dolorosa."   From the oblivion of
centuries it has been rescued by editors and translators of the present generation, Dr. Neale having given
his English version of this hymn to the public in

1866. As the "Stabat Mater" represents Mary standing at the cross, the "Mater Speciosa" represents her by the manger. As, therefore, the first is a hymn for Good Friday, the latter is a Christmas hymn of singular delicacy, beauty, and warmth of feeling. We quote a part of Dr. Neale's version:

"Full of beauty stood the mother
 By the manger, blest o'er other,
   Where her little one she lays;
 For her inmost soul's elation,
 In its fervid jubilation,
   Thrills with ecstasy of praise.

Oh! what glad, what rapturous feeling,
 Filled that blessed mother, kneeling
   By the sole-begotten One!
 How, her heart with laughter bounding,
 She beheld the work astounding,
   Saw his birth—the glorious Son!

.   .   .   .

Jesus lying in the manger,
 Heavenly armies sang the stranger,
   In the great joy-bearing part;
 Stood the old man with the maiden,
 No words speaking, only laden
   With this wonder in their heart.

Mother, fount of love still flowing,
 Let me, with thy rapture glowing,
   Learn to sympathize with thee;
 Let me raise my heart's devotion
 Up to Christ with pure emotion,
   That accepted I may be."

But the great hymn of this period, and of all periods, is the "Dies Iræ." It is commonly attributed to a Franciscan monk of the thirteenth century—Thomas of Celano—but the evidence as to

the identity of the author is by no means conclusive.
Thomas was a personal friend as well as pupil of St.
Francis, and was selected by Pope Gregory to write
his life. His native home was in a small town in
the kingdom of Naples; but so little is known of him
that not even the dates of his birth and death can be
accurately given. In truth, then, this great hymn
may be fitly characterized as "a solemn strain, sung
by an invisible singer." "There is a hush in the
great choral service of the universal church, when
suddenly, we scarcely know whence, a single voice,
low and trembling, breaks the silence; so low and
grave that it seems to deepen the stillness, yet so clear
and deep that its softest tones are heard throughout
Christendom and vibrate through every heart—grand
and echoing as an organ, yet homely and human, as
if the words were spoken rather than sung. And
through the listening multitudes, solemnly that melody flows on, sung not to the multitudes, but 'to the
Lord,' and therefore carrying with it the hearts of
men, till the singer is no more solitary; but the self-
same, tearful, solemn strain pours from the lips of the
whole church as if from one voice, and yet each one
sings as if alone to God." [6]

The hymn has been a force in the world of letters,
as well as that of religious thought and experience.
It has passed into upwards of two hundred translations, and has called forth the admiration of the most
eminent scholars. The sturdy Dr. Johnson confessed,
with Sir Walter Scott, that he could not recite it
without tears. Mozart made it the basis of his celebrated requiem, and became so intensely excited by

the theme as to hasten his own death. With what
power do those few stanzas burst upon us in Scott's
"Lay of the Last Minstrel!"—

"Then mass was sung, and prayers were said,
  And solemn requiem for the dead,
  And bells tolled out their mighty peal,
  For the departed spirit's weal;
  And ever in the office close
  The hymn of intercession rose;
  And far the echoing aisles prolong
  The awful burden of the song—
' Dies iræ, dies illa,
  Solvet sæclum in favilla;'
    While the pealing organ rung;
  Were it meet with sacred strain
  To close my lay, so light and vain,
    Thus the holy fathers sung:

That day of wrath, that dreadful day,
When heaven and earth shall pass away,
What power shall be the sinner's stay?
How shall he meet that dreadful day?

When, shriveling like a parchéd scroll,
The flaming heavens together roll;
When louder yet, and yet more dread,
Swells the high trump that wakes the dead!

Oh! on that day, that wrathful day,
When man to judgment wakes from clay,
Be thou the trembling sinner's stay,
Though heaven and earth shall pass away!"

This version by Sir Walter Scott is not strictly a
translation, nor yet an imitation, but rather one of
the many echoes which the "Dies Iræ" has awakened
in the literature of the world. It is, however, faithful to the spirit of the original, and of remarkable
power. The hold which it had on the mind of its

eminent author was shown by his frequent repetition
of it in the delirium of his final illness.

As already stated, the versions of this hymn may
be counted by the hundred. A single author collected about eighty versions into the German language
alone. A large number of excellent versions have
been made into our own language by Irons, Coles,
Earl Roscommon, Crashaw, Stanley, General Dix,
and others. Several of these are of marked excellence; but that of Dean Stanley has some advantages
for being set to music, while it is, at the same time,
very faithful as a translation. The opening line of
this version is:

> Day of wrath! O dreadful day!

The version of Dr. Irons will, however, be thought
by many to represent more vividly the spirit of the
original, though the meter is such as to make it very
difficult to find music for it, adapted to the ordinary use of a congregation. From this version we
transcribe:

> "Day of wrath! O day of mourning!
> See! once more the cross returning,
> Heaven and earth in ashes burning!
>
> O what fear man's bosom rendeth,
> When from heaven the judge descendeth,
> On whose sentence all dependeth!
>
> Wondrous sound the trumpet flingeth,
> Through earth's sepulchers it ringeth,
> All before the throne it bringeth!
>
> Death is struck, and nature quaking,
> All creation is awaking,
> To its judge an answer making!

Lo! the book, exactly worded,
Wherein all hath been recorded;
Thence shall judgment be awarded!

What shall I, frail man, be pleading?
Who for me be interceding,
When the just are mercy needing?

Righteous Judge of Retribution,
Grant thy gift of absolution,
Ere that reckoning day's conclusion!"

About a century earlier dates the more joyous but less famous counterpart of the "Dies Iræ," known as the "Dies Illa." Its author is unknown. It is well represented in the excellent version of Mrs. Charles:

Lo! the day, the day of life!

14

CHAPTER V.

HYMNS FROM GERMAN AUTHORS.

"THE hymns of Germany have been her true national liturgy. In England the worship of the
Reformed church was linked to that of past ages by
the Prayer-book; in Germany, by the hymn-book."
We can mark some connections between the hymns
and music of the Middle Ages and the psalmody of
the German church, showing the steps by which the
one passed over into the other.

The humble beginnings of German hymnology,
which has come to a development so marvelously rich,
were made in the ninth century. In the time of Charlemagne, the only part which the people were allowed
to take in the services of the church was to chant the
"Kyrie Eleison" in the litany, and that only on extraordinary occasions, such as the great feasts, processions, and the consecration of churches. But in Germany, during the following century, short verses in
the vernacular were introduced at such times, of
which the refrain was "Kyrie Eleison," and this was
the beginning of hymnody in the German language.
The oldest German Easter hymn dates from the
twelfth century. The Latin hymn, "In the midst
of life," one sentence of which stands in the English
Prayer-book, in the order for the burial of the dead,

and is said actually to have been taken by Robert Hall as a text for the preparation of a sermon, under the impression that it was a sentence of Holy Scripture, was written by Notker, a learned Benedictine, near the beginning of the tenth century. It was suggested to him as he was watching some workmen who were building the bridge of Martinsburg at the peril of their lives. The hymn attained to a wonderful celebrity, and was even used as a battle song, until finally its use in this way was forbidden on account of its being supposed to exercise a magical influence. It was early translated into German, and this version formed a part of the service for the burial of the dead as early as the thirteenth century.

The Flagellant fanaticism exerted an important influence in fostering and establishing the practice of singing hymns in the vernacular of the people. Processions of these pious pilgrims would go through the towns and cities, singing hymns and chants, which found ready access to the hearts of the people, and became a very influential factor in this extraordinary movement. The great Hussite movement, which stirred the church more profoundly, and interested some of the most cultured and spiritual men of the fifteenth century, gave new impetus and dignity to this tendency, so that really useful popular hymns were originated. In 1504 a considerable volume of hymns, which had been in use among the "Bohemian Brethren," was published by Lucas, one of their bishops. In the fifteenth century German hymns came to be used in special services and solemnities of the church, and, in some cases, even at the principal service and at mass. Mixed hymns, half Latin and half German, also contributed their influence to breaking down the barrier between the learned clergy and the common people, and also between the church and the home. Translations and adaptations of the old Latin hymns now begin to appear. In this later medieval period, too, we mark for the first time a type of hymn which has too often since then reappeared, and sometimes in forms peculiarly shocking and profane. Secular and love songs were, by slight changes, appropriated to religious uses, carrying the original melody with them into the service of religion. For instance, a popular ditty, originally intended for wandering apprentices, commencing

> " Inspruck, I must leave thee,
> And go my lonely way,
> Far hence to foreign lands," etc.,

was changed to

> "O world, I must leave thee,
> And go my lonely way
> Unto my Father's home," etc.

So in this country, and in this century, a song commencing

> "Thou, love, reignest in this bosom ;
> There, there hast thou thy throne ;
> Thou, thou knowest that I love thee—
> Am I not fondly thine own?"

has been published and sung,

> "Thou, *Lord*, reignest in this bosom," etc.

Another instance, still more grotesque, though scarcely more shocking, was furnished in the times of what was known as the Millerite excitement, in 1843. To the familiar and popular tune known as "The Old Granite State" such words as these were sung:

> "You will see your Lord a-coming,
> You will see your Lord a-coming,
> You will see your Lord a-coming
>   In the old church-yard;
> While a band of music,
> While a band of music,
> While a band of music
>   Will be sounding through the air."

Other verses were:

> "You will see the dead arising."
>
> "We 'll march up into the city."

A hymn is preserved from St. Francis, the founder of the Franciscan order, of a different type, but equally marked and peculiar. In this hymn he introduces "Brother Sun," "Sister Moon," "Brother Wind," "Sister Water," "Mother Earth," and "Brother Death" as praising the Creator.

But it was reserved for the church of the Reformation to show the true office of the hymn, and to illustrate its character. As the warmth of spring releases the streams from their icy fetters, and calls back again their rippling melodies, so did the light and warmth of the Reformation era bring back into the homes and hearts of the people their long-lost music. This is illustrated in the sudden and extraordinary multiplication of hymns, and the great variety of uses to which they were appropriated. When Luther arose there were not, so far as can now be told, more than one thousand hymns in the entire church; now there are more than one hundred thousand. Then the hymn was something grand, formal, artistic, suited for liturgical use, the peculiar and exclusive property of the priest, the choir, and the temple; now the church is beginning to learn that the whole universe is set to music; that the echoes of the " morning stars " are always resounding in our air; that wherever there is a worshiper, there may be, and ought to be, a hymn. As the earliest Christian hymn whose, author can be identified is suited especially to childhood and the life of the home; as the " Magnificat " and the " Nunc Dimittis " were primarily private and personal rather than public and liturgical; as the psalms of the Jews touch upon all conditions of their life, many of them seeming to be for the household or the individual rather than the great assembly, so again hymns became the liturgy of the people, and the words of joyous, holy song shook the world.

Martin Luther was born in Eisleben, November 10, 1483. His father was a poor miner, who supported his family by daily toil. He was educated first at the Latin school of Mansfeldt, then at the Franciscan school of Magdeburg, where he supported himself by singing from door to door; then at the school of Eisenach, where the wife of Conrad Cotta befriended and aided him; and finally at the University of Erfurth, from which he took the master's degree and also that of Doctor of Philosophy. At the age of twenty-two he entered the monastery of St. Augustine, and three years later he was made Professor of Philosophy in the University of Wittemberg. He posted his famous theses against indulgences in 1517, and three years later he took the boldest step of his life, in publicly burning the papal bull of excommunication. In 1522 his version of the New Testament was given to the public; in 1525 he was married; and he died at Wittemberg, February 18, 1546.

This great leader in the older Reformation was so passionately fond of music that it used to be said of him that his soul could find its fullest expression only through his flute amid tears. "Music," said he, "is one of the most beautiful and noble gifts of God. It is the best solace to a man in sorrow; it quiets, quickens, and refreshes the heart. I give music the next place and the highest honor after theology." A similar testimony he bears also to poetry, confessing that he has been "more influenced and delighted by poetry than by the most eloquent oration of Cicero and Demosthenes." His enemies said of him that he did more harm by his hymns than by his sermons; and Coleridge says "he did as much for the Reformation by his hymns as by his translation of the Bible." Thirty-seven of Luther's hymns have been preserved, some of them being versions of the Hebrew Psalms, others versions of the old Latin hymns, while still others are original both as to form and subject matter. The earliest of these is believed to be that one the English version of which commences

Flung to the heedless winds,[1]

which was called forth by the martyrdom of two young Christian monks, who were burnt alive at

Brussels. Interpreted by such an event, it is a sublime and characteristic testimony to the same faith
which is so resplendent in Luther's entire history.
But his great hymn, and perhaps, taken all in all, his
most characteristic production, is that commencing
" Ein feste Burg ist unser Gott "—" A strong tower is
our God." Rough and rugged, full of strength, but
with little beauty, it is eminently worthy of him
whose very words were half battles. It was composed at the time when the evangelical princes delivered their protest at the second Diet of Spires, in
1529, from which event the name " Protestant " had
its origin. The hymn at once became one of the
watchwords of the Reformation, as it has since come
to be regarded the national hymn of Germany. After
Luther's death, one day Melanchthon was at Weimar,
with his banished friends Jonas and Creuziger, and
heard a little girl singing this hymn in the street.
" Sing on, my little maid," said he; " you little know
what famous people you comfort."

One of the very best of the many English versions of this hymn is that by Rev. Dr. Hedge, commencing

A mighty fortress is our God.[2]

Even more characteristic is Carlyle's version:

A safe stronghold our God is still.

This hymn has had a notable history. As its origin
was coincident with the Protestant name, so it has
ever been regarded as one of the great representative
hymns of the Protestant church. It was sung by
that noble Christian hero Gustavus Adolphus, on the

morning of the day on which he sealed his fidelity to
God with his blood. The two armies had been drawn
up, and were waiting for the morning mist to disperse
in order that the struggle might begin. At the command of Gustavus the whole army joined in singing
Luther's grand psalm, and then the hymn which has
since been called by his own name, "The Battle-
hymn of Gustavus Adolphus:"

> **Fear not, O little flock, the foe.**[3]

Immediately afterward the mist broke, and the glory
of the morning sunshine came down upon the scene.
For a moment the king knelt down beside his horse,
in the presence of his soldiers, and repeated his usual
battle-prayer: "O Lord Jesus Christ, bless our arms
and this day's battle for the glory of thy holy name."
Then, passing along the lines, he spoke brief words
of encouragement, and gave the battle-cry, "God
with us!" Thus began that memorable battle which
laid low in the thickest of the fight the noblest king
and soldier Europe has had since the Reformation.

There are many interesting associations connected
with another hymn of Luther: "Out of the depths I
cry to thee." It was written in 1524, soon after its
author was fairly launched in his new career as the
leader of a great and difficult movement. It is an
impassioned and earnest appeal to God out of the
depths of his conscious weakness and helplessness.
It was eagerly taken up by the people, who were
bound to him by the same ties of danger and extrem-
ity which the very conditions of the Reformation
gave rise to. Later it came to be used as a funeral

hymn, and it was sung, amid tears and lamentations, at Luther's own funeral.

The hymn of Gustavus Adolphus is, in many regards, more perfect and better suited for ordinary use than that of Luther. It seems to have come from the royal author. whose name it bears, but in what precise form can not now be determined. It has, however, been conjectured that the substance of it, and perhaps much of the language, was written by Gustavus, and that his chaplain, Fabricius, threw it into its perfect metrical form; but it can not now be determined whether the original was in Swedish or German, though, as representing the king himself, the former would seem to have special interest. There are few better hymns of Christian trust and courage than this. A community in our own land, on that terrible Monday when we learned of the disastrous defeat at Bull Run, found in this old battle-hymn words adapted to the trying emergency:

> "Fear not, O little flock, the foe
> Who madly seeks your overthrow,
> 　　Dread not his rage and power;
> What though your courage sometimes faints,
> This seeming triumph o'er God's saints
> 　　Lasts but a little hour."

The Hussite movement was represented in the fifteenth century by the " Bohemian Brethren," and among these Christians, even before Luther arose, a very considerable psalmody was developed. This was one important source of the hymnody of the Lutherans. Both in doctrine and life the church of the Reformation was not a little indebted to such "reformers before the Reformation" as Huss and Jerome.

Rev. Michael Weisse (died 1540), a German minister in Bohemia, translated many of the Bohemian hymns and added some of his own. Among the hymns thus furnished is a very precious and popular funeral hymn—"Nun lasst uns den Leib begraben"⁽⁴⁾—to which Luther added one verse. The first line of the hymn by which he is represented in many modern collections is,

> Christ the Lord is risen again.

A hymn has been in common use in English congregations for a generation, and, by mistake of the translator, attributed to Luther. Its real author, however, was the Rev. Bartholomew Ringwaldt, who was born at Frankfort-on-the-Oder in 1530, spent his life as a Lutheran pastor at Langfeld, in Prussia, and died in 1598. That one of his hymns should be ascribed to Luther by so good a critic as Dr. Collyer is sufficient proof of his excellence as a writer of hymns. Many of his hymns were born of the sufferings which he and his people endured from "famine, pestilence, fire, and floods." The hymn above referred to is:

> Great God, what do I see and hear?

and was suggested by that greatest of hymns the Dies Iræ. It has marked power, though it must be confessed that the meter of the English version is not well suited to the dignity and solemnity of the theme.

Contemporary with Ringwaldt was the Rev. Mar-

tin Boehme (Behemb) (1537–1621), author of the
very beautiful and comprehensive hymn which Miss
Winkworth has translated, " Lord Jesus Christ, my
life, my light."[5]

Rev. George Weiszel (1590–1635), the author of
the hymn translated by Miss Winkworth, " Lift up
your heads, ye mighty gates," was born at Domnau,
in Prussia, and spent the last years of his life as pastor
at Koenigsberg. The hymn above mentioned exhibits rare felicity in lyric expression, and we are well
prepared to believe that his influence may be traced
in the more numerous hymns of his junior contemporary in Koenigsberg, Professor Simon Bach (died
1658), who composed one hundred and fifty hymns and
religious poems. In the place cited above the hymn
is in long meter, and in this regard gives no correct
idea of the original as reflected in Miss Winkworth's
version. To show the true form of the hymn, we
transcribe one stanza :

> " Lift up your heads, ye mighty gates;
> Behold, the King of Glory waits!
> The King of kings is drawing near,
> The Savior of the world is here;
> Life and salvation doth he bring,
> Wherefore rejoice and gladly sing
> Praise, O my God, to thee!
> Creator, wise is thy decree.

What Luther was among the singers of the Reformation era such was Paul Gerhardt (1606–1670) in
the period of the Thirty Years' War. Indeed, as a
writer of hymns he decidedly outranks his great
master and leader. Luther is represented in the

world of song by thirty-seven hymns. But very few of these are now used, especially outside of Germany. Gerhardt is represented by one hundred and twenty-three hymns, some of which are among the most spiritual and most ecumenical of modern hymns. Some of the choicest hymns of John Wesley are translations from this older master, who, in a higher sense than Wesley, "learned by suffering what he taught in song." Among the hymns in common use are:

O sacred head now wounded.

Extended on a cursed tree.

Here I can firmly rest.

Jesus, thy boundless love to me.

Commit thou all thy griefs.

Give to the winds thy fears.

The last two are very widely known, being parts of the same hymn in the version of John Wesley. The original was born of suffering. Gerhardt had come from his native Saxony to be pastor of a church in the city of Berlin. He had held this position ten years, when, on account of conflict with the elector in refusing to sign a pledge wholly to abstain from attacking the Reformed doctrines, he was ordered to quit the country. With his wife and little children, he set out on foot to return to his native home. The journey was long and toilsome, and, in the midst of it, having stopped one night at a humble village inn, his wife's heroism completely gave way, and she broke down in sobs and tears. Sternly crushing down the "climbing sorrow" in his own breast, Gerhardt spoke only words of cheer and confidence, reminding his wife of God's faithful promise: "Trust in the Lord. In all thy ways acknowledge him, and he shall direct thy paths." And then, in this dark hour of destitution and seeming friendlessness, with his overburdened wife and helpless children pressing upon his heart, he retired to an arbor in the garden and composed this precious hymn, which has brought strength and comfort to so many fainting souls:[6]

> " Who points the clouds their course,
>   Whom winds and seas obey,
> He shall direct thy wandering feet,
> He shall prepare thy way.
>
> . . . .
>
>   Through waves and clouds and storms
>   He gently clears thy way;
> Wait thou his time, so shall this night
> Soon end in joyous day."

The sober second thought of the elector, and the interest of his noble wife in behalf of the banished minister, resulted in his recall; but, fearing that even his silence had been construed into a promise to change the character of his preaching, he was led to make a new declaration of his views, which resulted in his permanent banishment from Berlin. Subsequently he was made Archbishop of Luebben, where he spent the last seven years of his life. But they were emphatically years of sadness; for his wife was dead, his only child was repeatedly brought to death's door, and he himself toiled on in the midst of constantly increasing infirmities. His refuge and refreshment was his gift of song, and many of his beautiful hymns were written here. The popular

German hymn, " Wake up, my heart, and sing," was written after he had passed a night of anguish on the altar-steps of the church at Luebben.

Gerhardt has been called " the prince of German hymn-writers." His hymns have penetrated all ranks of society, and into the company of all classes of worshipers, and are eminently songs of the heart. The mother of the eminent German poet, Schiller, taught them to her child, and some of them continued to be favorites with him during his life. Doubtless these hymns must be recognized as one factor, and it may be a very important factor, in the education of him who has been pronounced, next to Goethe, the greatest poet of Germany.

The excellent hymn-version of the Creed—

> . We all believe in one true God—

one of the most perfect compositions of the kind ever written, and specially suited for use on sacramental occasions and fellowship and covenant meetings, was written by Rev. Tobiah Clausnitzer (1619–1684.) He was educated at Leipsic, was sometime chaplain of the Swedish forces during the "Thirty Years' War," and was finally settled as pastor in the Palatinate.

Of the two Langes, who are represented in the hymnology of this period, Ernest (1650–1727) was a layman, and held the civil office of burgomaster, or chief magistrate, of his native town Dantzic. In 1710 the town was visited by pestilence, but so marked was the interposition of God in their behalf, that he was constrained to give expression to his gratitude, and several of his hymns were written for this purpose. Two of his hymns were translated by John Wesley, and are in common use:

> O God, thou bottomless abyss.

> Thine, Lord, is wisdom, thine alone.

Joachim Lange (1670–1744) was theological professor at Halle, and one of the earliest representatives of the Pietistic School in hymnology. He enjoyed the personal friendship of Francke, celebrated both as a philanthropist and writer of hymns. The hymns of the Hallean Pietists are not so much hymns for the people and for public worship, as for the individual soul and for the closet. They abound in the richest views of Christian experience and life. The best-known hymn of Lange was translated by John Wesley, and is of very high merit:

> O God, what offering shall I give?

In the same year with Joachim Lange was born Rev. J. Joseph Winkler (1670–1722), who was for many years pastor of the cathedral of Magdeburg. His hymns belong to this same Pietistic School. The two which are in universal use, and are among the most solemn and searching among those specially suited for ministers, are:

> Shall I, for fear of feeble man?

> Savior of men, thy searching eye.

Rev. Gottfried Arnold (1666–1714) wrote one hundred and thirty hymns, very few of which, however, are known outside of Germany. He was a man of marked and positive character, and his sense of fidelity to God not unfrequently brought him into collision with men. He was a warmly attached friend of the eminent Spener, to whose influence he attributed his own quickening into spiritual life. His hymn—

Well for him who, all things losing—

is one of the finest expressions of Christian duty and Christian privilege in the whole range of hymnology.

Few hymn-writers of the eighteenth century stand so eminent as scholar, preacher, and poet, as Johann Andreas Rothe (1688–1758). For many years he was intimately associated with the famous Count Zinzendorf, and pastor at the scarcely less celebrated Hernhutt. He wrote a learned work on the Hebrew Bible. To his power as a preacher Count Zinzendorf bears most emphatic testimony: "The talents of Luther, Spener, Francke, and Schwedler, were united in him." Some of the count's hymns were dedicated to him, and he dedicated to the count his own best-known hymn—

Now I have found the ground wherein.

This hymn is specially dear to Methodists, not only because of its superior merit, but also because of the wealth of associations which cluster about it. It represents the Moravians, who, under God, were instrumental in bringing the Wesleys into spiritual life and liberty. It was translated by John Wesley, whose best work in hymnology consisted in bringing the precious spiritual hymns of the Germans into the English language, thus making them accessible to the

15

multitudes, of which he became the spiritual leader.
Almost the last words of Mr. Fletcher, of Madeley,
were two lines from the second verse of this hymn:

> "While Jesu's blood, through earth and skies,
>   Mercy—free, boundless mercy- cries."

Few hymns in any language are so full of devout
and tender expression as those of Benjamin Schmolke
(1672–1737). His father was a clergyman. Benevolent friends assisted him to enter upon his studies in
the University of Leipsic, but he was soon able to do
something toward defraying his own expenses by publishing some of his earlier poems. The whole number
of hymns written by him was more than one thousand. As Rist said of himself, so might Schmolke
say: "The dear cross has pressed many songs out of
me." He was the subject of severe and extraordinary
personal afflictions. A destructive conflagration, which
destroyed half the town in which he lived, involving
the people in great suffering, the loss of two of his
children by death, his own hopeless invalidism by
paralysis, and finally his total blindness from the
same cause, were the dark background with which
contrasts the radiant glory of such words of resignation and trust as—

> "My Jesus, as thou wilt!
>   O may thy will be mine!
> Into thy hand of love
>   I would my all resign.
> Through sorrow, or through joy,
>   Conduct me as thine own,
> And help me still to say,
>   My Lord, thy will be done."

The best-known hymns of Schmolke are:

> Welcome, thou victor in the strife.

> My Jesus, as thou wilt.

Johann A. Scheffler—called also Angelus Silesius—(1624–1677) was a friend of the famous mystic, Jacob Boehm. He was at first a Protestant, but later a Catholic priest, and a zealous controversialist. Two of his hymns were translated by John Wesley, namely:

> O God, of good the unfathomed sea.

> I thank thee, Uncreated Sun.[7]

The fourth verse of this latter hymn was repeated by Richard Cobden in his dying hour:

> "Thee will I love, my joy, my crown;
> Thee will I love, my Lord, my God;
> Thee will I love, beneath thy frown
> Or smile, thy scepter or thy rod.
> What though my flesh and heart decay;
> Thee shall I love in endless day."

The most churchly of the poets of the older Pietistic School was the Rev. Johann J. Rambach (1693–1735), professor at Giessen. He wrote the hymn:

> I am baptized into thy name.

Wolfgang Christopher Dessler (1660–1722) was head-master of the grammar school at Nuremberg, and a Pietist. The following hymns are his:

> Into thy gracious hands I fall.

> O Friend of souls, how blest the time.

The version of the first of these was made by John Wesley. The second, though less known, has yet some marked felicities of expression:

> "When from my weariness I climb
> Into thy tender breast."

> "And when life's fiercest storms are sent
> Upon life's wildest sea,
> · My little bark is confident,
> Because it holdeth thee."

In the same class of Hallean Pietists is Rev. Christian Friedrich Richter (1676–1711), who was physician to Francke's celebrated orphan-house in Halle, and author of thirty-three excellent hymns. The following are John Wesley's versions of two of them:

> My soul before thee prostrate lies.

> Thou Lamb of God, thou Prince of Peace.

The great poet in the Mystical School in German hymnology was Gerhard Tersteegen (1697–1761). From Catherine Winkworth's "Christian Singers of Germany" we condense the following account of this most remarkable and interesting man. He was the son of a respectable tradesman, and after such education as he could get at the grammar-school of his native place, was apprenticed to his elder brother, a shopkeeper at Muelheim. Here, under the influence of a tradesman, he was converted, and was led to devote himself to the service of God. As his days were occupied, he used sometimes to pass whole nights in prayer and fasting. That he might have more freedom for spiritual exercises, he left his brother, and took up the occupation of weaving silk ribbons, living for some years entirely alone in a cottage, except that in the day-time he had the company of the little girl who wound his silk for him. His relations—who seem to have been a thriving and money-getting set of people—were so ashamed of this poor and peculiar member of the family that they refused even to hear his name mentioned, and when he was sick he suffered great privations for want of care.

His spiritual experiences were at first marked by violent contrasts. Upon the peace and comfort of his early Christian life a season of darkness supervened, and for five years he was the subject of extreme and painful doubts. From this fearful dungeon in "Doubting Castle" he was suddenly and gloriously delivered, and in his gratitude wrote with his own blood a new covenant of self-dedication. He began at once to devote himself to the spiritual welfare of those about him. Soon he found himself entirely occupied with a sort of unofficial ministry, which speedily took permanent form, and became his life-work. Peremptorily declining all pecuniary assistance, he opened a dispensary for his support, making it a means of ministering to the souls as well as the bodies of men. So famous did he become in this double ministry that people came to him from other lands— England, Holland, Sweden, and Switzerland—so that he found his strength and resources taxed to their utmost. But amid it all he maintained an unvarying humility, affectionateness, devoutness, and simplicity.

From such a life none but the most spiritual
hymns could come, and Tersteegen's are highly and
justly prized.[8]   Among them are :

> Lo! God is here! Let us adore.
>
> God calling. yet! Shall I not hear?
>
> Thou hidden love of God, whose height.
>
> O Thou to whose all-searching sight.
>
> Though all the world my choice deride.

Three of the above, like so many others of the
choicest and most spiritual German hymns of the
seventeenth and eighteenth centuries, are versions by
John Wesley.

One of the most saintly of the many saints of Protestantism was John Frederick Oberlin (1740–1826).
Though the sphere of his personal labors was exceedingly restricted, the sphere of his influence is world-
wide. He stands before us as a notable illustration
of what a Christian pastor, who devotes himself unqualifiedly to his work in the spirit of the Master,
may do. By his wonderful influence the words of
Isaiah were more than fulfilled—"The desert shall
rejoice and blossom as the rose"—for that rugged and
sterile mountainous parish of Steinthal, with its ignorant, degraded, and unprosperous inhabitants, became
a scene of thrift, purity, and prosperity. One morning, after preaching from the text, "He shall see of
the travail of his soul, and shall be satisfied," he made
an earnest appeal to his hearers to devote themselves
entirely to God, and then read a hymn, in which he
asked the whole congregation to join him. It was this:

> O Lord, thy heavenly grace impart.

Two famous Moravians, both bishops, made very material contributions to the hymnology of this period—Count Zinzendorf and Bishop Spangenberg. The history of Nicolaus Ludwig Zinzendorf (1700–1760) is too well known to require any sketch of it here. In an eminent sense he stands in church history and in hymnology as a representative Moravian, having renounced his civil honors and cares to devote himself to the religious work of the Moravian Brethren. The hymns[9] by which he is best known are all in versions made by John Wesley:

> Eternal depth of love divine.
>
> Jesus, thy blood and righteousness.
>
> I thirst, thou wounded Lamb of God.

The last of these is very familiar and very precious to all who look to Wesley as their spiritual father. The second was written on the island of Saint Eustatius on his return from visiting the Moravian missionaries in the West Indies.

Bishop Aug. Gottlieb Spangenberg (1704–1792) is second only to Count Zinzendorf himself in the history of the Moravian church, and was greatly his superior in theological culture. Educated at the University of Jena when the distinguished Buddaeus was professor in that institution, he gave such brilliant promise as to be himself employed as a lecturer in the university at the early age of twenty-two, which place he held for six years. In 1735 he became an assistant of Zinzendorf at Herrnhut, and acted as a kind of missionary bishop to the Moravian churches in England, the West Indies, and North America.

In Georgia he came in contact with John Wesley, who had gone out with Oglethorpe as a missionary to the Aborigines. The meeting was a most memorable one for Wesley, and was one important means of bringing him to a realizing sense of his great want. Wesley had sought an interview with Spangenburg to consult with him as to the best plans of missionary work.

"My brother," said the Moravian, "I must first ask you one or two questions. Have you the witness within yourself? Does the Spirit of God bear witness with your spirit that you are a child of God?" Wesley was surprised, and knew not what to answer. Spangenberg perceived his embarrassment and asked: "Do you know Jesus Christ?" Wesley replied: "I know he is the Savior of the world." "True," rejoined the Moravian; "but do you know he has saved you?" "I hope he has died to save me." Spangenberg only added: "Do you know yourself?" "I do," responded Wesley; "but," he writes, "I fear they were vain words."

This good bishop is represented in English hymnology by John Wesley's version of one of his very choicest hymns, such as, indeed, a bishop might write:

High on his everlasting throne.

Other German writers whose hymns are frequently met with in the collections are Matthias Claudius (1740–1815), author of that best of harvest hymns,

We plow the fields and scatter,[10]

and Rev. Carl Johann P. Spitta (1801–1859) one of
. the many modern Christian poets in Germany, whose

hymns are characterized by depth, inwardness, freshness, and catholicity. He wrote:

I know no life divided.

The precious seed of weeping.[11]

About three-quarters of a century ago, in the midst of a severe naval battle, the deck of the ship commanded by Captain James Haldane, was fairly swept clean by the broadside of the enemy. He ordered up another company from below, to take the place of the dead. As they came upon the deck, slippery with blood and strewn with mangled corses, a sudden and irresistible panic seized them. The captain, swearing a horrid oath, wished them to hell. A pious old marine stepped up to him, and, respectfully touching his cap, said: "Captain, I believe God hears prayer, and if he were to hear yours what would become of us?" These words, spoken in that terrible hour, were as a nail fastened in a sure place, and as a result this profane captain became a Christian and a minister of the gospel. Through his instrumentality his brother Robert was also led to Christ, and he, in turn, was selected by Providence as a minister of life to that old city of Geneva, where the poison of French infidelity and German rationalism had well-nigh destroyed the life of the church of the Reformation. Mr. Haldane's labors were specially directed to the students of the theological seminary, and among the fruits of them were such men as Merle D'Aubigné, Felix Neff, Adolphe Monod, and others of similar distinction. Among the fruits of that revival must also be mentioned

Cæsar Henri Abraham Malan (1787–1864), who was at that time a young pastor in the city. He had previously been awakened to a sense of his spiritual need by the influence of the Rev. Dr. Mason, of New York, who had visited Geneva. It was Mr. Haldane, however, who led him to the knowledge of the Savior. He began at once to preach the doctrines of grace with an earnestness and plainness such as was not wont to be seen in that old city, so rich in historic memories, but now fallen into the deadness and formalities of rationalism.

A special interest attaches to the memory of Dr. Malan as the instrument, under God, of leading the soul of Charlotte Elliott into life and liberty, and so of giving to the world one of the very best hymns which this century has produced: " Just as I am." He was the author of the French original of Dr. Bethune's hymn,

It is not death to die.[12]

Another version of this same hymn, not, however, from the French original, but from an excellent German version, has been made by Professor R. B. Dunn, of Brown University. It commences:

No, no, it is not dying.[13]

To Dr. Malan we are also indebted for several excellent church tunes, such as Rosefield, Hendon, and Welton. He was a man of marked individuality of character; and, by this precious funeral hymn and these tunes, and especially his noble example of Christian courage and fidelity, he has laid the church under lasting obligations to his memory.

CHAPTER VI.

EARLIER ENGLISH HYMNS.

IN many important particulars English hymns are distinguished from those of every other language. Many of them are translations of the best and most famous hymns of other tongues. Nearly all the great hymns of the mediœval time are represented by English versions. This is true, also, of the most cherished and most spiritual of the French and German hymns. The great body of English hymns have been produced in the modern period of church history, and hence reflect the most recent phases of church life and work. As among English-speaking peoples evangelical movements have taken a greater variety of form, and have incorporated more various methods than have been employed elsewhere, so here the hymn has been appropriated to a greater variety of uses. In addition to the ordinary demands of public worship and the necessities of the individual life, which, though they do not essentially change, are yet all the time becoming more perfectly interpreted and more adequately expressed, there are many institutions which have been called into existence by the life of the church in this period. The modern prayer-meeting, revival meetings, conferences, conventions, synods, Sabbath-schools, and reform movements, have

all created a demand for a special type of religious
service. Hence, in no other language is there so great
a variety of hymns; in no other has the hymn been
more perverted and degraded from its proper character; and in no other is the vast and varied wealth
of hymnology more fully exhibited.

The oldest English hymn now in common use—
"The Lord descended from above"[1]—is a translation of some verses of the Eighteenth Psalm, made
by Thomas Sternhold, who died in 1549. He was
"Groom of the Robes" to Henry VIII and Edward
VI. He made a metrical version of the first fifty-one
Psalms, which, with versions of the remainder made
by John Hopkins, were attached to the Book of
Common Prayer. . As to the character of these men,
as shown by this work, doubtless the judgment of
quaint old Thomas Fuller will be generally approved:
"They were men whose piety was better than their
poetry; and they had drunk more of Jordan than of
Helicon." And yet the psalm above cited fully vindicates, by its own intrinsic excellence, the taste and
judgment of those who have so long kept it in its
seat of honor.

With this should be associated that translation of
the One Hundredth Psalm made by William Kethe:

<blockquote>All people that on earth do dwell.[2]</blockquote>

Of its author we know almost nothing, not even the
dates of his birth and death. He was a clergyman,
was sometime a chaplain in the army, and shared the
exile of Knox, in Geneva, in 1555. The psalm was
first published in 1561, and is not only one of the

oldest, but also one of the most ecumenical of English hymns. It was used at the opening of the recent Pan-Presbyterian Council in Scotland (1877,) and also was the opening hymn of the Church Congress of Episcopalians in Boston, in 1876. The clearness and archaic simplicity of the version atone for its ruggedness; and when we call to mind the grand and heroic history of these Scottish Dissenters, of which these old psalms are in a special sense monumental, we can well understand why it should have a place of high honor in our hymnals.

Among these psalms, used by those Scottish sects who are opposed to the use of ordinary hymns, are not a few which are acceptable to all who "profess and call themselves Christians," such for instance as:

O God, to us show mercy.

The Lord 's my shepherd; I 'll not want.[3]

The associations connected with this last are peculiarly interesting. It was a favorite channel through which the sturdy Scotch people of the olden time poured out their souls to God in assured and grateful confidence. It was the language of individual trust, it beautifully befitted the worship of the home, and yet was equally in place in the great congregation. It was linked with the earliest memories of childhood, and it was the "strong staff and the beautiful rod" of the aged pilgrim. In Professor Wilson's touching little story of Moss Side, when Gilbert Ainslie's little Margaret was hovering between life and death, in the delirium of her fever, she kept muttering words which showed that she thought herself "herding her sheep

in the green, silent pastures, and sitting wrapped in
her plaid upon the lawn and sunny-side of Birk-
Knowe." At last, when she was almost exhausted,
and there was "too little breath in her heart to frame
a tune," with her blue eyes shut and her lips almost
still, she breathed out these lines of sweet and restful
confidence:

> "The Lord's my Shepherd; I'll not want;
> He makes me down to lie
> In pastures green; he leadeth me
> The quiet waters by."

The name of Bishop John Cosin (1594–1672) is
deserving of most honorable mention, because of his
translation of the "Veni, Creator Spiritus"—"Come,
Holy Ghost, our souls inspire."[4] Few men of his
time held a greater variety of distinguished positions,
or received more flattering testimonials of personal
popularity and influence. Though made to feel the
virulent opposition of his Puritan enemies, and to
suffer from their unjust charges of leaning toward
popery, yet he stands in the history of the church
fully vindicated, and a noble example of a man true
to the church, and true also to his own convictions.
He expended his emoluments, and the profits arising
from the sale of his works, liberally for the cause of
learning and religion, founding no less than eight
scholarships at Cambridge. His one hymn has a
higher place of honor than any other in our language,
having for two centuries and a half maintained its
place in the service for the ordination of elders. It
is a most satisfactory instance of "poetic justice," in
a sense much fuller and more perfect than that in

which the phrase is ordinarily used, that the hymn of Gregory, who taught Britain her first lesson in practical Christianity, should be the only one which has been given a place in the ritual of the English church.

Another bishop, whose hymns have come to almost equal honor, and in some regards even superior, is Thomas Ken (1637–1711). Early left an orphan— his mother dying when he was but five and his father when he was fourteen—he was brought up by his half-sister, the wife of the celebrated Isaac Walton. He was educated at Oxford; was first rector of Brightstone, in the Isle of Wight, and afterwards bishop of Bath and Wells. King Charles used to say: "I must go and hear Ken—he will tell me of my faults." He was one of the seven bishops imprisoned and brought to trial for resisting the tyranny of James II. His most enduring monument is his "Morning and Evening Hymns." Says one writer: "Had he endowed three hospitals he would have been less a benefactor to posterity." His grand old Doxology in long meter is heard wherever the English language is spoken. It is almost as catholic as the English Bible itself. The following hymns are his:

> Glory to thee, my God, this night.
>
> Awake, my soul, and with the sun.
>
> Praise God, from whom all blessings flow.[1]

The three great names in modern literature are Dante, Shakspeare, and Milton. But of the works of these three illustrious men, those of Milton stand forth as most evidently and unqualifiedly the product of a Christian culture. It is, therefore, a matter of special satisfaction to recognize in the hymnology of the English church the name of John Milton (1608–1704). Some of his best-known hymns are:

> Let us with a gladsome mind;
>
> How lovely are thy dwellings, Lord;
>
> The Lord will come, and not be slow;

which will be recognized as versions of the 136th, the 84th, and selected verses of the 82d, 85th, and 86th Psalms.

By the side of his should be placed the scarcely less illustrious name of Joseph Addison (1672–1719). He was the son of the dean of Lichfield, was educated at Oxford University, and married to the dowager countess of Warwick. As a writer of English prose he had no equal in his own time, and few equals in any time. "Whoever wishes to attain an English style," says Dr. Johnson, "familiar but not coarse, and elegant but not ostentatious, must give his days and nights to the volumes of Addison." And though he has been described as "so great in prose, so little in poetry," yet we have only to examine the little poetry by which he is represented in the world of letters, to be convinced how merciless and unjust this criticism is. Few finer passages can be quoted from any writer of Addison's time than the closing lines of Cato's Soliloquy:

> "The stars shall fade away; the sun himself
> Grow dim with age, and nature sink in years;
> But thou shalt flourish in immortal youth,
> Unhurt amid the war of elements,
> The wreck of matter, and the crush of worlds."

He is represented by such hymns as the following, each of which is a real gem of its kind:

> The spacious firmament on high.
>
> When all thy mercies, O my God.
>
> The Lord my pasture shall prepare.
>
> When rising from the bed of death.
>
> How are thy servants blest, O Lord.[5]

Rev. Richard Baxter (1615–1691), well known as the author of "The Saints' Rest," was an eminent Non-conformist minister. He was born at Rowton, Shropshire; became pastor of the parish of Kidderminster, where he was greatly popular and useful; afterward chaplain of a regiment among the Parliamentary forces, during which time he wrote his "Saints' Rest;" returned to Kidderminster, but was soon ejected by the Act of Uniformity; went to reside in London, where he occupied himself in preaching and writing, until he was arrested on a charge of sedition, and brought before the infamous Jeffreys, by whom he was adjudged to pay a heavy fine, and thrown into prison. His life was filled with activity and usefulness, and he enjoyed the friendship of some of the best men of his time—such as Matthew Henry, and others. Though he attained to a good old age, his whole life was one constant and severe struggle with disease; and the hymns by which he is known may well be added to the long list of those which have come up "out of the depths." In his final illness he was accustomed to reply to those who called to inquire after him, "Almost well," and in his death-

hour he became "entirely well." The process of
dying was to him, as to all God's saints, the process
of becoming immortal. His best-known hymn is:

> Lord, it belongs not to my care.[6]

How reasonable and consoling the first couplet in the
third verse—

> "Christ leads me through no darker rooms
> Than he went through before!"

And how satisfying the final lines of the hymn—

> "But 't is enough that Christ knows all,
> And I shall be with him!"

Though the name of Nahum Tate (1652–1715) is
eminent in English hymnology, yet the associations
connected with it are not all grateful. His active life
commenced as clergyman of a country parish in Suf-
folk, from which he subsequently removed to London.
But intemperance and improvidence cast a blight
over his life and a shadow upon his memory. In
connection with Nicholas Brady, he prepared the metrical version of the Psalms, which is now printed in
the Book of Common Prayer in place of the older
one of Sternhold and Hopkins, which version Montgomery justly characterizes as being "nearly as inani-
mate as the former, though a little more refined."
Nicholas Brady (1659–1726), his associate in this
work, studied at Christ College, Oxford, and graduated at Trinity College, Dublin. He was afterward
chaplain to a bishop and prebend to the Cathedral
of Cork, and later in life taught a school in Rich-
mond, Surrey.

The Psalter of Tate and Brady was first published in 1696, with tunes in 1698, and with a supplement of hymns in 1703. From this work several hymns in common use have been taken, though it is impossible to determine which were written by Tate and which by Brady. Among them are the following:

O render thanks to God above.

O God, we praise thee, and confess.

While shepherds watched their flocks by night.

As pants the hart for cooling streams.

O Lord, our fathers oft have told.

A very choice evening hymn has come down to us from this seventeenth century, written by John F. Herzog (1649–1699):

In mercy, Lord, remember me.

One of the really distinguished philosophers of England's early time was Henry More (died 1687), one of the first Fellows of the Royal Society; friend of the eminent Cudworth; defender of the philosophical system of Descartes, with whom he maintained a personal correspondence; and opponent of the famous Thomas Hobbes, who died eight years before him. He was educated at Eton and Cambridge, but refused the mastership in his college, as also all church preferment, and devoted himself with much enthusiasm to the study of philosophy. He was the author of the hymn—

On all the earth thy Spirit shower.[7]

Even at this day the thoughtful student can hardly
take into his hands a book more suggestive or more
stimulating than Mason's "Self-Knowledge." In
depth, solidity, clearness, and comprehensivenes, it
has few equals in our language. The young person
who makes it the subject of constant and loving study
is sure to be richly rewarded. John Mason, the
hymn writer (died 1694), was grandfather of the John
Mason who was the author of this treatise. Little is
known of his life, save that for twenty years he was
rector of a parish in Buckinghamshire, where he was
very highly esteemed for his piety and his devotion
to his flock. Baxter called him "the glory of the
Church of England." In 1683 he published his
"Spiritual Songs," to which were afterwards added
"Penitential Cries," mainly from the pen of Rev.
Thomas Shepherd. Many traces of these hymns of
Mason are found in the later works of Watts, Pope,
and the Wesleys. Of the one hymn of his which is
most used, David Creamer says that it is "certainly
one of the best specimens of devotional poetry in the
English language." The hymn is—

> Now from the altar of our hearts.

One hymn from the "Penitential Cries" of
Thomas Shepherd (1665–1739) has been preserved in
most of our modern hymn-books, though in a form
so much changed from the original as almost to destroy its identity. Indeed, in most books the hymn
is credited to Mr. G. N. Allen, who made the alterations, rather than to Mr. Shepherd, the original author.
It begins—

> Must Jesus bear the cross alone? [s]

The earliest of the considerable number of Baptists who have been eminent as English hymn-writers is Joseph Stennett (1663–1713), who spent his life as pastor of a small congregation of Seventh-day Baptists in the city of London. He was also accustomed to preach to other congregations on the first day of the week, which makes it pretty certain that his sympathy with his people was as Baptists, rather than as Sabbatarians. In addition to his duties as pastor, he also, for some years, received young men into his house to be trained for the ministry. He died in his forty-ninth year, and among his last words were: "I rejoice in the God of my salvation, who is my strength and my God." He published two small collections of original hymns—"Hymns for the Lord's Supper" and "Hymns on the Believer's Baptism." His familiar hymn—

> Return, my soul, enjoy thy rest—

is one of the most frequently used of our Sabbath hymns.

No name appears in a Christian hymn-book with more grotesque effect than that of Alexander Pope (1688–1744). Probably few men have ever acquired an eminent literary reputation who have been more utterly incapable of appreciating an evangelical experience. Born of Catholic parentage; acquiring the smatterings of an education at Catholic schools, until, at the age of twelve, he entered on the perilous path of self-culture; with a nature deformed and diseased; diminutive in stature and irritable in disposition; with much of the critical but little of the creative faculty; with an extraordinary facility for measured smooth-

ness, but showing little consciousness of the essence
and soul of true poetry; having little contact with
evangelical beliefs, and an utter stranger, so far as can
now be told, to evangelical experiences,—it were indeed
strange if he had written a true Christian hymn.
Many of his poetic utterances reflect that extreme
naturalism which amounts substantially to Deism, and
so are at the farthest possible remove from the warmth
and life of the Christian religion. He is represented
in many of our collections by his " Dying Christian "—

> Vital spark of heavenly flame.[9]

It seems to have been suggested by the Emperor
Adrian's Address to His Soul, as also by a fragment
of Sappho. Even for the English of the poem he is,
to some extent, indebted to an earlier rendering of
Adrian's words by Thomas Flatman. As a specimen
of literature it is not without interest, but it is very
far from being a *hymn*. It is utterly destitute of
warmth and devoutness, and dramatizes, as if for mere
literary effect, the holy experiences of the dying hour.
That it has so long been accorded a place in our
hymn-books is an unmistakable tribute to its rare
beauty; but it is not to be wondered at that it is now
very generally omitted from the latest collections.

There is one English hymn, dating probably from
the sixteenth century, whose history is specially interesting. It comes from an old Latin hymn, which
Dean Trench assigns to the eighth or ninth century.
We refer to that dearest of all our hymns on heaven—

> Jerusalem, my happy home.[10]

In a very old book of religious songs, now kept in the British Museum, it stands with this title—"A Song, Made by F. B. P., to the Tune of Diana." It has been conjectured—doubtfully by most, but confidently by some—that "F. B. P." is an *alias* for Francis Baker, Priest, who was for a long time confined as a prisoner in the Tower, and so that this is one of the many hymns which have come up out of the depth of suffering and bitter wrong. A later and more beautiful form of this hymn—"O mother dear, Jerusalem"—was given to the public by David Dickson, in the early part of the seventeenth century.

The hymn, as it appears in our modern hymnbooks, is considerably altered from the text as found in the book in the British Museum. It is called by Miller "the hymn of hymns," and certainly holds a very warm place in the hearts of Christian worshipers in every communion. A young Scotchman, on his death-bed in the city of New Orleans several years ago, was visited by a Presbyterian minister. He continued to shut himself up from the good man's efforts to reach his heart. Somewhat discouraged, at last the visitor turned away, and scarcely knowing why, began to sing, "Jerusalem, my happy home." A tender chord was touched in the heart of the young man. With tears he exclaimed: "My dear mother used to sing that hymn!" The tender memories awakened by the hymn opened his heart to religious truth. He was led through penitence into peace, and thus was made ready for the "happy home" whither his mother had already preceded him.

CHAPTER VII.

ISAAC WATTS (1674–1748) is pronounced by Montgomery the "father of modern hymnody"— "almost the inventor of hymns in our language." He was son of a school-master, and deacon of an independent church in Southampton, England, a locality which is embalmed in the imagery of some of his hymns. So insignificant was he in stature, after he had come to years of maturity, that when he offered his hand to Elizabeth Singer, who had already stolen his heart, she gave the death-warrant to his hopes by replying that "much as she might love the jewel, she could not admire the casket," and so missed the honor of becoming the wife of the most famous man of his generation. So precocious in intellect was he that almost his earliest cry was for a book ; and he actually commenced the study of Latin at four, of Greek at nine, of French at ten, and of Hebrew at fourteen, and this intellectual activity was continued through a long and most fruitful life. Says Dr. Johnson: " Few men have left behind such purity of character or such monuments of laborious piety. He has provided instruction for all ages, from those who are lisping their first lessons to the enlightened readers of Malebranche and Locke." And the judgment of this extraordinary critic in the matter of hymns is sufficiently indicated by such sentences as the following: "It is sufficient for Watts to have done better than others what no one has done well." "His devotional poetry is, like that of others, unsatisfactory. The paucity of its topics enforces perpetual repetition, and the sanctity of the matter rejects the ornaments of figurative diction."

Dr. Watts was a man of fervent and devoted piety. Descended through his mother from the old Huguenots, the traditions and memories of their bitter wrongs must have filled his soul with a hatred of tryanny, and a sense of the sacredness of the rights which had been purchased at such fearful cost. And the stories his mother told him of the time when his father was thrown into prison for his convictions as a non-conformist, and how she used to go and sit, day after day, just outside the prison bars, holding up her infant to comfort his father in his bonds, must have deepened and intensified this feeling; so that it is no wonder that this mild-spirited man was so clear and positive in his religious convictions, and, at the same time, so broad in his sympathies even toward those who differed somewhat radically from the common faith.

He preached his first sermon on his twenty-fourth birthday, and the same year was chosen assistant pastor of the Independent church, Mark Lane, London, and four years later became sole pastor. In this pastorate he remained for almost fifty years, though for most of the time he had an assistant, and such was the feebleness of his health that some of the time, for years together, he was unable to preach at all.

Often after preaching he would be compelled to take his bed, and have his room closed in darkness and silence.

In 1712 he visited the mansion of Sir Thomas Abney for rest and change of air, which led to his making it his permanent home. To a lady who once called to see him Watts said: "Madam, your lady-ship has called to see me on a very remarkable day. This very day, thirty years ago, I came to the house of my good friend Sir Thomas Abney, intending to spend but a single week under his friendly roof, and I have extended my visit to this family to the length of exactly thirty years." "Sir," said Lady Abney, "I consider it the shortest visit my family ever received." Here he found all the comforts of a home without its cares, and doubtless to this, as a ground condition, we owe much of the fruitfulness of his life. For four years after going there he was obliged to desist from preaching altogether; but all his life long his literary activity seems to have been incessant. In addition to his poetical and theological works, he wrote numerous other books and tractates—such as a work on logic, which was adopted as a text-book in Cambridge University; a treatise on astronomy, "Art of Reading and Writing English," "Guide to Prayer," "Improvement of the Mind," which at one time was very widely used as a text-book in the schools of this country, and is, beyond question, one of the best of his works, as it is certainly one of the best books on mental discipline ever written. He also projected a work on the "Rise and Progress of Religion in the Soul," which he was finally obliged to turn over to

his friend Dr. Doddridge to execute, and he did it
so excellently that it has been pronounced by the
North British Review the most useful book of the
eighteenth century.

Watts was eminently catholic in his spirit. In
this regard his own spirit and character were truthfully prophetic of the grand and universal mission
which his hymns have fulfilled. The memory of the
dark and cruel wrongs which his ancestors, and even
his own parents, had suffered from religious intolerance, seems to have wrought in his mind something
of the spirit which Coleridge so broadly expresses:
" I will be tolerant of everything else but every
other man's intolerance." This spirit of Christian
charity and fellowship was beautifully illustrated at
his funeral. Having lingered on to a good old age,
" waiting God's leave to die," when at last the sum-
mons did come, he was, at his own request, carried to
his burial by ministers chosen from three different denominations. And it was fitting that in 1861 the
various Christian denominations in England should
bring their offerings in common for the erection of a
memorial monument in his native town of Southampton. The monument itself is a fitting expression
of gratitude on the part of those who felt themselves
laid under a debt of obligation to his memory by his
hymns, which have come into such universal use. It
stands in a public square, and consists of a base eight
and a half feet square, surmounted by a pedestal of
polished gray Aberdeen granite, with three bas-reliefs of marble in the sides, upon which stands a
statue of pure white Sicilian marble, the whole rising

to the height of nineteen feet. One of the bas-reliefs represents a teacher in the midst of a group of children, and bears this motto :

" He gave to lisping infancy its earliest and purest lessons."

Another represents the poet himself, and, underneath, this line from his own pen :

"To heaven I lift my waiting eyes."

The remaining one represents the poet surrounded by globe, telescope, and hour-glass, with this sentence from Dr. Johnson :

" He taught the art of reasoning and the science of the stars."

The inscription on the tablet is as follows :

A. D. 1861.

ERECTED BY VOLUNTARY SUBSCRIPTIONS

IN MEMORY OF ISAAC WATTS, D. D.,

A NATIVE OF SOUTHAMPTON.

BORN 1674; DIED 1748.

AN EXAMPLE OF THE TALENTS OF A LARGE AND LIBERAL MIND,
WHOLLY DEVOTED TO THE PROMOTION OF PIETY,
VIRTUE, AND LITERATURE.

A NAME HONORED FOR HIS ENGLISH HYMNS WHEREVER THE ENGLISH
LANGUAGE EXTENDS.

ESPECIALLY THE FRIEND OF CHILDREN AND OF YOUTH, FOR WHOSE
BEST WELFARE HE LABORED WELL AND WISELY,
WITHOUT THOUGHT OF FAME OR GAIN.

" From all that dwell below the skies,
Let the Creator's praise arise ;
Let the Redeemer's name be sung
Through every land, by every tongue."

WATTS.

Only as a writer of hymns is the fame of Dr. Watts pre-eminent. When, at the age of eighteen, on a certain Sabbath, he was complaining to one of his fellow-worshipers at the Independent chapel where his father was deacon, of the character of the hymns sung there, the reply was, "Give us better, young man." He accepted the challenge, and the church was invited to close the evening service with a new hymn commencing:

> " Behold the glories of the Lamb
> Before his Father's throne;
> Prepare new honors for his name,
> And songs before unknown "[1] —

a hymn which is retained in many of our hymn-books, and is still sung with reverence and delight. Such was the beginning of the most illustrious career as a hymn-writer which, with not more than a single exception, it has ever been given to mortal to fulfill. The author of that first hymn has made more material contributions to the apparatus of Christian worship in the English tongue than any other man, and his hymns are familiar and precious wherever that language is spoken. Less prolific and less versatile than some others, especially than Charles Wesley, with whom he is most frequently compared, with less of poetic genius and less of spiritual fervor and joy, his hymns are so devout, so Scriptural, so catholic, and so simple, and, in the main, so correct in diction and in sentiment, that they meet a general want more perfectly than any other. Though Wesley wrote seven or eight thousand hymns, and Watts only six hundred and ninety-seven, yet it is probable that more of Watts's hymns are in common use than of Wesley's. A recent writer says: " Judging from the results of an examination of seven hundred and fifty hymn-books, it is safe to assign to Watts the authorship of two-fifths of the hymns which are used in public worship in the English-speaking world." In the " Hymns and Songs of Praise," one of the best and most broadly representative of the hymnbooks used by the Calvinistic churches of this country, Watts is represented by one hundred and ninety-one hymns and Charles Wesley by ninety-nine; while in the Methodist Hymnal, Watts has but seventy-eight and Wesley three hundred and seven. The facts as to actual use, however, may be considerably different from what would be indicated by these figures; and we need but to glance over the list of Watts's leading hymns to be convinced that they constitute a very large proportion of the staple hymns for public religious service. Among the most eminent of these are such as the following:[1]

> Alas! and did my Savior bleed.
>
> Am I a soldier of the cross?
>
> Before Jehovah's awful throne.
>
> Blest are the sons of peace.
>
> Come sound his praise abroad.
>
> Come, let us join our cheerful songs.
>
> Come, ye that love the Lord.
>
> Father, how wide thy glory shines.
>
> From all that dwell below the skies.
>
> Give me the wings of faith to rise.
>
> He dies! the friend of sinners dies.
>
> How vain are all things here below.
>
> How beauteous are their feet.

I 'll praise my Maker while I 've breath.

Jesus shall reign where'er the sun.

Let every tongue thy goodness speak.

My God, the spring of all my joys!

O God, our help in ages past.

The heavens declare thy glory, Lord.

There is a land of pure delight.

Unveil thy bosom, faithful tomb.

When I can read my title clear.

When I survey the wondrous cross.

Why do we mourn for dying friends?

Why should we start and fear to die?

Some of these hymns are, in a special sense, autobiographic. Nearly all of them bear, in a marked degree, the stamp of the poet's personal experience. It has been alleged that the hymn,

> How vain are all things here below,

was written on the occasion of the rejection of his offer of marriage by Elizabeth Singer, to which allusion has already been made. The bitterness of his disappointment and its lesson are reflected in such lines as these:

> "The fondness of a creature's love,
>   How strong it strikes the sense;
> Thither our warm affections move,
>   Nor can we call them hence.

> Dear Savior, let thy beauties be
>   My soul's eternal food,
> And grace command my heart away
>   From all created good."

To the character of the scenery about Southampton are doubtless due some of the most striking and beautiful passages of his hymns. It is situated on the south coast of England, at the head of Southampton Water, between the Itchen on the east, and the Anton on the west, with the Isle of Wight in the distance, at the mouth of the bay. This island is separated from the main-land by an interval of from one to six miles, and serves as a vast natural breakwater, making this port one of the safest and most eligible in the United Kingdom. The scenery of the island is of remarkable beauty, and the climate so salubrious that in one part the death-rate is lower than in any other locality in the United Kingdom. The tradition is that these conditions furnished the costume of expression for the hymn,

> There is a land of pure delight.

Certain it is that the language is such as exactly suits them, and by their aid we feel its force and beauty.

> "Death, like a narrow sea, divides
> This heavenly land from ours."

> "Sweet fields beyond the swelling flood
> Stand dressed in living green."

> "Could we but climb where Moses stood,
> And view the landscape o'er,
> Not Jordan's stream nor death's cold flood
> Should fright us from the shore."

There is little doubt that the imagery of one of the verses of another hymn may have been suggested by the same associations. Only one familiar with the sea, and accustomed to study its various moods,

would have been so felicitous in seizing upon and in-
terpreting the most perfect symbol of rest which
nature contains—water in repose:

> "There I shall bathe my weary soul
> In seas of heavenly rest,
> And not a wave of trouble roll
> Across my peaceful breast."

The hymn in which this verse stands has been perhaps as often used as any of his hymns. It was sung
on the field of Shiloh, the night after the battle, under
circumstances of peculiar impressiveness. A Christian officer had been severely wounded, and, being
unable to help himself, lay all night on the field.
Says he: "The stars shone out clear above the dark
battle-field, and I began to think about God, who
had given his Son to die for me, and that he was up
above the glorious stars. I felt that I ought to praise
him even while wounded on that battle-ground. I
could not help singing:

> 'When I can read my title clear
> To mansions in the skies,
> I'll bid farewell to every fear,
> And wipe my weeping eyes.'

There was a Christian brother in the brush near me.
I could not see him, but I could hear him. He took
up the strain. Another, beyond him, heard and
joined in, and still others too. We made the field of
battle *ring* with the hymn of praise to God."

Many volumes might be filled with illustrative
anecdotes bearing upon the use of some line, stanza,
or whole hymn even, which Watts has written. The
full history of his hymns, if it could be written,

17

would be a great part, and a very interesting part, of the history of Protestant Christianity among English-speaking peoples for the last hundred years. Scarcely another couplet in the entire range of Hymnology has been so often quoted in the great crisis-hour of individual spiritual history as

> " Here, Lord, I give myself away,
> 'T is all that I can do."

Few verses appropriate to the dying hour are so often quoted, and with such satisfying effect, as

> "Jesus can make a dying bed
> Feel soft as downy pillows are,
> While on his breast I lean my head,
> And breathe my life out sweetly there."

And how often have the lines of the previous verse been the experience of God's children:

> "O would my Lord his servant meet,
> My soul would stretch her wings in haste!"

Said Thomas Scott the morning of his last day on earth: "I have done with darkness forever—FOREVER. Nothing now remains but salvation and eternal glory—ETERNAL GLORY!" Was not this the brightness of the coming of the Lord to meet his servant in the dark passage-way?

When the good Bishop Beveridge was on his death-bed he was visited by a ministerial friend. " Bishop Beveridge, do you know me?" " Who are you?" said the bishop. Being told, he answered: " I do n't know you." Another friend sought recognition. " I do n't know you" was still the answer. His wife addressed him, but with the same result.

At length one said : " Do you know Jesus Christ ?"
" Jesus Christ?" said the dying man, as if the very
name had touched a new spring of life. " O yes; I
have known him for forty years. Precious Savior!
he is my only hope." Thus did the loving Master
support and cheer his trusting disciple as the waters of
the " dark and solemn ocean " were closing over him.

Dr. Doddridge wrote to Watts of the powerful
effect produced by the singing of one of his hymns
in his own congregation. He had preached from
Hebrews vi, 12 : " Followers of them who through
faith and patience inherit the promises ;" and at the
close of the sermon gave out the hymn :

> " Give me the wings of faith to rise
>   Within the veil, and see
> The saints above, how great their joys,
>   How bright their glories be.
>
> Once they were mourners here below,
>   And poured out cries and tears;
> They wrestled hard, as we do now,
>   With sins and doubts and fears.
>
> I ask them whence their victory came;
>   They, with united breath,
> Ascribe their conquests to the Lamb,
>   Their triumph to his death.
>
> Our glorious leader claims our praise
>   For his own pattern given,
> While the long cloud of witnesses
>   Show the same path to heaven."

So perfectly suited were these words to the matter of
the discourse, and so tender the associations awakened, that many could not sing for their emotion,
and many sung amid tears.

It is a matter of special interest that the memory of Watts is, by many associations, so closely linked with that of the Wesleys. He lived about ten years after the beginning of that grand evangelical movement in which the Wesleys and Whitefield were the chief actors, though probably he never came into very close personal contact with any of its chief agents. But he did read some of Charles Wesley's hymns, and never did one eminent poet give to another, then comparatively unknown, such a generous meed of praise. Said he: "I would rather be the author of that single poem 'Wrestling Jacob' than of all the hymns which I have ever written." Probably no other person ever agreed with him in this estimate, and these words should be quoted rather in honor of Watts than Wesley, in whose honor they have been so often quoted.[2]

It is an interesting fact that the last words which fell from the lips of John Wesley were written by Watts. When the supreme moment came he was struggling to repeat that grand hymn of gratitude and victory:

> "I'll praise my Maker while I've breath,
> And when my voice is lost in death
> Praise shall employ my nobler powers," etc.

This hymn Wesley began on earth, but finished it if he ever finished it at all, "before the throne of God."

Some of the very best of the hymns of Watts owe their present perfection and much of their usefulness to the finishing touches of John Wesley. The hymn "Before Jehovah's awful throne" is an instance in point. As at first written it commenced:

> "Sing to the Lord with cheerful voice,
> Let every land his name adore;
> The British isles shall scent the noise
> Across the ocean to the shore.
>
> Nations attend before his throne
> With solemn fear, with sacred joy," etc.

Wesley dropped the first verse altogether, and changed the first two lines of the second to read:

> "Before Jehovah's awful throne,
> Ye nations, bow with sacred joy;"

thus making a suitable beginning for a hymn which is almost unequaled in our language for strength and majesty.

Two or three slight changes made by Wesley in the hymn above mentioned as spoken literally with his dying breath, are felt to be such improvements as materially to elevate the character of the hymn. Watts wrote:

> I'll praise my Maker with my breath,

which Wesley changed to

> I'll praise my Maker while I've breath.

In the third verse Watts wrote:

> The Lord hath eyes to give the blind.

This Wesley altered to

> The Lord pours eyesight on the blind.

In a similar way did Wesley change, materially for the better, several lines in that glad song of Chris-

tian joy, "Come ye that love the Lord." At a
single stroke he cleared away the weakness and impurity of the first verse by changing it from the first
to the second person—"Come ye" for "Come we,"
etc. The first four lines, as originally written, stood
thus:

> "The God that rules on high,
> And thunders when he please,
> Who rides upon the stormy sky
> And calms the roaring seas," etc.

Wesley made the second line to read, "That all the
earth surveys."

In the hymn commencing, "My drowsy powers,
why sleep ye so?" Watts wrote in the second verse:

> "The little ants for one poor grain
> Labor and tug and strive."

Wesley reclaimed it from its uncouthness and vul-
garism, and elevated it into the region of lyrical expression by substituting:

> "Go to the ants! For one poor grain
> See how they toil and strive."

But the most striking instance of textual change,
elevating and transforming the character of a whole
hymn, is seen in the hymn commencing.

> "He dies! the friend of sinners dies!
> Lo! Salem's daughters weep around:
> A solemn darkness veils the skies,
> A sudden trembling shakes the ground:"

which, as at first written by Watts, stood:

> "He dies! the heavenly lover dies!
> The tidings strike a doleful sound
> On my poor heart-strings. Deep he lies
> In the cold caverns of the ground!"

These hymns are all dear to the universal church, and it is a matter of considerable interest that, as now sung, they are the joint product of these two eminent and honored representatives of the Calvinistic and the Arminian type of Christian belief.

Many of the hymns of Watts are a part of the universal language of English-speaking Christians, and are almost as sure to be known as the Bible itself. But a few of them have been selected by the critics as entitled to special mention because of their rare perfection as lyric poems. The two most frequently mentioned with the highest praise are :

My God, the spring of all my joys.

When I survey the wondrous cross.

As examples of special felicity in versifying the Psalms the following have been quoted :

O God, our help in ages past.

The heavens declare thy glory, Lord.

CHAPTER VIII.

THE prominence of the famous Wesley family in the general history of the Christian church is equaled only by its prominence in the history of Christian hymnody.

Samuel Wesley, Senior (1662–1735)—father of his more distinguished sons, Samuel, John, and Charles— was educated at Oxford, and was, for most of his life, rector of the parish of Epworth, in Lincolnshire. His grandfather, Bartholomew, and his own father, John, were both Dissenters, and were driven from their pulpits, fined, imprisoned, and, in the case of the father, crushed by the persecutions which they suffered as Non-conformists. In the exercise of that independence and self-reliance so characteristic of him, he started for Exeter College, Oxford, with less than three pounds in his pocket; yet with such energy and economy did he apply himself to the problem of self-support that, though during his entire college course he did not receive aid to the amount of a crown, he was able to leave college with ten pounds, after defraying all expenses. Notwithstanding the bitter wrongs which his father had suffered, and which drove him to his grave at the early age of thirty-four, he decided to enter the ministry of the Established Church, and in this ministry lived and died. His noble wife, too—one of the most extraordinary women who have ever lived—experienced a similar revolution in her views on the great and overshadowing question of Conformity. Her father—Dr. Annesley—was an eminent Non-conformist divine, but this his favorite daughter early came to clear convictions in favor of Conformity, and that, too, without at all interrupting the warm affection which existed between them.

In Samuel Wesley we mark a distinct prophecy of the remarkable poetical gifts of his sons. From the first he himself shows an irrepressible proclivity for rhyming. He wrote a "Life of Christ" in verse, as also "The History of the Old and New Testaments" in the same form. Dunton says that he would write two hundred couplets a day, a statement which in itself almost vindicates the remark of another that "the current of his verse was so rapid as to carry with it all the lighter rubbish of its banks, and to sink whatever of weighty value was cast upon it." Two of his hymns are in somewhat common use:

> Behold the Savior of mankind!

> What shall I render to my God?

This last must not be confounded with a hymn by Watts, founded on the same passage—Psalms cxvi, 13. The first was found written on a piece of music rescued from the flames of the Epworth rectory. In this fire John Wesley narrowly escaped perishing; and the first act of the father, when he saw that all his family were safe, was to kneel down with them to thank God for his protection and deliverance. As a memento of this interesting passage in the history of the Wesley family, as well as for its own intrinsic merit, this hymn is highly prized.

Samuel Wesley, Junior (1690–1739), was the oldest son of the foregoing, and, like him, was a Churchman. As to church order he stood at the very antipodes of his brothers John and Charles, being thoroughly High-church in his views, and utterly opposed to the irregularities of the Methodistic movement. He was educated at Oxford, was an excellent scholar, and an author of some reputation. For twenty years he was an usher at Westminster School, and for the last seven years of his life he was headmaster of the school at Tiverton. The following hymns are his:

> The Lord of Sabbath let us praise.
>
> The morning flowers display their sweets.

His literary taste, and probably also his churchly sympathies, led him to express in verse his views of the prevalent tendency to put the Psalms into meter and rhyme—a protest which, as there can hardly be any doubt, was directed particularly against Dr. Watts:

> "Has David Christ to come foreshowed?
>   Can Christians, then, aspire
> To mend the harmony that flowed
>   From his prophetic lyre?
>
> How curious are their wits, and vain;
>   Their erring zeal how bold,
> Who durst with meaner dross profane
>   His purity of gold!

The Psalms unchanged the saints employ,
  Unchanged our God applies ;
They suit the apostles in their joy,
  The Savior when he dies.

Let David's pure, unaltered lays
  Transmit through ages down
To thee, O David's Lord, our praise—
  To thee, O David's Son!

Till judgment calls the seraph throng
  To join the human choir,
And God, who gave the ancient song,
  The new one shall inspire."

The history of John Wesley (1703–1791) has often
been told, and need not here be repeated. The history of no minister, from the days of the apostles to
the present time, is more widely and universally familiar. The estimate in which he should be held is
already made up, and can not be materially changed.
It has come to be felt on all hands that his is one of
the grandest characters in all history—that his friends
and followers have no occasion to blush for him, as
he takes his seat in the very highest society of earth—
and that the career it was given him to fulfill had a
most influential bearing upon the history of Protestant Christianity among all the peoples who speak the
English language. Of all the movements which have
been set on foot in the sacred name of religion, no
one has been more catholic, more spiritual, or more
Christly in its genius and in its methods than that of
which John Wesley was, in some eminent sense, the
originator, and in which he was a chief actor. The
Churchman, Isaac Taylor, pronounces it "the starting
point of our modern religious history," and asserts

that "the field-preaching of Wesley and Whitefield, in
1739, was the event whence the religious epoch now
current must date its commencement."

But it is with the relations of John Wesley to
Christian hymnody that this sketch is solely concerned. His work here is of three kinds—alterations
of hymns written by others, translations of hymns
from other languages, and original hymns. Of his
work as a hymn-mender we have already given illustrations taken from the hymns of Watts. There is
little doubt that the hymns of his brother Charles
may be also much indebted to his more critical though
less affluent pen. It is by no means improbable that
some of these precious hymns may be the joint product of these brothers, just as certain hymns already
mentioned are, in their present form, the joint product of Watts and John Wesley.

But his most important contributions to hymnology were made in the form of translations. His eminent mission was to bring the spiritual hymns of the
Moravians, and the French and German Pietists and
Mystics, into the English tongue, and so into the
hearts of his followers. In them was struck the key-
note of Christian experience for himself and his
people. Among the most potent and stimulating influences which have ever come to the English churches
are the hymns of such men as Gerhardt, Tersteegen,
the Langes, Rothe, Winkler, Spangenberg, and Zinzendorf, and to them Methodism owes much of the
vigor and fervor of her spiritual life.

Considered as translations these hymns are worthy
of high praise. Clear, accurate, dignified, poetic in

diction, and forcible in style, they are, in their way, models. We read and sing them with no feeling that they were written in another language than ours. The only objection which can lie against them is as to the meter, which is in octo-syllabled lines; arranged, for the most part, six lines to a stanza, giving one of the heaviest meters ever employed in religious poetry, and one for which it is exceedingly difficult to find suitable music.

The following is a list of the principal translations of Mr. Wesley, which are still kept as hymns in the congregations:

O God, of good the unfathomed sea.	*Scheffler.*
I thank thee, Uncreated Sun.	"
O God, thou bottomless abyss.	*E. Lange.*
Thine, Lord, is wisdom, thine alone.	"
O God, what offering shall I give?	*J. Lange.*
Now I have found the ground wherein.	*Rothe.*
Though waves and storms go o'er my head.	"
My soul before thee prostrate lies.	*Richter.*
Thou Lamb of God, thou Prince of Peace.	"
Eternal depth of love divine.	*Zinzendorf.*
Jesus, thy blood and righteousness.	"
I thirst, thou wounded Lamb of God.	"
Extended on a cursed tree.	*Gerhardt.*
Jesus, thy boundless love to me.	"
Commit thou all thy griefs.	"
Give to the winds thy fears.	"

Into thy gracious hands I fall.	*Dessler.*
Thou hidden love of God, whose height.	*Tersteegen.*
O Thou, to whose all-searching sight.	"
O Thou, who all things canst control.	"
Lo! God is here! Let us adore.	"
Holy Lamb, who thee receive.	*Mrs. A. S. Dober.*
High on his everlasting throne.	*Spangenberg.*
Shall I, for fear of feeble man.	*Winkler.*
Savior of men, thy searching eye.	"
O Lord, within thy sacred gate.	*From the Spanish.*
Come, Savior, Jesus, from above.	*Mad. Bourignon.*[1]

The following original hymns are from his pen:

Father of all, whose powerful voice.

Ho! every one that thirsts, draw nigh.

O Sun of righteousness, arise.

Ye simple souls, that stray.

We lift our hearts to thee,

How happy is the pilgrim's lot![2]

Of these the last is the most autobiographic. Indeed, some of the verses are so exactly suited to Mr. Wesley as to be quite unsuited for the use of average mortals. Take, for instance, these of the original, which, for very manifest reasons, are not found in the hymn-books:

> "I have no sharer of my heart
> To rob my Savior of a part,
> And desecrate the whole;
> Only betrothed to Christ am I,
> And wait his coming in the sky,
> To wed my happy soul.

> I have no babes to hold me here,
> But children more securely dear
> For mine, I humbly claim;
> Better than daughters or than sons,
> Temples divine of living stones,
> Inscribed with Jesu's name."

Seldom has good poetry been used with such dismal effect as in these lines. We can not fail to recognize here the dark shadow of that most fallacious and pernicious doctrine of priestly celibacy. There is an evident implication that a man may be a better Christian and a better minister for being childless and unmarried. As we read these verses we can not repress a feeling of pity, not so much for the loneliness of the writer's lot—without "babes" and without a "sharer of his heart"—but because he seems to find in these essentially abnormal conditions matter for self-gratulation. There is, however, a half-truth in all this, and the complementary truth Mr. Wesley sets forth in other places in his writings most clearly and forcibly.

But the great name in Christian hymnody, contributed by the Wesley family, is that of Charles Wesley (1708–1788). He wrote more hymns—and we will add, more good hymns—than any other ten men who have written hymns in the English language. Watts wrote less than seven hundred, Doddridge less than four hundred, Montgomery less than two hundred, while Charles Wesley wrote from seven to eight thousand! Of course some of these are such as not even his most ardent admirers can find much pleasure in reading, but others exhibit a wealth and beauty of lyrical expression truly marvelous. A prominent actor in the most important evangelical movement since the days of the apostles, his hymns have the rare merit of reflecting every significant phase of that movement; so that if the question be asked to-day, What is Methodism as a creed, an experience, a life?—a more adequate answer can be found in these hymns than anywhere else, not excepting the Sermons of John Wesley or the Institutes of Richard Watson. It has been said: "Let him who would form a good English style give his days and nights to the study of Addison." With more propriety may it be said: "Let him who would understand that wonderful movement called Methodism, and especially him who would enter into and partake of its life—who would feel the thrill and glow and exhilaration so characteristic of it—give his days and nights to the study of the hymns of Charles Wesley." Next to the New Testament itself, they are the best body of experimental divinity ever written. No man can sing them heartily and habitually, "with the spirit and the understanding also," without coming to a just and discriminating sense of the real genius of Methodism.

In unusual measure these hymns bear the stamp of the author's personal history and experience. Even his letters to her who afterwards became his wife were often written in verse; and when we remember that he was at this time a clergyman, forty years of age, and leading a most active and laborious life, we shall realize how absolutely irrepressible his poetic proclivities must have been. Among the best known of his hymns are such as the following:

Jesus, lover of my soul.

O for a thousand tongues to sing.

A charge to keep I have.

Stay, thou insulted Spirit, stay!

Jesus, the name high over all.

How happy every child of grace.

Come, O thou Traveler unknown.

Stand the omnipotent decree.

Depth of mercy! can there be?

Arise, my soul, arise.

And must I be to judgment brought?

Love divine, all love excelling.

Light of those whose dreary dwelling.

Come on, my partners in distress.

Lo! He comes, with clouds descending.

Forever here my rest shall be.

Blow ye the trumpet, blow.

Soldiers of Christ, arise!

Thou God of glorious majesty.

And am I only born to die?

Come, thou Almighty King.

O Love divine, how sweet thou art!

Thou Shepherd of Israel, and mine.

Vain, delusive world, adieu!

Hark! the herald angels sing.

See how great a flame aspires.[1]

This list might easily be extended so as to embrace
as many more which are generally familiar and dear
to the heart of the universal church, but these will
serve as illustrative specimens. The Wesleyan Hymn-
book of Great Britain contains six hundred and
twenty-seven of his hymns, and many others are met
with, scattered through the various hymnals of other
denominations. Robert Southey says of them that
they have been "more devoutly committed to memory," and "oftener repeated on a death-bed," than
any others. But life is a more just and adequate test
than death, and with even more emphasis may it be
said that no hymns have ministered to the wants of
the human soul, in the great crises of spiritual history,
more frequently or more helpfully than these. We
hear among them voices for all phases and grades of
spiritual experience, and all forms of Christian work—
awakening conviction, penitence, pardon, assurance ;
rejoicing in sins forgiven, in communion with God,
in prospect of heaven ; the closet, the family, the
church ; evangelistic work, charitable work, reform
work,—everything which lies between the fearful ruin
wrought by sin and the glorious consummation of the
work of human recovery. Every condition in life,
every occupation, and almost every event, is here
represented. Among his general captions we find :
"Hymns for Watch-Nights," "New-Year's Day,"
"The Lord's Supper," "The Nativity of Our Lord,"
"Our Lord's Resurrection," "Hymns Occasioned by
the Earthquake," "Hymns for Times of Trouble and
Persecution," "Hymns for Methodist Preachers,"
"Hymns for the Use of Families," "Hymns for

Children," "Prayers for Condemned Malefactors,"
"Hymns for the Nation," "Funeral Hymns," etc.
Among the titles of individual hymns are such as
these: "For a Family in Want," "To be Sung at
Tea-table," "For a Persecuting Husband," "At Sending a Child to a Boarding-school," "A Collier's
Hymn," "For an Unconverted Wife," "For One
Retired into the Country," "A Wedding-song," "On
Going to Work;" and the more common captions,
such as "For Sabbath," "Bereavement," "Sleep,"
"Morning and Evening." To many a devout Methodist these hymns have been, as indeed they are suited
to be, "the key of the morning and the bolt of the
night." Indeed these hymns, beautiful and felicitous
as they often are in the mere matter of expression,
seldom seem like mere words, but like "a heart poured
out into a heart—a child-like, dependent human heart
into the great, infinite, tender heart of God." Of
this Bishop Wordsworth complains, and even finds
such sensuous and amatory suggestions in "Jesus,
lover of my soul," as to be shocked to hear it given
out in a promiscuous congregation, gathered from the
poor and sinful in a great city; but it may be safely
said that right-minded persons are more shocked at
the criticism than the hymn. This warm, glowing,
seraphic quality in Wesley's hymns is their grand,
distinguishing characteristic, and the one reason why
they will ever be placed, by many, above all other
uninspired compositions.

Their influence is well illustrated in that exceedingly choice, if not the very choicest of Mrs. Charles's
books—"The Diary of Mrs. Kitty Trevylyan." One

of her characters had been a poor, ignorant, and desperately wicked Cornish wrecker, but had been reached by the evangelists and brought to Christ, and is made to tell his story in this way :

" ' Yes, missis, my sin is the same, I think. I hate it more ; it 's seldom out of my sight. King David says, " My sin is ever before me;" and I find him pretty right. And the eyes of the living Lord are on me, searching me through and through, seems to me deeper and deeper 'most every day ; and I can 't avoid them any more than I could ; but, thank the Lord, *I do n't want to.* There 's the difference—I do n't want to. I would n't be out of the sight of his eyes for the world.'

" ' And what helped you thus at last ?' said mother.

" ' It was mostly the hymns,' said Toby ; ' first the Bible, then mostly the hymns; for they are the Bible for the most part, only set to music, like, so that it rings in your heart like a tune. It was the hymns, and what they said at the class-meeting. Before I went to the class, and heard what they had to say there, I thought I was all alone, like a castaway on a sandy shore, under a great sheer wall of cliffs; a narrow strip of sand, which no mortal man had ever trod before, and which the tide was fast sweeping over, bit by bit. To spell out the hymns in the book by myself was like finding foot-prints on the sands, and that was something. It made me feel my trouble was no madness, as poor mother called it; no mad dream, but waking up from the maddest dream that could be. It made me see that others had felt as I felt, and struggled as I was struggling, and had *got*

through! But when I went to the class, and heard them
sing the hymns, it was like hearing voices on the top
of the cliffs, cheering me up and pointing out the
way. Our class-leader is no great speaker, but he
has got a wonderful feeling heart, and a fine voice for
the hymns, and it's they that has finished Parson
Wesley's work and healed the wound he made:

> "Depth of mercy! can there be
> Mercy still reserved for me?"

That was the first that settled down in my heart. I
could n't listen any further, and I could n't get that
out of my head for days, until another took its place—

> "Jesus, let thy pitying eye
> Call back a wandering sheep;
> False to thee, like Peter, I
> Would fain like Peter weep.
> Let me be by grace restored;
> On me be all long-suffering shown;
> Turn, and look upon me, Lord,
> And break my heart of stone!
>
> For thine own compassion's sake,
> The gracious wonder show;
> Cast my sins behind thy back,
> And wash me white as snow.
> If thy bowels now are stirred,
> If now I do myself bemoan,
> Turn, and look upon me, Lord,
> And break my heart of stone!
>
> Look, as when thy languid eye
> Was closed, that we might live —
> 'Father' (at the point to die
> My Savior gasped), 'forgive!'
> Surely, with that dying word,
> He turns, and looks, and cries, ' 'T is done!'
> O my bleeding, loving Lord,
> Thou break'st my heart of stone.' "

"That hymn, Toby said, seemed to put a new picture in his heart. Instead of the pale face of the poor lad, lying lifeless on the sands, which had lately haunted him night and day, another countenance rose before him, pale and all but lifeless, but with the hollow eyes, large with pain, fixed in the tenderest pity on him. He understood that "God was in Christ reconciling the world unto himself." He felt that it was the face of the Judge that looked so tenderly on him from the cross; that suffering, beyond any he had ever dreaded, had been borne for him by the Lord himself—made sin for him. And he felt that he was forgiven.

"Then all day his heart seemed bursting with the joy of reconciliation, and he was singing—

> 'Thee will I love, my joy, my crown;
>   Thee will I love, my Lord, my God;
>   Thee will I love, beneath thy frown
>   Or smile, thy scepter or thy rod;
>   What though my flesh and heart decay;
>   Thee shall I love in endless day.'

Everywhere that dying face of his Savior seemed beaming on him in the fullness of pity and love, and those words—''T is done! Father, forgive!'—filled all the world with music. He could see or hear nothing else.

"'And now?' said mother.

"'Now, missis,' said Toby, 'I see all things once more as they are; but it seems as if everything were changed inwardly, though the outside is the same. The curse is taken out of every thing. Even that poor, dead lad's face, I see it now, and I am not afeared. For it seems to say: "Not to me, Toby, it's too late, I want nothing; not to me, but to all the rest, for my sake." And the two faces seem to get mixed up in my mind, Missis—the poor, drowned lad's and HIS—and still the words the dumb lips speak are the same: "Not to me; all is well with me; but to all the rest for my sake." And that,' concluded Toby, 'is what I live in hopes it will be given me to do before I die.'

"'How, Toby?'

"'Why, Missis,' he said, 'I watch for the wrecks more than ever I did in old time. I watch for the crews as I never watched for the cargoes. And one of these days it is my belief the Lord will give me to save some of them, and to see some poor, lifeless souls wake up to life again up there by mother's fire. And then I shall feel those two faces smiling on me up in heaven—the poor, drowned lad's, missis, and the blessed Lord's himself. And that will be reward enough for an angel, let alone that an angel could never know the shame, and the sin, and the bitter reproaches in my heart, that makes it like heaven to me to dare to look up in his face at all.'"

One of the most notable of Charles Wesley's hymns is that known as "Wrestling Jacob"—beginning, "Come, O thou Traveler unknown." The testimony of Watts in its favor has already been quoted. John Wesley indicated his own estimate of this testimony by incorporating it into the biographical notice of his brother, in the Minutes of the conference, at the time of his death. Dean Trench says of it: "Though not eminently adapted for liturgic use, it is yet quite the

noblest of Charles Wesley's hymns." Considered as a
poetical composition, this opinion might be generally
acquiesced in ; but considered as a hymn, this can by no
means be true. It neither belongs to the highest class
of Christian hymns, nor does it satisfy the highest
conditions of utility. It is by no means from the
mere accident of being without music well suited for
popular use that it is so seldom heard, even in the
social meetings, but because it is not well suited to
answer the purpose of a hymn. But its eminent
Scripturalness, its deep spirituality, its felicity of
style, its vividness, and its thoroughly sustained interest from beginning to end, bear eloquent testimony
to the wonderful genius of the author.

Robert Southey pronounces "Stand the omnipotent decree " "the finest lyric in the English language;"
but if the judgment of those who have made much
use of the Wesleyan hymns—and so have made up
their judgment by the test of experience rather than
of literary taste—is of any value, there are many finer
among the hymns of Mr. Wesley.

The hymn "O for a thousand tongues to sing"—
which has, from the first, occupied the place of honor
in the Methodist hymn-books of Great Britain and
America—was written on the first anniversary of his
spiritual birth, and so is, doubtless in an eminent degree, the outpouring of his own rapturous emotions.

> "Come away to the skies, my beloved, arise,
>   And rejoice in the day thou wast born ;"

and

> "Come, let us ascend, my companion and friend,
>   To a taste of the banquet above,"

were both addressed to his wife on her birthday.[1]

But beyond question the most popular, if not the most famous, of Charles Wesley's hymns is "Jesus, lover of my soul." Says Henry Ward Beecher: "I would rather have written that hymn than to have the fame of all the kings that ever sat on the earth. . . . It will go on singing until the last trump brings forth the angel-band; and then, I think, will mount up on some lip to the very presence of God." The last indication of life that Dr. Lyman Beecher gave was his mute response to his wife, as she repeated:

> "Jesus, lover of my soul,
> Let me to thy bosom fly."

"Two lines of this hymn," says Rev. Theodore L. Cuyler, "have been breathed fervently and often out of bleeding hearts. When we were once in the valley of death-shade, with one beautiful child in the new-made grave and the other threatened with fatal disease, there was no prayer which we said oftener than this—

> ' Leave, O leave me not alone!
> Still support and comfort me !'

We do not doubt that tens of thousands of other bereaved and wounded hearts have tried this piercing cry out of the depths."

To Margaret Wilson, the Scotch martyr, the terms of this hymn had a most apposite application, and to her was the prayer of this hymn most blessedly and eminently fulfilled. A young woman of eighteen, she had been informed against as a Covenanter, and was condemned to die by being fastened to a stake, where the slowly rising tide would come over her. To try her constancy still more severely, an older woman

was also fastened to a stake still lower down, in order
that the sight of her death-agonies might move Margaret. As the waters rose, and she saw her aged
companion wrestling with death, the heartless men
asked Margaret: " What do you see there?"   " I see,"
said Margaret, unmoved, " Christ suffering there. Do
you think we are the sufferers?   No, it is Christ in us;
for he sends none on a warfare upon his own charges."
She then chanted the Twenty-fifth Psalm, beginning—

> " Let not the errors of my youth,
>   Nor sins, remembered be ;
>   In mercy, for thy goodness' sake,
>   O Lord, remember me."

Afterward she repeated, with a cheerful voice, the
eighth chapter of Romans, ending : " For I am per-
suaded that neither death, nor life, nor angels, nor
principalities, nor powers, nor things present, nor
things to come, nor height, nor depth, nor any other
creature, shall be able to separate us from the love
of God, which is in Christ Jesus, my Lord."   And
then, as she was commending her soul to God in
prayer, the waters of the dark and solemn sea closed
over her.   She had found in Christ's bosom a refuge
from the nearer waters of earthly danger and death.

Several accounts have been given of the origin of
this hymn, but all are of more than doubtful authen-
ticity. The most elaborate and interesting of these
is given in Rev. Edwin M. Long's " History of the
Hymns," and of it Mr. Long says : " These interesting facts were given by Mr. Pilmore, who was an eye-
witness, to an intimate friend, Mr. Hicks, who stated
them to Rev. I. H. Torrence, of Philadelphia, from

whom l received them. The same statement was also
previously given to me by the aged Rev. Dr. Collier,
who received it from an Englishman, who was contemporary with Wesley." The story is this:

"Charles and John Wesley and Richard Pilmore were
holding one of their twilight meetings on the common, when
the mob assailed them, and they were compelled to flee for
their lives. Being separated for a time, as they were being
pelted with stones, they at length, in their flight, succeeded in
getting beyond a hedge-row, where they prostrated themselves
on the ground, and placed their hands on the back of their
heads for protection from the stones, which still came so near
that they could feel the current of air made by the missiles as
they went whizzing over them. In the night-shades that were
gathering, they managed to hide from the fury of the rabble
in a spring-house. Here they struck a light with a flint-stone,
and after dusting their clothes and washing, they refreshed
themselves with the cooling water that came bubbling up in
a spring, and rolling out in a silver streamlet. Charles Wesley
pulled out a lead pencil—made by hammering to a point a
piece of lead—and from the inspiration of these surroundings,
composed the precious hymn." [2]

One of the most solemn and impressive of all these
hymns of Charles Wesley reflects the scenery of
Land's End, even more vividly than do any of
Watts's that of Southampton. The second verse of
the hymn "Thou God of glorious majesty" reads as
follows:

> " Lo! on a narrow neck of land,
> 'Twixt two unbounded seas, I stand
> Secure, insensible;
> A point of time, a moment's space,
> Removes me to that heavenly place,
> Or shuts me up in hell."

The hymn above mentioned as praised by Southey—
"Stand the omnipotent decree"—doubtless derives

much of its special interest and impressiveness in that it was written "For the Year 1756"—a time when men were appalled by the terrible calamity of the great Lisbon earthquake. Read in the light of this fearful catastrophe, the sublimity of its almost unequaled utterances is fully evident:

> "Stand the omnipotent decree;
> Jehovah's will be done;
> Nature's end we wait to see,
> And hear her final groan.
> Let this earth dissolve, and blend
> In death the wicked and the just;
> Let those ponderous orbs descend,
> And grind us into dust!
>
> Rests secure the righteous man;
> At his Redeemer's beck,
> Sure to emerge, and rise again,
> And mount above the wreck.
> Lo! the heavenly spirit towers,
> Like flames o'er nature's funeral pyre;
> Triumphs in immortal powers,
> And claps his wings of fire.
>
> Nothing hath the just to lose,
> By worlds on worlds destroyed;
> Far beneath his feet he views,
> With smiles, the flaming void;
> Sees this universe renewed,
> The grand, millennial reign begun;
> Shouts, with all the sons of God,
> Around the eternal throne."

> Come, let us join our friends above,

was a special favorite with John Wesley. It is the concluding part of what was originally a long poem of more than a hundred lines; which poem has been divided into four hymns, which, in the Methodist

Hymnal, are made to follow each other in proper order. The part commencing,

Come, let us join our friends above,

is a tender and beautiful tribute to the memory of the pious dead. One of the most tender traditions of the later years of John Wesley is that which represents him as having, on one occasion, come to the chapel at City Roads, where he was to preach that evening; and as the shades of the evening were gathering around him, standing with his head bowed on his hand, as if holding communion with the invisible world; and then giving out this hymn, in which he seemed to gather up the precious memories which bound him to the first band of heroic workers, of which he was then almost the sole survivor:

"Come, let us join our friends above,
  That have obtained the prize,
And on the eagle-wings of love
  To joys celestial rise. . . .

One family we dwell in Him;
  One church above, beneath,
Though now divided by the stream,
  The narrow stream of death.
One army of the living God,
  To his command we bow;
Part of his host have crossed the flood,
  And part are crossing now.

Our old companions in distress,
  We haste again to see;
And eager long for our release,
  And full felicity.
E'en now, by faith, we join our hands
  With those that went before;
And greet the blood-besprinkled bands
  On the eternal shore."

ADDITIONAL NOTES.

BY THE EDITOR.

CHAPTER I.

(1) Dr. Schaff says that the number of German hymns can not fall short of 100,000. Dean George Ludvig von Hardenberg, of Halberstadt, in 1786, prepared a catalogue of first lines of 72,733 hymns, and the number, not completed then, has been greatly increased since.

(2) Of these two hymns, the first was composed for his wife's twenty-ninth birthday, October, 12, 1755; the second seems to have been generally "for Christian friends," and appeared in the author's "Hymns and Sacred Poems," 1749. It was of this latter hymn that the saintly Fletcher said: "When the triumphal chariot of perfect love gloriously carries you to the top of perfection's hill; when you are raised far above the common heights of the perfect; when you are almost translated into glory, like Elijah,—then you may sing this hymn."

(3) Composed during a solitary walk in the field, when the poet was tortured by an apprehension of returning madness. It was the last he ever wrote for the famous Olney collection.

(4) Part of the hymn found in the Olney collection, entitled "Looking at the Cross," and beginning—

> "In evil, long I took delight,
> Unawed by shame or fear,
> Till a new object struck my sight,
> And stopped my wild career."

(5) A selection from a poem of ten stanzas, entitled "Desiring Resignation and Thankfulness," the first stanza of which is—

> "When I survey life's varied scene,
> Amid the darkest hours,
> Sweet rays of comfort shine between,
> And thorns are mixed with flowers."

(6) From the Evening Hymn in the "Christian Year." The original has fourteen stanzas, of which the third, seventh,

278

eighth, and last three verses, are usually given in hymn collections.

(7) This, one of Wesley's hymns for children, is given entire in the Methodist Hymnal, No. 968, and begins, "And am I only born to die?" Two stanzas are here omitted.

CHAPTER II.

(1) "Poesy is of so subtle a spirit that, in pouring of one language into another, it will evaporate."—DENHAM.

(2) The Trisagion is said to have been first introduced into the Liturgy in the reign of the younger Theodosius (408–450), but it is probably much older. Tradition has it that it was supernaturally communicated to the terror-stricken population of Constantinople during an earthquake of St. Proclus (A. D. 434).

(3) The *Gloria* consisted originally of the few words in Luke ii, 14, to which subsequent additions were made—first in the Greek, then in the Latin church—until, in the fifth century, it is found substantially as in use to-day.

(4) There is a legend to the effect that Ambrose composed and sang the *Te Deum* by inspiration, when he baptized Augustine; also, that they sang it responsively. This latter suggestion has been poetically wrought out by Mrs. Margaret J. Preston, in "The First *Te Deum*" (see her "Colonial Ballads," 1887). It is generally believed to be a composite of some Greek morning hymns and metrical renderings of Scriptural passages.

(5) Farrar (Lives of the Fathers, I, 278) doubts the genuineness of this hymn, claiming that, while it is beautiful and interesting, it probably belongs to a later age.

(6) This version is found in the Methodist Hymnal, No. 885.

(7) The author mentions a dozen others by title, one of which deserves more than passing notice; namely, "Redeemer of the nations, come!" Dr. Schaff calls this the best of the Ambrosian hymns, full of faith, rugged vigor, austere simplicity, and bold contrasts. We subjoin the first and last stanzas (of seven) in Dr. Ray Palmer's translation:

> "O Thou, Redeemer of our race!
> Come, show the Virgin's Son to earth;

> Let every age admire the grace ;
> Worthy a God thy human birth !
>
> .   .   .   .   .   .
>
> With light divine thy manger streams,
> That kindles darkness into day ;
> Dimmed by no night henceforth, its beams
> Shine through all time with changeless ray."

The translation by John Franck, Trench calls one of the choicest treasures of the German hymn-book, and Bunsen says it is "even deeper and lovelier than the Latin." See *Lyra Germanica*, First Series, page 186.

(8) *Confessions*, ix, 6. " How greatly did I weep in thy hymns and canticles, deeply moved by the voices of thy sweet-speaking church ! The voices flowed into mine ears, and the truth was poured forth into my heart, whence the agitation of my piety overflowed, and my tears ran over, and blessed was I therein."

(9) Confessions, ix, 7.

CHAPTER III.

(1) The original is still in use in the Roman church, being sung on Good Friday, during the procession in which the consecrated host is carried to the altar. This hymn is selected as one of "the seven great hymns of the medieval church" by the editor of a work bearing that name, and published by A. D. F. Randolph & Co., New York.

(2) This famous hymn is said by Rev. John Ellerton, the translator, to be, with the same author's "Crux benedicta nitet," the earliest instance of elegiac verse in Christian song. The transfusion of Ellerton's, which finds a place in the hymn collections, is in a different measure from the original, which runs :

> " Salve festa dies, toto venerabilis aevo,
> Qua Deus infernum vicit, et astra tenet,
> Salve festa dies, toto venerabilis aevo."

Throughout the poem the first two lines of this verse form the third line of the other verses alternately. The festal day referred to is Easter.

(3) Besides Charlemagne and Gregory, the authorship has been claimed for Rabanus, archbishop of Mayence (776–856).

Dryden's version in English has been commended by Warton as "a most elegant and beautiful little morsel, and one of his most correct compositions." It opens:

> "Creator Spirit, by whose aid
> The world's foundations first were laid,
> Come, visit every pious mind;
> Come, pour thy joys on human kind;
> From sin and sorrow set us free,
> And make thy temples worthy thee."

(4) The translation by Ray Palmer is found in the Methodist Hymnal, No. 284. Miss Winkworth furnishes a translation of this hymn from the German for the "Lyra Germanica," which, according to competent authority, is a finer translation than any that professes to be from the Latin. We give the second and third stanzas:

> "Come, Father of the poor, to earth;
> Come, with thy gifts of precious worth;
> Come, Light of all of mortal birth!
>
> Thou rich in comfort! Ever blest
> The heart where thou art constant guest,
> Who giv'st the heavy-laden rest."

(5) See Methodist Hymnal, No. 1047, where it has been considerably altered. Dr. Neale, the translator, thinks it "extremely pretty" as a song, but not intended for Church use.

(6) Methodist Hymnal, No. 230. It is still in use in the Greek church, and Neale, in his "Hymns of the Eastern Church" (p. 92), quotes a graphic account of the celebration in which it is sung.

CHAPTER IV.

(1) The hymns of Bernard, cited here, are all in the Methodist Hymnal, the second and fourth being especial favorites with our people. "Of him who did salvation bring" was, at one time, credited to Charles Wesley; the matter and style of the poem bewraying, as was thought, the Wesleyan genius. It was discovered afterwards in a book of translations by A. W. Boehm (1673-1722), and has since been properly assigned. "Jesus, the very thought of thee," has been denominated "the sweetest and most evangelical (as the *Dies Iræ* is the grandest,

19

and the *Stabat Mater* the most pathetic) hymn of the Middle Ages." Trench, selecting fifteen of the forty-eight or fifty quatrains for his "Latin Poetry," remarks: "Where all was beautiful, the task of selecting was a hard one."

(2) For the benefit of Latin scholars we subjoin the text:

> "Sicut chorda musicorum
> Tandem sonum dat sonorum
> Plectri ministerio,
> Sic in chely tormentorum
> Melos Christi confessorum
> Martyris dat tensio.
>
> Parum sapis vim sinapis,
> Si non tangis, si non frangis;
> Et plus fragrat, quando flagrat,
> Tus injectum ignibus:
> Sic arctatus et assatus,
> Sub ardore, sub labore,
> Dat odorem pleniorem
> Martyr de virtutibus."

(3) The late Rev. S. W. Duffield essayed a translation, preserving the original measure, thus—

> "These are the latter times; these are not better times;
> 　　Let us stand waiting;
> Lo! how, with awfulness, He, first in lawfulness,
> 　　Comes arbitrating."

(4) Of the Stabat Mater (Dolorosa) Dr. Schaff says: "It is the most pathetic . . . hymn of the Middle Ages, and occupies second rank in Latin hymnology. Suggested by the incident related in John xix, 25, and the prophecy of Simeon (Luke ii, 35), it describes, with overpowering effect, the piercing agony of Mary at the cross, and the burning desire to be identified with her, by sympathy, in the intensity of her grief. It furnished the text for the noblest musical compositions of Palestrina, Pergolesi, Haydn, and others. . . . The soft, sad melody of its verse is untranslatable."

(5) The Stabat Mater (Speciosa) was brought to public notice through the researches of A. F. Ozanam (1852), and introduced more particularly to American readers by Dr. Philip Schaff, in an article in "Hours at Home," May, 1867.

The question of authorship is not settled, and Dr. Coles argues a twofold authorship of the hymns from internal evidence.

[6] Quoted from Mrs. Charles's "Voice of Christian Life in Song," one of the most scholarly and interesting works on the subject of hymnology.

CHAPTER V.

[1] Methodist Hymnal, No. 911. The two martyrs referred to are Henry Voes and John Esch, whose martyrdom took place in 1523. After the fires were kindled, they repeated the Apostles' Creed, sang the "*Te Deum*," and prayed in the flames: "Jesus, thou Son of David, have mercy upon us!" The original poem consists of twelve nine-line stanzas, and begins—

> " Ein neues Lied wir heben an."

The tenth stanza is the basis of the hymn quoted. Professor Bayne, in his recent Life of Luther, speaks of it as a "ballad—rugged, indeed, and with little grace or ornament of composition, but tingling, every line of it, with sincerity and intensity." The meter is preserved in the following:

> " With joy they stepped into the flame,
>   God's praises calmly singing.
> Strange pangs of rage, amazement, shame
>   The sophists' hearts are wringing;
> For God they feel is here."

[2] Methodist Hymnal, No. 166. The imagery of the hymn is derived from the forty-sixth Psalm. The hymn has commonly been assigned to 1529; but the recent discovery of a print dating apparently from February, 1528, has led Köstlin to assign the hymn to 1527, the year of the pestilence, and of Luther's severest spiritual and physical trials. Dr. Bayne says of Luther's hymns: "It may be said generally that they are characterized by a rugged but fundamentally melodious rhythm, a piercing intensity and expressiveness, with tender, lovely, picturesque touches here and there. Above all, they are sincere. They seem to thrill with an intensity of feeling beyond their power of expression, like the glistening of stars whose silence speaks of God."

[3] Methodist Hymnal, No. 569. The authorship of this hymn was long ascribed to Altenburg, a pastor in Thuringia; but recent researches, according to Miss Winkworth, have

made it clear that he only composed the chorale, and that the hymn itself was written down roughly by Gustavus himself, after his victory at Leipsic, and reduced to regular verse by his chaplain, Dr. Fabricius, for the use of the army.

(4) Translated by Miss Winkworth in "Lyra Germanica," second series, beginning, "Now lay me calmly in the grave."

(5) Methodist Hymnal, No. 694. The translation consists of eleven stanzas.

(6) Interesting and beautiful as the story is, it has to be said that Gerhard's ministry did not close in Berlin until 1667, and that the hymn was in existence in 1666. Kubler says it was first published in 1659.

(7) Methodist Hymnal, Nos. 119, 478. It is said that most of Scheffler's hymns were written before he entered the Roman communion. Schultze, a German missionary in Madras, in 1722, translated Scheffler's "Liebe, die der mich zum Bilde" into Tamil for his people, and it so delighted them that he translated more than one hundred of the best German hymns for their use, and they are still sung in South India.

(8) Miss Winkworth says: "His hymns have great beauty, and bespeak a tranquil and child-like soul, filled and blessed with the contemplation of God."

(9) Zinzendorf was a prolific writer. He is said to have composed about two thousand hymns, many of which were produced extemporaneously. The Brethren took them down and preserved them. Zinzendorf says of them, in speaking of his services at Berlin: "After the discourse, I generally announce another hymn appropriate. When I can not find one, I compose one; I say, in the Savior's name, what comes into my heart." Quoted by Josiah Miller.

(10) Methodist Hymnal, No. 1086. For an account of his life and criticism of his style, see Longfellow's "Poets and Poetry of Europe," p. 267.

(11) Methodist Hymnal, Nos. 755, 1010. The original of this last hymn was sung at the grave of the author when he was buried. A favorite pastime with Dr. Spitta was to sing in the evening, with his two daughters, hymns and tunes of his own composing, and so attractive was this performance that crowds were wont to gather at his window to listen.

(12) Methodist Hymnal, No. 993. This hymn was used at the funeral of the translator, Dr. Bethune, who died in 1862.

[13] The German version is by Albert Knapp: "Nein, nein, das ist kein Sterben." Duffield ("English Hymns") intimates that Malan's hymn was a version of Knapp's, and not, as Dr. Hemenway implies (whose view is also Dr. Schaff's, see "Gesangbuch" and "Christ in Song"), the other way.

CHAPTER VI.

[1] Methodist Hymnal, No. 152. The second verse of the hymn, as written by Sternhold, was:

> "On cherubs and on cherubims
> Full royally he rode,
> And on the wings of all the winds
> Came flying all abroad."

Duffield says it is related of the learned Scaliger—whether father or son is not stated—that he would rather have been the author of this stanza than to have written his own works.

[2] Methodist Hymnal, No. 11. This was the first British composition to which the tune "Old Hundred" was united, and, as is seen, gave its own name to the tune. The authorship is contested, Duffield, in his "English Hymns," assigning it to John Hopkins, who, with Sternhold, Kethe, and others, published a rendering of the Psalms.

[3] Methodist Hymnal, No. 156. Under the persecution of James VI., six ministers were banished for their independence of the Establishment, and were taken to Leith for embarkation. On the shore the parting from friends and dear ones was most touching. All joined in singing this psalm according to the quaint version, two verses of which are:

> "He doth me fold in cotes most safe,
> The tender grass fast by;
> And after driv'th me to the streams
> Which run most pleasantly.
>
> .   .   .   .
>
> And though I were even at death's door,
> Yet would I fear none ill;
> For by thy rod and shepherd's crook,
> I am comforted still."

[4] See Chapter III.

[5] The hymn "How are thy servants blest, O Lord!" is usually called the "Traveler's Hymn." It was composed on shipboard during a terrific storm, in which all was given up for

lost. While the captain, in terror, was confessing his sins to a Capuchin friar, Addison was solacing himself with the composition of this song of praise and trust.

[6] Methodist Hymnal, No. 669. This is part of a poem of eight double stanzas, beginning, " My whole, though broken, heart, O Lord," and entitled, "The Covenant and Confidence of Faith." It has this note appended: "This covenant my dear wife, in her former sickness, subscribed with a cheerful will. Job xii, 26." The hymn was a favorite with the eminent scientist Clerk Maxwell, who frequently repeated it during his last illness.

[7] Methodist Hymnal, No. 268. Considerably altered, and for the better, by John Wesley.

[8] Methodist Hymnal, No. 666. The first verse originally stood:

> "Shall Simon bear thy cross alone,
> And other saints be free?
> Each saint of thine shall find his own,
> And there is one for me."

[9] Methodist Hymnal, No. 969. For an interesting account of the evolution of this hymn, see article by Rev. C. S. Nutter, author of " Hymn Studies," in New York *Christian Advocate* of August 26, 1886.

[10] Methodist Hymnal, No. 1044. The hymn has been traced to the collection of " Williams and Boden " (1801), where it is credited to the *Eckington Collection.* Duffield conjectures that as Rev. James Boden, one of the editors, lived and died near Eckington, Yorkshire, this may have been his version of "F. B. P.'s" hymn. For a fine critical and historical sketch of this famous hymn see W. C. Prime's monograph, " O mother dear, Jerusalem " (New York, 3d edition, 1865). The Latin hymn referred to as given by Daniel (*Thesaurus Hymnologicus*) consists of forty-eight lines, and begins:

> Urbs beata Ierusalem dicta pacis visio.

The " F. B. P." version, as given by Dr. Bonar, opens:

> " Hierusalem, my happy home,
> When shall I come to thee?
> When shall my sorrows have an end?
> Thy joys when shall I see?"

and contains twenty-six stanzas.

CHAPTER VII.

Page 5. [1] It is only proper to state that the assignment of this hymn to that occasion is based upon a tradition which, according to Dr. E. F. Hatfield, an authority on the subject, "is probably founded on the fact that the hymn appears as No. 1 of his first book."

[2] Dean Stanley, however, said of the same composition: "It is not only a hymn but a philosophical poem, disfigured, indeed, in parts by the anatomical allusions to the shrunk sinew, but filled, on the whole, with a depth and pathos which might well excite Watts to say that 'it was worth all the verses he himself had written,' and induce Montgomery to compare it to the action of a lyrical drama."

CHAPTER VIII.

[3] See Chapter I, and note.

[4] The late Mr. George John Stevenson, of London, and one of the best informed Wesleyan hymnologists, entirely discredits this story as of "pure Yankee invention." There is certainly nothing in the hymn itself to indicate that the incident, if it had any existence at all, inspired the song. The hymn is found in "Hymns and Sacred Poems," 1740; bears the title, "In Temptation," and has five verses. The third verse, usually omitted from collections, runs:

> " Wilt thou not regard my call?
> Wilt thou not accept my prayer?
> Lo! I sink, I faint, I fall!
> Lo! on thee I cast my care!
> Reach me out thy gracious hand,
> While I of thy strength receive;
> Hoping against hope, I stand—
> Dying, and behold I live;"

and hints that the Scriptural suggestion is Matt. xiv, 28, *seq.* In temper and treatment the hymn is eminently contemplative and subjective, the very opposite of which might be expected from the spring-house episode.

Lectures and Sermons.

EDITED BY

REV. A. W. PATTEN, D. D.

INTRODUCTORY NOTE.

OUT of the great number of Dr. Hemenway's lectures, sermons, and addresses only a few have been selected for publication, for the reason that most of the material was in the form of skeleton and syllabus for class-room work. The lectures on Pastoral Theology and Biblical Introduction were those by which the Doctor most strongly impressed his students. It is, therefore, much to be regretted that we can not present these lectures in a completed form. His broad outlook as to the nature of a Methodist preacher's work, and his power as a preacher, may be vividly recalled by the selections given.

AMOS W. PATTEN.

LECTURES AND SERMONS.

I.

SPECIAL QUALIFICATIONS NEEDED FOR A METHODIST PASTOR.

THE *general* qualifications demanded in a Christian pastor are clearly indicated by the nature of his office. He represents Christ. He is to the flock, in some sense, instead of Christ. He is in the place of Him who possessed a perfect manhood. By what he is and by what he does he is seeking to bring humanity nearer this perfect model. To stand between Christ and his church, and to represent Christ *to* his church, calls for the highest qualities of body, mind, and soul.

But it is the object of this paper to indicate not the *general* qualifications needed in a *Christian* pastor, but the *special* qualifications demanded in a *Methodist* pastor.

I. ACQUAINTANCE AND SYMPATHY WITH THE HISTORY OF METHODISM.

Each of the great denominations, doubtless, has its providential mission. It exists not by the caprice or cunning or obstinacy of men, but by the will of God. It is the product of forces divinely originated, which could not find vent, and so created new organs of development. It is but reasonable to conclude that each of the great Christian denominations expresses some idea—presents some phase of Christianity more perfectly than any other; and there is no reason to doubt that all together may at last conspire to work out a more perfect Christianity than the world has yet seen. Under God's providence, men are often conducted to results of the value and blessedness of which they themselves had formed no antecedent conception. So, as I can not doubt, many denominational movements have been providentially originated and conducted with a view to results far higher and broader than the chief actors in them ever dreamed of.

Their leaders have builded wiser than they knew. Men have had their will in them, but God has also had his. Honest and devoted men, under some special inspiration, have hewn out some beautiful pillar of Christian faith, and God has builded it into his great spiritual temple. They have originated some sweet and simple melody, thinking thereby only to express their own experience more correctly, and God has made it one strain in the universal harmony. At the cost of much toil, suffering, and perhaps persecution, they succeed in opening a new channel by which the water of life may come to some land which before has been "dry and thirsty." God adopts it as a part of that network of gracious supply which shall ultimately spread the world over.

Hence each denomination has an individual character. It is distinguished from all others, not only

in *men's* minds, but also in *God's* mind. It has not
only a different creed, polity, name, manner of work,
but, deeper down than these, a different genius, a
different consciousness, and so a different mission.
Believing, then, that this consciousness may differ in
some degree from that developed in other branches
of the church and yet be Christian, and so this mission divine, it follows that every minister who would
be an organ of this denominational life should partake of this consciousness and recognize this mission.
He has no right to bear the name of a denomination
with which he is not in sympathy. He has no right
to assume to do what he is incapable of doing—to
seem to be what he is not.

It is, then, making no narrow or bigoted claim
that a Methodist pastor should be a Methodist; that
he should be familiar with this chapter in ecclesiastical history; that he should understand the genius
of Methodism, and be himself a partaker of it;
in short, he should comprehend this great spiritual
movement, and feel that some of its springs are in
his own nature. In this he goes down below all
questions of polity, economy, or even doctrine; he
leaves out of sight the *phenomena* which this new
force has actually produced in its historic development, to fasten upon the essence of the movement—
the principle in which all these new laws and regulations had their origin—the force which originated
these phenomena, but which, under other circumstances, might produce other and different results.

I repeat, then, in order to be fit to be a pastor
in the Methodist Church a man should understand

and appreciate Methodism—its dignity, its divine significance, its achievements of good, its adaptation to the wants of men, and so its promise of good in the future. He needs to see clearly and feel profoundly that this great movement is a God-originated one; that it has, under God, given such an impulse to Christian feeling on all sides as to become (as the Churchman, Isaac Taylor, has characterized it) "the starting-point of our modern religious history; that the field-preaching of Wesley and Whitefield in 1739 was the event whence the religious epoch now current must date its commencement; that back to the events of that time must we look necessarily as often as we seek to trace to its source what is most characteristic of the present time; and that yet this is not all, for the Methodism of the past age points forward to the next coming development of the powers of the gospel."

Especially does he need to see that Methodism was not the product of merely *mechanical* forces or of ingenious expedients; that it did not result from any particular economy or manner of work, as itinerant or lay preaching, for example, though its spirit may have found its natural expression in these, and the movement may have been greatly indebted to these instrumentalities; that it was not the work of any man or set of men, and so due to their sagacity, fidelity, zeal, or knowledge of evangelistic truth; but that it was eminently a providential movement, the product of spiritual forces—the inspiration of that infinite, life-giving spirit under whose influence all the vital forces of the church are originated. Hence it must be understood, as Isaac Taylor has so well characterized it, as resulting from a direct, earnest appeal to the religious consciousness, such as is characteristic of the teaching of Christ and his apostles, holding up every man, in the solitude of his own individuality, to the scrutiny of conscience and the searching glance of the omniscient eye. It was a simple preaching of the gospel, the great truths of which were emphasized and reiterated until they came to sink into the hearts of those who heard. It was a great movement of evangelistic philanthropy. It proceeded, with some measure of consistency, on the assumption that man needs the gospel, and that the gospel is for man. The inestimable worth of man and the fearfulness of the ruin to which he is exposed were on one side, and the ineffable love of God, as revealed in an atoning Savior, on the other. Methodism, in the simplest manner, with downrightness and earnestness, sought to bring these two counterparts together.

My brethren, let us see to it that this prime qualification for exercising a pastorate in the Methodist Church be ours. Let us strive to follow worthily in the footsteps of the fathers. The product of our preaching is not to be *theology* merely, but *religion.* Our business is not to *instruct* men *as an end*, but to save them. Fall into the history of Methodism. Catch the inspiration of this grand evangelic movement. Tone up your souls by studying the lives of the fathers. Practice the same simplicity, earnestness, directness, evangelic intensity which God so honored in Wesley's time. As we stand up to preach to the people, let us remember that, in the case of many of them, we have "but a half hour out of the week to raise the dead in," and let this reflection inspire us to strike our most telling blows for God and truth and souls. Then shall every sermon be a battle, short, sharp, decisive, victorious.

II. ACQUAINTANCE AND SYMPATHY WITH THE DOCTRINES OF METHODISM.

Methodism was not primarily a doctrinal movement. It did not result in any measure from an attempt to readjust the doctrinal statements of Christianity. And yet there has never, in the whole history of the Christian Church, been a more marked individuality of doctrine than among the people called Methodists. Their real creed is a very short and simple one; but they unite upon it, and it has contributed much to their marvelous success. It may be characterized as *evangelical universalism.* It recognizes the *all-fatherhood of God,* a truth obscured by Augustinianism and perverted by Universalism; the *essential and so the universal freedom and accountability of man;* the *universal prevalence of sin,* and the consequent *utter helplessness of humanity;* and the *all-embracing atonement of Christ,* providing a *full salvation for every man.* This system antagonizes the Augustinian doctrine of election at every point, while it emphasizes the spiritual privileges of the believer. It agrees, however, with Augustinianism as against Pelagianism in maintaining man's utter dependence for all good upon the grace of God. This system of doctrine, then, is *evangelical* as against all *rational-*

istic schemes, and *universal* as against all *partial* systems. With Protestants in general, we reject all papal additions to Christianity; and with all evangelical Christians, we agree in our beliefs as to a future state.

Such is the doctrinal position of Methodism. It makes little of the philosophical aspect of theology, but much of its practical aspect. It assumes that every characteristic doctrine of Christianity is for the sake of bringing men to salvation; that the doctrines and ordinances, as well as the living members of the church of Christ, all join in one grand, universal, impartial invitation, "*Come to Jesus.*" With these doctrines every Methodist pastor should be in sympathy. There must be in him no theological exclusiveness. He must cherish no restricted views of the grace of God. He must indulge no proclivities to bring merely speculative notions into his public teaching; for Methodism is in its genius eminently simple and practical. Especially must his words give no uncertain sound as to the general doctrines of grace. He must give no man any excuse for confounding Wesleyanism with semi-Pelagianism. He must always assume that all souls belong to God. He must see in every man the purchase of the Redeemer's agony. He must set forth the infinite fullness of provision made for the spiritual wants of men. He must make every man feel that if he dies eternally, it will be as a *spiritual suicide;* that if he plunges into perdition, it will be because he would not plunge into "the fountain filled with blood."

20

III. Acquaintance and Sympathy with the Polity and Usages of the Methodist Episcopal Church.

This polity is at once simple and complicated— simple in principle, but complicated in outward expression and adjustment. The one principle of which it is the outgrowth is that *of bringing all agencies of the church to bear upon all classes in the church*, and to secure for all efficient pastoral care and oversight. The development of this polity has proceeded in the light of Scriptural and ecclesiastical precedent and practical expediency. The result is a polity which, for variety and completeness of detail, has no equal among Protestant churches. But all this machinery is intended for a *living, militant church*, and so is entirely unsuited for one non-aggressive and dead. The adjustments of the Methodist Church will be a yoke of bondage to every unspiritual member; and especially so to a pastor in whose heart the flame of spiritual and aggressive piety does not burn brightly. The armor and discipline suited to war will only be burdensome to an ease-loving, non-resisting, compromising, contented advocate of peace.

And so the Methodist minister should understand and appreciate the economy of his own church—not merely its external, formal, and mechanical details, but its *genius and spirit*, its reason and principle. And he should be *loyal* to it—not, by any means, that it is perfect, and so changeless; nor even that it is the best possible, but as having much experience and success in its favor, and so not to be hastily and crudely tinkered.

IV. FAITH IN THE MISSION OF METHODISM.

" It is impossible to be a hero in anything unless one is first a hero in faith." " Fields are won only by those who believe in the winning." To be an efficient agent of Methodism, one must have faith in the mission of Methodism. We can only do our utmost to give Methodism to the world under the profound conviction that the world needs it. This conviction should be deeper than any that can be begotten by a knowledge of the marvelous successes of the past. It should spring from a recognition of the thorough fitness of this type of Christianity to meet a great and pressing demand. The results already garnered may well be accepted as a confirmatory comment on our conclusions touching this matter; but I would look deeper than these results for the firm basis of our faith. Does humanity need to be elevated? What will do this so certainly as that bringing of each individual soul into a sense of freedom, and so accountability before God, which is characteristic of all Methodist preaching? What will give a man to feel the dignity and inestimable worth of his own nature so fully as to show him the place he occupies in the impartial love of the infinite Father and the impartial grace of the divine Savior? What do guilty men so need to see as the cross? What does wretched and despairing man so need to know as that Jesus Christ, by the grace of God, tasted death for every man? And what means so effectual in publishing these great central, vital truths of religion as those which Methodism employs?

V. The Methodist Pastor needs Some Special Practical Adaptations.

1. *To the Masses.*

It has thus far been the peculiar glory of Methodism that it is a religion of the people. Hence the man who is fitted for her ministry must be capable of adjusting himself not to the learned merely, the rich, the aristocratic, the luxurious and ease-loving, but to the common people—the hard-working, practical masses, who make up the bone and sinew of society. He must not be dainty and fastidious in his tastes. He must be capable of wielding an influence over men incapable of judging of the quality of his culture and indifferent to the beauty of his diction— men who may judge very correctly as to the soul and essence of his teaching, but have no appreciation of hair-splitting distinctions and fine-spun theories. In short, he should aim at popular power. For, while it is the cry of *monarchists* across the water, "*God save the king!*" and of timid and time-serving *ecclesiastics*, "*God save the church!*"—of *demagogues* and *politicians*, "*God save the party!*" and of *patriots*, "*God save our country!*" let it be the cry of *Methodists* everywhere, "*God save the people!*" for if they are saved, everything else worth saving will be saved also.

There is a kind of clerical exclusiveness which many indulge or affect, and which stands in direct opposition to this practical adaptation of which I speak. There are some clergymen of what George MacDonald calls "the pure, honest, and narrow type," who seem, in every point and line of their countenances, marked as priests, and apart from their fellow-men. By their dress, the tones of their voice, and their general demeanor, they seem to say: "Stand by yourself! Come not near me, for I am holier than thou." They are, they would seem to say, to common men as the Sabbath to common days, or the church to common houses; but, more correctly, they are like funerals to common events, or corpses to living men. In the unsullied whiteness and unwrinkled blackness of their costumes, in their cold stateliness of aspect and their hollow and priestly tones, they remind us of death rather than life—of the dark and solemn under-world rather than the bright and joyous heaven to which it is their business to invite men. They move among men with a mingled pomposity and solemnity, "as if the care of the whole world lay on their shoulders—as if an awful destruction were the most likely thing to happen to every one, while to them is committed the toilsome chance of saving some." As they enter the places where men congregate—market, shop, railway depot, public hall—the language of their manner is, "*Procul, procul, O profani!*" When they speak to common men, they either patronize them or tolerate them, or endure; and, manifestly, it is with a very generous and praiseworthy patience. They seem to imagine that their ministerial duties are to be done in a mechanical way; that men are to be regenerated by their magical priestly touch, or their lofty and

impressive ceremonials; and so their whole life seems
to flow out through these channels.

This type of men, though found in every denomination, have certainly no legitimate place in the
Methodist ministry. They are made up in about
equal parts of Puritanism and ecclesiasticism, and are
thoroughly out of harmony with the genius and spirit
of the Methodist denomination. The Methodist minister must be every inch a man. He must be ready
to give to other men his hand and his heart. He
should be most broadly, profoundly, and intensely
human. Not by pompous ceremonial and cold and
formal utterances will he seek to save men, but by
vital influences.

2. *To the Itinerancy.*

As not every good Christian would be suited to,
or by, the Methodist Church, so not every good minister would be suited to our peculiar system of itinerancy. It imposes marked and peculiar conditions
of ministerial service. It requires a man to maintain
a monkish abstinence from worldly entanglements,
and yet allows him to be burdened with domestic
cares. He may have a family, but they can have no
home except that blessed home whose walls are built
of the affections of loving hearts. He must form
and cherish warm attachments to people from whom
he is soon to be separated. His affections must take
quick root, and not unfrequently deep root, in a soil
from which they must erelong be torn away. He
must surrender into the hands of others some of the
most interesting and important questions of life. It
must be decided *for* him, and not *by* him, *where* he

will labor. It must be determined *for* him, and not *by* him, what shall be his *compensation* for labor and what the *conditions* of his labor. And sometimes it may seem to him that these questions are wrongly and even unworthily decided; that men, under the influence of low and selfish motives, have improperly interfered with decisions on which his usefulness and the welfare and comfort of his family depend.

Thus unqualifiedly to commit our dearest interests, and, what is more, the interests of those dearest to us on earth, into the keeping of others, demands the fullest faith in God and the fullest faith in men. A timid, suspicious, morbidly sensitive temper would not be consistent with the conditions of this service. There are those whose affections are like hooks of steel, and yet they are so sensitive that the slightest breath will throw them into painful agitation. Such men, especially if at all disposed to bitterness or jealousy, would endure the friction of our itinerancy badly. The *local* attachments of some men are so strong as, in some measure, to disqualify them. Lack of either physical, mental, or moral stamina may unfit a man for this life of hardship and heroism. Indeed, the Methodist itinerancy is related to what are called settled pastorates, much as the life of the soldier is related to that of a civilian, and the special qualities and conditions demanded are clearly and fairly indicated by this comparison.

3. *To the Methodist Pulpit.*

The Methodist pulpit, however numerous and marked may be the individual exceptions, is a place where the gospel is preached earnestly, plainly, pointedly, and effectively. It is not a place for essays, theological, moral, literary, or any other kind. It is not a place for lectures or orations, either religious or political. It is not a place for abstrusities, profundities, or platitudes. It is not a place for dry and harsh polemics. It is not a theater for oratorical display— for intellectual gymnastics or mere word-painting. The preaching of the Methodist pulpit should not bristle with hard, naked, angry propositions. It must not be narrow, dry, hard, nor cold; nothing suited to the select few merely, but to all. It must not address the intellectual nature mainly, but the spiritual nature. Its profiting must be seen, not in the world that now is, but in that which is to come.

If it be said that all these characteristics pertain to the Christian pulpit as such, in whatever denomination, I reply that they pertain, *in an eminent degree*, to the characteristic Methodist pulpit. And there are many who would be acceptable in other pulpits who would not be acceptable in ours, as there are also many who do effective work among us, but would not be so successful in any other denomination.

To be best suited to our pulpit, a man must be positive in his convictions, fervid in his feelings, plain and downright in speech, and simple in manner; of broad sympathies, and capable of wielding a fair measure of popular influence. Extemporaneousness of address is naturally associated with these qualities, and they express themselves most perfectly in this way, and yet I can not write it down as in the highest and most absolute sense essential.

Such are some of the special qualifications needed

for the pastoral work in the *Methodist* Church. But I will not refrain from adding that these must be allowed, in no manner, to set aside, or supersede or .atone for the absence of, the still broader and more fundamental qualifications which are needed in a *Christian* pastor. It will be a sad day for us and for religion when our ministry becomes more Methodistic than Christian, more Wesleyan than Protestant, more effective for denominational propagandism than for Christian evangelization. Loyalty to the denomination should be simply the outflowing of that still deeper and more all-comprehending loyalty to Christ, to conscience, and to truth. Adhering to this principle, we shall, in our measure and in our special department of influence, help the Church to realize that beautiful description of the poet Montgomery:

" Distinct as the billows, but one as the sea."

II.

RITUALISM IN THE METHODIST EPIS-
COPAL CHURCH.

I USE this term, not in its narrow and technical
sense, but in the broad and comprehensive sense
of *order in religious service;* and, hence, as opposed
to all dispositions and tendencies to subject such
service to the whims or caprices, the carelessness or
the ignorance, of him who may happen to have it in
charge. The apostle does indeed direct us to "turn
away" from such as have the "form of godliness, but
deny the power thereof;" but it would be a strange
and unwarrantable inference from this, that we have
any right to be indifferent to decent and appropriate
forms in religion. On the other hand, this passage
itself implies that the form of godliness is a matter
of distinct and important notice—indeed, that it is so
good that there may be danger of substituting it for
the substance. The question in this matter is not between forms and no forms, for nothing real and actual
can be without some type or mode of development;
it is rather between a good form and a bad or indifferent one. A tree can not grow without assuming
some shape; a river can not flow without selecting
some course; so religious service can not proceed
without taking some definite order, which, by long
custom, will come to be an established form.

And this is a feeling that holds with all classes alike. The Non-conformists of Great Britain came at last to insist on their Non-conformist usages with almost the same rigidity and intolerance that had been exhibited by the Conformists themselves. The old Covenanters of Scotland were even more inflexible in their demands that no religious service should be said at the open graves of the departed, than are the members of the Church of England in theirs, that in every instance must the rites of the church be performed over the baptized dead. There is a denomination of Christians in this country who would regard it a sacrilege, never to be forgotten or forgiven, if the minister should introduce into divine service a single one of the sacred Psalms in Watts's metrical version. There are many single churches in this country, and even whole denominations of churches, who would be quite as much shocked and surprised, should the minister, to their knowledge, make use of a single previously composed prayer, as would the High-churchman should the priest extemporize a portion of the liturgy. Even minor peculiarities among those who dissent from the doctrine that the church must fix the forms of worship, and dictate the language of prayer and praise, confession and profession, come to be invested with the same sacredness and are clung to with the same tenacity, as ritualistic forms themselves. A Presbyterian minister who should go on his knees in public prayer, in the presence of his congregation, would do so at the imminent risk of position, reputation, and usefulness. Were a Methodist minister to practice uttering a brief invocation, as he stands up to read the opening hymn in the Sabbath morning service, he would be almost sure to lose caste by it to some extent, and to incur the charge, which would sooner or later come to him, of being "half-Presbyterianized." So jealously do the people regard even those peculiarities which, to an outside observer, would seem to have the smallest possible value and significance. Hence, then, I repeat it—the question is not whether there shall be set and established forms in religious service, but it is simply whether these forms shall be good or bad, appropriate or inappropriate; and, also, to how great an extent these can be adjusted beforehand. Hence, then, there is much practical importance investing this question of order in religious service, and it most certainly demands the careful attention of every one called to direct the worship of the sanctuary.

I. First, then, let us briefly consider this subject as connected with the ordinary services of public worship on the Lord's-day. The Disciplinary directions are: "Let the morning service consist of singing, prayer, the reading of a chapter out of the Old Testament and another out of the New, and preaching. Let the afternoon service consist of singing, prayer, the reading of one or two chapters out of the Bible, and preaching. Let the evening service consist of singing, prayer, and preaching." . . . "Let the Lord's Prayer also be used on all occasions of public worship in concluding the first prayer, and the Apostolic Benediction in dismissing the congregation." In addition, every minister is charged to choose appropriate hymns, and not to "sing too much at once; seldom more than four or five verses."

Such is, substantially, the sum of the Disciplinary directions on this subject. It will at once be seen that in reference to some points usually deemed important, and even some that most would hold essential, there are no directions given. For instance, we are not told what services should follow the sermon— whether prayer, singing, and benediction; or, singing, prayer, and benediction; or, prayer and benediction; or, singing and benediction; or, the benediction alone. We are not told what posture the minister shall assume—whether he shall stand in prayer and benediction, or kneel in prayer and benediction, or kneel in prayer and stand in the benediction. There are one or two general directions given in reference to public religious service, that are not without value, which are well worthy of careful attention by every minister, old and young. To some of these I may refer farther along. In the light of the Discipline and experience we are able, then, to read certain rules which should govern a preacher in this matter.

1. Obey the specific directions of Discipline, so far as they are at all applicable to your circumstances. I append this modifying clause because there are, manifestly, some clauses in these articles on public worship not adapted to every case. In such cases it is Methodistic to retain the spirit of the rule, even if compelled to depart from the letter. A general model is held up to view, which it is our business to imitate so far as practicable. Many of us, for instance, have no afternoon service, but do have an evening service.

Which shall govern us—the directions for afternoon
or evening? Afternoon, I should say, as being the
second and important service of the day. If the
services are at different places, I would not omit the
reading of the Scripture at any service.

2. Be able to bear these parts assigned us by the
Discipline well. The hymns should not only be carefully selected, but the Scripture also, *and both should
be well read.* It was said that multitudes used to attend upon the ministry of the eloquent Dr. Mason,
of New York, just to enjoy his reading. Good reading is a charm in religious service which every one
feels, and no preacher has a right to be indifferent to
it. His reading may not be artistic—he may not
have all the vocal graces of the actor or professional
elocutionist—but a minister of the gospel has no excuse for not exhibiting in his reading the excellent
qualities so well set forth in the eighth verse of the
eighth chapter of Nehemiah: "So they read in the
book in the law of God distinctly, and gave the sense,
and caused them to understand the reading." The
minister should be able to recite the Lord's Prayer
according to the form in the Methodist Ritual. This
is a rare accomplishment. In my observation, cover-
ing several years since my attention has become fixed
on the point, I have heard less than a score of individuals recite the Lord's Prayer with perfect accuracy.
Not long since I raised the question in a select company of ten ministers, several of them eminent, and
not one of them could recite the Lord's Prayer according to the Methodist Ritual. I know of no excuse for such carelessness in reference to a form that

most of us use at least three hundred and sixty-five
times in a year.

3. The Discipline suggests attention to what may be
denominated the proprieties of religious service: "Let
your whole deportment be serious, weighty, solemn."
The personal character, and manner, and spirit of the
minister, have so much to do with the interest and
profit of the sanctuary service, as to be worthy of the
most careful attention. Among the most common
faults here, some of which are expressly mentioned in
the Discipline, are:

(*a*) *Egotism.* A man's manner may announce his
important self quite as distinctly as his words. And
nothing can be more offensive. The man who, like
Æsop's fly seated on the end of the axle, is continually exclaiming, "See what a dust *I* raise;" or like
the lily, who imagined that by retiring into its bulb
it would take all the summer with it,—is capable of
rendering religious service, which is otherwise entirely correct in form and respectable in talent, absolutely repulsive.

(*b*) Another serious fault is *Levity.* I do not allude so much to that perverted taste that leads a
minister to indulge in quaintness, eccentricity, puns,
or even buffoonery in the sacred desk—for there are
few, comparatively, capable of offending in this way—
but to all disposition to treat religious service as a
matter of little importance. This will show itself by
haste, irreverence, flippancy, trifling thoughts and
words, and especially by the use of sermons which
are really impromptu, or are made to appear so. The
preacher will sometimes find himself led to make use

of a subject or train of remark hastily caught up, and sometimes very much to his own satisfaction and the profit of his audience, but this should be the exception and never the rule. No minister, laboring in the ordinary routine of his profession, has a right to bring unbeaten oil into the sanctuary; and to do so habitually, indicates unpardonable indolence and levity of character.

(e) *Affectation.* "In man or woman, but most of all in man that ministers and serves the altar, in my very soul I loathe all affectation." It is a greater evil, because more offensive, than rudeness or awkwardness.

So much has been written in reference to the general course of service in the Lord's house, assuming that the disciplinary directions are authoritative and infallible. If I may, however, travel so far outside of my record as to inquire whether the order of service, laid down in the Discipline, is capable of improvement, I should venture to suggest that my own taste and judgment would be much better satisfied were our service, like that of most other churches that have no liturgy, to commence with an invocation, and our sermons to close by prayer. I should be glad to commend this suggestion to him who is to represent us in the next General Conference.

II. In the second department of my essay—which I here promise shall not be very extended—I propose some random suggestions bearing on our ritual proper. I doubt not, as it now stands, it is perfectly intelligible and easy to be conducted, and yet the cases in which its forms are used with perfect propriety and correctness are not numerous.

1. There is a single point in the baptismal service, in reference to which I have noticed some confusion of usage: The people are directed to stand while the Scripture is read. *When shall they sit down?*

2. Persons who receive baptism as adults answer to certain questions in the presence of the congregation, and this is called their *baptismal vow*. Is there anything corresponding to this for those who were baptized in infancy? My own practice has been, and shall be until this is better provided for among us, to call forward such, with those about to be baptized, and have them respond to the questions with them. The only difference I make between them is, I do not ask them if they will be "baptized in this faith," and do not apply water to them.

3. Are candidates for adult baptism expected to answer the questions at all? I have seen these questions proposed to persons that stood as immovable as statues; the answers were read to them, while they gave not the smallest token of assent in any form. I would in every instance have it understood beforehand, if practicable, and require each candidate to answer with his voice, and that not in unison, but singly and successively.

4. Are our ceremonies in receiving persons into the church always as solemn and impressive as they should to be? Receiving persons to relations which may be *changeless forever*, is a very different matter from admitting them into a temperance society or Masonic lodge. And yet it is frequently one of the loosest and most careless services of the church.

5. The form for the Holy Communion is probably

21

better observed than any other among us, because it
is, in most cases, in the hands of experienced men;
and yet there are not wanting evils even here.

(*a*) In most of our strong and well-established
societies it is not administered with sufficient fre-
quency. There is no reason why Baptists, Congregationalists, and Presbyterians should commemorate
Christ's death monthly, and Methodists only once a
quarter. I think our churches would be profited by
a more frequent observance of this ordinance.

(*b*) It is frequently administered in such haste as
to destroy, in a great measure, the interest of the occasion.

(*c*) The beauty of the service is frequently greatly
marred by random talking by those who are distrib-
uting the elements. Better to confine yourself strictly
to the form in the Discipline, than to say a careless
or inappropriate word.

(*d*) While much of the service may undoubtedly
be omitted, it seems to me that not all the closing
services should ever be omitted.

6. The forms for Matrimony and the Burial of the
Dead, as a matter of practice, I find myself obliged
greatly to abridge, and in some instances to modify.
They are adapted to more formal occasions than ordinarily present themselves. I find my *material* in
them, and seek to conform to their spirit; but can not
always, consistently with my own views of propriety,
conform strictly to their letter.

III.

OUTLOOK OF METHODISM.

I DO not essay to predict what will be, but rather to point out what may be and ought to be. What will be depends, in great measure, on the sagacity, fidelity, and obedient service of men; what ought to be is indicated by the providence of God. What has been and is, we know, though imperfectly; the one thing needful is, that we may have eyes to read its deep lessons aright.

Methodism has thus far had a wonderful history—a history replete with the goodness of God and the heroism of men. Every impartial church historian will concede this, even though he may not fully sympathize with the movement. It is no arrogant claim to make, that Methodism has been selected by Providence to do a work in developing Protestant Christianity which could have been done by no other class of methods or agencies; as Isaac Taylor says: "The present religious epoch must, in some important sense, take its date from the field-preaching of the Wesleys."

Notably is this true with regard to this country. It has achieved here a work which would have been impossible under any other economy or any other class of men than such as Methodist preachers have been. The breadth of their theological views, their freedom from scholastic methods which separate from the people, their hearty sympathy with the masses, their fertility in expedients, their direct and downright methods, and especially their singleness of aim in seeking and saving the lost, gave them a special adaptation for the work which they were called to do in this land. To no other class of men, and in particular to no other class of ministers, is this nation so much indebted. Had it not been for such men and such methods, it is clearly to be seen that American history must have been very different from what it has been. All honor, then, to our fathers—those now lingering among us, as well as those who have passed on to their reward. The best we need to ask for ourselves is, that we may be worthy to follow in this high succession.

The Methodist Episcopal Church, especially in this Middle West and North-west, is now in a transition state. This is true, not only in that sense which applies to every living organism at all times—for it is in the nature of life to manifest itself by working changes—but in that special sense which applies only to critical periods in the history of living organisms. Hitherto, in this region, the evangelistic aspect of our work has been most prominent. The typical Methodist minister has been a "circuit rider," going from place to place, literally, to carry the good news of salvation. The rude, temporary churches, which sprung up everywhere in his path, in due time gave place to other churches; also, for the most part temporary, but more attractive and commodious, and indicating a more advanced stage of church life. But recently, and particularly within the past dozen years, the third stage—that of maturity—has, in many places, been reached. The permanent church edifice has been built, often of brick or stone, and so complete in its appointments as to be adequate to the wants of a fully developed and well-organized church. All over the territory of this North-west stand beautiful churches, which represent an untold amount of toil, prayer, solicitude, sacrifice, and in many instances positive suffering, on the part of the people. I know strong business men who have builded their lives into the church, as they have not done into their private business; who have expended on the house of God an amount of energy and painstaking which they have not bestowed on their private affairs. Now, the building of this local church is the terminus *ad quem* as to material development; if there be further progress, it must be in another and a still more important direction. What is now needed is not so much development as strength; not so much the starting of new enterprises as the turning of old facilities to the richest spiritual account. The growth which the church now needs is not only extensive, but intensive; not merely expansion, but depth and solidity.

Definitely, then, what are the key-notes of our future progress?

1. First of all, the time is now come for the best development of our local church life. Up to this time our poor societies—and all our societies are poor; the exceptions are so rare that we hardly need to take them into account at all—have been straining every nerve to solve that problem which Carlyle calls "the

first and simplest of all philosophy, that of keeping soul and body together." Like the rapidly growing boy, all their vitality has gone into their body, and they have had nothing left for the wants of their higher nature. But now the time has come for a higher life than that of the physical and material. The energy, which for so long has been expended in simply building up material organs of life, may now be available for higher uses. The outward growth must find its complement in inner growth. Hence, those organs of church life, such as class-meetings and other spiritual means and instrumentalities, may be turned to the richest account. Our class-meetings are a strange anomaly. They are our best and poorest meetings. Some of our members would have them distinguished from every other class of religious duties, and made tests and standards of Christian character. This must be construed as indicating a possibility in this meeting which is not ordinarily realized. The time has now come when all that is best in this meeting should again come to the front. We want in this meeting less of cant, and more of culture; less of the mechanical, and more of the spiritual; less of old and stereotyped repetitions, and more of fresh and vital truth. The minister finds that his social meetings draw on him even more severely, in some directions, than his public work. It is sometimes easier to preach a sermon, as sermons go, than to lead a prayer-meeting. And if the minister has any good thoughts, he is pretty sure to find good use for them in such meetings as bring him face to face with his fellows, with no barriers of office between. But the class-leader, who is often a man of no superior thought or culture, expects to keep up the spiritual interest of his class without special study or other means to qualify himself for his most sacred function. Is this reasonable? Do men, in these days, enjoy a special inspiration? Has not the time come when this most important class of men shall be more and better qualified for their pastoral work?

May not the financial life of the church be improved? Is it not still true that, in too many of our churches, we are "living from hand to mouth" in a most improvident way? For the most part, these great and fundamental interests are managed as no one would think of managing his private business. A rare thing it is for a church to have a financial history which it is pleasant to contemplate. All this must be improved. Hitherto there may have been some excuse for confusion here, but now no longer. Let it be the definite ambition of each church to have a financial plan which they can work with good effect. It is by no means certain that just the same in all details is suited best to every locality; there may be more or less variety, but there should be *a* plan, and it should be *well worked.* More truly than it was said with regard to governments, that "that which is best administered is best," may it be said as to plans of church finance, that that one is best which is best worked. What is most important is, that every church have a plan and adhere to it, and that the minister have as little to do with it as possible. Nothing is more unfortunate than for the financial life of a church to be tossed to and fro by successive

pastors, who may each have his peculiar idiosyncrasy
to illustrate. All the pastor can reasonably ask is
that there be a plan, and that it be faithfully attended
to. Inquire at the beginning of the year definitely
what are to be the expenses, and then ask what sources
of income shall be depended on to balance. Let
nothing be left to that limbo of vague uncertainty to
which such matters are too often relegated. Unless
there is special reason for supposing that the church
may, in the course of the year, strike a flowing well
or a bonanza, let the question be persistently urged
at the beginning of the year, until the receipts are
made to balance the expenses.

Another class of men who are to be reformed by
the proper development of our local church life is
local preachers. The Wesleyan idea of lay preaching
is scarcely recognized or illustrated in some portions
of the Methodist Episcopal Church. All our local
preachers are likely to be either embryo traveling
ministers, or worn-out, unacceptable, or secularized
preachers. Too rarely is it the case that a pastor, in
going to a new charge, looks forward with any special
hope or satisfaction to a large element of this kind in
his officiary. In some cases these men called local
preachers, instead of being in any special way helpers,
are in a special way obstructionists. Instead of
placing on the altar the offering of a holy, self-sacrificing, cheerful service, they are spies, croakers, dead-
weights, and yet in an official position.

Is it too much to hope that this institution of lay
preaching—which has in past time been thought so
characteristic of Methodism and so potent for good,

but which seems among us to have degenerated into
utter insignificance—may be again elevated into its
proper character? Now and then, outside of our denomination, do we have an example of really useful
and influential lay preaching. The Moody movement
has brought to the front a very considerable number
of lay helpers, whose character and work answer more
nearly to the Wesleyan pattern than anything which we,
as a denomination, can show. And in some sections of
our own church we have local preachers who are in
every way ornaments and vindications of the office.
The thing that is wanted is, that this institution may
everywhere be brought back to its primitive efficiency.
Our Young Men's Christian Associations illustrate,
in many cases, the value of that which Methodism
has almost allowed to die on her hands.

2. Another direction in which we are to make
progress is in the religious care of our children. The
saddest fact that confronts a pastor of experience in
the church is that, in too many cases, the most important of his religious families run out,.so far as the
church is concerned. The second or third generation
is entirely graceless, or indifferent, or actually infidel.
And any person who has been in the habit of grap-
pling with the practical problems of evangelization
as they arise, will say that positively the most dis-
couraging sign of the times is the slender hold which
our blessed Christianity seems to maintain on the
children of our religious families; so that, if they
were not being continually re-enforced from without,
the church would not hold her own as to numbers.
There is here something greatly wrong. It is very

much that, in some cases, the laws of moral optics
have been reversed, so that Christian workers see
distinctly only the interests which are the most distant, and their eyes are holden from discerning the
need and the danger of those who are nearest. There
are among us a good many Mrs. Jellabys, who are
practicing telescopic philanthropy. At all events, the
church greatly fails with reference to the very class
as to which she ought most and best to succeed. Possibly something has come from the change of base in
the matter of Christian nurture. The Sunday-school
has come in, and too many parents have allowed it
to assume the entire control of this most sacred interest. Let it, then, be renewedly emphasized upon
all our people, that the most sacred of all their
duties is to help their children to solve the problem
which is presented to each for solution; that no other
work, which can be done for God and his church, is
so important as this of training the children for the
kingdom; that every parent is to see to it that his
children are placed in the loving arms of the Savior
of children.

3. Finally, we must raise the standard of ministerial efficiency. As has already been said, the character of our work has been very much changed of
late. Our preachers are less evangelists and more
pastors, in the full sense. Their main work is not to
bring men into the church from without, but to take
care of those who are already in the fold. To anchor
a man to the truth, so that he is safer from falling,
is as real a service to the kingdom of God as to bring
in a new recruit from without. Now, then, the pastor

is set for the spiritual care and culture of the flock. He is to feed them with Christ's words. He is to lead them into the fertile pastures of the Lord and by the side of the waters of rest. He is to keep them, feed them, fold them, defend them, minister to them.

IV.

GOD'S REQUIREMENTS;

OR, THE TRINITY OF SPIRITUAL CHARACTER.*

"What doth the Lord require of thee, but to do justly, and to love mercy, and to walk humbly with thy God?"— MICAH VI, 8.

THERE is one class of facts with which the careful and critical student of the Bible comes to be familiar which are both interesting and instructive, but are not without their suggestions of difficulty; and these are the reappearance of matters of Biblical history, with material additions, such as are not found in the original narrative. For example, Paul, in his address to the elders of Ephesus, whom he had called to meet him at Miletus, says: "And to remember the words of the Lord Jesus, how he says, It is more blessed to give than to receive;" and yet we read the entire Gospel history, from beginning to end, without finding any intimation that the Lord Jesus ever employed any such language. And so we are made to know that Paul, and those whom he addressed, had access to some source of information as to the life and words of Christ of which we to-day have no knowledge.

---

* Sermon preached in the Methodist Episcopal Church, Evanston, Ill., November 6, 1881.

Again, the Psalmist, in recounting the experiences of Joseph in the Egyptian prison, says that his "feet were hurt with the fetters;" and yet, in the original narrative, though it is very minute and circumstantial, no mention is made of this, thus leading to the conclusion that the writer, in his acquaintance with the personal history of Joseph, was not limited to our book of Genesis.

In one of the epistles, the names of the magicians who "withstood Moses," in that fearful contest which he waged in behalf of the God of Israel against the gods of the Egyptians, are set down : "Now as Jannes and Jambres withstood Moses, so do these also resist the truth;" and yet, in the original account, neither the names nor the number of these magicians are given. And so it appears that Paul had other information as to this most central passage in the history of the Hebrew people than that which we find in our book of Exodus.

But the most remarkable illustration is found in connection with the text. Few passages of personal history in the Old Testament are more notable or more interesting than that of the prophet Balaam. And it is given in a very minute and circumstantial way, even the attitude and words and all the proceedings of the principal parties being most graphically set forth. And yet it is reserved for the prophet Micah, writing almost a thousand years after Balaam's time, to record his most searching and pregnant utterance : "O, my people, remember now what Balak, king of Moab, consulted, and what Balaam, the son of Beor, answered him from Shittim unto

Gilgal; that ye may know the righteousness of the Lord. Wherewith shall I come before the Lord, and bow myself before the high God? Shall I come before him with burnt-offerings, with calves of a year old? Will the Lord be pleased with thousands of rams, or with ten thousands of rivers of oil? Shall I give my first-born for my transgression, the fruit of my body for the sin of my soul?"

To all this, which expresses most unmistakably and distinctly the spirit of materialistic and ritualistic heathenism, come, in reply, the grand and solemn words of the text—a voice from the primitive monotheism which this strange character, Balaam, must be taken as representing: "He hath showed thee, O man, what is good; and what doth the Lord require of thee, but to do justly, and to love mercy, and to walk humbly with thy God?"

Of the many important questions which have engaged the attention of men, doubtless one of the most important is that anciently proposed by the psalmist: "Who shall ascend into the hill of the Lord, and who shall stand in his holy place?" It is manifest that if the doctrines of theism be true, this question is invested with the highest interest to every spiritual being. It is a question of interest what relations I sustain to men, though they are truthfully described as but the small dust in Jehovah's balance, but "as the grass of the field which at evening is cut down and withereth;" yet it is a question of inconceivably greater interest, What relation do I sustain to the everlasting God, with whom there is no variableness, neither shadow of turning? It is a question of interest, Where shall be my earthly home, and who shall constitute my earthly friends? Shall I live in an atmosphere warm and congenial, or in one chilling and deathful? But rising above this question, as do the heavens rise above the earth, is that other question: "Shall I my everlasting days with fiends or angels spend?" And so one of the great objects of the Christian Scriptures is to set forth to us the style of character upon which God hath placed the seal of his approbation—to answer the question: "Who shall ascend into the hill of the Lord, and who shall stand in his holy place?" And one of the most intelligible and comprehensive of the many epitomes of human duty scattered throughout the word of God is this which we have read as the text for this morning: "What doth the Lord require of thee, but to do justly, and to love mercy, and to walk humbly with thy God?"

The theme suggested by this text, and to it your attention is now invited, is, GOD'S REQUIREMENTS; OR, THE TRINITY OF SPIRITUAL CHARACTER.

I use the term "trinity" because it expresses the exact truth, and is the only term which does express the truth. Spiritual character is essentially a tri-unity. It contains three essential elements, and only three, and these agree in one. If either of these is absent, all seeming goodness is spurious. If any other principle is admitted as co-ordinate with these, they are not genuine, but base counterfeits. It is no more possible to admit another into the holy of holies of spiritual character than to seat another by the side of the infinite God, and upon his own throne.

I use the term "spiritual" as being of the widest possible import, and as directing our attention to results rather than processes. I do not say Christian character—I do not know whether this phrase would be practically equivalent or not—but spiritual character, believing that goodness is one in all beings and in all worlds. And it seems to me to be well sometimes to turn away our attention from these processes—these questions of repentance and consecration and faith; the Church, the ministry, and the sacraments; the things we are to do, and the experiences which may come to us in doing them—and to fasten our attention upon that one grand result unto which we must come, in order to enter into the life of God. Whether we are Methodists or Quakers, Romanists or Liberalists, Externalists or Mystics; whether we profess this creed or that, or have had this or that form of what is called experience,—it is well for us sometimes to confront that changeless standard unto which we must conform or we can not enter into life. The scaffolding is at best but temporary, and must soon be thrown down. The great question is—and it is one which shall brighten or shadow the eternal ages—when this has fallen, will the temple of spiritual character stand perfect and complete, column and arch and dome of everlasting strength? Upon these three essential elements of character let us now fix our attention.

I. JUSTICE.

As is characteristic of the Old Testament, the text uses a concrete and individualizing phrase to set forth what is universal. It is not the "doing justly" that

God demands, but justice; not a form of life, but a quality of character. It is no more necessary to do justly than to speak justly, to think justly, or to feel justly. Just as the one great ocean is known by different names as it washes different shores, so this universal principle is called by different names as it has to do with different relations. It is justice in administration, truth in language, righteousness in general character, and holiness in nature. In one word, it is rightness, rectitude, a thorough and perfect adjustment of the soul to God, and so to all its spiritual relations—holiness of heart, and, by consequence, holiness of life.

1. *This justice must be fundamental.*

This is the first, as it is also the decisive, test of genuineness. Justice which is not authoritative is not justice at all, but may be most delusive and dangerous self-seeking. Right doing, with a view to interest or advantage, is not right doing, but may involve the very audacity of uttermost rebellion, just as it has been well said, "The devil never lies so badly as when he tells the truth."

Perhaps the deepest and most comprehensive of all tests in morals and religion is this: Which is first, holiness or happiness? that is, which of these is the ultimate and sacred thing which carries in its bosom all possible values? Is right doing right doing for the reason simply that it produces a happiness? or is it better to say that it produces happiness because it is right doing? Is all possible good gathered up in this one word happiness, and do all tests and standards of excellence come forth from it? or is there a

higher and more sacred thing out of which all spiritual harmonies do flow? This question is the touch-
stone of all the theologies. With equal clearness does
it draw the line between the Calvinist and the Arminian, and between the Liberal and the Evangelical.
If there is such a thing as essential and immutable
justice, then an arbitrary election to eternal life or an
arbitrary reprobation to eternal death is an impossibil-
ity. Equally so is salvation by mere prerogative,
which is the last and highest point where the Liberal
and Evangelical part company.

But though all the great controversies of all the
ages revolve about this question, the intuitions of men
upon it are in perfect agreement. It is universally
felt that the one sacred and fundamental thing against
which nothing can prevail, by the side of which
nothing can stand, whose absolute authority no one
can dispute, which is solitary and supreme as God
himself, is righteousness. We can conceive of God
as laying aside his happiness, but who can think of
him as laying aside his holiness? We recognize him
as inflicting suffering, but who does not feel the blas-
phemy of inquiring whether he ever inflicts sin? We
sometimes ask whether Christ's divinity suffered in
the atonement, thus proving that there is not in our
thought any clear sense of utter incongruity between
the nature of Christ and suffering; but who does not
recognize such an incongruity between him and sin?
But the general consciousness of men may be gleaned
from current aphorisms and adages. What is meant
when it is said that "it is better that ninety and nine
guilty persons go unpunished, than that one innocent

person should suffer," unless it be that the one and only fatal mistake which the State, as the individual, can commit, is that of doing wrong; that while there is loss, and perhaps peril, in suffering wrong, there is ruin in doing wrong, for it unsettles the only foundations upon which the State can be built?

Here, then, is the beginning of all excellence. There is absolutely no good if this be wanting. There can, by no possibility, be any genuine "mercy," or philanthropy, or "walking with God," unless there is first personal righteousness. One may speak with the tongues of men or of angels; his whole life may be crowded with philanthropic endeavor and with heroic achievement; he may give all his goods to feed the poor, and his body to be burned, and yet, unless there be in his deepest soul absolute rectitude as before God, he can not stand in the judgment, nor in the congregation of the righteous.

2. It must be universal.

It must pervade the whole being, just as the soul pervades the body; it must constitute the warp and the woof of character; it must enter into every thought, purpose, aspiration, affection, motive, principle, and every outward form of conduct. The difference between a bad man and a good man is, that the former sometimes does wrong. Of course he does not and can not antagonize the divine administration at every point. This, if it were possible, would be instant and utter suicide, extending even to annihilation. The thing which characterizes a bad man is, that he, at some times, and in the presence of certain temptations, does wrong of set intent, and thus proves that it is in his heart to do so. What God demands is spiritual symmetry and integrity—soundness and wholeness; or, as the theological term is, holiness.

One serious defect in the piety of the present day is in the lack of the ethical element—of a delicate, high-toned, and controlling conscientiousness. Men pray not to be made right, but to be saved; and to be saved is, in their thought, to be rid of physical evil, rather than spiritual—of suffering, rather than sin. The type of religion which prevails is largely of the bustling, sentimental, hymn-singing order; our church-life is often ostentatious and luxurious; but it does not, so certainly as we might wish, infuse into men and women that sturdy, downright, positive rectitude which guarantees fidelity in any relation in which they may be placed. The great want of society to-day, as ever, is not as to the amenities, refinements, or decorations of life—good as these may be—but thorough honesty and trustworthiness; truth in character and truth in life. Here is the great, though for the most part inscrutable, secret of these fearful disasters which, from time to time, shock and terrify civilized communities of the latter day—the falling of bridges, the foundering of ships, the starting of conflagrations, the collapse of buildings, and the wrecking of railway trains. Though it can not often be proven, there is little reason to doubt that, in the majority of this class of calamities, the real culprit was some dishonest and unfaithful worker—some man who held a precious trust unworthily, and wrought as pleasing men rather than God.

"In the elder days of art,
Builders wrought with greatest care
Each minute and unseen part;
For the gods see everywhere."

II. MERCY—"*To love mercy.*"

I use this term, taken from the text itself, as suggesting the truth, rather than expressing it. Our language contains no single term which sets forth fully and adequately the precious thing here intended. Benevolence is too weak and neutral, mercy too special and narrow, philanthropy too low and worldly. Neither of these expresses the principle of self-sacrifice, which is the characteristic and distinguishing thing in this aspect of goodness. I mean that which was illustrated by Saint Paul, when he said, "I am debtor both to the Jews and to the Greeks"—debtor, not because of what he had received of them, but because of his power to do them good; thus recognizing that grand and fundamental principle in Christian living, that every man owes every other man all the good he can possibly do him consistently with the rights of others. More beautifully is this expressed in another place: "Yea, and if I be offered upon the sacrifice and service of your faith, I joy and rejoice with you all;" that is, the apostle is willing to be poured out as a libation—to be lost, and to disappear, and be forgotten altogether—if thus he might render the sacrifice of those for whom he labored acceptable in the sight of God. Still more fearfully expressive are the words in the ninth of Romans: "I could wish that myself were accursed from Christ for my brethren, my kinsmen, according to the flesh." But this

principle finds its crowning illustration—and here it
may be most confidently and perfectly identified—in
Him "who, though he was rich, yet for our sakes
became poor, that we through his poverty might be
made rich;" who, "forasmuch as the children are
partakers of flesh and blood, he also himself likewise
took part in the same;" because "it behooved him
to be made in all things like unto his brethren,"
that "he, by the grace of God, might taste death for
every man."

The grandest thing and the most precious thing
in all this world is a truly consecrated soul—one that
continually offers up itself in flames of holy love on
the altar of God and of humanity. Such a man belongs to the nobility of heaven. He is a worker together with God. In so far as it is possible for a
finite being to be so, he is a savior of men. For
what this dead world needs is not forms, nor creeds,
nor systems—not polish, nor pruning—but life. It
is not by mechanical appliances, nor spiritual legerdemain; not by robes and tonsures, incense and attitudes and priestly manipulation, that the terrible
necessities of our ruined humanity must be met. The
world may totter under its weight of cathedrals; its
pile of ghastly uniformity, as to rites and ceremonies,
may have a base as broad as Sahara, and all be but
a splendid mausoleum of the dead. The one agonizing prayer of sinful humanity is for life; and until
this is answered, we have no other wants, and can
have no other blessings. And so he who becomes in
his own character and nature a channel of the divine
life, a port of entry from the skies, climbs up to the

very throne of human achievement. All others come short of life's great end; these, and these alone, constitute the peculiar family of the Most High. In the end, as I can not doubt, we shall find that the lamp of sacrifice sheds its light in every part of the divine dominions. It will fully appear that the cross is planted in the very center of the spiritual universe, and that the dying cry of the Divine Victim is the key-note of all spiritual harmonies. "Give me a place to stand," said Archimedes, in his enthusiasm at discovering the principle of the lever—"Give me a place to stand, and I 'll move the world." And hence this is the question which men are asking—"*Pou sto?*"—where can I stand? Where is the real center of power? Take your stand at the cross, and you will come to the maximum of your possibility. The weakest and obscurest worker, standing here, shall really move the world. The glory of those who shine so brightly and beautifully in the Christian heavens, is a gleam from the world's great altar-fire.

Hear the story of one of these: "In journeyings often; in perils of waters, in perils of robbers, in perils by mine own countrymen, in perils by the heathen, in perils in the city, in perils in the wilderness, in perils in the sea, in perils among false brethren; in weariness and painfulness, in watchings often, in hunger and thirst, in fastings often, in cold and nakedness."

By the side of this—which I can not but regard as one of the most eloquent passages in all literature—I will place another characteristic specimen of the Christian life, taken from an obscurer source. A century ago, the United Brethren, at much cost of toil and hardship, had succeeded in establishing their mission at Gnadenhutten, in Eastern Ohio. One night, as the mission family were at supper, the barking of the dogs alarmed them. One of the Brethren opened the door, when instantly a volley was fired by Indians in ambush. He fell dead, and his wife and several others were mortally wounded. The door was secured, and the well and wounded took refuge in the upper story of their fort-house. The Indians at last fired the building, and all but three of the missionaries perished. One sick woman gained the cover of a friendly thicket, and escaped to tell the tale. "The last time I saw my sister," said she, "she was kneeling, and I heard her say, in a clear, sweet voice: ''T is all well, my dear Savior!'" What angel in heaven ever stood on a lofter height of consecration and of victory?

III. RELIGIOUS DEVOTION—"*To walk humbly with thy God.*"

We have tarried, perhaps, too long in the outer court of the temple of spiritual character, but it has been to learn again the simple but all-comprehending lesson of truth. We have lingered a moment in the holy place to learn the lesson of sacrifice. And now we come to the grand and crowning privilege of humanity—that of entering into the holiest of all, and experiencing the rapture of divine communion. "To walk humbly with God" describes a perfect life, and that, too, in its divinest aspect. Heaven is not higher as to its essence, but only as to its accidents.

Of the blessedness of this life I may not now

speak. It were as easy to throw upon canvas the glory of the New Jerusalem, or to set forth by musical notation the songs of the angels. He has had but a poor experience who has not known joys which were absolutely ineffable, and which to attempt to speak would be sacrilege. There is "a peace that passeth understanding," and a "joy that is unspeakable and full of glory."

The struggle to express this joy of divine communion has created the richest passages in all literature; and yet when we have climbed up to the highest height of expression, we feel that we are no nearer this overarching heaven than we were at the first. Here originated that hymn which, by general consent, is regarded as the best Watts ever wrote:

> "My God, the spring of all my joys,
>   The life of my delights,
> The glory of my brightest days,
>   And comfort of my nights!
>
> In darkest shades, if thou appear,
>   My dawning is begun;
> Thou art my soul's bright morning star,
>   And thou my rising sun.
>
> The opening heavens around me shine
>   With beams of sacred bliss,
> If Jesus shows his mercy mine,
>   And whispers I am his."

Still more expressive, and perhaps more familiar, is the language of Count Zinzendorf, as translated by John Wesley:

> "How blest are they who still abide
>   Close sheltered in thy bleeding side!

> Who thence their life and strength derive,
> And by thee move, and in thee live."

But more tender and more adequate are the beautiful lines of the devout Dessler, written almost two hundred years ago:

> "O, Friend of souls, how blest the time
>   When in thy love I rest;
> When from my weariness I climb
>   E'en to thy tender breast!
>
> The night of sorrow endeth there;
>   Thy rays outshine the sun,
> And in thy pardon and thy care
>   The heaven of heavens is won."

I linger only for two general remarks:

1. All partial characters are spurious—the mere moralist, the mere philanthropist, or the religious enthusiast. Integrity in all spiritual relations is the only guaranty of genuineness.

2. This trinity in character answers to the Trinity of persons in the Godhead. In the quality of thorough and perfect righteousness, we are harmoniously related to God as God, without any distinction of persons. The spring of all real sacrifice, as well as its most perfect illustration, is found in the Lord Jesus; and so this quality binds us to the second person in the Trinity. And, finally, divine communion is, to us sinners, the special and blissful product of the Holy Ghost; and so, such a character as this text sets forth is, indeed, the "triune shadow of Jehovah," and all they who possess it enter into eternal fellowship with God the Father, God the Son, and God the Holy Ghost!

V.

THE VICARIOUSNESS OF HUMAN LIFE.

"Bear ye one another's burdens, and so fulfill the law of Christ."—GALATIANS VI, 2.

THE theme suggested by this text, and which, as I have thought, may profitably guide the meditations of this hour, is, THE VICARIOUSNESS OF HUMAN LIFE; by which is meant that every life which is under the divine ordering and conforms to it; every life that illustrates the divine idea of humanity, and so has any claim to be considered a true and typical human life,— will manifest itself in bearing the burdens of others, in a kindly, fraternal, and helpful sympathy for all who stand in need of it.

I. Now, there are some things which can by no possibility be transferred, and the very first step toward defining more clearly the territory of thought brought to view in this text, is to bethink ourselves of this fact, and to consider what some of these are; for if all things could be thrown off and laid aside at will, there would remain no firm basis of individuality, and society would be chaos.

The most fundamental and the most solemn attribute of human life is its utter solitariness. There is a sense in which every individual man is isolated and apart from every other man, as really as though they dwelt in different worlds. This solitude is changeless, and it is invincible. We can not get below it without falling out of being. We can not rise above it unless we can rise above God, who maketh us to differ. We can not evade it or ignore it, unless we can escape from ourselves, or repeal Heaven's first and most sacred law, written with the pen of God on every individual nature: "Every man shall bear his own burden."

1. For instance, one can not transfer his mission and work, of whatever sort it is. It was waiting for him when he came into the world. It does not depend, and it never did depend, upon his choice or caprice; it is possible for him to mar it, but it was never possible for him to make it. The individuality of a man's work is as perfect and as immutable as that of his nature. God's plan has something for us which no other can do. There are words which the world needs to have spoken, and which God is waiting to have spoken, which we only can speak. There is some corner, some dark recess, which will remain dark forever, unless our little light shine therein. There is some humble note in the everlasting anthem which no voice but ours can strike, and the harmony will not be perfect without this note.

And so the obscurest life may have a nobility and a sacredness just as inalienable as the most illustrious, because it is under the interested eye of God; because it has a divine meaning in it and a divine energy behind it; because it is a part, an essential part, of God's great plan, which embraces us and all things. The man who feels that he has come into the

world on God's errand, and is fulfilling it hour
by hour and day by day; that he is a divinely
selected medium of blessing to his own family, to the
community in which he lives, to the congregation in
which he worships, to the Sabbath-school in which he
labors, and to the friends with whom he associates,—
has in this a consciousness of dignity and a sense of
personal worth and success that nothing else can, by
any possibility, give. Assured that his life is producing immortal fruit, he can well afford to look down
on all earthly good. If God needs him, and has a
place for him in his plan, he is safe, and should be
content. The earth carries just as lovingly on her
bosom the humble violet as she does proudly on her
brow the majestic cedar; and who shall say that one
may not, from the lowliest place, see as far into the
deeps of heaven as from the loftiest?

2. A man's personality is alienable. There is
given to every one a "name which no man knoweth,
save he that receiveth it." God fits us for our work;
and as it differs, so do we. I do not say *because* it
differs. The reason may be, and I think is, deeper;
but it is certain that we differ as our work. There is
something we can do better than anybody else—one
sphere in which each may be master—a throne on
which he may sit, and a crown for him to wear. In
this sphere, not only is there no rival, there is absolutely no other. The man's adapted nature is the
only door of admission thereto. Every other is as
hopelessly excluded as the blind man from the gor-
geous hues, and the deaf man from the rapturous harmonies, of the universe.

Brethren, I pause to thank God for this most fundamental of all rights,—the right to be one's self; the right to stand in one's one place, no matter how obscure; to build on one's own foundation, no matter how narrow; the right to think one's own thoughts, to cherish individual beliefs, and to give individual expression to the same. In this world, where no two things are alike, where all variety blends in all unity, I accept with grateful loyalty the mandate which holds my personality in eternal separation from all others, and thus stamps it with indestructible value.

3. And this view covers personal weaknesses and infirmities. These also are a part of our individuality, and can not at will be laid aside as an ill-fitting garment. The complete circle of human goodness has never, in but a single instance, been perfectly filled out. Every other man, but the one Divine Man, is but a fragment or a caricature, ill-proportioned and grotesque, overdone or underdone, eccentric or fantastic. "He will be immortal," says quaint old Thomas Fuller, "who liveth till he be stoned by one without fault." We all feel, if our life amounts to anything that can be called experience, that we have not come to the ideal perfection, or to that perfection which is practicable to us—indeed, that we are terribly otherwise. Our minds are clouded by error and warped by prejudice; our hearts have taken in other guests than purity, honor, and disinterested love; and all this expresses itself in our outward lives. Who of us can say that there is no jealousy in our dispositions, no bitterness in our feelings, no overreaching in our dealings, no conceit in our self-esteem, no untruthfulness

in our utterances, no intolerance in our judgments, or hypocrisy in our professions—none of that radically impious love of the world with which the love of the Father makes no compromise? Alas! the history of the church abundantly shows that a man may be a saint, that he may belong to the highest circles of sainthood, and yet have failings and foibles, frailties and imperfections. Peter may have been too impetuous; Paul too inflexible; John too introspective; Luther too convivial; Wesley too despotic; and yet each one of these grand representative men exhibits his most characteristic excellences in the same direction with his most characteristic faults. So that the highest strength of a man is likely to be bound up in the same bundle with his most dangerous weakness.

Now, individuality in this low and narrow sense is practically indelible; and hence there is special need of charity in our judgments of each other. In this great battle which each must fight for himself, of right against wrong, of purity against impurity, of self-will against God's will, "every heart knows its own bitterness."

> " Who made the heart, 't is He alone
>   Decidedly can try us;
> He knows each chord, its various tone ;
>   Each spring, its various bias.
> Then at the balance let 's be mute—
>   We never can adjust it.
> What 's done we partly may compute,
>   But know not what 's resisted."

4. There is in this text, then, no principle of agrarianism; no law against nature seeking to bear

down and sweep away the personal distinctions of
men; no command that he whose burden is already
up to the full measure of his strength shall attempt
the impossible thing of carrying his brother's load.
This law, "Bear ye one another's burdens," must be
interpreted consistently with that deeper and higher
law, "Every man must bear his own burden." Let
us fix it, then, as the one focal point of our consciousness toward which everything must converge, and from
which everything must proceed, the citadel of our
self-hood, the immovable center of our spiritual life,
that *duty is personal;* that it always speaks to the
individual conscience; that every man must give account of himself to God. Hence, the vicariousness
which I allege of human life does not at all come
down into these deepest depths.

II. We turn now to the burdens which are trans-
ferable, and to which the command of the text applies:

1. The first group of these is found in what are
called our temporal affairs. "The first practical problem in all philosophy," as Carlyle says, "is that of
keeping soul and body together," and, as many of
us have found long ere this, it is a problem not easy
to solve. With care and poverty, sickness and accident, carelessness and ignorance, cutting away at the
bond of union, it is not an easy matter to preserve
and keep it. It is not so *simple* a problem as might
at first appear. "Man does not live by bread alone."
Not alone must our grosser physical necessities be
met, but those which are more subtle and ethereal,
which take hold of the rarer and richer products of a
Christian civilization. The question is not simply,

how to keep our *physical* nature from starvation,
but how to keep our *mental* nature, our *social* nature,
our *esthetic* nature, our *moral* nature, from starvation.
So that this hand-to-hand fight with want and poverty, in which so many of us are engaged, is a great
deal more hotly contested than would at first appear,
and it brings to most of us the varying fortunes of
victory and defeat. With a majority the issue hangs
in suspense from first to last, so that very few indeed,
even in the most prosperous communities, ever
come to feel that they have built up an adequate barrier between themselves and families and want. There
is always a possibility, a dreaded possibility, that all
resources may at last fail, and those we love be turned
out upon the world shelterless and dependent. Not a
few feel that their hold on competency and comfort is
by the frailest of tenures—health, particular occupation, the fortunes of trade, and such like uncertain-
ties—so that the tenure is liable at any time to be
broken. And thus in every circle are those living
under grinding and depressing conditions, like men in
a sack trying to run a race, or prisoners let out to
work in the quarry or to macadamize the street, yet
tethered to their bondage by ball and chain.

Of all this I by no means complain. I have no
suspicion that the universe is badly managed, that it
has fallen out of the hands of our wise and tender
Father into the power of some malignant tyrant who
delights to lay upon men unnecessary and cruel exactions. I have no doubt that the grand outcome will,
when it is reached, vindicate all the intermediate steps.
If this world is a spiritual gymnasium, it ought to

23

afford some pretty vigorous exercise. If it is a train-
ing-school for immortality, it ought to be such as to
develop and perfect our highest powers, so that, when
we graduate from it, it shall be with strong, symmet-
rical, and thoroughly cultivated natures. If it is a
battle-ground, it were well that it should be the battle-
ground of humanity, and perhaps, also, of the spiritual
universe. Let all the hostile forces that can ever
meet us, meet us here and now, only so that all the
divine resources which can ever be available to us
shall be available here and now; and then shall the
issue, when we reach it, be decisive, and the victory
permanent.

We may not complain, then, of the hardship of
self-support. It gives a rest, a significance, and a
value to life, which would be otherwise impossible.
The little, loving sacrifices and tender plannings and
willing toils which are interwoven into the possessions
of the poor, make them a thousand times more precious than the decorative ciphers which fill the homes
of the rich. Show me a man who inherits this earth
to the very fullness of the promise, and I will show
you one who paid the price of wise and thoughtful
planning, and patient and persistent toil, for the ac-
quisitions he made. One of the most fearful curses
that can come upon a human life is that "insupport-
able weight of emptiness" which they feel who have
nothing to do but to fill up every day from brim to
brim with trifles.

But though we may not accuse God's plan which
requires us, each one for himself, in some sense to
create the value which he would find in outward

things, and makes it impossible that any wealth should
be thrust upon us as from without, yet, on the other
hand, we must not fail to see that, because of these
" heavy burdens and grievous to be borne," Christianity
comes in with its special help and alleviations and
inspirations. It comes demanding that men who are
Christian in every other department of life shall not
be unchristian here. It comes enjoining us to remember that all we are brethren. It would sweep away
all artificial distinctions, such as are based on mere
fortune and not on culture or character or intrinsic
worth. It comes enjoining on all the duty of simple
living and humble loving, and this is the gospel's
perfect remedy for the most serious evils that afflict
society. It comes forbidding that the burdens of
God's poor should be wantonly increased by oppres-
sion and cruel exactions; by overreaching in business;
by any contrivances to obtain an undue or unfair advantage; by any and all expedients to interrupt the
natural flow of supply to demand, and thus to divert
nature's reward of honest toil into the coffers of the
crafty human parasites who live on the life of their
fellows; by carrying the oppressive tyranny of fashion
into all circles of human life, even into the house of
God itself; and by whatsoever in our business habits,
and in the ordering of our daily lives, tends to make
this problem one of greater difficulty and security to
the poor "brethren of our Lord" that may be found
in every community.

Carry to those who need it a tender and considerate sympathy; assure them of your sense of identity
with them in their trials; lift the burden from their

hearts; chase away the shadow of despondency, if not
despair, that is beginning to fall across their lives;
help them to a richer strength and a nobler courage;
and, in so far as the way can be opened without
working a sense of dependence and degradation in
them, minister unto their need of your bounty. " He
that seeth his brother have need and shutteth up his
bowels of compassion against him, how dwelleth the
love of God in him?"

2. The second group of our burdens are those
which come out of our mortal condition,—infirmity,
disease, suffering, and death.

In these is the whole world kin. The rich and
the poor meet together on the bed of pain and in the
narrow house appointed for all living. The solemn,
inevitable hour marches steadily on for each one of
us, whether we wake or sleep, rest or labor, suffer or
rejoice. We all stand in the presence of this dread
certainty; and so there is a sense of common exposure and common peril. The grave that opened
yesterday to receive my brother, may open to-morrow
for me. His mortal agony, which I could not allevi-
ate, is a truthful prophecy of my own; for

> " Soon shall death's oppressive hand
> Lie heavy on these languid eyes."

I can not at this time discuss the dark and difficult problem of physical evil. I would, however,
express the faith I have that it is all light in the presence of the cross. As I have already said of some
of the hard conditions of our present life, I have no
suspicion that these come from a malign power. God

hath put all things in the Christian inventory,—losses and crosses, defeats and disappointments, sicknesses and bereavements, and even our mortal pain and anguish.

There is no ministry on this earth which is holier than the ministry of pain, unless it be the ministries which itself invokes. "How often have I thought myself at home, save until sickness roundly told me I was mistaken!" "If the good Lord had not put thorns in my pillow, I should have slept away and lost my glory." How many a man has had occasion to say, substantially, with Whitefield, "that notwithstanding his sickness continued for six or seven weeks, he should have occasion to bless God for it through the *ages of eternity!*" How many of us would to-day be walking altogether in the light of this world, looking only at the things which are seen, had we not been

> " Compelled
> By pain to turn our thoughts towards the grave,
> And face the regions of eternity ?"

"Of all the know-nothing persons in this world," says Thomas Hood, "commend us to the man who has never known a day's illness. He is a moral dunce; one who has lost the greatest lesson in life; who has skipped the finest lecture in that great school of humanity, the sick-chamber."

But the ministry of sickness and suffering is specially valuable, in that it calls out the Christ-like sympathies of others, and gives them legitimate play. It throws wide open the door of Christian duty. It makes it possible for us to be literally followers of

Him who himself took our infirmities and bore our sicknesses, and whose miracles were wrought in the direction of human relief. In nothing is the Christian more Christ-like than when he is seeking to relieve the terrible pressure of sin and suffering upon individual members of our race, carrying light to dark homes, and joy and courageous hope to sad and despairing hearts. The necessity that is sometimes on the parent thus to minister to his own child, or the child to his parent, or neighbor to neighbor, is one of the most potent, purifying, and unifying influences which God has sent out into this world.

3. But the most important class of burdens are spiritual; for the one real burden of humanity is sin. This is the one terrible fact in the history of this planet, and in the history of humanity. Nothing else has power so to weight us down as that we shall miss the immortal prize. Eliminate this from the nature of man, and he rises to heaven with a momentum which no power in the universe can overbear. Fail to eliminate it, and he sinks, not into poverty and misery and obscurity merely, but into the very depths of perdition itself.

Hence the one need of humanity, in the presence of which there is no other, is the need that this burden shall be borne. And it is this terrible need which unlocks the deep mystery of the incarnation itself. The one mission on which Christ came to this world is to bear the sin of the world. The one comprehensive description of Christ in his relations to men—that which carries all others in its bosom—is that to which, in our Sunday-school studies we have recently given attention : "Behold the lamb of God, which taketh away [or better, beareth] the sin of the world." And this is our work with reference to each other, just as absolutely as it is Christ's work. Our mission is laid in his mission; our life is but the outflowing of his life, so that they are not two, but one. A Christian is to be in his sphere just as really a savior of others as is Christ in his sphere.

Here, then, is our great work. It is a blessed thing, a good and Christ-like thing, to lighten the ills of poverty to our fellow-men ; to walk by the side of the weary and heavy-laden ones, and give them the support of our strength and sympathy. But how much better to bring them to know and to have the true riches! It is divine, as well as in the highest sense human, "humane," to minister to the sick and suffering and dying; and yet the most blessed of all ministries to them is that which brings into their hearts that divine alchemy of the grace of God which transmutes *all things to gold*—all things, for even sickness and suffering and decrepitude and mortal anguish become precious treasure in the Christian's inventory.

III. Such, then, is the general sweep of the exhortation of the text. With what divine simplicity and authority do these truly characteristic words come to us! By what weighty sanctions is this command enforced—sanctions of duty and of interest, of sympathy and of gratitude, of humanity and of religion, the promise of the life which now is and of that which is to come!—especially by that highest of all considerations, the essential nature of spiritual life. For life is

shown in these, that it appropriates and that it *gives.*
If it fails in either of these functions, it fails fatally.
He who does not devote himself to the welfare of
others, is dead while he liveth. There is no hell so
fearful as that which the consummately selfish man
carries about in his own breast. The verdict expressed
by our words *inhuman* and *humane,* is universally approved. He who never manifests toward the needy
and unfortunate a spirit of helpful sympathy, is pronounced *inhuman;* that is to say, he ceases to be a
man. He gives the lie to his own proper nature, and
voluntarily descends, not to the level of the brute, but
to that of the demon. And just in the ratio in which
a man rises to the full dignity of self-sacrifice, rejoicing in the most literal and comprehensive sense to give
himself for others—going with a generous helpfulness
to all who stand in need of what he can give or do,
counting not his life dear only so he can bless and
save his fellow-men—just in that ratio is he in the
deepest and fullest sense humane, does he attain to the
richest and most characteristic human life.

I know of no words more full of tender suggestion
than those words of Christ recorded in the 25th
chapter of Matthew, as spoken by him in vindication
of his own decision in favor of those whom he had
placed on his right hand: "Inasmuch as ye have done
it to the least of these my brethren, ye have done it
unto me." O, if we could but recognize in the men
and women about us the real brethren and sisters of
our Lord; if we could realize that he does absolutely
identify himself with them, and treat what is done for
them as done for himself; that, having given himself

for us, he makes it possible for us to give ourselves to
him in deeds of love and mercy to our fellow-men,
how would we rejoice to bear, as much as in us lies,
the burdens of our sinful and our suffering brethren!
May God inspire us with patient, loving, self-sacrificing zeal, to walk thus literally in the very steps of
our blessed Master!

VI.

THE CHARACTER OF A TRUE LIFE.

"For me to live is Christ."— PHILIPPIANS I, 21.

I DOUBT whether any other sentence ever written, inspired or uninspired, condenses so much practical truth into so small a compass as this which I have just read. And if any man comes to understand this truth perfectly, and to appropriate it fully; if any man comes to a profound and thorough experience of this life of Christ in the soul, he will thus solve the all-important problem of *personal excellence*, and the equally important problem of *personal usefulness*. And in some manner, let us remind ourselves, this problem of life must be solved, for life is henceforth to everyone of us an unfading reality.

The time was when we had no conscious existence, when our names had never been spoken, when our places in this universe were unfilled, when our seats in the great family of God were unoccupied; but that time never shall return. We have commenced to prosecute an endless journey. We have entered upon a path which we must tread unceasingly. We have received a boon from which we can not part. We have taken life for "richer or for poorer, for better or for worse," and death can not separate us. The time may indeed come when we shall desire to die, but we shall not be able. In the deep and bitter agony of our hearts, produced by the fearful prospect before us, we may call upon the rocks and the mountains to fall on us and crush us; but prayers of this sort will never be answered. So long as an indestructible nature can live, so long as God shall occupy the everlasting throne, so long shall you and I experience the inconceivable bliss or the untold misery connected with a never-ending life.

But though we exercise no agency as to the *fact* of life, we must exercise a controlling agency as to the *character* of our lives; or, in other words, though what has been called "the nameless secret of existence" may not be unlocked at will by any one of us, the question of life in its highest and fullest sense must always wait for an individual answer. It is true we may not be able to determine with perfect freedom the *outward form* that our lives may take; as to whether we will be rich or poor, learned or unlearned, men of eminence or men of comparative obscurity,—these questions are often determined for us by the providence of God. But every question upon which depends not merely the hue and coloring and accidental form of our lives, but also their tone and spirit and essential character, must be answered by ourselves, and can be answered by no other. Whether we will be honest or dishonest, true or false, virtuous or vicious, spiritual or sensual; whether we will find our highest excellence in the nature which constitutes us brothers "to the insensible rock, or to the sluggish clod which the rude swain turns with his share and treads upon," or in that higher nature which we share with angels and with God,—these are ques-

tions which each man must answer for himself. Not
all the love of heaven, and not all the sympathy of
man, can repeal, or in any measure modify, the law
which is written as in letters of fire in every human
conscience: " Every man must bear his own burden."
That is a sad refrain which comes up from the old
Scotch song:

> "There 's nae room for twa, ye ken ;
> There's nae room for twa.
> In the narrow house where all maun lie,
> There 's nae room for twa."

And if there's no room for two in our graves,
there's no room for two in our standing-places in
life—in our portion of the great harvest field—in our
seats in the mansions of glory.

I know that life is sometimes represented as a
voyage; but no two of us go in the same ship. I
know that it is a *journey,* and yet we do not travel
the journey of life in caravans. Every man is alone
in his distinctive personal endowments, alone in the
position he occupies and the relations he sustains;
alone must he fight the battles of life, and meet its
stern and solemn issues; alone must he contend with
the last fell destroyer, and alone must he confront the
awards of eternity.

I have one more preliminary remark; and O that
I had emphasis with which to utter it! Everything
that is precious to us is involved in this matter of
life. I know that we are constructed to feel a deep
interest in questions which are purely mechanical and
incidental—questions of form, place, occupation, and
of outward relation; but when we come to see things

as they really are, when the revealing light of God's truth shall shine in the hidden chambers of our souls, and give us to see the solemn realities in whose presence we do continually stand, then, O then, it is that we are made to feel that absolutely nothing has any value at all that lies without the domain of spiritual character. I care what relations I sustain to *men*, though I know they are but "the small dust in Jehovah's balance," but as "the grass of the field which to-day is and to-morrow is cut down and withereth;" and yet, after all, I profoundly feel that the great question is: What relation do I sustain to the everlasting God, with whom there is no variableness, neither shadow of turning? It is a matter of interest with me, Where shall be my earthly home, and who shall constitute my earthly friends? Shall I live in an atmosphere warm and congenial, or in one frigid and deathful? But rising as far above this question as do the heavens rise above the earth, is that other question :

> "Shall I my everlasting days
> With fiends or angels spend?"

I repeat it, then, this question of life is the *supreme* question. It carries in its bosom all the blissful and all the fearful possibilities which are wrapped up in a deathless nature. If this problem is rightly solved, the door is opened into an illimitable paradise ; but, on the other hand, if this problem is not solved, it shall be written as the final and fearful sentence of our probationary history, " And the door was shut."

If, then, it is true that we are to live forever, and that each man for himself must determine the char-

acter of this unending life, and that upon the character of this life all precious things do really depend,
can any theme be more appropriate to this hour than
THE CHARACTER OF A TRUE LIFE? To this theme
I invite you this hour.

The language used in the text is of most extraordinary, and yet, as regards Paul, of *characteristic* boldness. It implies that every one who truly lives, is in
his measure and sphere an anointed one—a prophet
and a savior. To live is not to *enjoy* Christ merely,
though it is certainly this; not to *imitate* Christ; not
to preach him and serve him, though of course, all
these are involved; but "to live IS CHRIST." That
is, in the case of every individual who truly lives, it
will be as though Christ were again incarnated in,
him; and hence his life will be a reproduction of
Christ's life, and identical with it in nature and essential qualities. Let us avail ourselves of this suggestion for the purposes of this hour.

I. A TRUE LIFE IS AN EARNEST ONE.

I use a term that *suggests*, rather than fully expresses, my meaning. It is too narrow and too intense to set before us broadly and adequately that
dynamic element in character on which I would first
insist. The foundation-attribute of every successful
life must be the attribute of *power;* not latent power,
or dead power, but power projected into action—living force. This needs to be plainly stated, and especially to every young person. There must be a cause
if there is to be an effect. If you would have your
life crowned with golden results, you must pay the
price. Real success can not be inherited, or bought,

or obtained by chance, or brought down from the
skies by faith and by prayer—it must be wrought out.
We are living under a reign of law, and every form
of good has its exact and unchangeable price affixed,
which, under no conditions, will ever be commuted.
Every really precious thing must be consecrated with
the baptism of tears and blood. Weariness of muscle,
of brain, and of heart, lie between us and our goal.

"The lottery of honest labor is the only one whose
prizes are worth taking up and carrying home." Labor is the one universal currency of heaven; "the
gods sell everything good for labor."

And so the one quality of character which is primal
and fundamental—a quality without which our lives
are a failure from the beginning, and we are dead
while we live—is *earnestness.* Let our souls be vital
in every part, through and through. Every point of
our characters should stream with energy. To begin
with, let us bring the *quantity* of our life up to its
proper maximum. " In youth, work; in middle age,
give counsel; in old age, pray."

There are two terms which are very often confounded, and the practical confusion of these lies at
the foundation of many very damaging mistakes, both
of theory and practice; and these are, *life* and *existence.*
And yet no two terms are more distinct. All the difference between the body living and the body dead—
between the living, sentient soul and the body which
is its servant and minister; yea, all the difference
which separates the insensible rock and the sluggish
clod from the highest archangel which stands before
the throne,—all that difference, then, is between life and

mere existence. The rock as truly exists as does the angel; the difference is, that the angel *lives!*

If, then, life and existence are not the same, it follows that they may have different measures. Existence is measured so as to show its dimensions in space and duration, by feet and miles, days and years, but life can not be so measured. Many a young man dies, as we lament, prematurely. His sun is said to have gone down while it was yet day. We mark his last resting-place with a broken shaft, as if to say that his life was an unfinished thing, imperfect and fragmentary—a comparative failure; and yet, as I can not doubt, in the sight of God his life was really richer, more complete, and crowned with more golden fruitage than the life of many another who has died at threescore and ten, and seemed to go down to the grave like a shock of corn fully ripe and ready for the harvest.

> " We live in deeds, not years; in thoughts, not breaths;
> In feelings, not in figures on a dial.
> We should count time by heart-throbs."

Here, then, is the outer court in the temple of spiritual character where all stand together and on a common level; where Christian and infidel, Jew and Gentile, the spiritual soldier and the earthly warrior, Paul the persecutor and Paul the apostle, Cæsar the earthly monarch, and Christ the Spiritual King, Wesley and Wellington, Luther and Loyola, Newton and Napoleon, meet and mingle without distinction.

II. A True Life must be a Loyal One.

Loyal to God and to his universe; loyal to truth and righteousness. And this means a profound and controlling sense of the sancity of law and of right. This is the *holy place* in the temple of spiritual character. He who enters here belongs to the kingdom of God. He has crossed the line of demarkation which separates the children of this world from the children of light.

The great question in morals and in practical religion is this : Which is first, holiness or happiness? Is an act right because it promotes happiness; or does it promote happiness because it is right? This is the great question of all the ages, carrying in its bosom all the great issues which have been raised, not only in morals, but in religion itself; and yet, if I mistake not, the intuitions of men upon it are all one way. Various are the tests which may be applied to ascertain what these intuitions are; but when they are applied, the result is invariably the same. For instance :

1. We can conceive of God as *laying aside his happiness* in some sense and in some degree, as, perhaps, may be involved in the very idea of the atonement; but who can conceive of God as laying *aside his holiness?*

2. We can think of God as *inflicting unhappiness*, as indeed he does on all hands in the common course of nature and providence; but who can conceive of God as *inflicting sin?* The antagonism between God and spiritual evil is so absolutely perfect as to amount to an exact contradiction, so that we can no more think of God as originating Satan, in his character as Satan, than we can think of him as casting down his own throne.

3. And what mean these popular adages which,

24

whether true or false, certainly express the common judgment of men? " Better that ninety and nine guilty persons go unpunished than that one innocent person should suffer unjustly." What is this but saying that the one mistake irretrievable and fatal which society can commit is the mistake of *doing wrong.* For such a mistake as this there is no possible compensation. It unsettles the very foundations on which the whole fabric of society rests.

Then let us fully confront this one, all-comprehending basal truth, that the one sacred thing in the universe is *righteousness.* He who has it has the key which will unlock an illimitable paradise. In this bark he may safely undertake to navigate the ocean of eternity, and adopt Whittier's words of calm and joyful trust :

> " I know not where His islands lift
>   Their fronded palms in air ;
>   I only know I can not drift
>   Beyond His love and care."

The sublimest spectacle in the universe is the man who takes his stand, and maintains it, upon eternal truth ; who recognizes the absolute supremacy of principle ; who stands forth as a visible illustration of the kingdom which can not be moved, but abideth forever, asking not what is politic or expedient or agreeable, but what is true and what is right. Such a life strikes its roots down into that which is eternal. It takes hold on God ; it makes us realize the dignity and the worth of man ; it is absolutely invincible.

> " For right is right, since God is God,
>   And right the day must win ;

To doubt would be disloyalty,
To falter would be sin."

Like that eminent Christian father, Athanasius, the greatest man of his time, and one of the greatest of all time, who, when he was told that the entire church was yielding to the God-denying heresy, and so he and his cause must fail, bravely lifted up his voice in banishment, " *Athanasius contra mundum* "— " Athanasius against the world." And Athanasius, as against the world, was the victor; for the entire church rejoices to confess its faith in that creed which is called by his name. Or that man of iron, John Knox, to whose fervent spirit "the fire of surrounding martyrdoms but gave a rush of quicker zeal," and when the ax of tyrants threatened, firmly stood his ground until the idols fell and Scotland was free; over whose grave an enemy pronounced the eulogium: " Here lies one who never feared the face of man." Or like that grand heroic daughter of his, who, when she pleaded so earnestly for the life and liberty of her husband, John Welsh, and received an intimation from the king that he would grant her request if she would bring her husband to promise to desist from his rebellious preaching, held up her apron before the king, her eyes flashing fire, and exclaimed: " Please, your majesty, before I'd ask my husband to do this, I'd catch his head here."

One of the most familiar passages of personal history that could be cited is that one which illustrates, with peculiar clearness and impressiveness, the quality of character on which I now insist. I allude to that most memorable chapter in the personal history of Luther, in which he was called to stand before the Diet of Worms. It was a scene of fearful excitement, and Luther himself was almost the only person who seemed entirely calm. When called upon to retract the heresies of his writings, "he made answer in a low and humble tone, without any vehemence or violence, but with gentleness and mildness, and in a manner full of respect and confidence, yet with much joy and Christian firmness." He said, if in anything he had used severe and bitter language to men, he was wrong; "but as to doctrine," said he, "I can not submit my faith either to pope or councils. If I am not convinced by Holy Scripture, if my conscience is not thus bound by the Word, I can not and I will not retract; for it can not be right for a Christian man to speak against his conscience." And then, having uttered these final words, which must in all probability seal his fate, he looked around upon the assembly before which he stood, and which held in its hands his life, and said: "Here I stand. I can do no otherwise. God help me. Amen." So came to its birth the new Protestantism, the fundamental principle of which is loyalty to God's revealed truth— a principle destined to work a full and thorough reformation and purification of the church of the living God. The only sanctification which is recognized by the Word of God is the sanctification through the truth; any and all other forms and methods of sanctification are born of fanaticism, and must tend only to spiritual despotism, and then to corruption.

You remember how, in that battle on which, at the beginning of the present century, the fortunes of the civilized world were made to turn, when the genius of Napoleon had been baffled and thwarted by the talent of Wellington, so that the fortunes of the contest had turned against the French, as a last resort the command was given for the charge of the Imperial Guard. It was near the close of one of the most fearful days in the world's history; scenes of carnage had been witnessed more appalling than language can describe. France, England, Europe, the civilized world, were looking upon the struggle which must decide their destiny. Then it was that the fortunes of the day were committed to the Imperial Guard, whose steps had never before moved but in the path of victory. With no sound of fife or drum, no shout or huzza, the guard commenced its march across that dreadful plain, and as the artillery of the allies was turned upon them, mowing down their ranks at every discharge, there could only be heard along their lines, "Close up! close up!" as they pressed steadily on. And when it became fully evident that they had failed, and that a few more discharges would annihilate them, the allies in admiration of their bravery ceased firing, and sent the message, "Brave men, surrender;" and it was in that terrible hour that this mere handful of men, standing in the very "jaws of death and in the mouth of hell," returned the immortal reply, "The guard dies; it never surrenders."

O, could the ranks of truth be filled with men of such invincible spirit as this, the glad shout would speedily go up that the kingdoms of this world have become the kingdoms of our Lord and of his Christ.

III. A True Life must be a Consecrated Life.

This is the holiest of all in the temple of character—the place where God dwells; where the Shekinah beams; where man and God meet, and the divine interpenetrates and pervades and transforms the human; where is that secret conduit through which the life of God flows down into this world of death. For what this dead world needs is life. Not forms, nor creeds, nor polish, nor pruning primarily; not by mechanical appliances, nor spiritual legerdemain; not by robes, and tonsures, and incense, and attitudes, can the terrible necessities of our ruined humanity be met. The one, earnest, agonizing prayer is for *life*; and until this prayer is answered we have no other wants and can know no other blessings. The world may totter under its weight of cathedrals; its pile of ghastly uniformity as to religious rites and ceremonies may have a base as broad as Sahara, and all be but a splendid mausoleum of the dead.

The lamp of sacrifice is the only one which can cast its rays into the dungeon of sinning and suffering humanity. There must be those who are willing to live for the world just as Christ was willing to die for the world. Every truly consecrated soul is a living soul, and becomes a channel of the divine life, it is a golden link binding humanity to God—a tree of life whose leaves and fruit are for the sustenance and healing of the nations.

1. Such a life is *in harmony with the universe.* Everything in nature finds its end out of itself. The sun shines not for itself, but for the world. The rain

falls not for itself, but for the world. The flowers bloom not for themselves; they bloom to fill our air with fragrance and our hearts with beauty.

2. And so of man. A man has not a *parental* spirit who has it not in his heart to sacrifice for his child; a child has not a *filial* spirit who is not willing to sacrifice for his parent; a *brother* is not truly such who is not willing to share his brother's sorrows, and extend a helping hand for his relief; a husband is not worthy of the relation who does not take his wife for poorer as well as richer, for worse as well as better, and for sickness as well as health; a man is not a *patriot* who has it not in his heart to sacrifice himself, if need be, for his country's good. Indeed, a man does not even get a glimpse of the high possibilities before him as an artist, a poet, an architect, a philosopher, or a worker in any of the high fields of human achievements, whose heart has never glowed with an enthusiasm which would lead him to forget himself in his work, and make him rejoice to sacrifice himself for his work. If, then, a man is not a father, a child, a brother, a husband, a patriot, an artist, or a hero, who has not learned obedience to the great law of sacrifice, may we not put all this together, and rise to the highest generalization where we can see the whole truth face to face? A man is not a man, he does not illustrate the divine idea of humanity, unless he has come to this great birth experience of self-crucifixion.

3. We have seen how this law of sacrifice is wrought into the very texture of the universe, so that he who lives a selfish life sets himself against all the

forces of the universe, visible and invisible, and so becomes a monstrous blot upon its fair pages. But I desire especially to say that this law of sacrifice constitutes the very substance and essence of Christianity; so much so, that a man does not even conceive of the Christian life who is a stranger to this law. "Ye know the grace of the Lord Jesus Christ, who, though he was rich, yet for our sakes became poor, that we through his poverty might be made rich; who, being in the form of God, thought it not robbery to be equal with God, but made himself of no reputation, and took upon him the form of a servant, and was made in the likeness of men; and being found in fashion as a man he humbled himself and became obedient unto death, even the death of the cross."

Such is Christ and such is Christianity. And they who share most fully the life of God, will illustrate most clearly this great law of sacrifice. Look upon another picture, such as we have been so long familiar with that, as I fear, we fail to recognize its sublimity.

"In journeyings often, in perils of waters, in perils of robbers, in perils by mine own countrymen, in perils by the heathen, in perils in the city, in perils in the wilderness, in perils in the sea, in perils among false brethren, in weariness and painfulness, in watchings often, in hunger and thirst, in fastings often, in cold and nakedness."

Now let me put by the side of this picture, which seems to me to be one of the most wonderful ever sketched, one from a humbler source. One week ago last Wednesday, there was celebrated in Eastern Ohio, at an obscure place called Gnadenhutten, the centennial of a sad tragedy which marked the early history of Christian missions on this continent. The Moravians, with much heroism and sacrifice, had planted a mission, hoping to Christianize and then civilize the wild men, aborigines of this continent. The mission had been established, but it was at a fearful expense of suffering, and toil, and hardship. On the night of the 24th of May, 1782, the mission family' were alarmed while at supper by the barking of a dog. As one of the brethren opened the door to ascertain the cause, a company of Indians, lying in ambush, fired upon them, and he fell dead, while his wife and others were wounded at his side; but they succeeded in barricading the door of their house-fort, and the well and wounded rushed up-stairs. But their refuge was a vain one, for the Indians persevered in their attack and fired the building, and all but two perished in the flames. One woman, sick and wounded, crawled unobserved from the burning house, and succeeded in concealing herself in the bushes, and so lived to tell the story. "The last time I saw my sister," she said, "she was kneeling on the burning roof in prayer, and I heard her say, in a clear, sweet voice, ''T is all well, my dear Savior.'" In that hour of terrible surprise and mortal agony, when the hopes of her life and the treasures of her heart had perished in an hour, so perfect is her consecration that she sweetly confesses, "'T is all well, my dear Savior."

[NOTE.—It was thought best, for the sake of completeness, to allow the passages in this discourse which are repeated in the sermon on "God's Requirements," to remain.—EDITOR.]

VII.

THE CHRISTIAN MINISTER.

"For he whom God hath sent speaketh the words of God; for God giveth not the Spirit by measure unto him."—John iii, 34.

THE first question which arises on the reading of this text is one of interpretation. What is meant by "God giveth not the Spirit *by measure* unto him?" Doubtless there is, at the very outset, some suggestion of contrast between the way in which *God* gives and the way in which *men* give. *Men* give "by measure"—with a rigid and calculating parsimony, lest the supply become exhausted, and they bankrupt! God's goodness is an ocean of unwasting fullness. It can not be exhausted and it can not be diminished. It is infinitely, gloriously the same, "yesterday, to-day, and forever." He is able to do for us "exceeding abundantly above all that we can ask or even think."

And so we have here an anticipation of the "therefore" of the great commission : "All power is given unto me in heaven and in earth; go ye therefore into all the world, and preach the gospel to every creature." Thus, in effect, saying, I who send you am the everlasting and universal King. I stand on the very throne of earth and heaven, and give my law to all things, all men and all angels; and in

sending you forth I put you in league with all the
forces of the visible and the invisible universe.
Going on my errands, you march with all the host
of God. The winds shall never be contrary. The
lightnings shall not leap forth angrily and destruc-
tively upon you. "The stars in their courses" shall
not fight against you, as they did against Sisera,
God's enemy; but every one of them shall shed
down upon you perpetual benediction. God will
give his angels charge concerning you, and he will
give the whole material and spiritual universe charge
concerning you. Going on Christ's errands of mercy
and salvation, you will find an open path to success
and victory; and, if you do but mark them well, you
will see all along foot-prints still glowing with living
light from the everlasting throne.

But a more specific contrast is here suggested;
namely, between the Christian minister and the priests
and prophets of the old dispensation. To these God
gave his Spirit, but it was "by measure." It was limited to special times, places, and relations, and did not
come in all the glorious fullness which characterizes
the Christian age. To them it came as an influence
external, mechanical, and fitful; to the minister it
comes as a personal agent, warm, vital, and bringing
the exhaustless resources of life. The prophet was,
at certain times, caught up into the mount of spiritual vision, where he talked with God face to face, as
a man talketh with his friend. God comes down to
the minister, and walks with him up and down the
ways of his ordinary life, giving him that sense of
sympathy and support which only the living presence

of an almighty Friend can give. The priest, at certain times and in a prescribed place, waited upon God in holy service; the minister serves in a universal temple, and all his days are days of God.

In this text we have a perfect description of THE CHRISTIAN MINISTER.

I. HIS CHARACTER—*"Sent of God."*

II. HIS WORK—*" To speak the words of God."*

III. HIS ENDOWMENT—*The fullness of the Divine Spirit.*

I. HIS CHARACTER—"Whom God hath sent."

1. First of all, then, he is described as one "sent." He is not his own master. The very essence of his ministerial character is *service.* He has

> "A work of lowly love to do
> For the Lord on whom he waits."

" Whosoever will be great among you, let him be your minister; and whosoever will be chief among you, let him be your servant: even as the Son of man came not to be ministered unto, but to minister, and to give his life a ransom for many."

Now, it follows that precisely here is the test of genuineness, and also of value, in a minister. That life which contains most of spiritual service is most perfectly conformed to the Christian pattern ; and, on the other hand, the life which contains most of self-seeking, no matter though it be prosecuted with consummate adroitness and success, will be most absolutely abnormal and unchristian—an organized rebellion against the order of heaven and the spirit of Christianity.

2. But there is here also a suggestion of *aggress-iveness.*

The minister is one who has a mission. He is not simply to keep guard, to stand on the defensive, to hold the fort, as we have been singing in all these years, *ad nauseam;* but he is to go forth to aggressive warfare. Christ himself says: "Think not that I am come to send peace on the earth; I am not come to send peace, but a sword." The fundamental assumption of Christianity—that without which the Christian religion would be a grand impertinence—is that the world is wrong; that the established order of heaven has been reversed, and hence the only hope of humanity is in radical reconstruction. The audacity of human rage did not go one whit beyond the truth when the apostles were described as the men who "had turned the world upside down;" for this is the exact aim of Christianity, and she will not be satisfied until it has been fully accomplished. Her spirit with regard to all other religions is that of holy intolerance. She is working steadily to the ideal of making this earth a universal temple, in which every member of the human race shall be a devout and spiritual worshiper—all, rich and poor, cultured and ignorant, ruler and subject, black and white, kneeling together on our common earth, and repeating in blessed unison, "Our Father who art in heaven." For, while it is the cry of monarchists across the water, "God save the queen!" and of politicians here, "God save the Union!" and of timid ecclesiastics, "God save the Church!" let it be the cry of Christians everywhere, "God save the people!"

for if they are saved, everything else worth saving
will be saved too.

Joseph Cook once said that the grand characteristic of Mr. Moody—that in which he shows his gen-
eralship more than anywhere else—is his power to
set other people to work, and "in so setting them to
work as to *set them on fire;*" and in this single phrase
Mr. Cook gives an excellent description of a Christian worker. Men who have been so set to work as
to be set on fire, are the men for whom the church
is waiting.

We need to fix it a little more deeply in our minds
that we belong to a militant church, and must either
conquer or die. No man who has not this spirit of
determined aggressiveness—this unflinching purpose
to turn everything to account for the Master and his
one work of saving men—is a minister at all. Nay,
he is not even a Christian in any full and normal
sense. He may, indeed, belong to that class who
shall be saved "so as by fire," for it can never be
told where the line is which separates these from
those who shall be finally lost—a fortunate wave may,
at the very last, carry the imperiled one into the port
of everlasting deliverance—but this is no truthful
illustration of the real genius of Christianity. He
that is content to stand idle all the day in the ecclesiastical market-places because no man hath hired
him, or to sit in the seats of spiritual ease and expa-
tiate on the good things of the kingdom while men
are dying all around him, or to spend his time gazing
wistfully into the heavens because he expects ultimately to enter them, will need something more than

the consecrating hands of a bishop to make him a true minister of the Lord Jesus. And if I believed that it is the necessary influence of the schools, and especially of the theological school, or any other course of preparatory training for the ministry, to conceal, or in any manner to obscure this truth, I should pray in behalf of Methodism and spiritual culture, in reference to them all, "Good Lord, deliver us!"

We have, of late, been singing quite too much—

> "O to be nothing, nothing,
> Only to lie at His feet!"

For lying at the feet of Jesus is not the special business of the Christian in this world. When the time comes, and the word comes, it is quite as important, and quite as Christian, to go forth into the "highways and hedges, and compel them to come in." There are a good many people who are more willing to pray for the New Jerusalem to come down from heaven, than to labor to build it up on earth. "It is a blessed thing to go to heaven in a chariot of fire, but more blessed still to leave behind those who shall weep by the cast-off mantle of flesh, and exclaim: 'My father! the chariots of Israel and the horsemen thereof!'"

3. The mission of the minister is a *divine* one—he is sent *of God.*

He goes on God's errand as definitely and authoritatively as does an angel. He goes to men with a message, which is just as really from God, and just as certainly fraught with vital interest to the race, as was that message of wondrous import which the angel

Gabriel brought to the lowly Jewish maiden of Naz-
areth, whom he saluted as the most highly favored of
women, because she was to be the mother of the Son
of God. He enters the ministry, not because of a
general desire to do good—to be fully consecrated and
loyally obedient to the divine will—but because of
the solemn pressure of Jehovah's authority; because
he has come to have a deep and abiding conviction
that he is called to this work, as really as though the
Divine Master had spoken his individual name from
the skies and imperatively summoned him to this
post of duty.

I regard this as a most vital matter. For my
young brethren who are just entering the Christian
ministry, I pray, more than for any human qualification—more than for superior natural endowments or
high educational attainments—more than for extraordinary gifts and graces, a clear and distinct sense of
a personal divine call. Without this, you are no minister; with it, you may feel that you are "linked with
Omnipotence." You should be in the ministry because of your conviction that God wants you there;
not for your own sake, but for Christ's sake, and for
the sake of your perishing fellow-men; and there, not
to make a *convenience* of the ministry until something
more lucrative or more inviting shall offer—a specu-
lator, or money-broker, or politician in disguise, while
the deluded people unsuspectingly believe that you
are in good faith a minister laboring with consuming
desire for the salvation of their souls—but there to
save souls, to serve the Master, to put down error, to
drive out sin, to pour light into dark minds and bring

peace and consolation to sad hearts, and by all possible means to bring back to the race its lost purity and perfection. The apostle speaks of some who have entertained angels unawares; were he writing to-day, he would also be able to speak of families and churches who, while thinking to open their doors to God's messengers, have found to their grief and humiliation that they were entertaining money-brokers or insurance agents unawares. Who shall tell to what extent the shock, which all this gives to the faith of God's people, makes against the success of Christianity in the very places where it ought to be most gloriously victorious

(a) He who feels that he is in the ministry at the command of God, will be likely to be faithful to his calling. He will not caricature the ministerial office by turning aside, for slight reasons, to follow other professions. By his heroism and self-sacrifice, he will make it possible for the church to believe that men do enter the sacred office from the highest motives. And, instead of shallow editorials on the "Decay of Pulpit Power," written by men who rarely or never see the inside of a Christian church, it will be felt and acknowledged on all hands that the pulpit, with such men in it, is a center of power, and that the influences proceeding from it are more vital and influential than any other. The order of Heaven will be maintained, and God's truth placed on the throne of this world.

(b) This sense of a personal divine call *will hold the minister to God's own idea of this work.*

Living in the solemn presence of a "thus saith

25

the Lord," he will not find it comfortable to walk in the slimy ways of the ecclesiastical politician. He will be so busy in exhorting other men to make their calling and election sure, that he will have little time to think of his own calling and election to fat benefices and high offices. Think of Moses coming down from the holy mount to concoct some scheme for placing himself at the head of a dynasty; or Caleb and Joshua planning to turn their exploring tour to private advantage, keeping a sharp lookout for the rich pasture-lands, the living springs, or the eligible town-sites, which they would make haste to secure when once the land should be occupied; think of Paul laying in with Ananias, on the occasion of that first visit, to secure for him the "best thing" in the infant church; or John, making all haste to get himself back to Ephesus from the Patmos Isle, to make sure of a copyright of his sublime visions,—and the sacrilege would not be a whit more real, though it might be more grotesque, than that which may be committed by ecclesiastical place-seekers in this nineteenth century, and in the Methodist Episcopal Church.

(*e*) This conviction of a call from God will *clothe the ministry with power.*

Next to the fact of life in God, this is the one grand qualification for an effective ministry. Even a rude and uncultured man, with a clear conviction that he is God's messenger, will wield a power incomparably greater than the most cultivated and richly endowed representative of the schools who takes up the ministry simply as a profession. A sad day would it be for the Methodist Church were she to exchange this characteristic sense of a divine call on the part of her ministers for the best products, and all the products, which the schools can afford. Were she to lose this holy impulse and this sweet authority, and take instead all her colleges and her theological schools, it would be a fatal exchange. When our Methodist Samson consents to be deprived of that which has been hitherto a visible sacrament between him and God, the uncircumcised will be sure to triumph.

And so let me say to my younger brethren who are just now entering the holy ministry, Go, summoned by the voice of God. Go as God's messengers. Christ sends you. The blessed Spirit arms you with his divine authority. You go as legates of the skies, just as really as though you were angels from heaven. Go, then, as Christ's representatives. As you enter. the house of woe, may the stricken ones see Christ, the Consoler, in you! As you stand up before the people, may Christ, the Great Teacher, stand with you and speak his words through you. And when you minister at the altar—applying the baptismal water, breaking the bread, and dispensing the cup—. may your ministry and your benediction be that of the invisible Christ, who, having been translated from this realm of sense, makes men the organs and channels of his grace and life.

II. But the text sets forth *the work* of the minister—" *To speak the words of God.*"

Not his own words—his personal conceits and speculations; not the words of other men, for he may call no man master; not the words of the church, though it is indeed the body of Christ—but the message of the Divine Father to his sinful and erring children. The one thing which must not be absent from the Christian pulpit is the word of God. Take this away, and we have no Christian pulpit at all—no true ministry, no church, no Savior, no life, no hope—nothing but darkness, despair, and death, everywhere and forever! The one deprivation which carries all possible miseries in its bosom is a "famine of the word of God;" and it is this, the world's great want, which the preacher is set to supply.

But let him take no narrow and illiberal view of the "words of God." For—

1. Some of the "words of God" are written on the face of the material universe.

Nature articulates God's thoughts and feelings—his purposes and his character. His words are written in characters of light on the deep-blue of the overarching heavens, and in characters of green and gold, scarlet and vermillion, all over the face of this beauteous earth. They are proclaimed from the clouds by the "fire-tongue of thunder," and scratched ⊦by the "fire-pen" of the volcano upon the adamantine rock. They sweep up from the mighty deep in the "voices of many waters," and they are borne to us in the soft music of the evening zephyr; indeed, "there is no speech nor language where their voice is not heard."

Every word of God is holy; and every man who is able to understand and interpret these, so as to lodge them more perfectly in the minds and hearts of other men, has a holy mission—one which neither he nor his fellows have a right to disparage. The professor of natural science has his commission from God as truly as the professor of revealed religion. And he has a right to stand by his side—not *above* him and not *below* him, but by his side—as a fellow-worker in God's great harvest-field of truth. The last use to which the Bible should be put is to wield it as a bludgeon against the votaries of science. I know of but one thing more nauseating than for men, who have hardly learned the alphabet of science, to stand up in Christian pulpits and spend their breath in "refuting" Darwin and Huxley, Tyndall and Herbert Spencer—without ever having read a chapter that either one of them has ever written—and that is for men, who have never learned the alphabet of revelation, to assume to dispatch with a contemptuous sneer Moses, Paul, John, or, more frequently, the Bible as a whole. In the same way might a blind man, out of his own poor and mutilated experience, annihilate the whole science of optics, or a deaf man "refute" all the laws of sound.

Let not the minister of religion thus turn God's harmonies into discords. Let him not begin his work by denying the God of nature. And let him not contradict the facts of nature, "lest haply he be found to fight against God." Rather let him be a reverent and loving student of nature. Let him often seek rest and inspiration by holding "communion with her visible forms." Let him breathe the "unsectarian air." Let him bask in the beams of the catholic sun. Let him go back and stand with the old Hebrews, who saw God in everything, and communed with him

everywhere, never allowing any barricade of second
causes to shut him off from human view.

2. The "words of God" are written on the pages
of human history.

For the very idea of history assumes that the
career of humanity is a development, the unfolding of
a germ, and so that it proceeds according to a plan—
that it had a beginning, and tends to a conclusion.
If the successive generations of men are but so many
waves of one great changeless sea; if the ebb and flow
of human affairs is but an unprogressive oscillation
between extremes eternally fixed; if the stream of
human events flows ever on in one weary, monotonous go-round, evermore repeating itself, then is history impossible.   History is an expression of the
thought of God, who implanted these wonderful po-
tencies in the original germ; an expression, too, of
peculiar significance and sacredness.   God's words are
written here in characters of light and life, and of
darkness and blood; of freedom and serfdom, and of
prosperity and disaster; of beauty and order, and of
chaos and ruin.   A careful and comprehensive survey
compels the conclusion that "God is the judge; he
casteth down one and raiseth up another."   •

But, in admitting God to the field of history, the
minister must not exclude man.   He must still recognize his responsible agency and his creative power.
He must not think of the race as "a patent engine,
to be ruled over with valves and balances."   He
must not think that sinners can be molded, or chis-
eled, or sand-papered into saints; or that, if the proper
ingredients be skillfully mixed, right character can

always be produced. He must never think that mechanical processes or manipulations or evolutions can
solve the solemn problem of spiritual life and character. He must fully understand that God can, and
does, maintain a government over *free* beings; that
man is indeed the "arbiter of his own destiny"—and
yet that that destiny is the last and most adequate
expression which God can make of himself in the
realm of finite existence.

3. But all possible revelations meet in one personal revelation, who is styled, by way of eminence,
" *The Word of God;*" and it is the one great and
comprehensive work of the minister to make this revelation known—to cause men to see it and receive it.
In this sinful and deathful world of ours there is but
one thing worth saying—but, O for grace to say it
aright, with our lips, our hearts, and our lives!—
" Behold the Lamb of God that taketh away the sin
of the world!"

Now the words by which this personal revelation
of God is made known to men are pre-eminently the
words of God, and it is these words which it is pre-
eminently the business of the minister to speak. His
one work is to clear away all obstructions which lie
between men and the word of God; to lay the Bible
on the hearts and consciences of men, and lodge its
saving truths in their deepest consciousness, thus
making it a controlling force in their lives. The
minister's science, his department, and his text-book,
is the Bible. He is under the same obligation to
know the Bible and how to use it as the doctor to understand medicine, the astronomer the telescope, or

the mason the trowel. To this extent his obligation
is imperative. He may not ignore it, for he can not
escape it. If he lacks this, no matter what else he
may know, he is a charlatan. No matter how dignified and impressive in personal bearing, how shrewd
and enterprising in financial affairs, how thoroughly
versed in ecclesiastical and canon law, or how adroit
and successful as an ecclesiastical politician; no matter how perfectly he may comprehend the church as
a mere machine, and feel himself competent to "run
it;" no matter how eloquent or learned, how polished
in manner or amiable in spirit,—if he lacks a knowledge of the Bible, and the ability to use it as an instrument of spiritual edification, he lacks the *founda-
tion-element* of a true ministerial character.

But what is it to know the Bible? Is it to become so familiar with the original languages of Scripture that we can stand face to face with God's inspiration, with no human authority to intervene? Is it
to know the archæology of the Bible, so that no land
shall be so familiar as the Holy Land; no city as
Jerusalem; no people as that people among whom
Christ lived and died, and of whom, according to the
flesh, he came; no dress, dwellings, trees, plants,
flowers, fruits, customs, observances, so well known
as those which go to make up the frame-work of
Scripture? Is it to have the memory richly stored
with the very words of the Bible, so that the Holy
Spirit shall always find ready instruments for any
work which may need to be done upon any part of
our nature? Is it to understand the great truths of
the Bible, so that we are mighty for theologic and

polemic strife? All these, indeed, but incomparably more. It means that the grand inspirations of Scripture have taken possession of our souls. It means that we have come to read in our Bible the dialect of heaven—the speech of the immortal life. It means that every foot of the outer court is familiar ground; but it also means that it has become so because we have so often passed through it on our way to the holiest of all.

And what is it to speak the words of God? Is it to interlard one's discourse with the very words of Scripture, as if there were in these some mechanical virtue, and then roll them over the congregation with majestic arsis and thesis like the waves of the sea? Is it to select and have at command texts of Scripture which shall serve as so many sharp-pointed weapons upon which to impale our theological enemies? Is it to make the Bible a framework by means of which to exhibit to the admiring gaze of our congregations the splendid triumphs of our genius and treasures of our learning? Is it to practice our ingenuity upon it to see with what felicity of alliteration, what grotesqueness of grouping, and with what kaleidoscopic variety of permutations we can bewilder the congregation, and especially the Sabbath-school? Is it to make a verse of the Bible the point of departure for a theological or philosophical disquisition, couched, not in the language of the people, but in that of the schools, upon which men pronounce the very doubtful encomium that it would "read well in a book," and during the delivery of which "the hungry sheep look up but are not fed?"

Not thus is the genuine ministry of the word. He truly speaks the words of God who brings their life-power to bear upon the natures of men, and makes it as though they were standing face to face with the Omniscient One, who brings them to recognize his all-comprehending infinity, his rightful sovereignty, his spotless purity, and his parental sympathy.

Let me repeat it: the first and great business of the minister is to bridge the chasm between God's written word and the people, and to bring them to understand it, not merely as to its outward form, but especially as to its spirit and life. And so if there be anything that hinders this, that makes the minister unintelligible, that keeps him away from the people, it is vicious, and ought to be eliminated. Whether it be a clerical costume, a ministerial tone, a bookish style, a monkish air, lack of delicacy in thought and feeling, daintiness of manner, cloudiness of view, moroseness of temper, sluggishness of feeling,—anything, whatever it be, that operates as a non-conductor between the preacher and the people, is evil, and should, at whatever cost, be removed. The same Master who requires us to cut off a right hand, or to pluck out a right eye, if it hinder us from entering into life, would certainly require us to lop off an excrescence, or an eccentricity, if it hinders others from entering into life. Mrs. Charles, in that excellent book of hers devoted to the Wesleyan reformation, puts some very sensible words into the mouth of one of her heroes who is looking forward to the Christian ministry: "I am going to Oxford, and when I have learned how the old Greeks and

Romans used to speak, before I take orders I should like to go to another university to learn how the poor, struggling men around us speak and think; to live among the fishermen of the coast, to go to sea with them, to share their perils and privations, that I may learn how to reach their hearts when I come to preach; and then to live among such as these poor miners, to go underground with them, to be with their families when the father is brought home hurt or crushed by some of the many accidents; and to speak to them of God and the Savior, not on Sundays only and on the smooth days of life, but when their hearts are torn by anxiety or crushed by bereavement or softened by sickness or deliverance from danger."

It is especially to be deplored when a man's learning comes between him and his highest usefulness; when these intellectual treasures which have cost us so much of time and toil and money become mere impedimenta in the spiritual campaign upon which we have entered. And yet there is danger of just this. Having struggled heroically to acquire Hebrew and Greek, science and theology, because we know we need these for our work, it requires some good judgment and some heroism not to thrust them in the faces of our suffering people. Plainness and simplicity are royal virtues in every department of character, but they are especially Christ-like when brought into the speech of the pulpit. The Rev. Mr. Romaine, of the last century, had some reputation for learning, and was, at the same time, a very popular preacher. But his sermons gave little indication

of his learning; on the contrary, he always spoke in
the simple language of common life. Some of his
admirers were dissatisfied with this, and wished him
to speak more learnedly. On the following Sabbath,
when the time came to announce his text, he read it
first in Hebrew, and, looking over the congregation,
remarked: " Not one of you understands that." Then
he read it in Greek. " I think one or two of you understand that." Then in Latin. "Perhaps half a
score of you know that." Finally he read it in English, saying, " All of you understand that. In the
church I had rather speak five words with my understanding than ten thousand words in an unknown
tongue."

The preacher is an interpreter, and he is the
best preacher who is the most successful interpreter,
who is most successful in translating the truth of
God into the experience of men. Now this is quite
as much a matter of the heart as of the head,
and hence it is quite as necessary that the words of
God be spoken affectionately as that they be spoken
intelligibly; and so, of all men, the minister must
have depth and tenderness of Christian sympathy.
The cross is eloquent because it shines upon us with
the radiance of love, and every man who uplifts this
blood-red banner must do so under the same holy inspiration. The warmth of love will sometimes subdue the soul "that laugheth at the shaking of a
spear." Not as a theologian or a rhetorician or an
orator may the minister do his work, but as a man
and a brother, as a witness for Jesus, as one who has
felt in his own heart the bitterness of sin and the

power of an endless life, and so is able to testify to
the ability of Christ to "save unto the uttermost."
Without this heart-experience his sermons will have
a dry, metallic echo as of voices long since dead, "as
sounding brass or a tinkling cymbal."

III. And, finally, let me mention the ENDOWMENT
OF THE MINISTER; namely, *the Holy Ghost.*

That which distinguishes and characterizes him
is the holy anointing which rests upon him as a
"tongue of fire." As a religion without the Holy
Ghost would not be Christianity, so a man without
the Holy Ghost would not be a Christian minister.
He may be as eloquent as Chrysostom, as irresistible
as Luther, as gentle and lovable as Melanchthon,
as logical and theological as Paul, as winning as
Fletcher, and as persistent as Wesley; yet if he
have not the Holy Ghost resting upon him as an
invisible garment of power, he is not a minister at
all. He may speak with the tongues of men and
angels; he may "give his goods to feed the poor,"
and his "body to be burned;" "he may know all
mysteries and all knowledge;" and yet, unless he is
called and endowed of the Holy Ghost, he is not a
minister. As well expect vision without light, or
sensibility without life, as to look for spiritual service
without spiritual endowment. As life to organism,
as fire to powder, as the electric spark to the electric
wire, such is the Spirit of God to all human appliances for the salvation of men. Without it they are
nothing and dead; with it they rise into the highest
realm of power. Only the tongue of fire can preach

the gospel successfully; only the Holy Ghost can make a man a "burning and shining light."

O that some angel from God's right hand would come down in this holy hour, and speak again to our deepest consciousness this one all-comprehending secret of ministerial success! O that the Divine Spirit would open to our view the unseen world, with its one eternal Light, before whose shining all earthly lights grow dim and disappear; that he would make us to hear that Voice, before which all earthly voices sink into silence; that we might catch some glimpse of that great white throne, before which we must soon stand and give account for the most precious trust ever committed to mortals!

On the famous Eddystone light-house, off the south coast of Cornwall, in the English Channel, is the inscription, " *To give light to save life.*" God has placed us on the coast of a more dangerous sea, which is even now all bestrown with spiritual wrecks, and has given us a light to guide the imperiled to a place of safety. Let us, my brethren, make it the one motto of our ministry, " *To give light to save life.*"

VIII.

FIDELITY TO TRUTH.

"Thou desirest truth in the inward parts."—PSALMS LI, 6.

THIS is God's fundamental demand of every moral being. Nothing is so offensive, even to men, as insincerity. It matters little what other qualities are present if that of truthfulness is wanting. No subtlety of intellect, no amiability of temper, no attractions of person, no agreeableness of manners, no advantages of fortune or position, can by any means atone for falseness of heart. He who is untrue to us is foul and loathsome in our sight. The man who is actuated simply by selfish motives, who gives no satisfactory proofs of loyalty, who casts away one only to take another into his special favor and confidence, who is continually, by word and by manner, assuring us that we dwell in the innermost sanctuary of his affection, and yet is ready to turn from us altogether so soon as we cease to be able or willing to serve his selfish ends, is a foul stench in the nostrils of every truth-loving man, and can retain neither the respect nor the love of any who know his real character. Men who are controlled simply by considerations of policy, mere diplomatists and politicians, continually pulling invisible wires to compass their individual ends, usually succeed in securing the contempt of every decent man; and as a general rule they do not achieve any permanent success for themselves. Few men have ever been so richly gifted as the famous diplomate, Talleyrand, and few have ever gained for themselves a more conspicuous and assured place in the pillory of everlasting infamy. Shakespeare's Iago is the most representative man of this type in all literature, and Shakespeare dared not make him succeed. The truth of human nature and the drift of human history alike combined to demand the speedy downfall and punishment of such a heartless villain.

And if insincerity is so offensive to man, how must it be to the omniscient God, "who searcheth the heart and trieth the reins!" While all forms of wrongdoing must ever be odious in his sight, he yet denounces, with peculiar solemnity of emphasis, those who are false of heart, and are, as Christ denominates them, hypocrites. And hence it is that all God's claim upon us is summed up in that one most comprehensive word, "righteousness;" for all is met if but this be met.

The theme which is suggested by this text is, FIDELITY TO TRUTH.

I. IN THE CONVICTIONS OF OUR MINDS.

Here is the beginning, and yet there are many who ignore any special obligation at this point. It is a crime to be dishonest in deed or untruthful in word, but they have a right to think and to believe as they please. The obligation to truth in the forms of our conduct is fully recognized; but not always is it clearly seen that the same obligation extends to the substance of character which lies beneath these con-

stantly changing phenomenal forms. It is admitted
that the streams which come out upon the surface of
our lives, and into the light of public observation,
should be pure, but it is sometimes forgotten that the
same necessity pertains to the hidden fountains from
which they come forth.

But this view is both unphilosophical and unscrip-
tural. "As a man thinketh in his heart, so is he."
No principle is better established than the power of ha-
bitual thought to mold character; or the absolute dependence of the activities of the outer life upon the
will, of the will upon the sensibilities, and of the
sensibilities upon the intellect; so that whatever af-
fects this, conditions the whole character. Feeling
will be like thought, and volition will take its hue
and coloring from the emotions. And so the first
and most comprehensive test of our loyalty is as
to the attitude we assume and maintain with reference
to the truth. He who is upright in his inmost soul
will feel an unqualified preference for the truth above
everything else. He will "buy the truth" at whatever
price; no price can be too high to pay for it. More
than interest, more than friendship, or riches, or ease,
or honor, or the blandishments and delights of social
life, will he prize his relations to the kingdom of the
truth. He will say with Zwingli, "For no money will
I part with a single syllable of the truth." Like
Cranmer, he will thrust his right hand into the fire
rather than it should be raised to falsify the truth.
With the holy martyrs, he will burn at the stake, and
bless Heaven for the flame, rather than that the truth
shall be denied or betrayed.

26

This absolute loyalty of the intellect to the truth stands opposed,

  ' 1. To *prejudiced views.*

All judgments formed before the case has been inquired into, before the evidence has been adduced, and before the answers have been made and candidly considered, are prejudgments, and so are of the nature of prejudice. He who is under their influence can not be loyal to the truth, and is liable to serve the interest of error with extraordinary effectiveness. A great and controlling prejudice may so obtain the mastery of the soul as to make it absolutely incapable of thinking and feeling and acting justly.

There is an Arabian tale which records the fate of a ship whose pilot unfortunately steered her into the too close vicinity of a magnetic mountain. The nails and rivets were all attracted and drawn out, the planks fell asunder, and total wreck ensued. Such is the influence of a master prejudice. The man navigates his vessel successfully until he comes within the influence of this prejudice, when, lo! the bolts and rivets are drawn out, the seams open, the timbers fall apart, and himself and all his treasures are tossing in the angry waves. If he manages to get together his floating wreck, and again to set sail, it may go very well with him until he comes near another magnetic mountain, when the disaster will be repeated. This mountain prejudice may be in the realm of science, or theology, or reform, or practical religion. Wherever and whatever it be, if it be a prejudice it is fraught with danger.

2. It is opposed to *partial views.*

Truth is a jewel with as many facets as there are finite intelligences in the universe. No two look upon the same face, and so there is a sense in which all the views of finite minds must be partial. The view which another has must be different from that which I have—not only because we occupy different positions, but because we differ in our ability to recognize and discriminate truth. It is, then, no impeachment of a man that his intellectual horizon is limited, and does not include all; the fatal mistake is when he assumes that all truth is in his own consciousness. The testimony which any honest man bears as to his own thought is valuable, and should always be respected; but when he takes the next step of denying all views which differ from his, he perpetrates the egregious fallacy of mistaking a very small part, the merest infinitesimal division, for the grand and illimitable whole. Truth does not ask any man to be false to his own convictions, even if such a thing were possible; it only asks that a man shall so far understand himself as to realize how limited his widest survey is, and so to concede to others the same sacred right which he claims for himself.

Christianity has much at stake here. There are many precious truths and many precious experiences involved in this great work of human salvation. It is not strange if different aspects of the work strike different minds as of paramount importance. Repentance, faith, the atonement, the incarnation, the sacraments, the church, the priesthood, baptism, the advent,

the millennium, the future life, the gift of the spirit,
the higher life, divine communion, have each in its
turn been so treated as to convey the implication that
it contains the whole; and as the result, the Christian army is rent into factions and divisions which
have raised the shout of war against one another.

3. And finally, not to mention more, this is opposed to *selfish and reckless views.*

Here is our great danger. A narrow and bitter
intolerance is bad enough, but not so injurious as a
certain unscrupulousness and recklessness which men
show when their selfish interests are at stake. " If
these things are true," said a notable infidel with reference to the Bible, " I am ruined." Said the vile
and wicked Colonel Charteris, " I will give thirty
thousand pounds to any man who will prove to my
satisfaction that there is *no hell.*" There can be no
question that one of the main causes of infidelity is a
certain willful predetermination that the Bible shall
not be true. Men will not come to the light lest
their deeds shall be reproved.

And as in religion, so in all matters where human
interest is at stake. But a few years since an invisible
line drawn across the map of this country marked off
the limits of loyalty and revolt, so that the masses on
either side were arrayed in deadly hostility against
each other. Was this because of any radical and universal difference in their mental constitution which
made it necessary that they should take opposite sides
in a matter of such vital importance? or was it not
rather because of the contagion of passion? When
has the civilized world ever looked upon a more dis-

appointing spectacle than that of our famous Electoral Commission, in which the most eminent jurists of the Nation, chosen as being above all paltry party considerations, divided on that great question, fraught with such momentous issues, eight to seven, strictly according to their party affiliations? Who can doubt that there was in the minds of these eminent men, though they themselves may not have been aware of it, an element of prejudgment?

Many a man has spent his time belligerently hunting his Bible for proof-texts which shall support and vindicate him in the beliefs he has already formed, who has never thought of opening his Bible humbly and prayerfully to ascertain what is there revealed.

Against all these prejudiced, partial, selfish, and reckless views stands thorough intellectual honesty. Fidelity to truth requires that the intellect shall be absolutely under the dominion of the conscience. It is not true that a man has a right to think as he pleases, unless he pleases to think what is true.

II. In the Feelings of our Hearts.

This aspect of this subject is invested with peculiar sacredness. The heart is the citadel of life, and our supreme interest is always here. A man's real character is made up of his loves and his dislikes. To do wrong to another in our hearts is to do an injury for which there can be no compensation—an injury to him, indeed, but a still more fatal injury to ourselves.

1. One of the most flagrant forms of this is in *indulging unfounded suspicions.*

In civil society every man is innocent until he is adjudged a criminal; and he can not be convicted as

a criminal so long as there is a valid doubt in his
favor. Shall there be in the heart of a Christian man
a regard for another's most sacred rights, less careful
and conscientious than that which characterizes the
administration of civil society? It needs to be more
clearly seen, and more thoroughly emphasized, that
we have no right to think evil of another wantonly,
even in our inmost soul. It is a form of injustice
more damaging than deeds of fraud or words of
slander.

2. Equally does this law of truth *condemn extravagant partialities.*

For these disturb the harmony which can be based
only on the truth, and are sure to be followed by un-
reasonable prejudices. Oscillations toward one extreme
must be counterbalanced by those toward the other.
Though at first view it may seem generous and Christian to place a high estimate on one's friends, even to
the pitch of extravagance, but in the end this will be
found to rob our lives of symmetry and equipoise, and
to obliterate the lines and features of our own personality. A man's most sacred duty is to *be himself*
in thorough faith and loyalty; and anything which
interferes with this is to be condemned. It is not
well when, from excess of friendship and good feeling, one binds himself, body and soul, and delivers
himself even to his wisest and most devoted friends.

3. And so this principle of truth in character *for-
bids all undue elation or depression.*

We are living in a mixed condition of affairs, and
shall be likely to pass through some strait and difficult places; and, on the other hand, our capacity is so

limited that a very small good will sometimes fill it to overflowing. A slight success makes us feel that victory is assured, but a little failure leads us to give up everything as lost.

People who are subject to these extreme alternations are very poor material to work into any great movement. They are generally strong and enthusiastic when they are not particularly needed, but in great exigencies are not to be reckoned on. When the victory has been gained by others, they will swell the hosannas of the multitude; but when circumstances are unpropitious, they are ready to exclaim with Jacob, " All these things are against me."

Not so they who are thoroughly adjusted to the truth. The sources of their strength are in the invisible world; they care not for the varying fortunes of a day, for they feel that they are partakers of the nature of Him with whom there is no variableness, neither shadow of turning, and who is the same yesterday, to-day, and forever.

> " Truth crushed to earth shall rise again ;
> The eternal years of God are hers."

III. In Our Words.

Speech is one of the grand distinguishing prerogatives of rational and spiritual being. As the life of the tree expresses itself in its characteristic form and structure, building up this visible monument to its own God-given nature, so does rational life build up the temple of human language; and that which gives this its high value is that it is the unfolding and the embodiment of the spirit. Words are the pledges we

give to each other, betokening the thoughts and the
feelings which would be otherwise invisible and in-
audible. They constitute the circulating medium by
which the intercourse of life is carried on, and there is
no greater social crime than making and circulating
counterfeit coin. Carlyle says that "lying is the capital crime." It is so because it severs the ties of
mutual confidence which bind us together, and makes
real spiritual intercourse impossible. Could it be
conceived as universal, all social life; all family life,
and indeed all rational life, would die. This world
would be turned back into its primitive chaos, darkness, and death.

The obligation to truth in language is often emphasized as to business and social life, and I do not
propose at this time to discuss these aspects of my
subject; but I desire to call attention to one department
of life, in which, as I judge, there is special danger
that we forget the law of rigid truth in language;
namely, our religious life. There are several sources
of danger here. First, we are likely to express, not what
is true, what but we feel *ought* to be true. Then, again,
our religious exercises are sometimes ritualistic, and
sometimes perfunctory—that is, performed for others
as well as ourselves—and so it awakens no lively concern if they are not the exact setting forth of what
characterizes our individual experience. And still
again, the use which has sometimes been made of
"subscription" has been very demoralizing. When
men are required to subscribe to a creed in order to
enjoy the privileges of a national university like Oxford, there is a premium offered for infidelity to con-

science. The effort to check the tendencies toward heresy in the great schools of the church by requiring, on the part of the professors, subscription to a minute and exhaustive creed statement, put forth as an ultimate and unchangeable standard, is fraught with the same danger. And so it needs to be more strongly emphasized that it is more important that a man be loyal to his own convictions than even to the church itself; for he can not be loyal to the church unless he is true to himself. And if there be any place where a man should be at special care in no way to cloak or dissemble, it should be when he comes into the immediate presence of God, and also when he meets with the children of God in common worship and fellowship.

IV. And finally, leaving the special features and aspects of this subject, I would gather all that remains to be spoken into one by saying, that we should be faithful to truth IN THE SUBSTANCE OF OUR LIVES.

We should be right in thought, pure in feeling, and upright in speech; but higher than all, and comprehending all, we should be *true men and women.* What we do, determines our relations to our fellows; what we are, determines our standing as before God. And when he says to us that he "desires truth in the inward parts," he means us to understand that his one grand claim upon us is for righteousness of character and holiness in nature; that we shall recognize in an honest and practical way that we belong to God, that we do steadily and unqualifiedly hold ourselves on the altar of consecration. The man who sincerely, continually, and obediently asks, "Lord, what wilt thou

have me to do?" and who makes it his one and only
business to do the things which are made known—
not as unto men, but as unto God—illustrates in his
own character the words of this text.   He sets forth
in his own living example the blessedness and the
stability of a life which is truly devoted to duty and to
God; for what God wants is not right forms of action,
nor right forms of speech and of feeling, considered
in themselves, but living natures, which shall reflect
his own image.   He is most effectually served and
honored by those whose characters are more eloquent
than their words, and whose spirit of sanctity is more
contagious and more fruitful than their best and most
beneficent deeds.   What is wanted is men and women
who show by the steadiness and equipoise of their lives
that they belong to the "kingdom which can not be
moved," but abideth forever.

This type of character is the only guarantee of
permanent *commercial prosperity.*   Laws can not adequately protect us; business methods and usages can
only have a regulative influence; our only safe ground
of anchorage is in the men who hold their own integrity as absolutely above all price.   Said Edward
Everett of his friend, Abbott Lawrence: "I verily
believe, that if the dome of the State-house, which
towers above his residence on Park Street, should be
changed to a diamond, and laid at his feet as a bribe
to a dishonest transaction, he would spurn it as the
very dust he treads on."   In such men is the only real
stability of our commercial life.   The men who can
be trusted are sovereigns here as everywhere.

And so also for the State.   So long as public

functionaries are honest, and believed to be honest, republican government is possible; but if this faith shall die out of the popular heart, this possibility will die with it. In the dark days of our own Republic there was always one quenchless light: We could not doubt the honesty and the patriotism of our God-given President. We were by no means certain as to his competency; there were grave doubts as to his qualities of statesmanship, but no one doubted his truth; and in this was our strength. Had it been otherwise, our way to an assured and established nationality would have been longer and more perilous. And to-day the men who give strength and stability to our civil life are those who commend themselves to us as sincerely patriotic and incorruptible.

But especially are such true men the great *need of the church.* There are plenty who will kindle bon-fires on the heights of Zion, but too few who are burning and shining lights. There are plenty who will join in the hosannas, but too few who, by patient and self-sacrificing labor, are hastening on the latter-day glory. The great need of the church is not better creeds, though it may, for all I care now to say, need these; it is not more perfect forms and more suitable instruments and accessories of Christian work and worship, though often, doubtless, these are needed; it is not a deeper and broader and richer culture, and this is everywhere and always needed,—the great want is for more of truthful characters and lives, men and women who, like the grand old martyrs of the ancient time, can die for Christ, but will not deny him.

And the promise to such is, " They shall walk with me in white, for they are worthy."

N Sunday. February 16, 1890, MRS. HEMENWAY died suddenly of heart disease, at her home in Evanston. A few weeks before, she wrote, in response to a request for the facts of her life, these significant words:

"As regards my own life, in Evanston or elsewhere, it has been too quiet and uneventful to be mentioned except as the privileged homemaker of one of the purest, truest, and best of men, who fully appreciated the meaning of that sacred word, Home."

In her character strength and beauty were harmoniously united. Her noble life was filled with unselfish devotion to her family and friends, and of faithful service to God. What part of that great debt the Church owes to Dr. Hemenway is due primarily to the faithful ministries of his wife, we can not tell; but he certainly recognized her sustaining and inspiring influence as one of the most precious facts of his life.